Outside Our Parameters

Helen Lawrence

Helen Lawrence—Bruce Mines, ON
Paperback ISBN: 978-1-7381274-2-9
eBook ISBN: 978-1-7381274-3-6
Title: *Outside Our Parameters*
Author: Helen Lawrence
Digital distribution | 2025
Paperback | 2025

Published in the United States by New Book Authors Publishing

Dedication

To Armita and John, the first to hear this book idea (and then promptly argue for two wildly conflicting endings. I hope this one satisfies).

ACKNOWLEDGEMENTS

As the cover of a book is the first thing readers see, it follows that the first person I thank should be Sandra, who drew the cover and the map. Thank YOU! When we discussed what the cover should be, I had no ideas. I told her the plot, characters, answered any questions she had about the book, and then she came up with the brilliant cover that put the sector environments as clearly as I had been picturing them. Thank you Pam Hawdon, Pam Hawdon Photography, for the great author's photo!!

Thank you to Dr. Masson, as the idea for this book came to me during one of his lectures in Science Fiction and Subcreation. Also, sorry, because I spent the next twenty minutes writing down this idea and figuring it out. Thank you to Dr. Lee, whose Creative Writing course allowed me to actually start writing and getting past that point of no-return. Thank you to all who have listened to me excitedly explain that I had a new book idea, or listened as I explained what I was working on within the book. Thank you to everyone who has ever been encouraging about my writing, or bought my last book, it means *so much*. Also, shout out to James, who I guess I never told I wrote a book and questioned me about it almost a year later. That was a fun interaction. Thank you to my family for listening, being supportive, and giving me both space to write and all the board games that give me good breaks. Thank you to my roommates, Sandra and Daniela, I know I talk out loud to myself a lot, it's all part of the process, thank you for learning to ignore it, and for being awesome roommates in general. Thank you to Elizabeth and Malia, my amazing beta readers, for all your encouragement and corrections! Thanks Mom for raising me to love books and a variety of genres. Thanks Dad for all the conversations on random topics I think up that we follow through to their logical conclusion even when the first question probably wasn't super logical. Thank you God, for placing these people in my life to encourage me, for gifting me both skill and love of writing, that I might continue to develop the skill, and for your many blessings.

CHAPTER ONE

Jun

I used to be brave. So, I'm told. But I'm sure my mother's stories make me seem more heroic than I really was. And anyways, what six-year-old isn't confident? You're completely unaware of danger at that age.

I hate hearing the stories. Mom means them to be encouraging, I know she does. But all they do is make me feel worse and give Taro more reason to look down on me. All her stories of how I was basically a mini bodyguard for her while she was pregnant with Emi, and then I became a bodyguard for Emi. How many times I protected Emi from danger, usually in the form of bullies, but once a crazy dog. An incredible story, if it is true. Barely any dogs are left, and I only remember seeing one once.

Mom has told me the stories many times, but I don't have any memories of them. What I do remember is the first time I stole.

Dad had injured his leg and couldn't work. Taro was already working, with one of my uncles. His tiny salary couldn't keep us fed for the amount of time it would take Dad's leg to heal properly. I overheard Mom and Dad talking about how they were going to feed us. I could hear the worry and uncertainty in Mom's voice. They were talking about Mom finding a temporary job, which would leave Dad watching me and Emi during the day. All I knew was I wanted to help. I was so stupid back then.

The next day, I saw my opportunity. It was nothing unusual. Two soldiers were harassing some street vendors, demanding a percentage of the day's earnings in order to let them stay open. The vendors were pleading, but it was no use. The soldiers had nothing better to do, and they would pay the price. The vendors begrudgingly parted with some of their wares. One of the soldiers started tossing the cords into a pouch on his belt.

No thinking happened on my part. I saw my chance, and I took it. Before the soldier could close the pouch, I started running and ran right into him. Coins tumbled to the ground and so did I. The soldier swore and I froze on the ground, not daring to look him in the eye.

"Watch where you're going, boy," he growled, grabbing back his coins.

I stammered an apology, my muscles trembling. But I wasn't scared. I was exhilarated.

"He's just a kid, let him be," his companion said.

"Don't do that again," the other spat.

They left, but not before I got a cautionary kick in the ribs. Nothing broke.

I could feel my heart pounding in my chest. Adrenaline was rushing through me. I got up, shoving the coins into my pocket.

I did it! They hadn't noticed I had covered plenty of cords with my body.

I rushed home, eager to give Mom and Dad the money. I don't know what I was expecting. Mom was first excited, but her excitement only lasted an instant before it was replaced with suspicion. I explained what I did with great pride in my genius idea, not even bothering to gloss over the kick in the ribs. It hadn't fazed me.

Mom lectured me. I protested that the soldiers didn't need the money— they were stealing for no reason. We needed it! I couldn't understand why I suddenly felt like I'd done something wrong.

Dad took the money. He said to her, in an undertone, but I still heard, "No point in returning the money now. He'd only get in trouble."

Mother sighed and drew me onto her lap. "Listen, Jun, I love your desire to help us. I do. You have a wonderful heart. But just because you feel brave enough to do something *doesn't* make it a smart choice."

"But I want to help, Haoya!" I protested, flailing my arms. They were not appreciating my help.

"I know." She hugged me. "And you can. Maybe you can help your Otōsan at the marketplace. But don't have anything to do with the soldiers. You can get into serious trouble. Don't do anything like this again." She searched my face, wondering if I understood. "Be like a rabbit, Jun. Be my little Usagi. Rabbits have a great sense of danger. They know when to run. Please, know when to run."

"I will," I promised.

But I didn't mean it. Or maybe I didn't understand. I was high on my first paycheque and eager to make another for my parents. Nothing had gone wrong! And Mom was having trouble finding a job.

So I tried again.

The soldiers caught me.

That was the first time I felt fear— *really* felt fear. Nothing like my small concerns before, childish worries. My insides were melting and shifting, all I could hear was this high-pitched hum, and my heart was beating faster than it ever had before. I cried and fell to the ground. The soldiers didn't even need to beat me up to punish me. My mind did it for me. I returned home trembling and bawling.

Mother comforts me. She tells me I can do anything, but not everything is smart to do. Reminds me to become like a rabbit.

And I do. But not by choice.

外

"Can't you walk for two seconds without flinching?" Emi asks, nudging me in my ribs. "We haven't even left the marketplace yet."

But the marketplace is the problem. Few other environments can boast the chaos that the Sentā gage marketplace can. Vendors call out at random bursts, attempting to draw customers to their booths. What little existing traffic flow is constantly disrupted by people swerving at the last second. Others haggle over prices or argue with family members over the necessities of purchasing an item.

I come to the marketplace regularly. I've never gotten used to the chaos.

But "sorry" is all I say.

Empathy is not Emi's strong point.

She shrugs and shakes her head, probably wondering how she got stuck with such a cowardly older brother. It's not by choice. I want to tell her that. But I say nothing and focus on weaving through the crowds to exit the marketplace.

I'm relieved when we make it onto the streets. The foot traffic is steady and reliable. Just keep your eyes open and make sure to get out of the way of people pulling carts. Everyone keeps to themselves, intent on getting to their destination, and they only talk to those they are travelling with, which keeps the noise at a dull chatter. And, being so close to the marketplace, with so much traffic, muggings aren't an issue. They usually aren't in our sector anyway. Nobody has enough money on them to make it worth such a risk.

"I'm surprised Haoya was gonna let you go by yourself," Emi says, breaking the silence I would've happily maintained.

"Which part surprises you?" I ask.

"All of it," she answers. "You going somewhere by yourself. Haoya trusting you with an important task."

She says it without malice, but it stings nonetheless.

Emi swipes a bread roll off a cart an unsuspecting vendor is hefting to the marketplace. I gape at her as she munches. Happily swallowing her first bite, she adds, "Haoya should have sent me. I ended up coming anyways."

"*You* couldn't have gone alone," I say, shaking off the shock of seeing my sister steal so nonchalantly. "The pharmacy is in Sector 5."

"But *you* can go alone?" She brushes some crumbs off of her pants.

"I can take care of myself," I say, realizing how hollow the words sound.

"Wrong." Emi brushes her hands together as she finishes the roll. "You have the ability to take care of yourself, which is way different."

"How is that different?"

"Having the ability is much different from knowing how to use said ability."

There's nothing I can say to this, so I say nothing. Emi remains silent for the rest of the walk. I don't know if she realizes my desire for silence or if she is focusing on finding another cart to swipe from. Either way, I'm grateful.

When the pharmacy is in sight, my steps slow. Emi rolls her eyes and shakes her head.

"Good luck," she calls, veering to the right to visit her friend Patrice.

"Wait!" I want to shout that even walking that far alone into Sector 5 is dangerous and she should come back. But we would both know I'm only trying to delay. I force the words down.

Emi turns, gives me a thumbs up, then makes shooing motions.

I release a long breath and keep heading toward the pharmacy. My hands fiddle with the edge of my shirt. My stomach churns in a way so familiar and so despised.

I try to take deep breaths and repeat the words Mom told me in my head.

My hands are still fiddling. The desire to turn back is only increasing. I remind myself people are watching, and I don't want to appear anxious, even though I am. Or weak. My hands stop. But my brain latches onto the 'people are watching' part. Now I'm thinking about all the ways I could mess up in front of people. They could laugh at me. They could dislike me. What if—

I push those thoughts to the side, where they continue to fight for my attention. Trying to ignore the roiling of my stomach, I open the pharmacy door and step inside.

My brain analyzes the interior, scanning for possible threats.

Five customers. Two employees: one helps an older gentleman and the other is behind the medicine counter. No one pays me any attention except for a young child who stares, unblinking. I flinch when we make eye contact. He looks old enough to have entered the judging stage, but I've guessed that wrong before.

I hurry over to the counter. The worker is busy counting bottles and making notes on his clipboard. He doesn't notice me.

I stand there, hoping he'll notice so I don't have to say anything. I also hope no one's watching me stand awkwardly at the counter. I'm starting to sweat. Thoughts crowd my brain.

I can't stand here forever.

How has he not noticed me yet?

Is he ignoring me?

Is this the wrong place—

"Excuse me," I blurt out, too loud.

The worker turns. I feel other eyes in the store glance my way, and I shrink in on myself.

The worker smiles a customer-service smile. "What can I do for you?"

My hand goes to my belly as if I can hold the anxiety captive there. "I would like, um…" I have to clear my throat. "That is, my Hao—Mother sent me here…" I cringe internally. 'Spit it out!' my mind yells. "I'm here to pick up my mother's pregnancy pills. Her name is Hanae."

"I'll check if they're in," the worker says. He walks away and disappears around a corner.

If they're in?

I stand there, frozen, my hand still clutching my stomach.

What do I do if they're not in yet?

He returns quickly, leaving no time for me to dwell in my thoughts.
"Here they are." He sets the bottle in front of me. "It's 5 cregs."

My heart sinks. I had thought Mom gave me extra, just in case.

"I, uh…" I grab the pouch out of my pocket. "It's all in cords."

My cheeks burn, although I don't know why. Anybody from Sector 4 would pay with mostly cords, only the occasional creg. But this worker, with his expensive clothes and hair treated by products we could never dream to afford— he is from an Upper Sector. The only ones trusted to hand over medication. 5 cregs was an amount he probably forked over without any second thought. He could probably afford 5 specs with the same amount of thought!

The worker wrinkles his nose. "Entirely cords?" he asked.

I clutch the pouch in my hands, the sound of my heartbeat pounding in my ears.

I want to run. My body is on edge, my muscles are tense.

He's staring at me.

My face is red. I can feel it. But I can't leave. The lives of my mother and my sibling in her stomach could depend on these pills. To give birth having taken the prenatal pills throughout pregnancy was to have only a 12% chance of something going wrong. But without the pills, there was a 63% chance, with so many options for disaster.

Slowly, I open the pouch and pour the coins onto the counter. It takes a while to empty the pouch.

I hear someone grumble behind me and wince. I don't dare to glance at how big of a line it is. But it bugs me that I didn't notice when it formed.

It takes an eternity for him to count the coins.

I try every technique my mom has ever taught me to de-escalate my anxiety. Grounding. Deep breathing. Square breathing—usually a favourite. But it is no use. The anxiety is an out-of-control avalanche and I'm the poor schmuck who got swept up by it.

I'm about to pass out, so I dig my nails into the palm of my hand. My head clears a bit. Pain is an effective if unfortunate grounder. My mom discourages it, but if it works, I'll use it when I need to.

The worker finishes counting. He nods, and hands over the bottle.

I grab it. I rush out, keeping my eyes on the ground. I look up only enough to avoid bumping into people.

I'm outside.

I gulp in the fresh air.

My head clears some more.

It's over. I did it.

How successful I was could be debated, but I've achieved what I was sent for.

The waves of anxiety recede as I make my way further into Sector 5 to Patrice's house. I'm left with the familiar feeling of frustration. Nothing about that situation necessitated my body's reaction. No fight or flight was needed. But it's always like that.

I retrieve Emi after fulfilling the painful obligation of small talk with Patrice's Mom. Nice lady, but small talk is always the worst.

"You did it?" Emi asks as we leave the house.

"Yep." I pat the pocket where the bottle is, making the pills rattle.

Three boys are lounging on the porch of the house we're passing. At the sound of the pills, one's head jerks around to stare us down. I avoid making eye contact. The sooner we are out of Sector Five, the better.

"Wow!" Emi exclaims.

"You don't have to sound so impressed."

It stings. Such a mundane task shouldn't get such a reaction. But I don't dwell on that for long. The three boys that had been on the porch must have run around because they are now coming out of the shadow of the house in front of us.

"Sector 4!" one calls out. "Stop right there!"

I grab Emi's wrist and go to turn left—we're a minute's walk from our sector, I can see it—but they rush in front and block our path.

They grin at us. I stare back, intense dislike rushing in. Sector 5 is one of the most dangerous of all sectors. Sector 6 is middle class, so Sector 5 inhabitants are both frustrated they've barely missed being middle-class and convinced of their superiority over the rest of us poor-class folks. Plus, they've got this stupid trend right now of putting half their hair in a bun on the side of their head and leaving the other side down. It's ugly.

"What?" I ask. My voice only quavers slightly. I hope.

Emi moves in closer to me.

My body kicks itself back into fight-or-flight mode. Good. This situation warrants it.

They scan us up and down, apparently deciding we don't amount to much. The tallest one spits at my feet.

"What're you doing in our sector?" he asks.

"We were just leaving," I say. My heart is pounding.

I'm frustrated with myself. They should have left us alone. I'm tall, broad, and bulky, I should be intimidating. But my brother has told me my thoughts show clearly on my face, and right now, my thoughts are all terrified. My face needs to learn to whisper.

Emi clings to my arm.

The tall one raises an eyebrow at her. "I saw you coming outta that house. You friends with someone here?"

Emi nods. Her body is trembling.

"Trying to make your way up in the world?" another sneers.

I'm starting to tremble a bit too and desperately trying to hide it. Whatever comes next, I don't want it.

"Just leave us alone," I say. "We're heading back to our sector."

The tallest considers this. Then he says, "I'll make you a deal. Give me the pills in your pocket and we won't cause any trouble."

"They're pregnancy pills."

"I don't care." He holds out his hand. "Hand them over."

"No!" I say automatically. "My mother needs them!"

Plus, the pills are designed for their specific recipients, factoring in any pre-existing health concerns and supplying what that person needs most during pregnancy. So, they have literally no value to him. This is a power play, nothing more.

"Wrong answer."

They all step forward.

I step back. I attempt a deep breath. I don't want to fight. Punches hurt. And if I get seriously injured, I can't help Mom out around the house. What if they have weapons on them? What if they knock us down and take the pills?

Emi leans forward. "Leave us alone," she squeaks. "We didn't do anything."

"Shut up." The one closest to her shoves her to the ground.

Before I even realize what I'm doing, my fist connects with his throat, sending him back reeling and coughing.

I step in front of Emi.

The other two rush at me. I can only dodge so much, otherwise I leave Emi open, so I take a few hits. But I give just as many in return.

Emi scrambles away.

I don't think, only react and act.

The fight doesn't last long. The one I punched in the throat never rejoins. Once he's done massaging the breath back into his throat, he shouts, "C'mon, give it up! Let's go!"

The other two immediately fall back, and they race off together.

I'm breathing hard. Nothing hurts yet, but I know once the adrenaline wears off, it will be a different story.

I rush over to Emi.

"Are you okay?"

She nods, her eyes big. "That was… you were awesome!"

I manage a half-grin. "Would have been more awesome if there wasn't a fight at all."

Emi shrugs. "But you kept them from getting Mom's pills."

I freeze. Pat my pocket.

No!

"Emi, the pills! They're gone!"

No, no, no, we spent so much money on those! We can barely afford to buy the amount Mom needs, let alone replacements. I can't breathe; my mind is spinning with the thoughts of having to tell my parents I lost the pills.

"Jun!" Emi waves her hand in front of my face.

I jump.

She waves the bottle. "It fell out of your pocket during the fight."

"Oh."

She shakes her head. "C'mon, let's get you home."

The adrenaline is wearing off, and as we walk, I start to limp.

Emi slips her arm around my waist, which is a sweet gesture. But since she's half my size, I only allow myself to lean on her so much.

As we slowly make our way back, a thought occurs to me.

"Emi, you told Dad you were coming with me, right?"

Her silence is all the confirmation I need.

I groan. "Why?"

"You only had to do a pick-up; how long could it take? I thought we'd be back before he finished telling his story."

"Which story was he telling?"

"Izanagi and Izanami."

I have to admit, if we hadn't gotten delayed by those jerks, we might have made it back in time. The story of Izanagi and Izanami is pretty long, to begin with, it being our creation myth. But especially the way my Dad tells it. Embellishments, and acting out everything, with different character voices. He was born to be a story-teller, not a fruit vendor. But there's not enough money in story telling—not in our sector at least. There's barely enough in selling fruit.

"We have to go to the market, then," I say.

"Why? You're hurt, we need to go home."

"What if Dad's noticed you're gone and he's worrying? We have to."

I grunt and shift my weight. A few of my ribs are protesting every step. I remember taking two hard hits there. They'll definitely be bruised for a while. I'm lucky if I haven't broken anything.

"I could go by myself," Emi offers.

I shake my head.

This part of our sector is usually safe. But when I think about her going alone, my brain concocts all sorts of worst-case scenarios.

"I'll rest when we get to the market," I say.

My leg is too sore to keep walking. I need the rest. And someone I can put more of my weight on.

CHAPTER TWO

Kyra

"What is your face doing?" I ask.

Maria's face is contorted, her eyes squinting, lips scrunched towards her nose. It's distracting. "I'm thinking," she says.

"Don't do it in my direction."

I refocus on typing the commands into Computer D4130m. The computer beeps and a mechanical voice says, "File accessed. Subject Lia Foster, Sector Three. Information at your disposal."

I step away from the computer so Maria can see.

"Wow." She almost presses her nose to the screen, as if she's farsighted. "So that's what the files look like! I mean, I've seen them in training before, but now I'm seeing in on the actual computer!"

"It's the same file."

"No, but it's the real thing. Not that those ones weren't, but this is on the actual computer! It's different."

I sigh. Newbies.

"Think you can call out the file?" I ask.

Maria nods eagerly.

With two quick taps, I close the file.

Maria starts before I have a chance to say anything. She uploads it properly. First try. Rather fast. I make a note on my clipboard.

"How'd I do?" she asks.

"Good." I scan the paper for anything we have yet to do.

"Am I the fastest trainee you've worked with?" she presses.

"You're only the second I've ever worked with." I lift the paper to double-check the one below. "The bar isn't high."

"Do you really have all your computer locations memorized?" Maria asks.

"Of course." The only item left on the agenda is to have her find her way back.

"How many computers do you have?" she asks, voice full of awe.

I glance at her. Why is she still talking? "I'm in charge of 52 computers."

"No way!" She sounds starstruck.

"The computer does 87% of the work. It's not impressive."

"But you've memorized the location of *52 computers*?"

I shrug. Most Individual Overseers have 40-50 computers. 52 isn't anything crazy. She's been in training for two years, she should know this.

Maria's eyes narrow. "Prove it."

There are so many better uses of my time.

Maria crosses her arms. "I'm not going to believe you."

I narrow my eyes at her. I'm not about to have my skills questioned by someone two days out of the classroom. Not when I've been doing this since I was twelve.

I grab from my clipboard the sheet listing all my computers and their individuals listed. I put it on top and hand Maria the clipboard.

"Pick a name. Any. I'll lead you to their computer."

Maria scans the page. "Rohan."

My brain whirls, figuring out where his computer is located.

"Rohan's computer is on floor eight," I say.

"Then let's go! I want proof."

"I'm not going four floors down to prove a point. Pick a closer name."

"How am I supposed to know which names are on this floor?" she complains.

"I'll pick, then." I mentally scan my list. "Kate Dunlop. She's floor 12."

Once again, my brain kicks into action, figuring out where Kate's computer is in relation to us.

"Follow me."

Straight. Right.

I lead her through the hallways with walls made up of computers on top of computers, from floor to abnormally high ceilings. Hallways intersect with others at random or come to a dead end. It's a maze, and I've memorized it.

Left. Left. Straight.

The fans hum in the background, a noise I scarcely register anymore. The computers are working 100% of the time, and they need to be kept from overheating.

Left. Right.

As we walk, another question occurs to Maria.

"Ooh, and is there really a way to wipe the computer?" she exclaims. "That severs the connection to the individual?"

I sigh. I see why she needed two years of training. This topic would have been covered, but she must not retain any information. "Yes, there is," I answer. "But it's only used for after the individual is dead. To clear the computer so it can be synced to a new individual."

"How is that done?"

"You don't need to know."

We take another right turn.

"Why not?" she pesters.

"Because if the time comes where it needs to happen, someone with a higher security clearance will do it."

"Do you know?"

"Yes."

I stop at a waist-high post in the middle-left of the hallway. Its surface is a tiny, black electronic pad.

"Why do you know?" she protests.

"I've been here for 10 years and I have 52 computers. I *have* a higher security clearance. Can I call the computer down, now?"

She nods.

I scan my fourth finger on the electronic pad, then say, "Kate Dunlop, individual G549k."

A whirring noise different from the humming of the fans fills my ears. I know where to look, but Maria's head is whipping around in every direction trying to locate Kate's computer.

To my right, and about halfway up, a computer ejects out from the wall, then on two tracks it sinks until it's at my eye level.

"Woah…" Maria breaths. "That will NEVER get old."

I breathe a laugh. She'll discover the excitement lasts about two weeks. For her personality, maybe even a month.

I reach under the computer and pull the keyboard out and down, then lock the arms so it will stay still. I type in my password, and the computer turns on. Then, as I did before, I type in the commands to pull out Kate's file. Proving it's her.

"That was insane!" Maria exclaims. "Let's do another one! Who else is on this floor? Ooh, I've got an idea! Stop me when you hear a name on this floor!" She starts reading from my clipboard.

I listen in faint amusement. This takes so much more time than me plucking another name from my memory.

Then she says the name 'Jun Hirano.'

"Stop," I say automatically, even as my stomach swoops.

"What?" she asks.

"Jun is on this floor."

"You don't look pleased about that," Maria observes.

I frown. "Why should I feel anything about it? Follow me."

As we walk, I smooth my emotions back into place.

Once again, I lead Maria to a computer. I bring out Jun's file as proof, and once again she regards me in awe.

"Let's do another one!" she exclaims, lifting the clipboard.

"No," I say, stopping her before she can start going through the names again.

"Why not?" She's fairly pouting.

"I've proved myself. Now we both have other duties to attend to." I hold out my hand for the clipboard.

She hands it over, then waits.

I stare at her.

She realizes. "Wait, you're not going to lead me out?" Her eyes widen.

"No."

Her eyes fairly bulge out of her head and her face goes pale.

"I'm not sending you off to get lost. In this job, you have to be able to make it out of here. Do your best. If you get lost, use your walkie-talkie. Security will get you out."

"Oh, that's true!" She brightens. "No better way to learn than on the fly!" She takes off.

I wait until she's out of view before turning back to Jun's computer.

Dismissing the file, I pull out the security cameras. Sector 4 has few of them, but one is located in a marketplace where Jun's dad works and, occasionally, so does he. I scan through the crowds, easily finding them. They're sitting at his father's booth. Jun has his stool pushed back so he can lean his back against the wall. His eyes are closed. Odd. I hope he's alright.

Why?

I come to myself. Hastily, I turn off the computer and send it back up to its resting place.

To be caught lost in thought, watching one of my individuals could be disastrous. Rules are rules. The way of life remains unchanged. My feelings are insignificant.

So are his.

So are most of the population.

CHAPTER THREE

Kyra

Matthew knocks on my doorframe. "Special delivery." His voice lacks his usual enthusiasm.

I tear my gaze away from my work. "What do you mean…?" My words die when I see what's in his hands. It's a letter. I stare at it.

He's gripping it gingerly between his thumb and first finger like it's something germy he doesn't want on him.

"Well, I don't want it," I say finally, breaking the stretch of silence.

"Yeah, I know you don't!" he exclaims. "But I couldn't throw it out without first showing you, that would be rude."

"How is it in your possession?" I ask, holding out my hand.

He deposits it in my hand, then says, "She gave it to Braxton."

I raise an eyebrow.

"My brother," Matthew elaborates, his tone bitter.

"Right."

Matthew mentions his brother so infrequently, that I often forget he exists.

I contemplate the letter. It's written in her thin, elegant, perfect script. It's in Farsi. Of course. Mother has always insisted on writing everything in Farsi, though few still speak it, and even fewer who can read it. Why bother, when everything else is done in the standard tongue?

"My mother and her stubbornness," I say, spinning the letter around to inspect the wax seal on the back, "Never cease to amaze me."

"You could try reading this one," Matthew ventures.

I glare at him over the envelope.

"Just an idea," he says hastily, raising his hands. "But c'mon. You haven't read one in six years. Things could have changed. Maybe she feels bad."

I lean over, dropping the letter into the trash can. "I can't read Farsi anymore."

Matthew sighs. Aside from his brother, he's close to his family and visits them often. It pains him that I haven't seen mine since I first got selected for this job.

"Don't you ever miss them?" he asks.

"I was a disappointment at birth and ignored until I was selected for this job. Why would I miss them?"

Matthew shakes his head. "I'll see you for tea at *48."

I've already turned back to my computer. "Yeah."

He leaves.

But I can't focus on work. The letter might be in the trash can, but it sits at the front of my mind. I spin around and stare at the trash can.

It's been seven months since she's written a letter. Why keep trying?

I know why. I'm the only child with a government job and it reflects poorly on her not to have a relationship with me. She's maintaining the illusion. Even if she barely interacted with me before I was selected.

My parents were expecting a boy. They had already had my sister and doted on her. As soon as they could after me, they had my brother. I was forgotten. Except when my siblings needed someone to pin the blame on. I wasn't sporty and didn't have one area of expertise, because I loved gaining knowledge in all areas. So, I learned to blend in and take care of myself. Stay neutral.

Until the day the government officials appeared at my door.

I take the letter and rip it in half several times. The pieces flutter down.

Then I return to work. What good is it to dwell on the past? I blink away the tears threatening to form and get back to work.

The day reaches *80 faster than I wanted. I contemplate going home instead, but it's only a fantasy. Everyone has to attend. So I get up, grab my backpack, and head out. Everyone else is leaving as well. We're all going to the same place.

The auditorium.

People file into the rows and rows of seats, all clustered around the empty space in the middle. I search for Matthew, but it's hard to locate anyone in this sea of people. So, I take a spot in one of the highest rows, sitting between two people I've never seen before.

Luckily, they're not chatty.

It takes a few minutes for everyone to file in and find their seat. The room is quiet aside from a few hushed conversations. The mood is a mix of electric and somber. People's opinions about these are diverse.

Then the Director walks into the room. A silence falls so prominent I can hear his footsteps from where I am. In his booming voice, he addresses us in a speech that never varies. He reminds us how lucky we are to be here. How honoured we should be for having been selected for these jobs. The consequences of disobedience.

Then they bring out the transgressor.

It's a man in his mid-thirties. I don't know him.

Half of the crowd gains energy, shouting curses, some even rising to their feet. A few look uncomfortable, unsure, even sympathetic. The rest, myself included, sit in neutral silence.

The Director continues in his smooth, even voice, which echoes around the room. "Crimes must be punished. We wish to encourage you all to follow the parameters we have set in place. You are allowed the freedom of your own choices. This does not mean all choices are allowed. Let this be a reminder to you."

Then he steps away.

This is the sixth one of these I've witnessed in my ten years here. I'm getting used to watching the whipping.

The man cries out when the whip bites into his flesh, but his cries are almost entirely drowned out by the roaring of the crowd. My coworkers.

It's no secret the price of disobeying orders. He made his choice.

It's why I couldn't make a choice, years ago.

When they're finished, he gets dragged from the room. He'll be placed in a jail cell for all to see, without food or water for days. As a further warning. Depending on the level of his transgression, they might be merciful and execute him. Or they'll let him waste away. Or worse. But I've only seen that once.

We're dismissed. Matthew somehow finds me, Jasmine at his side.

"Hey, we're going to get coffee and a cinnamon bun at Leslie's. Wanna come?" He smiles brightly.

"Yeah, sounds good."

As if it was just a normal work-day.

CHAPTER FOUR

Jun

We arrive home late.

I had thought the rest would help, but it only gave more time for the adrenaline to wear off and the bruises to form. Even leaning on Dad, it takes twice the time to get home.

Once we get close enough, Dad lets Emi run on ahead to tell Mom why we're late.

Dad and I both duck our heads as we enter our house.

A dish clatters as Mom drops the bowl she had been cleaning into the cleaning bucket.

"There you are!" she exclaims.

I drop into a chair. Dad goes over and kisses Mom on the forehead.

"How was your day?" she asks him, but her eyes are watching me, full of worry.

"The usual," he says quietly, rubbing her back. "How do you feel?"

Her hand goes absent-mindedly to her stomach. "The usual," she echoes back. "Thank you for picking up the medicine, Jun," she says to me. "I am so sorry you got injured because of it."

I shrug. "It's fine."

It's not fine.

I never want to get out of the chair. My ribs are on fire. What if I've cracked them? I try to calm my racing heart by reminding myself that the situation would be manageable. I can still sort the fruit for my father, I just can't deliver it to the marketplace myself.

"I wish we had something for you," Mom says, slowly rising to her feet. "I sent Taro out to see if anyone has ice. But I doubt he'll be successful."

Even if someone in our neighborhood managed to have some ice, they'd never give it up for me.

"Emi told us what happened." Mom drops a kiss on the top of my head. "You were very brave. I'm proud of you." Her voice drops to a whisper. "What have I told you? You're capable."

I drop my gaze to the floor and mumble, "Thanks."

"She's right, you should be proud of yourself," Dad says.

I'm not.

I'm glad I was able to stop them from taking Mom's medicine. I'm glad I kept Emi from getting hurt. But I can't give myself the credit for it.

If it had been up to me, I would have over-analyzed so much that I would never have gotten around to throwing the first punch. My instincts took over. My instincts saved us. The small part of my brain that operates like it should.

I wish my instincts would take over more often.

"Someday you'll be able to see it for yourself, my Usagi." Mom makes her way back to her seat. "You can do anything you put your mind to."

My mind is exactly the problem.

I absentmindedly rub my stomach, in which anxiety has begun to rise up again.

It's like my body has programmed itself to release a burst of anxiety every time my mom tells me I can do anything. Which happens all the time. It used to fill me with determination. Now it only highlights how incapable I am.

To distract my thoughts from spiraling, and because I'm hungry, I grab one of the bowls of soup left out for Dad and me. Emi watches enviously as I eat. It's watery, and the meat is close to spoiling, but the carrots are great. And I'm so hungry.

Dad grabs his and puts it in front of Mom. She frowns.

"No, my love, you need your strength," she says.

He shakes his head. "You need it more."

Before Mom can keep protesting, he heads back to their room.

Her frown deepens. She gets up, grabs the bowl, and follows him, muttering about making him eat.

I grin to myself, but it's quickly chased away. Mom should be eating more. She's growing a whole human being in her stomach. But we don't have enough. Her stomach's growing bigger, but the rest of her is shrinking. Will the pills even do much if she's too weak to give birth?

Taro returns, providing a welcome distraction from my thoughts.

He sees me, and announces, "No ice."

I shrug. "I wasn't expecting any."

Taro walks in fully and flops on the chair Mom just vacated. He studies me.

I try to ignore him and focus on the rest of my soup.

"So," he says. "You got beat up."

"No!" Emi objects. "You heard me tell the story; he fought those guys!"

"And got beat up in the process," Taro says.

I say nothing. My usual tactic with Taro. He works as much as he can and, aside from it tiring him out, it builds resentment at my inability to get a job.

It's not that I don't want to get a job. Well, it is. I'm terrified at the thought. But I want to want to. I want to be able to help my family.

But I can't express these thoughts to Taro in a way he'd understand. In his mind, I'm a coward.

Taro scoffs and shakes his head.

I'm about to reach the end of my soup.

Emi grabs a protein bar from the plastic bin and takes a bite. She coughs, puts her hand over her mouth, and barely manages to force a swallow.

She stares at the bar, then announces, "That is disgusting with an aftertaste of decaying souls."

Taro reaches across the table and plucks it out of her hands. "That's why they're so cheap." He takes a massive bite.

Emi looks relieved she won't be required to finish the bar.

I finish my soup and stare at the bottom of the bowl. Gone too soon.

"Ugh, close your mouth," Emi exclaims. Her nose is wrinkled almost to non-existence as she watches Taro work through mouthfuls of crumbly and dry granola, mystery meat, and dried fruit (that had definitely begun the rotting process by the time they started to dry it), all held together by some substance that may or may not be technically safe for humans to consume.

"Ugh." Emi shakes her head. "I don't understand how Haoya can stand to eat those things. She has, like, one every hour."

Well, at least she's getting some calories in.

"She's pregnant, she doesn't have a choice." Taro finishes the bar and wipes his hands. "She needs the calories."

"What I don't understand," Emi says, grabbing a grape and flicking an ant off it, "is why they chose to get pregnant again." She pops the grape in her mouth, grimaces, but swallows it.

"They didn't choose; birth control is too expensive. Use your brain." Taro flicks Emi's forehead as he gets up from the table. "Or better yet, be like Jun and don't say anything."

I bite my tongue. I'd love to retort, but what is there to say?

Taro has fire in his eyes. "Feel like getting a job anytime soon? I physically cannot work any more than I already am, neither can Paoya and what we're making now isn't enough to feed six people."

"I'm trying, I—"

"You're trying? No, what you're doing is sitting in this house all day. Doing nothing. Pretending something's keeping you from doing the right thing."

I slump back into my chair, my eyes resolutely trained on the floor. He's right, but there's more to it.

"You can't even look at me! You know I'm right!"

My heart is sending out tendrils of electricity, making my chest hurt.

"Why are you yelling?" Mom sounds bone-tired. "Taro, again?"

"Yes, again. And again. And again, until he finally gets a job!"

This is when Mom always comes to my defense. When she shuts Taro down and gives me so much encouragement my insides squirm from the weight.

But she doesn't this time.

"He does more around this house than you give him credit for, Taro. Go to bed. You need the rest. Be thankful you don't have the struggles Jun does."

Taro scoffed. "He should be the thankful one. You defend him while he gets to sit at home all day." His eyes bore into mine. "I will go to bed because I have to be up before the sun rises. So we can *survive*."

With that, he walks away.

When he nears Mom, she reaches up and swats him on the back of the head. She says something to him in a low undertone and he responds in kind. Taro allows her to give him a brief hug, then disappears into the room he, Emi, and I all sleep in.

Where are we going to put the baby when he comes?

Mom sits beside me at the table.

I realize Emi has left.

Dirt swirls along the floor, and stirred by some faint breeze enters through the doorway. We don't have a door.

"I'm sorry," Mom says finally. "I wish I could make him understand." She rubs her belly, her eyes faraway.

Mom's fighting a losing battle. Taro will never understand. But I'm cursed with understanding him. I know. I must look pathetic. That's certainly how I feel.

"It's okay," I say, my voice glum.

Mom's shoulders pinch. "It's not okay, my Usagi. He's right."

My stomach drops into my feet. I press my hands to my thighs to keep them from shaking.

Her eyes are sympathetic, but her voice is firm in a way I've never heard before. With love and steel, she says, "We need you to get a job, Jun. We can't—"

"I know." My voice is too high-pitched. "I know, we'll have an extra mouth to feed and we barely eat enough as it is."

"It's not just the baby. What you say is true. But there's more than that. It's Taro."

"Yeah, I know, he works his butt off every day and he's gonna get sick if he keeps working this much." He's such a hero, working and making up for my ineptitude.

Mom shakes her head. "That's not what I'm talking about. He wants to get married."

This surprises me so much that my hands stop shaking.

Mom chuckles softly. "Yes. He has a girl. I've met her, she's so sweet."

Taro has a girl? Mom's met her? I'm not surprised or hurt that Taro has never mentioned her to me. I shouldn't be hurt that I've never met her. But I'm at the house more often than I'm out. Taro specifically brought his girl to the house to meet Mom at a time when I was not there.

I tune back in to what Mom's saying. "He'd never leave us before we could survive without him. But he also can't support us and them at the same time."

"Which is why I need to get a job," I supply tonelessly. My hands haven't resumed their shaking. I don't feel anxious. I feel numb.

Mom pats my knee. "I know it's terrifying." She sighs. "We need this. We need the money. And I don't want Taro to have to put his life on hold for us. If you make yourself do it, your brain might realize there's nothing to be afraid of. It could actually be helpful to get over your fears."

I frown. "Might?"

Mom sighs and hunches her shoulders. "Sometimes we just have to ignore our brain. Fight against it."

I look away. I want to ask a question, but I have to steady myself enough to actually compose the words. "Why am I like this?" I mumble. "Emi doesn't care what anyone thinks of her, and I've seen Taro do the stupidest things without thinking at all. Why do I have to psych myself up just to leave the house?"

I risk looking back at Mom and wish I hadn't. Tears gather in her eyes. Gone is the firmness and all that's left is love and empathy.

"I don't know," she whispers. "I'm sorry. It may never get easier. It may never go away. But you can learn to live with it. You always have a choice— it does not control you. Remember how you were as a kid? You never thought twice, either. You were so brave. And reckless. Anxiety can be a helpful tool for discerning dangerous situations and reacting appropriately. You just have to help your brain see which situations warrant it."

Mom's words do little to warm my heart. It feels like she just threw every angle she could at me in an attempt to make me feel better. And I have rebuttals for all of them.

The anxiety most definitely has control over me. I'm powerless to shut it down or redirect it. It reduces me.

How can I be like I was then? I was a child! It's been years since I've felt that brave. Something in me has changed.

How am I supposed to fight against my own brain? I am my brain and it's decided for me. What is there left to do?

Mom's watching me closer, leaning forward, her eyes full of concern. She's waiting for a reply.

The words are like sawdust in my mouth. I force them out. "I'll try, Mom. I'll look for a job."

She gives me a smile and sits back in her chair. "I'm proud of you. So proud. Taro says a bakery not too far from his work is trying to hire. You'd be good at that. You've been helping me cook for years."

I try to grin, but I think it comes out as more of a grimace. "I'll try," I say again. But my heart feels hollow.

I have to do a lot more than try— I have to succeed. For all our sakes.

CHAPTER FIVE

Kyra

I'm eating supper in my apartment, trying not to spill any of my soup onto my book. There used to be over 4,000 species of snakes. Insane. Sector 10 has a zoo, but it only has fifteen different types of snakes. Some of them are barely staying alive. How sad.

Matthew's shouting in his apartment, the one beside mine. He's excited about something. It could be anything from a pay-raise to his favourite cookies being on sale. Felicity, my other neighbour, never makes any noise. She'll be forced to retire any month now. She's 73. When she does, she'll move into one of the apartment complexes for Individual Overseer retirees. Then someone new will move in. Hopefully, they also don't make much noise.

I'm getting off the couch when Matthew knocks on my door. I know it's Matthew because he's the only person who ever knocks on my door. He's also the only person in this apartment complex I know past their name.

"Go away!" I shout, putting my empty bowl in the sink.

He opens the door and sticks his head in. "Kyra! You'll never believe— where'd you go?"

I stick my head out of the kitchen. "What?"

"Ocean's Eleven is showing on the Screen!" he exclaims.

"Really?"

"Yes!" he shouts. "Let's go!"

I grab my coat and wallet, joining him in the hallway.

"I've also invited Jasmine," he tells me as we head to the elevator.

I roll my eyes. "It's not really inviting when you're attached at the hip, is it? More like, expected."

He shakes his head. "You'll understand. One day."

"I don't plan on ever being that clingy."

He just wiggles his eyebrow.

Waiting for us outside is Jasmine, who immediately throws her arms around Matthew. I give him a lot of grief, but they're actually cute together. Standing beside Jasmine is a man I don't know. I groan internally.

Matthew introduces me to the stranger once he's done hugging like it's been a year since he's seen his girlfriend.

"*And* he works in the Computer Upkeep Department," he says, concluding his two-minute pitch for this guy. Then he grins at me.

I give the guy a half-smile. I don't know where Matthew keeps finding these guys or why he keeps trying. It never works. But seeing Ocean's Eleven is worth it. It's been at least three years since the last time it was shown.

The government sector is surrounded by the city walls and Sector 10. All of the government worker's apartment complexes are in the same area, and from there, it's only a 20-minute transit to get to the closest Screen in Sector 10. They only show one movie per day, across all the Screens in Sectors 10 and 9, so you have one chance if it's one you want to watch.

The night passes pleasantly enough. Ocean's Eleven is fantastic, just like last time. The guy is fine. His presence isn't as irritating as others, even though he has no interesting or original thoughts to contribute to conversations. But Matthew once brought along a guy who couldn't stop asking me questions about what was happening in the movie. Ruined the experience. So, I'm at least thankful this guy keeps silent during the movie.

Afterwards, I'd love to return home, but the other three want to go shopping. I haven't bought anything non-essential in years, but in the spirit of fun, I consent. Especially after Matthew points out my books aren't 'essential' and I don't have a good defense. We wander the streets for a while, enjoying the different coloured street lights, glancing into shop windows selling every conceivable good. Most aren't necessities. Street cars pass by, and the people inside drinking, chatting, or watching for their stop.

Sector 10 always sits ill with me after overseeing my individuals in the poor sectors all day. What one of these people will spend tonight could change the lives of a family in the lowest sectors.

At Jasmine's insistence, we enter a store selling pointless baubles to decorate shelves and desks or serve as paperweights.

The guy grabs one that catches his attention. It's a blue-purple fusion of glass in a somewhat spiky shape. 5 cregs.

The number smacks me in the face. At first, I can't figure out why the amount should make my stomach roil. Then I realize. It was only recently Jun spilled 5 cregs worth of cords across the pharmacy counter to pay for his mother's pregnancy pills.

"Cool." He says, turning it over in his hands. "I like this. I'm gonna buy it."

"After five seconds of consideration?" I ask.

"What's to consider? It's only 5 cregs. Practically nothing."

"It has no function or purpose," I point out.

He shrugs. "Yeah, but it's cool. I like it."

I frown. "Okay. I'm going home." I head towards the door.

He grabs my arm. "Wait, why? What's wrong?"

Matthew and Jasmine rush over.

I shake his arm off. Why the need for physical detainment? "I don't want to be out anymore. I went along with the shopping, but now I'm done. I'm going back home."

"Right after I decided to buy this?" The guy waves the bauble. "My spending habits are that repulsive to you?"

"No." Somewhat. "I'm just done being out."

He crosses his arms. "I think it's because I'm buying this. But why should it offend you?"

I glare at him. "No, it's because you have the personality of a brick. And I don't want to be around you anymore."

Matthew clicks his tongue sympathetically. "Sorry, dude. You just got nope-zoned. Goodnight, Kyra."

I bid them goodnight and head back.

Sitting in the subway, I try to figure out why I was so bugged by everything tonight. I'm sure I've spent 5 cregs on impulse purchases before, but I can't think of an example in recent years. The books don't count. They keep me sane. But they also remind me of the world we've lost. At least here, in the city. The view of the flashes by the windows is nothing but concrete and support beams with the occasional emergency exit door.

I run my hands down my face. Work might be affecting me too much. I do have everything I need. Not spending my money on fun things doesn't do anything to help those who have no money to spend.

The people surrounding me on the subway will never know what that level of poverty feels like. It's rare for anyone in Sector 10 to drop at all, and never more than three sectors. On their own merit?

I shake my head. No more of those thoughts. They can lead to insubordination, which can lead to execution. I have no desire to be executed, so I banish all thoughts of this nature from my head for the rest of the night.

CHAPTER SIX

Jun

By the time I venture into the kitchen, Mom is the only other person still in the house. I waited on purpose, but it wasn't hard. Taro leaves excruciatingly early in the morning. Usually, I don't hear him leave. I wake up when Emi does, as would anyone who isn't a light sleeper. She makes enough noise to raise the dead. But she loves her sleep, so she wakes up as late as possible. If I wait in bed for only ten minutes, she and Dad have already left for the market.

Mom is sitting at the table, mending one of Taro's shirts. When she sees me, she smiles and sets the shirt down.

"Good morning, my rabbit. I left a cup of water for you." She nods at a cup on the table.

I grab it and drink it in its entirety.

"How much water do we have left?" I ask. "Do I need to go to the well today?"

Mom takes a moment to gather her thoughts.

I place the cup back on the table. Should I sit? Is it awkward that I'm just standing here? But if I need to go get water, I should head out right away, so there's no point in sitting.

"You could go today," Mom says slowly. "But Taro plans on coming back on his lunch break. He'll take you to the bakery we talked about. So you can apply for a job."

I sit with a thud. My legs lost the ability to hold me up.

Mom's face is sympathetic, I think.

"I know its soon, Usagi, but you want to secure the job before someone else takes it."

I nod. "I have enough time to make it to the well and back before Taro's lunch," I say. "I'll do that. Then we don't have to think about the water for a few days."

I get up. I grab the yoke and the empty buckets.

"Stay safe," Mom says.

It's funny how easy getting water is now. I used to struggle immensely to carry the water back. I had to rest so often. Now, I'm much stronger. I feel the weight, but it no longer strains me.

Maybe getting a job would be the same way?

I shake that thought away. I don't want to think about it. I'm getting water so I don't have to think about it. Not to avoid Taro. I'll be back in time. Getting a job is too important.

I hardly need to think about where I'm walking. I make the journey twice a week. But I do think about it. My eyes constantly scan for possible threats. I hold the yoke and buckets firmly, and close to me, on the off chance someone might try to swipe them.

The reality settles in a hard lump at the bottom of my stomach.

I have to get a job. No matter how I feel about it, I have no choice.

The thought is somewhat freeing. I can feel anxious about it as much as I want. But I have to do it.

Before my brain can wreck this resolution, I'm determined to think of it no more. Instead, I focus on where my feet are stepping. Who's walking beside me? What turn is next?

A street is blocked by a collapsed house. This provides excellent distraction and only minor panic as I scramble to re-route myself.

I reach the well at a reasonable time. Only one person is drawing water, so I wait for them to finish. Another person reaches the well, but they recognize that I'm next and wait for me to go first.

Fill the buckets. Place them on the yoke. Place the yoke on my shoulders.

I can head home now.

Now my focus is on walking steadily and not spilling water, which also means avoiding hitting anyone in the head with a bucket. This takes up most of my concentration. It's my greatest fear when carrying the water back. These buckets could seriously hurt someone. And, knowing my luck, I'd bump into some touchy buff guy who'd dump the buckets and beat me up for it. Today especially, I don't have time to go back for a refill.

I'm so focused on not hitting anyone that it takes most of the walk back to realize anxiety has been growing in my chest. But as soon as I realize it, it smacks into the forefront of my mind. I stumble from the sudden intensity.

Water sloshes out of the buckets.

Steadying myself, I attempt deep breaths.

'Just get home,' I tell myself. 'Get home, then it can be panic time.'

But it wells up inside of me. I don't want to go home, not if it means the next step is a job interview.

The next stretch of time is a smear in my mind. Forcing one foot in front of the other. Gripping the yoke tighter. Uneven breaths.

I make it home.

Taro lifts the buckets. He puts them down.

I let the yoke fall.

"Were you trying to cop out?" Taro hisses in my face.

He grabs my arm. Yanks me along.

"You can do it! You can do anything!"

But Mom's words of encouragement are quickly fading into the background.

We're in front of the bakery.

Taro sighs. He stands in front of me. "Listen, I have to go. You were late, now I'm going to be late." He claps my shoulder. "You got this. Don't go home till you have the job."

Then he leaves.

And I'm there.

In front of the bakery. The 'help wanted' sign stares me in the face. Daring me. Mocking me.

I want to cry, which only makes me mad. I'm applying for a job! Why do I tremble like I'm about to be executed?

I can do this. Just ignore my senses.

Two steps forward. That's all I manage.

I turn and begin pacing. Maybe if I can get the energy out, I'll be less nervous. My hands are doing something, but I'm not sure what. They're not a part of me right now.

My feet move forward, twist, forward. My eyes are unfocused.

'I have to, I have to,' plays on repeat in my mind.

Except I already know I have to. Knowing doesn't help the anxiety— if anything, it heightens it. If I fail—

No, I can't even think about that.

I might throw up.

I'm dimly aware of one of my hands rubbing my stomach in a useless attempt at soothing.

How long I pace, I don't know. My skin is crawling, stomach-churning, a mantra repeating in my head.

Eventually, and suddenly, like hitting a brick wall, it's too much. I have to go inside or implode.

I stop, square my shoulders, and start inside.

Before I realize I'm even doing it, I'm turning on my heel and sprinting away.

An alley comes up on my left. It looks safe. I duck into it and crouch down.

Then I pass out.

When I wake up, the sun is setting.

It takes me a few minutes to get my bearings. I've never woken up in an alley before.

I stand too fast, making my head spin. Once my head clears, I find it hard to breathe.

With a shout, I punch the brick wall. Pain bursts in my knuckles. But what is my pain compared to the pain I've caused my family?

Taro's words ring in my head.

How can I go home? Face my family, whose survival depends on me getting a job. And I couldn't even make it inside the bakery.

I have to go home. Mom will be sick with worrying. Plus, I haven't eaten yet, and my stomach is curling in on itself.

The thing is… how do I get home?

I was not paying attention when Taro led me to the bakery.

My heart beats faster. I scan my surroundings, hoping for a landmark to tell me where I am.

Am I gonna die?

Oh. Wait.

I laugh as my heartbeat slows back to its regular pace. I'm two streets over from my water route.

It takes a little bit of figuring out, and some backtracking, but I get to the route I walked this morning. Now I know how to get back home. And fast. I want to get off the streets as quickly as possible. Night time is a bad time to be out and alone.

I should be left alone, for the most part. From further away, I appear intimidating enough, especially in the dark. But if they get close enough to read my eyes, they'll know a fearful coward lives within the bulky frame.

So I rush home.

As my house comes into view, my steps unintentionally slow.

Taro should be asleep. He's definitely in bed. He gets up too early.

He's not stupid. I know he's figured out I've failed my interview. But I can't face him yet. I'm glad I'm returning too late to see him.

Yet, I don't know that I want to face Mom, either. Her encouragement. Her acceptance. I've failed. I don't want to hear how I'll be able to do it next time.

I hope Dad's the one waiting for me.

Although, everyone works so hard. I don't want to be responsible for anyone's lack of sleep.

What if no one's waiting for me? Wait if they don't care enough to make sure I get home safe?

I rush and close the final distance, reaching the entrance way.

I freeze.

It's Taro.

He stares at me with eyes that could drill holes through metal.

"Have a seat," he says.

But my feet are bolted to the floor, and I can't move.

He signs, leans forward, and rubs his eyes. "Listen, I'm exhausted, so I'm going to make this brief." His eyes meet mine with no pretense. "You failed."

It's not a question, but I nod confirmation anyway.

"You're gonna tell Haoya you succeeded."

"What? But that's a lie—"

"For now. But you will go and stand in front of the bakery every day until its the truth."

"What about wages?"

"I'll supply you with the wages until you get your job."

"...huh?"

My brain can't comprehend the way this conversation is going.

"Taro, Haoya's gonna notice if you suddenly are getting half the amount of money you usually do."

He shakes his head. "I never give Haoya the full amount."

My jaw drops.

"She doesn't let me," he continues. "She makes me keep a portion for myself. To save up. For the wedding." He's no longer meeting my eyes. "I have enough saved to get you through a few days. This is not letting you off the hook. It's to give you a chance to succeed without the added pressure."

"Thank you."

He gives a sharp nod and stands up.

"Wait, so, we're just gonna lie to our parents? What are we gonna say?"

"We?" He grins lopsidedly. I haven't seen his face carrying this much amusement in a long time. It makes my heart warm, even if it's at my expense. He says, "I leave before they wake up. You're the one who's gonna have to lie. Goodnight."

He leaves.

My shoulders drop.

Great.

I'm grateful. So grateful. I never would have expected this from Taro.

But now I have to lie.

And I have to get the job. I have to.

This isn't going to be a fun couple of days.

CHAPTER SEVEN

Kyra

"Excuse me, Kyra…"

I spin in my chair and face my office's doorway to greet Matthew.

He grins at me. "Don't worry, it's only today's orders. Nothing about last night, promise." Without waiting, he reaches in and places a folder on my desk. "How is this lovely day going for you?"

"That depends on whatever orders they've given me."

I grab and open the folder. My eyes scan the first file. Orders to increase whatever hormones necessary to elevate Jun's state of general anxiety. Closing the folder, I toss it back onto my desk.

"Orders you don't like?" Matthew asks. Is he still here?

"It's not up to me to like or dislike them," I mutter, leaning back in my chair.

Matthew nodded. "It's about Jun, isn't it?"

I glare at him.

He shrinks back. "Hey, I'm not judging. I never judge. You know that."

"I do. I just…" I sigh.

"Does it still bother you?" he asks, his voice cautious.

I freeze.

"Sorry, I shouldn't have asked," he says quickly, backing into the hallway.

I let him leave.

Does it still bother me?

It would, if I let it. But I don't. I do what it takes to survive here. Even your thoughts have to be in line. So I stifle the rising emotion and grab the folder. I stare at Jun's order.

2437, 25 May

For: Kyra de27
Individual: Jun Hirano; L864k
Orders: Level Increase

Individual is close to applying for a job. This event is not in his designated future. Increase anxiety response by 2%. May increase further depending on the individual's response. Completion before *38.

I check my watch. *36. I should get on this.
    Then Matthew reappears in my doorway. No more folders.
    "Tea time this afternoon? Around *64?" His eyes glint with mischief.
    He's invited someone else. Again.
    "No."
    He deflates but accepts without argument.
    "Hey, Matthew?" I say before he goes too far.
    He pokes his head back into my doorway. "Yes?"
    "Do you feel empathy for any of your individuals?"
    "Oh, all of them." He nods many times. "Of course. They're all humans, and they've all got their tough breaks."
    "Doesn't empathy make your job rather difficult?"
    He considers this. "No, I don't think so. This is the way things are. It makes me more grateful for where I am."
    Grateful…
    He must sense I'm not going to reply further because he waves and leaves.
    Grateful.
    I stare at the ceiling.
    Am I grateful?
    Before this, I was in Sector Nine. Almost as good as it gets. I would have led a successful life, never doubting I made it entirely on my own merit and abilities. I would have never known I never had a choice.
    Now, my choices are my own. Possible consequences include torture and death. But I also no longer have to live with my family. Pros and cons.
    I'm not grateful for either option. I shouldn't have to be.
    Time to do my job.

I grab the rest of the folders to take with me. I'll read them in the elevator. Then I head to Jun's computer.

Once I reach his computer, I call it down. His is the top one in his column, and it always takes a long time.

I turn his computer on and pull the keyboard out. Bringing out Jun's hormone trackers, I observe their current statuses. Elevated cortisol, and overactive adrenaline, he's getting close to hypothyroidism, constantly fluctuating oxytocin, and lowered dopamine. He's a mess. No other individual of mine is this tampered with. Most wouldn't get this far and still be functioning. It's remarkable what the human mind can accustom to.

I type in the command. Increased cortisol and a spike of adrenaline. My finger hesitates over the enter key.

This is the first time that Jun struggles against his anxiety and has produced an extreme response. And it would mean so much to his family if he could throw it off. His mother is about to bring into the world a baby that will never have a chance at anything other than misery. Having another mouth to feed will be the slow death of them all. Unless Jun can get a job.

I hit the key.

It's not my job to make the decisions. Only to enforce them.

Many others are in similar circumstances. And they're all fighting. To increase their station. Their quality of life.

Futile.

Your life is determined by who you are born as.

And none of us have any say in that.

After I send Jun's computer back up, I check the next file. A routine notice from computer D339w. The individual is considering a life-changing possibility and I need to confirm the course of action.

A standard file. And located on floor 11. As I head out of the maze, I check the next file.

It's not a typical transcript, and once I register its meaning, I stop walking. My hands grip the paper tighter.

2437, 25 May
For: Kyra de27
Individual: Matteo Rossi; J334O

Assessment Request: Transferability

I can feel myself clenching my jaw, and work to relax it. Matteo has much potential. I'd be a failure at my job if I didn't recognize it. But this is the first of many individuals I've been asked to give an assessment on.

Someone, many years ago, stood in this same place. Viewed a request for an assessment on me. Wrote a recommendation. Introduced me into a world where my choices are compliance or death.

Can I force this life onto someone else?

Can I risk not giving an accurate report?

As I return to my office to write the assessment, my mind is plagued by memories.

The officials appearing at my house. Forcing me to go with them. Telling my family I was being honoured, being recruited to serve the government. My family didn't understand then, and they have no idea now. They only knew I would not be returning. I could never be allowed to return to my old life once the truth was revealed to me. Eventually, once they were sure I wouldn't tell anyone the truth I'd learned, I was cleared to be able to leave the government sector. Go visit my family, if I wanted. I did once. A mistake. I haven't again.

I didn't know what I was agreeing to. How could a ten-year-old possibly understand? But I understood it would be a chance. Something different than pretending the four other people in your house didn't exist and have a tiptoeing existence.

The following months are hazy. Destroying my brain's connection and dependence on my computer was a time-consuming, delicate process. It required operations, with long recovery times in between. I thought then that they were being overly cautious, and I still think so now. If it was as dangerous and painful as they said, they would break connections to torture criminals before execution. A grim reason to believe something, but such are the bosses I work under. I wish I had known that then.

I was eleven when I started training. Just turned twelve when I got my first computer.

Who would go through all of that to rebel?

As I'm penning the last words of my assessment, the tiny computer in the corner of my desk pings.

I glance up. The screen's flashing with a green light.

An individual emergency? Who could possibly be constituting an emergency? I make sure all my individuals live well within their set parameters.

I grab the computer and tap the screen, silencing the light. Instructions pop up.

'5% correction insufficient. Attempting a job interview now. Rectify situation.'

His individual number is listed at the bottom, but I don't need it. I know this is about Jun.

My heart sinks.

He fought against the anxiety. Enough to actually be attempting a job interview.

If it's true, he's claiming a choice himself in a world set up to allow for none.

With a start, I jump out of my chair and hurry to Jun's computer.

I call his computer down and open Jun's live feed. I have to focus since the camera is not close to where he is. He's standing outside of a dingy building. It might be a cafe— or sector 4's version of it, anyway. A 'Help Wanted' cardboard sign, ink bleeding, rests against the steps.

Jun is pacing, wringing his hands, muttering to himself. Occasionally, he stops, facing the door... then resumes his pacing.

I want him to succeed.

The realization horrifies me. Bad memories rise like bile in my throat. I know the cost. I can't let him succeed.

The job wouldn't make much difference in his life quality, anyways, I reason.

Jun stops. Squares his shoulders. Faces the doorway.

My hand reaches out towards the keyboard. I know I need to interfere, and cause him a panic attack that indirectly forces him to turn back.

I can't bring myself to type the command.

Suddenly, Jun shudders, turns on his heel, and races off.

I immediately turn off his computer and send it away.

I see no reason to increase his anxiety levels. Or watch him any further. He won't be getting a job today.

Why does that make me sad?

I can't afford that reaction.

CHAPTER EIGHT

Kyra

"Kyra, what did you *do*?" Matthew exclaims, appearing in my doorway. His voice is pitchy and raised.

I gape at him. "What did I do?"

He stares at me, eyes wide, taking up half his face. "You'd better figure it out and quick, cause Liliya wants a meeting with you. *Now.*"

My pulse quickens. Liliya rarely means good news.

"Thanks, Matthew." I stand up.

"Be careful," he pleads.

I nod, then leave. As I walk, my brain is scrambling to figure out what I've done to necessitate a meeting. I followed all the orders I received today. What could I have done wrong?

No one stares at me as I walk by, so it can't be horrible.

Too soon, I'm knocking on the door to Liliya's office.

"If you're Kyra, come in," comes the voice of a person bored with life. "If you're not, go away."

I take a second to steady myself. Liliya does not respond kindly to any weakness. I breathe out slowly, letting all signs of emotion leave me. Then I enter.

Liliya is sitting in her chair, which she's turned to face the door.

"Come in," she says. Her elbow rests on her chair's arm and she uses her fingers to prop up the side of her head.

I enter only enough to shut the door behind me.

"Why didn't you increase Individual L864k's anxiety level?" she asks.

This is about Jun. I must choose my words carefully. "I received the orders to do so at *36, and I completed them no later than—"

"No," she interrupts, voice still low and unwavering. "Why did you not increase after the emergency alert?" Her eyes don't blink enough.

I think back to the alert. It held no instructions to increase his levels further, only to immediately rectify the situation.

"The alert gave no direct instructions," I say. "And I was wary of increasing the levels again on the same day. Usually, it takes three days for levels to stabilize. I was monitoring and, had he proceeded, I would have caused a panic attack. He turned back, so I didn't need to."

"It was a close call." Her eyes drill into mine.

"I was there to monitor." *I know my job.* "If he attempts another job interview today or tomorrow, then there would be cause to raise his levels further. Or perhaps I would suggest something less harmful, like a further decrease in oxytocin or serotonin."

Liliya sighs like it takes focused concentration. "You don't feel sorry for him?"

"What difference would it make if I do? I'm just doing my job."

"Hmmm." She turns her chair back to her desk. "You may go now."

Trying not to appear too eager to escape, I quickly leave her office. I feel like I hold my breath until I reach the false safety of my office. If only I had a door to close.

I sit and take a slow breath. In and out.

Tread carefully.

Liliya asked if I felt sorry for him. Was her question borne out of only this incident? I know we must be monitored. Have my lingerings added together and they're questioning my loyalty? Or are they remembering how I behaved years ago? I've been the perfect employee since then, but they don't forgive easily.

If they decide I can't be trusted, I must be prepared.

Death is a necessary step that holds no appeal to me yet.

I release my thoughts and refocus on work.

When the time comes for me to head home, I decide to walk. I need to clear my head, and the crowded subway is not an adequate place. The only exit is still through the subway. I take the elevator to the basement level. Then, instead of hopping onto the subway, I take the stairs almost directly to my left.

The fresh air rolls down the stairs to greet me, and I breath deeply. I wish the window in my office opened. The air circulation system is flawless, but nothing can match the movement and refreshing nature of free, outside air.

I get out onto the street. It's tiny, with no cars. Transportation in the government sector is almost entirely by subway. I can count on my hands the number of people I can see on the street with me.

It's a sunny day, but the sun's rays don't have a chance to meet me. The buildings are too tall and too close together. For brief moments, gaps allow the sun to hit me and its warmth douses me. But with the next step, I'm out of its reach.

My thoughts swirl around in my head as my shoes clack on the pristine streets. It didn't use to be this difficult to mind the computers. To keep detached from my job.

This is it. My life. I'm heading back to my apartment the exact same as all my coworkers'. We all live in the same apartment buildings, here in the government sector. It's about a fifteen-minute walk for me. I'll eat supper, read, exercise, and go to bed. Tomorrow I'll do it all over again.

These streets don't even have a rock for me to kick.

I wonder what my family's life is life. Then I scoff. Why should I care? I don't pursue that line of thought.

My life is not so bad. I am assured of my position. Good food, if repetitive. Some time to pursue my own interests. A good retirement home. As long as I do my job, I am assured my life won't get worse. A lot more than many can say.

Like Jun.

Life is the way it is. That's all.

Before I reach my apartment building, I get another shower of sunlight. I stop for a moment, to bask in it. Turning my face towards the sun, eyes closed, I breath in deeply. It's so wonderfully fresh outside.

But I can't stay long. I must turn aside and enter my apartment building. Lingering is not encouraged.

Yes, life could be much worse.

CHAPTER NINE

Jun

I don't sleep.

Well, I'm sure I must have. But the sort of sleep where you drift in and out, never conscious of where the sleep begins and ends. It wasn't a restful night.

I trail into the kitchen long after everyone else has left.

"Jun!" Mom exclaims immediately.

I freeze. All this time awake and I still haven't landed on a lie.

"Haoya," I say instead.

The word doesn't fall flat so much as it trips and stumbles into a black hole.

She frowns. "What did you come back so late? What happened?"

I settle for saying the one lie that's certain. "I got the job."

Her face lights up. "Jun!" She hurries over and hugs me. "I'm so proud of you! I knew you could do it!"

It's like a fist is squeezing my heart.

She's so happy.

I'll face any amount of anxiety to make this job a reality. To properly earn her praise.

"But, then why didn't you come home? Why were you so late?"

"Training," I blurt out. "Actually, I've gotta leave. I'm gonna be late!"

"Oh… okay. Yes, of course! Go, go work."

I grab a protein bar from the table and rush out.

I hurry to the bakery. I have to get the job!

What if someone's taken it? Mom was so proud. I can't imagine having to tell her I lied—

I can't breathe. I stop walking and focus on taking deep breaths.

No one's got the job. That would be crazy bad timing. No way. It'll be okay. I'll go, and I'll get the job today. I don't want to keep lying to Mom. We need this money.

We *need* this money.

I start walking again, determined.

The job is mine.

I fail.

Taro meets me as he's heading home from work. One glance at my face, and he knows. He takes a small pouch out of his pocket.

"Here, it's your earnings from today. 3 cords."

I swallow and take the pouch. "Thank you," I choke out.

He hits my shoulder. "Tomorrow."

But tomorrow fails too.

I can't explain the surges of anxiety as I stand in front of the bakery. But then, I can never explain the anxiety.

I stop by the marketplace on my way home. I can't quite deal with seeing Mom yet. Hearing her praise when, in reality, I failed again. The money from Taro burns a hole in my pocket.

Dad is telling another story. People are crowding around his booth, the wares forgotten. But a few drop a cord or two into a tip box. We are all hungry for entertainment.

I give the crowd a wide berth, slipping behind a booth a few down from my Dad and working my way up. The other workers are used to this, but my cheeks still burn with embarrassment.

I sit beside Dad, on a second stool. Emi must be at home, helping Mom, since I can't. But who's helping Dad? We can't do everything.

Dad's telling the story of Issun-Bōshi. The crowd hangs on his every word as he makes dramatic gestures and different voices for the characters.

When he's finished, the people disperse. Dad sits back in his chair, tired. His old leg injury still bugs him, and standing for long aggravates it. But it makes the people happy.

"How'd it go today?" he asks me.

I inspect my hands. "It went well," I say carefully.

"Ah, you'll get it tomorrow."

I stare at him. "How…"

"You would be a lot prouder of yourself if you had gotten the job. But—" He slaps my knee— "I believe in you. Maintain the lie for your mother. She's so happy for you."

I blink back tears, feeling only worse. I nod.

Then, shattering the moment, a man from Sector 5 approaches the booth. Not unusual. Many from 5 shop in the Sentā gage. Almost all of them are difficult customers.

I keep my eyes trained on the man as Dad rises to his feet to greet the new customer.

Almost immediately, the man begins complaining and haggling over the price.

"4 cords? You expect me to pay this much?" He slaps the amount onto the table. "For one apple?" He waves it in my father's face. "Can you go any lower?"

My father's face remains stoic, his voice steady as he replies, "I bought them for 3 cords each. I have a family to feed."

"So do I!" the man exclaims.

I eye his shirt. Definitely made in Sector 6. What a waste of money for something only slightly superior.

"No," he says, "I'll pay you 3 cords for this apple! Nothing more!"

He goes to grab the cords off of the booth but stops. "What… I put four here! Now there's only two."

He glares at us.

My father shrugs. "I wasn't looking. You must be mistaken."

The man glowers at me.

I just look back. My heart is racing and my hands shaking, but he can't see them below the booth. "How could I have taken them?" I say. It's an innocent enough question, but with a challenge behind it that I've found works quite well. To accuse me is to say they didn't notice me taking their money right from under their nose, and no one wants to admit that.

The man grumbles, grabbing another cord from his pocket and slapping it on the table. Then he leaves.

"Your mother wouldn't approve," Dad says as he collects the cords. But there's a twinkle in his eye.

I open my hand, revealing the two cords I'd grabbed, and hand them over to him.

"We need to make a profit," I say. "He'll survive the loss."

"Sneaky." Dad grabs them from my hand. "Thank you."

"Well, if I can't intimidate people, at least I can make sure we still get paid," I mutter.

Then my eye catches someone entering the marketplace. My pulse spikes and I'm immediately on my feet.

"It's Aunt Hilda," I hiss. "See you at home!"

Then I rush out, ducking, weaving, and avoiding her eyesight completely. She makes me so nervous. Always demanding when I'm going to do something for my family, condemning me in her shrill voice. She's not really my Aunt, she's my Dad's cousin, but she demands the title.

I make my way back, preparing my lies and my happiness so Mom doesn't suspect. But I can't prolong this lie. And I don't know how much more Taro has saved up. Or if someone else might take the job. I need to succeed soon.

I really can't sleep that night. The guilt of someone else snagging the job is already upon me. Choking me.

I will enter the bakery tomorrow. Even if it kills me.

I leave with Taro that morning. The bakery might not be open yet, but I will have plenty of time to prepare.

Taro and I part ways. The bakery isn't open, so I sit and lean against the wall of a neighboring building.

The anxiety is welling up inside of me, building in intensity, to the point where I'm so lost in thought I miss when the baker arrives and opens up.

I suddenly become aware of the smell of baked goods wafting my way.

I stare at the door.

I stand up.

Abruptly, I'm at peace.

The sensation is so sudden and so foreign that I'm almost more uneasy about it. Is this a new and awful trick of my brain?

But the feeling stays. It's solid. I can do this. I am capable. My family needs me, and I won't fail them.

I walk into the bakery. The door creaks.

"Hello, what do you want to order!" comes a rushed shout from the kitchen.

"I'm actually here to apply for the job," I say, the words falling easily from my mouth.

Something heavy drops. The baker curses softly. Then she appears in the doorway, wiping her hands on her apron. Her hair is short, her face is red and sweaty, and her clothes are stained with ingredients.

"You're hired," she says.

"Just like that?" To be sure, I don't know how job interviews work, but I didn't think it was so easy.

She nods. "Can you follow instructions?"

"I'd be too scared to do otherwise," I answer honestly.

"I thought you had that look about you. First order: get rid of the 'help wanted' sign. Then come to the kitchen."

She gets me to grab one of the stones she must have dropped. I never thought about having to have multiple fires and stone ovens set up if you want to cook lots of food. Then she introduces herself as Carla and starts showing me how to work.

She is incredibly knowledgeable. Her instructions are seamless, issued at just the right time to act on without time to forget. I forget myself. My worries about making mistakes fade away. Her written recipes are so well laid out, that no one could mess up following them.

She handles all the customers! What a relief. That I couldn't handle.

Taro comes by and tells me they've all been given the rest of the day off. Unheard of, so he's going home, then to visit his girl. He makes sure I'm okay to walk back, then fairly sprints away.

At some point after that, I notice the familiar feeling of anxiety bubbling up. I resolutely ignore it. My mom was right. I can do more than my brain wants to let me believe. From now on, I'm going to ignore it. Unhelpful, broken signaling.

The day goes fast. Everything is sold by early afternoon, and then, I'm exhausted.

Carla chuckles at me. "You'll get used to it," she says. "The long days on your feet. But for now, go home. Come back tomorrow."

She hands me my pay. I clutch the coins. I earned this.

I walk on air on the way back.

Until I reach my home, and find it destroyed.

CHAPTER TEN

Kyra

Jun keeps trying again. It's now *80, and I should be going home. But I can't.

Aside from quick trips to other computers, I've been monitoring Jun's computer all day. All day he's been pacing in front of the bakery. I can't bring myself to release enough anxiety to cause him to turn away completely. It would probably be a mercy. But part of me wants him to make it. Even knowing if he makes it inside, I'll have to make him leave.

How can it be my job to make sure a family starves?

The thought is too familiar. Bile rises in my throat as the bitter memories rise to the surface. I grip my head, trying to keep my thoughts contained. If I don't ensure they starve, I risk my life. But what is my one life against their six?

I slump in my chair. It's comfy, but not enough to be a suitable substitute bed. Because I can't go home. I have to be here in case Jun sets out early. Taro leaves for work early. Judging from Jun's body language on their walk back home, I'm worried he's decided to leave when Taro does.

They have beds somewhere, for this purpose. But I hadn't decided early enough for them to link my office's alert system to one in a sleeping room.

I stare at the ceiling, debating whether I should try sleeping on the floor. At least I'd be properly horizontal.

I'm trying not to think about Jun. About how admirable he is. About the evil I'm doing to him and his family.

What does it matter if one family in Sector 4 goes against their parameters? Even if Jun had a job, their situation wouldn't improve by much. Not enough to matter to anyone else…

Except for me. Would I receive the death penalty? Or a few whips and days without food or water?

Will the slow death of watching his whole family die when I could have helped them be worse?

If I've done it once, I can survive it again.

Miserable and unsure, I curl up as best I can on my chair…

Green light flashes. A thin wail fills a sleepily quiet space.

I wake with a start, almost falling out of my chair.

An emergency.

Jun.

I stumble to my feet and walk towards the elevator on legs still half-asleep.

I step out of the elevator into the maze of computers. Before I take any more steps, I stop and force myself to wake up more. Venturing into the maze half-asleep could make me severely lost.

I shake my limbs. Do a few jumping jacks. Speak aloud, just to hear my own voice. Punch the air a few times.

Fully awake, I set out for Jun's computer. I'm not concerned about rushing. Jun has to walk all the way to the bakery. I'll make it to his computer before then.

Indeed, I have to wait in front of his computer for ten minutes before he reaches the bakery. And then it's not even open yet. He sits and stares at the building. He doesn't move.

My head keeps nodding, then jerking back as I realize I'm falling asleep. I do my best to watch intently, but he's not doing anything. He doesn't even notice when the baker does come.

I survey his vitals. Elevated heart rate, spiking adrenaline, and cortisol are rapidly rising.

His frozen form draws my attention back to him. My heart breaks. He woke up so early. So he could try more.

The computer doesn't track their emotions, but if it did, Jun's love for his family would be high.

What does it matter if he gets the job? If their lives go from struggling to bearable?

He deserves the job. If we can help those who don't try to excel at life, surely we can reward those who try exceedingly hard.

I type in a command I've never typed for Jun before. A reduction of cortisol and adrenaline. An increase of oxytocin and dopamine. It's a dramatic change but for the positive. I've counteracted the anxiety and reduced him to a neutral state. How long ago was he in one? It won't hold for long. The brain has habits and patterns and it would take more than this to erase his anxiety. In a day or so, the levels will start creeping back up, until he's back at his usual state.

But now he has an actual chance to get the job.

I grin to myself as he stands and walks into the bakery.

Something tugs in the back of my head. I should be worried. Why? He's getting the job. They'll survive. They'll still be stuck in a miserable state of poverty, but they'll survive.

Then I head back to my office to get what sleep I can before Matthew comes around to hand out the day's files.

Except it's not Matthew that comes to my door. It's a man I've seen before only in passing, silently trailing behind Liliya. He's tall and broad, and his face has lines from scowling. Intimidating.

My insides shrivel up. My mind instantly jumps back to only a few hours ago when I helped Jun. Fully awake now, I curse my past-self that went against direct orders. I signed my death warrant.

"Kyra," he says, "You need to come with me."

I was a fool. Even half-asleep, why couldn't I think about what would happen to me?

"Right," I say. "I'm coming."

I stand and follow after him. I expect him to lead me to Liliya's. Instead, we get into the elevator and he presses floor 7, which requires him to scan his ID. We're going to see the leaders.

I'm screwed.

If I'm smart, maybe I can get out alive. I don't think second chances are handed out often, but if I exaggerate the lack of sleep, perhaps I have a chance. I have an otherwise perfect record.

My mind whirls with strategies as we step off of the elevator.

This floor is identical to a regular office floor except all the offices have doors and are much further apart.

He leads me to the first door on the left and opens it.

It's a meeting room, containing one table, rectangular. Three people sit at it, facing the door. The room contains no other furniture.

I walk in. The door shuts behind me with a thud.

Liliya is one of the three. The other lady doesn't concern me. But the man stops me in my tracks. The Director. I've only seen him in person six times before.

He sits in the middle, glasses resting so far down his thin nose that he's not looking through them when he scrutinizes me. His suit is crisp, his posture stiff and uncomfortable.

"Miss Kyra," he says. "Please stand in front of us."

I move to the center of the room. Standing for this interview is probably meant to throw me off. But I'm walking out of here. Whatever it takes. I usually have excellent posture, but I let myself sag a little. My eyes I let droop as if they're heavy.

"Miss Kyra," he says again. "Do you know why you're here?"

I rub my eyes. "Um, I'm not sure," I mumble. "Did I do something wrong?"

The other woman cackles to herself. "Something wrong?" she repeats, voice shrill.

I flinch. Then act like I'm trying hard to think. "Did I do something wrong with Jun?"

The Director clears his throat. "You disobeyed clear, direct orders and allowed— nay, enabled Jun to operate outside the parameters that have been set for him. Do you remember your training?"

My blood runs cold. "Yes," I whisper.

"So you know how grievous of an action you've taken?"

I rub my eyes again. "I… I'm sorry, I'm trying to think. I'm exhausted."

Liliya frowns. "Why are you tired?"

"I slept here last night. It was awful." It was whatever, but I needed to do whatever I could to get them on my side.

"Did you not sleep in one of the many rooms available for our workers for this purpose?"

"I tried, but once I had decided to stay, I told Ben about it, and he said it was too late to install a connection between my office and a room."

"Why didn't you tell him sooner?" The Director asks.

"I didn't know. It was only at *65, when Jun and Taro were heading home, that I thought Jun might try to get up and leave with Taro the next morning. So I went to Ben and he said it was too late."

Silence.

I continue. "I was awoken at *18, so, I was right to stay overnight."

"Were you?" The Director asks. "He was only able to enter the bakery after you typed in your commands. Today might have been like all the other days." He folds his hands on the desk. "Why has he been allowed to try multiple days? Even *that* is borderline insubordinate."

This is a dangerous question. Carefully, I say, "He already has such dangerous levels, far beyond any other individual I have—"

The other woman thumbs her fist on the table and shrills, "Because he's the only one who keeps fighting!"

I acknowledge her comment with a nod. "He fights, yes, but it still gets him nowhere. I was hesitant to increase them if his present levels proved to be sufficient."

"They would have been— had you not interfered," The Director says.

I lower my head. "I certainly did not intend to."

Even now, I don't quite understand. I wish I hadn't. It was the actions of a foolish dreamer, the girl I was all those years ago.

"Kyra, these parameters are set for a reason. Everyone has their place in society, and it's dangerous for them to transcend it."

Except when it's in *your* best interests.

"Do we need to worry about you disobeying again?"

"No." I shake my head. "I promise— this was a culmination of poor sleep and many days weariness on overseeing a usually inactive individual. I have no thoughts of insubordination. This was a mistake."

The Director sits back in his chair and regards me.

My heart thumps in my ears. I stand still and straight, waiting for the verdict. There's nothing I can do now.

"Go home, Kyra," The Director says. "Take a few days. Rest. We'll rectify the L864k situation."

I nod. "Thank you," I say formally. But not overly grateful.

The Director waves his hand once in dismissal.

Once out of the office, I allow myself to relax. They gave me a second chance. I did it.

What a waste.

Now they're going to remove the job from Jun. I'm going to be under observation for a while. Not worth it. In fact, Jun will be worse off for getting the job and then losing it.

From now on, I must be careful to follow every aspect of every order I get.

I return to my office to grab my effects before heading back to my apartment. It takes no time to gather what I need.

As I go to leave, I crash into Matthew, who has launched himself into my office.

"Matthew! What on earth?"

"I heard you were going home for a few days, I had to say bye!" he says loudly. But his eyes are darting around.

"You'll survive without me for a few days."

He laughs. Too loud, too forced. Then he hugs me. In my ear, he whispers hastily, "They're planning to kill you." He pulls away. Searches my eyes.

"You know I'm not a hugger," I say.

He grins sheepishly and shrugs his shoulders. "That's why I didn't ask."

"Thank you."

He nods. With an effort, he holds himself back from saying more.

"Go," I say quietly.

He hesitates, then leaves.

They aren't forgiving. And I was a fool to believe them.

How will they do it? Maybe someone is waiting for me at my apartment, to arrest me for later torture. An example was just made, will they make another one so soon?

Or will they kill me quietly? When I never return for work people will speculate. But that's all they can do. My apartment might have been built with some sort of fail-safe. An "accidental" gas-leak. An explosive. A way for an assassin to get in. If they built all the apartments specifically for us, they definitely put in some sort of fail-safe.

Either way, I can't risk going back.

My brain isn't connected to a computer. I have money and knowledge. I can make it. I can run.

I grab my backpack and leave. As I'm heading down the hall, something tickles in the back of my head. I'm forgetting to do something. I turn around swiftly and go back to my office.

Everything is in my backpack, what could I be forgetting?

Should I change my passwords? The question pops in my head before I'm sure why it would be necessary.

If they're planning on killing me, then someone has to take over my individuals. But why would I change my passwords? There's no purpose, and they'd figure out how to get into the computers eventually.

I'm about to leave my office again when I think of Jun. My stomach drops.

They lied to me. Jun's not safe. Will they kill him?

It will be my fault if they do.

My stomach sinks. I have to make sure he's alright. If they go for him, he doesn't stand a chance. I need to change my passwords. No, only the password into Jun's computer.

It's risky. If someone's watching, they'll see I accessed the computer. But they have no reason to be concerned about me. I bought the bait. If it weren't for Matthew, I would be heading back to my apartment, congratulating myself on surviving and vowing never to get emotionally involved again.

I take a deep breath, then head out into the hallway. I walk slowly, as if tired as if time were at my disposal.

No one is in the elevator, and I reach Jun's computer without having to make small talk with anyone. Or explain why I have my backpack, ready to head home in the middle of a workday.

I call Jun's computer down. It always takes longer than I wish, but I'm more than just impatient this time.

"Hurry up," I mutter.

If they put an alert on my name, I've just sent off a signal. They'll know I'm accessing Jun's computer. They'll know something's wrong.

Jun's computer reaches the end of its track. I hastily assemble the keyboard and type in my password.

Next, to change my password.

It's easily done, everyone knows how to do it. Passwords are routinely changed every four months for security purposes. But we have to provide Computer Security with our changed password. If all goes well, they won't know I've changed it until they try to log in to this computer.

I go through the motions.

'Password computer specific' is a box I've never checked before, but it gives me great delight to do so now. When it comes time to enter my new password, I make the most random and complicated one I can. I slide my hands over the keys at random, then hold down shift, hit some numbers, more letters, and some capitalization.

It'll be difficult for them to figure this password out. I hope.

I wish I had time to give Jun a boost of bravery, but I can't risk it.

Password changed, I sent the computer back to its resting place and hurry for the elevator. Someone I don't know is in it, but luckily they get out as I go in. I take the elevator to the basement level and hop onto the subway. As I slide in a seat, I allow myself to breath a sigh of relief.

This is possible. It's achievable.

Now what?

Sector Four is easily reached. And when they realize I never reached my apartment, they probably won't think I would go to Jun's sector. Or it will be the most obvious choice. Either way, I must go. Jun has no idea what is about to happen.

The subway ride isn't long. I'm the only one who gets off at my stop. Not surprisingly, this is not the time most workers get off.

Once off the train, I pause. The stairs in front of me will take me to the base of my apartment. Not a good choice.

I turn and backtrack. At this station, I have one other stairway option, which comes out on the same street, further down.

As I climb this staircase, I reflect on the best way to get out of the government sector, and then to Sector 4.

I recall the map of the city.

The subway doesn't run to Sector 4, of course. I need to get there as fast as possible if I want to help Jun.

I reach the outside world and breathe in the fresh air.

My plan is set.

First, I must stop at a Withdrawal Booth. Take out as much as I can without raising suspicion. But even a little will go far in the poor sectors.

Then, I'll take the subway to Phoenix station. Go as far as it'll take me into Sector 7, which isn't to the end. Then I'll take a bus to the boundary, and cut through Sector 6 to be in 4. No problem.

I set off.

CHAPTER ELEVEN

Jun

Our house is a charred, collapsed ruin. Smoke furls upwards from the burnt wood, the scorched remains of what used to be my home. Ashes drift up the path towards me.

I freeze.

Did I make a wrong turn?

No. I never make a wrong turn. There's the Jamesons' house to the left, old man Lin's "house" to the right.

What—

What happened?

We had nothing to create fire in our house. I think we still had 2 matches, but those were precious and saved for only absolute necessity. Nothing was concerningly flammable. I can't imagine any scenario where *this* amount of damage could be done.

I can see charred figures in the rubble. My stomach flips in on itself and I can taste bile rising in my throat.

"Jun," a feminine voice says, and at the same time, a hand clasps my shoulder.

I whirl around, my hands automatically shooting out in front of me, ready to fight.

I've never seen this girl before. She's wearing lavish and formal business attire, perfectly fitted, with no wrinkles. On her back, a pristine backpack made out of stronger material than some of the houses in this sector. Is she wearing makeup? She's not from this sector. Her eyes pierce mine.

"How do you know my name?" I ask.

She frowns. "I can't explain right now. Your life is in danger." She surveys the remains of my house. "I'm sorry about your family."

"They might have survived it," I say. But even to my ears, my voice sounds hollow.

"No. They wouldn't allow that."

I don't know who she's talking about, but it confirms my worst suspicions. It knocks me to my knees. Nothing that could have happened by accident would remain so isolated to my house. Everything around it is untouched.

"Jun, I know this is hard, but we have to move. Now."

She's so calm. Something this horrifying should evoke *something* out of her. And how does she know my name? What does she know about this? What does it mean that she knows about it?

I surge back to my feet and step up to her. Usually, my height is enough to make people back up. But she doesn't move.

"What do you know about this?" I hiss.

"You need to get somewhere safe first," she says, face stoic. "I'll explain, I promise. But we need to get hidden before they send someone else after you or they figure out my password, otherwise we have no chance."

My eyes widen and the breath is squeezed from my gut. "What?" My brain can't comprehend what she could possibly mean.

She rolls her eyes. "What more can I say to convince you? Your life is in danger. Let's move."

I'm about to give whatever snappy retort I can muster when my attention is caught by someone far in the background behind her.

All my muscles tense up. My mind goes blank and suddenly I'm calm in the most adrenaline-high way.

"We have to hide," I say.

"Exactly what I've been saying."

I take off, passing old man Lin's house and taking an immediate left. I weave between houses, focusing on getting further away in both directions, moving more and more north-east. I don't pause to look back. That will only slow me down, and I can't afford any delays.

After a few minutes, I come across a little run-down tool-shed. The door's open. I think I'm far enough away now, so I duck inside.

I take a few steadying, deep breaths. Then I turn around.

"Aagh!" I jump back, knocking my head against a shovel hanging from the roof. "What are *you* doing here?"

The girl followed me. Now she stands between me and the door.

"Why would I have stayed?" She eyes me like she can't believe my stupidity. "I came all the way from the government sector to keep you alive."

"Can you say any sentence that makes sense?" I want to shout, but it's imperative we stay hidden.

"Who did you see?" she asks.

Why does she never answer my questions?

"The Cigarette," I answer. "He's an infamous sector 4 assassin."

"How'd you know it was him?"

"Only one person can walk openly around here with a cigarette in his mouth. Advertising you have a supply of matches to waste— that would get anyone else jumped or robbed."

"Duly noted." She nods like she's actually making a mental note of it. "Now what?"

"I don't know," I say. "If he saw us enter this, we're as good as dead—"

"He didn't. I was watching. We lost him."

"Okay. If we leave, we run the risk of bumping into him. But we can't stay here forever…"

My adrenaline is crumbling under the weight of indecision, and my breath is becoming rapid and shallow.

"We have to risk it," she says, matter-of-fact. "If we're on the move, we can keep moving. But if he finds us here, we're toast."

"Perhaps literally," I mutter. But she's right. "We have to get out of sector 4."

"We're not far from sector 3—"

I scoff to myself, earning a glower from her.

"What, surely you were joking?" I say.

Her eyes narrow even further, but she drops the subject. I can't tell if a glimmer of uncertainty passes through her eyes or if I imagine it.

I huff. "Are you going to tell me your name now?"

A moment passes where we regard each other.

"Kyra," she says finally.

"Nice to meet you," I say. "And when we get to safety, you're going to tell me how you knew my name."

She nods.

I find cracks in the walls on all sides and peek out through them. I don't see anyone, but there are many houses he could be hiding behind. Kyra said she was watching, but he still could have figured it out.

"Okay, I guess it's safe enough to go out," I say, turning away from the wall.

She's gone.

I rush out.

Kyra is walking east toward sector 5. How does she even know where to go? Why didn't she wait for me to take proper precautions?

I scramble after her, easily catching up.

"Why didn't you wait?" I demand.

"I told you, I was watching. How would he know we were there?"

"He's gonna know exactly where we are if you keep walking around in those clothes."

"It's fine, I'll trade the suit with someone."

"No one's going to trade with you."

"Why not? It's far superior material to anything you could get here."

"That's exactly it. No one here could wear it. They'd get jumped for it."

She stops walking. "Oh," she says. Her eyebrows furrow and her mouth pulls down.

"We can't stop!" I exclaim, my eyes darting around, worrying I'll see The Cigarette emerge from the shadows.

She resumes. "I'll have to steal some clothes."

"You can't do that!" I'm so indignant my voice squeaks. "How could you take from people who have so little? Most of us only have one or two pairs of clothes!"

She rolls her eyes and stops walking, taking her backpack off.

It's on the tip of my tongue to remind her, *again*, that we can't stop. But she drops to the ground, silencing my words. My eyes bulge. She rolls around in the dirt, effectively getting her shiny, fancy suit dusty and dirty. She grabs some mud and rubs it on her arms and legs. Her hair, which is long and luxurious, she ties at the back of her head in a messy and unstable bun.

She stands back up, grabs her backpack, and walks on.

"Wha- what was that?" I ask. "You just willingly ruined something that must have cost—"

"It was the only option."

She's way too casual. The price of her suit would have fed my family for *months*. But she's right, she was too conspicuous before. This is better.

We round the corner of a house and I almost run into the tall, lanky figure of The Cigarette.

I shout and punch him in the face.

Kyra grabs my sleeve and starts running. I follow.

"Does he have a gun?" she shouts.

Before I can reply, a loud sound cracks and seems to split the air, echoing between houses. I've never heard a gunshot so close. For a moment, my breath catches and I struggle to regain it.

"Never mind," Kyra mutters.

"This way," I say, veering to my right.

But then I only hear my feet pounding into the ground. I turn around, and Kyra's no longer behind me.

Where did she go? Do I go back for her? How could she possibly know her way around? I need her to tell me what she knows!

The Cigarette appears and I stumble backwards. He's holding what I assume is a gun. I've never seen one before, but I've been warned of them. He grins at me as he advances, still managing to hold his cigarette in his mouth. Wouldn't that get annoying?

I keep going backward, but I can't move fast enough to escape. But if I turn around, he'll shoot me for sure.

I trip over a bucket and fall to the ground. My right elbow hits the ground first and bursts with pain. But then the gun sound comes again, and the pain in my arm is completely overshadowed by a searing, intense pain starting in my upper left shoulder and quickly spreading so my whole shoulder feels aflame.

The Cigarette is at my feet now, pointing the gun at my head.

I brace myself. But I'm about to join my family. That can't be all bad.

But then Kyra jumps out from an alley, swinging her backpack like a club. It hits The Cigarette on his side, knocking him away from me. Kyra knocks him to the ground, then hits him with the backpack a few more times.

I stare at the sky, listening to the dull thuds of her backpack hitting his body, and his spitted curses, and I try not to pass out from the pain. She's got this.

Then the gun sounds again, and I jolt into a sitting position, which does no favors to my shoulder. But it's not Kyra who's been shot.

She stands above The Cigarette, holding the gun. It's smoking. His face is bloody, and I tear my gaze away.

"How'd you know how a gun works?" I ask.

She rushes over and crouches in front of me. "You're bleeding out, you have bigger concerns than my knowledge of a gun."

I wince and crunch my neck to inspect my shoulder. Red crimson flows out of me, staining the shirt that's been my only one for years. I've never seen blood on me like this before.

"Listen," Kyra says, staring into my eyes, "we have to get away from the dead body. People will have heard the gunshots."

My brain is going fuzzy, but I manage to say, "But we killed him. We're not in danger anymore."

Her eyes are apologetic. "No. We're in even more."

CHAPTER TWELVE

Kyra

After a few steps, it's apparent Jun can't move much further. Our walking pace is slowing to a shuffle. I want to move further from the dead body, but I'm not strong enough to move Jun if he collapses. We have to hide. On their own, the local authorities wouldn't care we got rid of an assassin. But if my bosses sent him, they'll alert every soldier stationed here to find us.

I scan our surroundings. Jun's not my only Sector 4 individual. I find a house I recognize. Markham's at work right now, and recently lost his wife, so his house will be empty.

"Jun, I can't carry you. You have to walk a little more. I know where we can hide."

"It hurts."

"Dying at their hands will hurt more. One foot in front of the other. You can do it."

It's a tedious process, but we make it to Markham's house. I open the door and lead Jun inside. He doesn't seem to register we technically broke into someone's house. I'm sure he would raise a fuss about it if he was clear-headed.

My apartment was bigger than this house. It's one room. The "kitchen" is in the left corner, in complete disarray. The bed is on the right. In the middle, a table, two chairs. Potted plants are scattered about in various stages of dead or dying. No bathroom. I had noticed an outhouse outside, it must be communal.

"On the bed," I instruct Jun, straining my muscles to help him reach it. Once he's on the bed, he tries to lay down. I grab his shoulders, holding him still. "Not yet. I have to clean and dress it first."

"With what," he mumbles, swaying as he attempts to stay seated.

I swing my backpack off and set it down. A puff of dirt rises from the floor. I grab my first aid kit. It's limited, but the supplies are clean. From the looks of it, nothing in Sector 4 is clean.

I open it, then pause. Jun's face is green, forehead beaded with sweat. I'm surprised he hasn't passed out yet.

Should I leave the bullet in his shoulder? Maybe it won't impair his mobility. It will only hurt more trying to get it out.

No. This is no sophisticated, small bullet from an upper sector. This is a large, clunky, lead bullet. It might not even be lead, but a concoction of metals that could poison him. I have to remove it. He'll have to bear the pain.

I stand up, scissors in my hand. I try to cut the fabric around the wound, but he grasps my wrist. A child could've shaken his hand off, but I pause.

"It's my only shirt," he says weakly.

"It's already ruined."

"Am I going to die?"

"No. But you will be in pain."

He blinks several times and doesn't let go.

"Can you trust me with this?" I ask.

"Why on Earth should I trust you?" he muttered. But he drops his hand.

Quickly, I cut away at his shirt and expose his shoulder. He's lost a lot of blood. I grab my water bottle from my backpack and flush the wound enough so I can see what I'm doing.

All I have to remove the bullet with are my scissors and a scalpel. I wouldn't trust any utensil from Markham's kitchen near an open wound. But I do grab a cloth that appears sanitary enough and give it to Jun. I don't need to tell him to bite on it. He does so without hesitation. His face is set, determined.

I grab the kit and place it on the bed so I'll be able to reach the gauze pads.

"I'm sorry," I say, then get to work.

The cloth helps muffle the scream that immediately rips from Jun's throat. I focus on removing the bullet as quickly as I can. It doesn't feel long for me, but I don't doubt the pain is excruciating for Jun.

Bullet out, I drop it on the ground and reach for a gauze pad. I manage to place it over the wound site right before Jun faints. He faints forward, his body now leaning against mine.

I sigh. Great.

With one hand keeping the gauze in place, and applying pressure, I use the other to remove the cloth from Jun's mouth. Then I attempt to gently lower him onto the bed, but his weight is too much for only one hand, and he flops down heavily.

"Sorry," I mutter.

I bandage the wound, using plenty of gauze, and tape it in place. Then I rearrange him into a more comfortable position, getting his legs properly on the bed and propping him upright as best I can.

Now it's the first time since the subway I can take a deep breath and pause. Now what? We can't stay here. I've got no pain meds. Are there enough cameras in Sector 4 for them to track us down easily? If a camera caught us going into this house, we're dead. And they can mess with Jun's head any way they want, once they crack into my computer. I check my watch. How much longer until they do? I'm glad it's not yet. Jun doesn't need to deal with being shot *and* however they decide to mess with his levels.

I frown at my watch. I doubt this sort of technology is common here in the lower sectors, if existent. Another thing to help me stand out. But I can't give this up. I need to be able to know what time it is.

Jun sighs deeply in his sleep. I stare at him.

What have I gotten myself into? I had one of the best lives I could hope for, and I threw it away. For what? Only to make his and my life worse.

"Useless," I mutter, sliding my watch so it sits higher on my wrist, hidden by my sleeve.

The chances we both survive this are slim. When they can control Jun's brain again, he'll be incapacitated.

If I want to have any chances of survival, I ought to leave now.

CHAPTER THIRTEEN

Jun

I'm in pain. Pain like I've never felt before. My shoulder still feels on fire. I groan, and try to shift into a more comfortable position. Pain bursts in my shoulder and shoots down my arm.

"Take it easy, boy, looks like you've been shot," a voice says to my right. It's a man's voice.

I *was* shot. By The Cigarette.

Who spoke?

My eyes fly open and I jolt into a sitting position. The sudden movement must have been a bad idea, because my head goes fuzzy and my vision dims.

Next thing I know, I'm prying my eyes open, staring at a wooden ceiling pockmarked with spider webs.

The voice sounds again. It's a comfortable, dad-like voice in its slow drawl and easy speech. "Yeah, that was the opposite of taking it easy. Sit up slower this time. I'm not gonna harm ya. Truth be, I almost knifed ya last night. Strange man lying in my bed. Till I saw your shoulder wound. But when I saw that bandaging I almost knifed ya again. Till I saw your face."

My brain moves slowly. Too much information. "My face?" What could he possibly mean?

"It's yer house that just blew up, yeah? Your family? Whole sector's talking about it."

I catch my breath. My family. My eyes well up.

"I'm sorry," he says. "I know how that feels."

Something in his voice touches my heart. I tentatively stretch out my right hand. This bed is big. Big enough for two people.

I try to sit up gently, using only my right arm. My stomach contracts in an effort to help, and with a grunt I manage to sit up slowly. My head whirls, but I don't pass out this time.

The man is sitting at a tiny table. He's sitting in a chair facing the door, drinking something out of a mug. A mug sits opposite him, at the other chair. The mug is dusty and undisturbed. A spider climbs down the handle and scuttles away. This whole place has been collecting dust and dirt for a while.

He's an older guy, probably around the same age as my Dad. It's like I've been punched in the gut. I take a deep breath and wipe my eyes.

"People thought you died too," he says.

"I was supposed to die."

He looks at me. His face is one of a man in pain, but my guess is it's nothing to do with my situation. "What are you mixed up in, boy?" he asks.

I sigh. "I don't know, Kyra was going to— Kyra! Where is she?" I cast my eyes about the room as if there's a section she could be hiding in.

"She the upper sector who had those sterile bandages for your shoulder? Ain't nothing in this sector that clean."

"Yeah, have you seen her?"

His eyes turn apologetic. "You were the only one here when I came in."

I drop my gaze. How could she leave? She promised to explain everything to me.

"She left me."

"Yeah, but she fixed you up real good first. You woulda bled out on my bed if she hadn't. That's gotta count for something. 'Course, she also stole some of my wife's clothing, so that's something too."

I don't miss the waver in his voice when he says 'wife.'

"I'm sorry," I say sincerely.

He waves his hand. "Ah, guess she doesn't need it anymore, yer friend can have what she took."

"No, I mean… I'm sorry about your wife."

He becomes preoccupied with his mug and blinks away a few tears. "Yeah…" He wipes his face and turns towards me again. "So you don't know what you're mixed up in? Word is they found The Cigarette. Dead. Shot with his own gun."

I don't know how I ought to reply.

He nods. "Didn't think you'd be surprised. That you or your upper sector friend?"

"It was Kyra. But she's not my friend. I don't…" I grimace, and admit, "I don't know who she is. I don't know anything about her."

He whistles. "You're really in it, boy."

"I guess so. Or maybe not, since she left. I don't know."

"Well, my advice is you don't go anywhere for a while. You probably lost a lot of blood. Need to recover."

"But—"

He waves his hand. "Don't worry, you can stay here. As long as you need. I'm headed off to work now anyways. You can eat whatever you can find in here. There ain't much."

He stands up, leaving his mug on the table. He grabs a worn out work-bag barely holding together.

Just before he leaves, I manage to get out, "Thank you."

He acknowledges it with a nod, but doesn't bother turning around.

Then I'm alone.

What now? I ought to be panicking. Usually, I would be. It's not that I feel peace, either. Too much has happened. The grief thuds in my chest, dull, unrelenting, pain beyond any gunshot wound. But there it stays. I can't weep. I can't wrap my head around this new world that doesn't have my family in it.

At some point I realize I've fallen asleep because I'm being shaken awake. My name is being spoken, soft and urgent.

"We have to go."

That's not the man's voice.

I open my eyes slowly. "Didn't think I'd be seeing you again," I say, my voice hoarse.

"You thought I abandoned you?" Her disapproval of my lack of faith is clear.

"Well I don't know you! I have no reason to believe you'd come back. Especially when—" I sit up. "Kyra, you! You *stole* the man's dead wife's clothes! Do you realize that?"

She stares at me. "You told me my clothes were too conspicuous, which they were. And no one was using them."

While she's right, she needed a change of appearance, I can't believe she'd be so callous about this!

She's put her hair in complicated braids, disguising how long her hair is. Hopefully after a few days of no washing, her hair will blend in better. And she's washed away any traces of the makeup she had been wearing. I guess she didn't need me to explain how conspicuous that was. Walking around Sector 4 for only five minutes would be enough for any sane person to realize no one here wears makeup except the few female soldiers.

"You promised you'd explain everything," I say.

"And I will. But we need to get somewhere safer." She pulls her sleeve up and checks something on her wrist. She frowns. "We need to get moving. Fast."

I really want to be able to fold my arms in defiance, but I know my shoulder would never allow it. And she's piqued my curiosity.

"What's that?" I ask.

"A watch."

I frown at the unfamiliar word. "The word doesn't help me if I don't know what it means."

She rolls her eyes. "Forget it, I can explain later. We have to go."

"Why?"

She groans. "Because people want to kill us, Jun!"

"Us?"

"I was marked for death the moment I helped you."

"Then go. Save your own skin. I'm injured, I'd only slow you down."

She gives me a look I can't decipher, her face a mix of regret and concern. "I can't."

"Why not?"

"I'd like to. It'd be a lot simpler. I'd be more likely to survive. But I owe you this debt."

Her words are cryptic, barely explaining anything. Something holds me back. I nod. "Alright. So at least explain why you left me yesterday."

"I had a few things to accomplish. And I didn't think anything I said could explain my presence to Markham. Someone from an upper sector, with something who was shot. He probably would've killed me."

"He almost killed me," I mutter.

She waved her hand. "An injured and unconscious man who's from this sector? He would at least give you a chance to explain yourself before killing you."

"Thanks for your concern."

"You're alive."

I notice the absence of her backpack. "Hey, where's your bag?"

"I traded it for a less conspicuous one." She reaches down and grabs a brown sack, worn, patched and re-patched.

"Perfect. You found someone to take your good one?"

"I went to Sector 5."

My eyes widen. "How much did you *do* last night?"

"Enough talking, we need to move."

She holds out her hand. She lends a surprising amount of strength as I grip her hand and stand up.

"Have you eaten anything yet?" she asks.

I shake my head. "He said I could help myself to whatever I could find, but I don't want to take anything from him. He's already done enough for us." I eye her clothes. She won't easily earn my forgiveness for the stealing.

"What I have is better quality," she says.

"So if his was better quality you'd take what little he has?" I ask indignantly.

"He offered," she says, reaching into the brown bag. She hands me a cheese roll, definitely from Sector 5. It's in a brown paper bag. "But no. I have enough money we don't need to take from anyone."

I take one bite of the cheese roll and am assaulted by flavour. My stomach rumbles and I realize how long it's been since I've eaten anything. Certainly it's been a long time since I've had anything this high quality. I stuff the rest in my mouth. Crumbs fall out of my mouth as I work to chew. As delicious as this roll is, it's now sucking the moisture out of my mouth.

"Wow. Need another?" She's trying, but it's hard for her to keep the disdain from her voice.

I nod, not trusting my mouth to work since it's so dry.

Kyra's holding a shirt she wasn't before. "Put this on," she orders. "Your old one is no longer in one piece."

My hands automatically reach out and take the shirt. "Is this one of his shirts?" I exclaim, then cough around the dryness. I shake my head adamantly.

"No, it's not. His only shirt is on his back. I bought this one. Put it on, you can't walk around shirtless with a bloody bandage on display."

I obey. Even though I try to move my left arm as little as possible, any movement makes me wince. Once I'm finished the surprisingly frustrating ordeal, Kyra is holding another roll in her hands. And a plastic bottle filled with water. I stare at it.

"Where did you get *that*?" I ask in disbelief.

"Sector 5." She hands it to me.

"You definitely paid way more than necessary," I say, taking it. I turn it over in my hands. The plastic is so clear. The water so clean. How does the bottle even get formed? My head tilts as I study it.

"Of course I did. They bought it from Sector 6 for more than they could afford to resell to all the wannabees in Sector 5."

I nod, half-listening.

"Jun, we have to get moving." She sounds tired of having to repeat herself.

Her voice breaks the spell of awe.

"Right! Sorry." I take the second cheese roll she's been holding out for me. "Where are we going?"

I'm less anxious than I have memory of ever being before. Like there's a chance we might survive whatever disasters Kyra knows about. Normally, theories would crowd my mind, each more dramatic and terrible than the last, about who's after me and how this could go wrong. Today, my head is empty. No thoughts. It's glorious.

"I know I said different yesterday, but right now, getting out of Sector 4 is the first objective," she says.

"Why?" I mumble, mouth full of a bite of cheese roll. A few dry flakes fly out.

She wrinkles her nose. "This is the first place they'll search for us. By now the whole sectors knows what happed to your family. You're too recognizable. The best plan is to get to Sector 5 and then we can figure out our ultimate plan."

"What do you mean our 'ultimate plan'?"

"Not important right now."

She's irritating.

"We should head to Sector 3 and then sidestep into 5."

"Why are you suggesting that again?"

She glares at me. "Why not? It's the best plan to get out of 4 the fastest."

"You're kidding, right?"

The way her face hardens gives me the impression I have 10 seconds to start explaining or she's going to abandon me to my fate. Or punch me in the face.

"Sector 3 is *the* dangerous sector. You don't go there unless you want to lose everything on you. And I mean everything."

"It may be dangerous, but remaining in 4 is risky."

"Less risky than 3."

"It would be a fast cut-through."

"Do you want to reach 5 with your backpack and money?"

She groans in frustration. "How bad can it be? Besides, look at you! Why would anyone mess with you?"

"Sector 3 messes with *everybody*."

And usually, just talking about it would be causing me worry. But I only feel what I judge to be the proper amount of trepidation and desire to avoid the sector entirely. Ever since I applied for the job, I haven't felt as anxious. It's starting to get unsettling. Why am I so calm?

"Jun, you're not listening to me!" Kyra snaps, voice raised.

I jolt back to reality. "Sorry. Listen, I appreciate you wanting to get out of here fast, but I'm not going to Sector 3. Ever."

"It can't be that much worse than 4."

"It is."

She glowers at me.

I don't know why she's getting so mad and refusing to listen. I'm the one who's lived here my whole life, not her. Why would she think she knows better?

Her expression is unreadable. In a negative way. Without saying anything, she goes outside.

Well, what does that mean? Is she leaving? Maybe she needs a minute to think. But I thought she was in a hurry.

I sigh and run a hand down my face. I really wish I knew what was actually going on.

I get up. Before I reach the door, it opens and she appears.

"We have to go," she says.

She's the one whose been delaying us!

"I'm *not* travelling through 3—"

"Not 3, fine, but some soldiers ahead have started searching houses. I think they're looking for us."

She is far too calm when she says that. And I'm far too calm in receiving it! Why am I not panicking? I'm only moderately anxious and my heart rate barely increased. What is going on?

"Then let's go," I say.

Somchow, my shoulder protests at the movements of getting up and walking. Why would my shoulder, all the way at the top of my body, be mad about the actions of the lowest part of my body? The pain thrums through me and I feel close to fainting. But I take deep breaths and shove the feeling down. We need to get going, get away. I can rest later.

I let Kyra lead the way. Somehow, she knows where she's going. Has she ever been here before? She certainly knows a lot about the area. Who is she, really?

She leads the way around buildings, peeking around corners, giving any soldiers a wide berth.

An unsettling thought occurs to me. What if *she's* not someone I can trust? What if she's part of this 'they' after me?

No, that can't be right. She saved me from the Cigarette. She patched my gunshot wound. Why would she if she wanted to hurt me?

'It could be a trick,' my brain persists, 'For something worse.'

But I just don't know what would be worse than slowly bleeding to death in the streets of 4.

No, I can trust her. At least as far as keeping me alive.

"Now will you tell me what a watch is?" I ask after we've been walking for a while. We haven't encountered any soldiers recently, so I think we're out of the danger zone.

"It's a way to tell time," she answers simply.

"How? That's incredible!"

"Not important right now." She glances around a corner before going onto the next street.

"But we can only tell by the sun," I say. "How is that tiny thing able to know?"

She doesn't answer, so I give up, instead asking for some more water. She hands me the bottle and I enjoy the cleanest water I've ever drunk. Except, suddenly, I can't even enjoy it. Once you get used to something, even if it sucks, anything new feels weird. I can't appreciate how pristine it is, only register the absence of the dirt and the overpowering copper taste. That's what our water tasted like. And I went to one of the best wells in Sector 4. Emi and I used to joke that, eventually, we would get superpowers from all the metal in the water.

The processed, filtered water turns to sludge in my mouth. I can't drink anymore.

A mother is sitting on the side of the road, back leaning against a building, trying to shush her sobbing toddler. Kyra walks by, never turning an eye.

I stop. Apology is written in the mother's eyes as she glances at me. But I lean down and hand out the water bottle. It's only half full, but her eyes shine as she takes it from me.

"Bless you, thank you!" she exclaims as she removes the lid.

I nod, not trusting my voice to speak. She drinks first, then gives the rest to her son.

Kyra has stopped walking, and she's staring, waiting for me to catch up.

"Don't tell me it was a waste," I mutter as I reach her. "If you can afford to buy the water at all, you can buy more."

But when I look at her face, I see an expression I didn't expect.

Her jaw works and her gaze is captured by the mother helping her son hold the water bottle, the unfamiliar object giving water they've been deprived of.

She shakes her head. "It's fine." Her voice catches and she clears her throat aggressively. When she faces me again, her face is blank. It's unsettling how fast she removed her expressions. "I told you, I have a lot of money on me. We can buy whatever we need. Now come on, no more delays."

CHAPTER FOURTEEN

Kyra

I can't stop seeing Jun giving the water away. Before I handed him the water bottle, he hadn't drunk anything since early afternoon the day before. He had to be thirsty, and it has to have been the best water he's ever drunk.

He didn't think twice.

When was the last time the mother drank water?

I shake my head. I need to snap out of it. I can't solve everyone's problems. Jun and I are in enough danger without concerning myself with other people. These lower sectors hold numerous people in the same position as that mother, and that's just how this world works.

A quick glance behind me shows Jun is still following me. He walks with a spring in his step I've never seen before. He glances at everything around him with mild curiosity instead of his usual constant scanning for possible threats.

They haven't cracked my password yet. It won't be long. I need to explain everything to him while he still has a rational brain to process it.

And yet.

He's going to hate me.

But he'll need me to stay alive. Once they hack their way into his computer, they're going to incapacitate him.

I barely lift the edge of my sleeve to check the time on my watch. *75. Later than I would like, and we're only now crossing into Sector 5. Jun slept too long. But, he was shot, and had lost a lot of blood. I can't begrudge him the sleep.

Jun stumbles into my shoulder.

"Sorry." He shakes his head, and stops walking. "Woah." He takes a deep breath.

I stop, too. "What's wrong?"

"Got light-headed," he says. "I'm okay now."

I purse my lips. "You need to eat. Two cheese rolls isn't enough, and you're still weak from blood loss."

"Okay, do you have more cheese rolls in your backpack? One will do me for the rest of the day, assuming you don't plan to walk all night, too."

I reach up and pull back the collar of his shirt. He flinches, but then realizes what I'm doing. The bandage is mostly blood.

"Your bandage needs to be changed."

"Is something wrong?" he asks hastily, anxiety creeping back into his voice.

"Not necessarily," I answer.

His eyes widen.

"It clearly hasn't clotted yet. Which is fine. I couldn't stitch it, and we've been walking for a few hours. I'll change the bandage. If you don't move around like crazy in your sleep, it'll probably clot overnight."

"Oh."

His shoulders relax, but not completely. Understandable, I imagine it would be unsettling to be shot and wounded.

"What's the status on a cheese roll?" he asks.

"I only bought four, and we each ate two. I have money, we can buy more food."

He frowns. "It's going to be more expensive in Sector 5."

I shrug. "I told you, I have enough money."

He shakes his head and glances back at Sector 4.

What now?

"We should buy from someone in 4," he says.

"Why? The quality of food will be better in 5."

"The quality doesn't increase as much as the price does. It's not worth it."

His tone holds a note of warning. I swallow my response and take a breath. I don't think the money difference is enough to be concerning, but it's not worth getting into another argument with him.

"Okay, let's go back to 4," I relent, starting to head back. "It's about as dangerous as barely being in 5. Same amount of cameras."

"Hold up." Jun gets in front of me, cutting me off. "Cameras?"

I hesitate.

He steps closer to me. "Kyra, what are you talking about?"

"The government has cameras put up," I answer. "All over."

"And the government's the people who want me dead?"

"Yes."

For a moment, it seems like he stops breathing. "Where are they?" he asks.

"You won't be able to see them. I can't see them. I only remember where they are. And there's not as many as you think there are. They don't have as many cameras in the lower sectors, because they're not as concerned with what happens to the people here."

His eyes turn harsh. "How do you know that and how do you know where they are?"

Now is not the time. He's tired, hungry, and in pain. He won't receive it well.

"Jun, I know I promised I'll explain. And I will. But now is not the time. We're tired, we're hungry, and I need to tend to your wound. I swear, I'll explain everything in the morning. First thing."

For a moment, I worry he won't relent. But, he nods, and moves to the side.

"Then let's get supper."

We manage to find a small vendor as they're packing their wares onto a tiny wagon. She gladly sells the rest of her stock to me, which isn't much. Between Jun and I, we can carry it all. She names her price and I survey our food. She would barely make a profit, so I pay her more. It's not much to me, but it'll make a huge difference for her, and whatever family she might have.

We search around for a few minutes before finding an alleyway between two houses. It's short, dry, and has a broken down-house partially obscuring the entrance. The house will keep us hidden. One of the roofs hangs out past the wall, which means we'll have some shelter if it rains.

Now we can eat.

"This… is questionable." Jun's holding the stew in his mouth, not swallowing.

"Don't talk with food in your mouth, it's bad manners," I instruct. "Besides, you're the one who insisted we get food from 4."

He shuts his mouth, and forces a swallow. His whole body shudders. Then, he cocks his head to the side. "You know… the aftertaste is not bad. I enjoyed about 10% of the experience."

I scoff. It can't be as bad as he makes it out to be.

As soon as the soup's in my mouth, I freeze, as Jun did. He laughs.

"Too much for your upper sector pallet?" he teases.

"You did the same thing!" I exclaim around my mouth-full of soup.

He raises an eyebrow and shakes his head. "Don't you know it's bad manners to talk with food in your mouth?"

I give him the harshest glare I can muster. Then I do my best not to think about it, and swallow.

The soup almost makes a reappearance, but I manage to keep it in my stomach. Jun's making fun of me. His eyes are dancing with mirth.

I take a steadying breath. "Whatever is in the soup has definitely gone bad."

Jun shrugs. "It was probably bad when she bought the ingredients. It's cheaper." Then he digs back into the stew, showing none of his previous hesitation.

We finish our food in silence. At least this is better than going hungry.

I'm grabbing my first aid supplies out of my backpack, to change Jun's bandages, when he says, "I'm sorry we're not out of 4 yet, but it's better than being in 3. Believe me."

I open the kit, considering my next words. I need him to be able to trust me when I tell him everything tomorrow. Also, as much as it stings my pride to admit, he's probably right. He's lived next to Sector 3 all his life. How can that compare to watching through the eyes of computers?

"I pushed the issue when I shouldn't have," I say. "Also costing us time. This is about as safe as we could get. And it's probably better to be farther away from Sectors 1 and 2. Now take off your shirt."

He uses only his right arm, wincing a bit. I wish I had bought medication. I can't imagine the pain he must be in.

Carefully, I peel away the old bandage. It's crusted with blood, sticking to his skin. I use some water to separate it, trying to use as little as possible.

"Kyra… why don't we want to be closer to 1 and 2?" His breath ruffles my hair. "I know Sector 2 is where we get our fruits and vegetables from. Well, what little that does come here."

He's almost right.

"Exactly. They're the sectors forced to work for the government. Nothing but hard manual labor, military enforcement, and poor rations. We don't want to be near those extra soldiers." As I speak, I kick myself for not having realized that danger earlier. How poorly does he think of me after our argument?

I have to use more water to clean the wound, but risking infection is too dangerous. We'll be heading to Sector 5 tomorrow, I can buy more water.

He sucks in a breath as I wipe around the bullet hole.

"Plenty of people travel to those sectors for work because they can't find anything else," I continue, grabbing a fresh gauze pad. "Sector 4 is left pretty much alone. Sector 5 would be, too, but they're actively seeking attention."

"Yeah, they're the worst."

I hold his gauze pad in place, place a larger bandage on top, then grab some tape. My eyebrows furrow in concentration as I try to tape sparingly, but so the bandage won't move as he shifts in his sleep.

"Done," I say, grabbing my kit and going back to my side of the alley. "Try not to jostle it in your sleep."

"I'll try."

There's a moment of silence, that I personally feel is awkward. Perhaps he doesn't.

"Kyra, what *is* your plan?" he asks.

"We're getting out of this place. Beyond the city walls."

His eyes light up. A spark of hope. "We can do that?"

"It's dangerous. But yes."

He grins to himself. "Well… goodnight," he says, resting his head against the wall.

"Goodnight."

I lay down, resting my head on my backpack. I close my eyes.

"Kyra?"

"Yeah?"

"Promise you'll tell me everything tomorrow?"

"Promise."

CHAPTER FIFTEEN

Jun

Everything hurts. My bullet wound isn't even the worst of it, my neck is. Whatever odd positions I assumed as I slept have not done my body any favors. Kyra at least had her backpack for a pillow. She's still asleep.

It's a little chilly, but just in an early morning sort of way. With the rising sun, it'll get hot soon enough.

As my body wakes up, my shoulder wakes up more too, the pain steadily increasing and making its presence known. I try to ignore it and relax, not hold myself in tension.

I wonder when Kyra will wake up. I know it's no use trying to go back to sleep. My brain is awake and alert, ready for action. Probably for the best. Apparently people are trying to kill me.

One would think, between my house exploding and getting shot, I'd be able to wrap my head around the idea. But it makes no sense. What have I done would make somebody want to kill me? Or even take notice of me.

Or kill my family, too.

I try to swallow the lump rising in my throat, but it refuses to budge. I stare at the sky.

"I hope," I whisper, "I hope you're happier up there. I hope you have lots of food. You'll never go hungry again."

Kyra stirs, then sits bolt upright. Her head whips around, taking in our surroundings, then me. "Did you speak?"

I nod.

"Oh." She relaxes. "What time is it?" She checks her watch. "Oof. Overslept."

"What? I thought the upper sectors got to sleep in?"

She snorts. "I'm not exactly 'upper sector.'"

Great, now's the time when she explains. I lean forward. "What are you, then?"

She hesitates. "Shouldn't we eat first?"

No way. I'm done waiting for answers. I need to find out if I was wrong to trust her. Something tugs in my mind. Something she mentioned the first day, when we were hiding in that shed.

"You said you came from the government sector," I say. "To keep me safe. I thought there were only 10 sectors."

She won't meet my eyes.

I persist. "Why are people trying to kill me? Why *did* people kill my family?"

"There's… a lot to explain," she begins haltingly.

"So explain it," I say. I'm not compromising. She's clearly uncomfortable or nervous or whatever. But I don't care. Somebody— or some group— killed my family, and now they're after me. "I already know this world sucks," I add. "Just tell it to me straight."

She takes a deep breath, then says, "Those pregnancy pills don't only help create a safe pregnancy and healthy baby."

Okay. Not where I thought she'd start. I lean back against the wall, trying to show I'm listening by my body language. Trying to help her be more at ease, because I had been leaning forward like I might lunge at her.

Her gaze is unflinching now and she meets my eyes, determined. "Those pills connect the brain of the baby to a computer housed in the Control Centre in the Government Sector. Everyone, in all the sectors, is connected to a computer. Every computer is run by an IO, Individual Overseer. The computers… control your brain. For the most part, people's lives are predetermined, and parameters established for the computer to operate within. The IOs make sure no-one breaks those parameters. Or, they enable those the Selection Committee chooses to be elevated, or to fall."

"Stop." My head is spinning. "What are you saying?"

"The government controls the hormones your brain activates and secretes. Thereby… controlling you."

My voice is hoarse when I ask, "My anxiety?"

"Product of some typed commands into a computer."

I stand up. My shoulder protests at the sudden movement, but that barely concerns me right now. She stands up, too.

"Jun, I know this is a lot, but you need to listen."

"No, stop!" I hold up my hand. "How do you know this?"

"I was assigned to your computer. You were my individual." Her gaze is unflinching. Unapologetic.

I step closer to her, forcing her to back up until her back hits the wall. She should feel a lot more scared than she looks.

"You did all that to me?" I hiss. "You put anxiety in my head? *Debilitated* me? Do you know how *ashamed* I always felt? And it wasn't even me! I was being controlled. WHY?"

"Your mother was an extraordinary woman—"

"You don't get to talk about my mother!"

"—I trained under the woman who had your mother as an individual. She showed me your mother's levels. At the time, they were the most elevated levels I had ever seen. I couldn't understand why they were necessary."

She's not answering my question. I hate hearing her talk about my mother. It hurts, but it's more than the sting of loss. I don't want to hear about someone I love so much from someone I no longer trust.

Krya continues. "I was told that those levels were necessary. That your mother was so capable, anything less would allow her to rise about her station. And they don't want that. Then, I was assigned to you. You have her same capability, her same strength. So I was ordered to do the same to you. To never let you succeed."

"What are you talking about, I'm not strong! I'm weak, then, if what you're saying can even be trusted! Mom did all those things, she raised a family, even with you messing with her brain. I couldn't even get a job. I'm weak, that's why it affected me so bad."

"No. It affected you so bad because the levels were so intense. They had to be intense because you are so strong."

I hit the wall beside her head. "Don't try to flatter me! Not when you're telling me you're responsible for making my life hell all these years. How am I supposed to trust you?"

"Because I went against orders, reversed those levels and enabled you to get your job. Because I left my sector to come find you. Because I saved you from bleeding out to death. And because I'm going to help you escape."

I know she's right. What I felt that morning I walked into the bakery was like nothing I'd ever felt before. It wasn't even my own merit. I didn't overcome my anxieties, she reversed them.

This is too much. It's like she told me to draw water from a well with no bucket, I can't even begin to wrap my head around any of it.

"I'm sorry," she says.

"Why did you do it?" I ask.

"I had no choice. Like everyone else, I was plucked from one of the higher sectors as a child because they saw potential in me. My connection to my computer was destroyed, and I was trained to be a Control Officer. The price of disobedience is death. I had to leave."

My heart plunges into my stomach, where it cracks in two. I can't breathe. Untamed dread bursts forth in my stomach. This time, I know it's all my own feelings.

"You disobeyed…" I say, and she freezes. "You let me take a job. The same day I got the job, actually got it, my house blows up. The Cigarette is sent to kill me."

She doesn't say anything, which is probably good. She stays still, like she's accepting her fate.

"It's your fault." My voice breaks.

She looks at me. Her eyes are misty, probably the closest she's ever gotten to crying. She's shown no concern for the people of sector 4, she killed The Cigarette, she stole clothes from a man's dead wife without a second thought, and with all the money she says she has, she's not given any away to those who need it more than us.

"I'm sorry," she says.

"Yeah, well," I inspect the ground, blinking rapidly, "Sorry doesn't bring me back my family."

"No. But it could save your life."

When I speak, my voice is hard as ice, and I don't recognize it. "Do you think there's any way I would trust you after this? You're the reason my family is *dead*."

"I know, I know, and I'm *sorry*. But you need me to survive this. Survive them."

"Why would I need you? I'm the one who's been surviving in the poor sectors my whole life. You've been in an office, a plushy government job, paid to stand by and watch us suffer."

She shakes her head. "No, you don't understand. I changed the password to your computer. That's why you haven't felt any anxiety return. But they will code their way in. When they do, they are going to hit you with everything they have. It could kill you. It'll definitely debilitate you. You won't make it on your own. You don't even know where you're going."

I step closer to her. Narrowing my eyes, I lower my head so our faces are on the same level. "I don't need you," I hiss. "My life would be better off without you in it."

"Jun, wait!" she shouts as I take off.

I run. I don't know where I'm going. My home is gone. My family is gone. But I run anyways.

As I run, people shout, gasp, and move out of my way. Curses get shouted at my back. I think I knock somebody over.

My eyes blur, and it takes me a minute to realize it's because they're filling with tears.

My foot hits something hard. I stumble, but manage to put my hands out to stop myself from hitting the ground. But in the same instance, my shoulder buckles, and gives out, my shoulder hitting the ground with a thud. Pain rips through my arm. I roll over, lying on my back. My chest is heaving.

It's silent, except for my breathing. No-one's around.

"Argh." I manage to sit up, but the pain almost makes me pass out.

Once again, I scrunch my neck to get a glimpse of my shoulder. Oh no. Blood seeps to the edges of my bandage, then trickles down my chest, staining my shirt as it goes.

I don't have anything clean to replace the bandage. So I apply pressure to the area with the palm of my hand. I wince at the sensation, but keep my hand firm.

Gingerly, I stand up. This might have been a bad idea. I don't know how to get out of this city. Until last night, I didn't even know that was possible.

I'm in a residential area. I don't recognize it. I stumble down a random, winding path through the houses.

How can I trust her? How do I know she didn't tell me lies? I don't know why she would fabricate such a story, but I still can't trust it. I don't know what to trust anymore. My mind is spinning and the world refuses to make sense.

Unbidden and unnoticed, my hand has stopped putting pressure on my wound and is instead rubbing my stomach, as if to sooth it. A normal habit, but suddenly it feels so foreign.

A bubbly feeling springs up inside my stomach, gurgling and rising. My breath quickens, and I my heart beat speeds up. The world spins around me, and my mind is consumed with fear.

I can't think. I can hardly stand.

My knees hit the ground, but I don't feel it. Dimly, in my mind, I register that this is what Kyra said would happen.

I try to breath, but brain can't send the command around the crowding chaos of panic.

My eyes roll into the back of my head, and darkness takes over.

CHAPTER SIXTEEN

Kyra

My head is on a swivel as I walk, examining all my surroundings as I try to find Jun. I'm following the trail of grumbling people, and faint shouted curses in the distance.

He's faster than me. But I also can't assume he ran in a linear line. Any alleyway he could've ducked into.

I should've known he would react badly. Of course he would. It's a horrifying reality to suddenly be made aware of. Years of being on the other side of the computer has calloused me. But I had to tell him. He had to know. And I had to do it before they were able to mess with his head. How could I have made it any more digestible?

I check my watch carefully, not letting anyone else see it. *30 It's now been almost 2 full cycles since I changed my password. Our technology is advanced, and our coders the best. If they haven't gotten in by now, they're getting in any minute now.

I increase my speed, but not to a full run. I can't risk running right past him.

So far, he hasn't strayed from a main path. I doubt he was thinking about his direction. It looked like he wanted to escape.

At some point, he's going to start. And then he could take any turns, go anywhere.

I'm surrounded by houses now. This main path cuts right through a massive sprawl of a chaotic residential section. It's quiet, and I see no one. Everyone must be at work.

Jun could have gone anywhere here, and I'd never find him.

I sigh, and stop walking. What am I doing? He is capable. He doesn't want to see me. I don't blame him. Maybe he could make it.

No. I shake my head. He's injured. That alone is enough reason to find him. He doesn't have the supplies to take care of himself. If his wound gets infected, it would be disastrous.

A figure on the ground catches my eye. It's Jun!

I rush over.

He's not awake. But breathing. It's shallow and uneven, but better than nothing.

His shoulder is bleeding again.

Quickly, I add bandages on top of the old ones, taping them in place. Those were my last. Unfortunate, but how could I have know there'd be a bullet wound to deal with? I can buy more in Sector 5. Hopefully.

I check his head to see if he hit it anywhere when he passed out. No bumps or bleeding that I can find.

Now what?

I can't move him by myself. He's taller and broader than me, and much stronger. It should be fine to stay here until he wakes up. No one's around. We're in full view of the main path, and closer than I would like. But I can't change that.

So I wait.

It's awkward to sit beside an unconscious body, waiting for them to wake up. So I draw in the dirt a map of the city and all the sectors. Getting out isn't going to be easy.

I try to recall how big each of the sectors are. How long will it take us to get out— assuming Jun can travel at the average speed. Assuming he changes his mind and comes with me.

Jun's breathing changes. It hitches, pauses, then he takes a deep breath. He groans.

I want to speak up, let him know he's safe. But my voice might have a negative impact. So I stay still, keep my eyes on the map in the dirt, only glancing at Jun out of the corner of my eye. My knees are up, my arms and chin resting on them.

He shifts a few times, opens his eyes, and slowly sits up. He knows I'm here, but he doesn't say anything.

Moments pass, where he focuses on restoring his breathing pattern, and I focus on inspecting the dirt.

Finally, he says, "I don't usually pass out this often."

"Not your fault. Being shot will do that to people."

He studies his shoulder. "Did you clean my bandage again?"

"Had to. Your bandage wasn't soaking up any more blood."

Inside my backpack I find a bunch of some kind of granola bars wrapped in a cloth from last night's purchase. I grab one and hold it out to him. He takes it, and eats in silence.

Then he notices the map.

"This is the city?" he asks.

I nod.

He inspects it. "Where's the exit?"

"Here." I point. "In Sector 2. They're the only Sector allowed to pass through the wall, outside. They plant and raise animals."

"Really?" he asks, meeting my gaze for the first time since he woke up. The awe is evident in his face. "They're allowed *out*?"

"They get food for the Upper Sectors. Nothing grows well in the city, so they grow it outside. As a result, it's heavily regulated. Walled on all sides, with entrances into it only in Sector 3, allowing the soldiers in, and the people who come in for jobs."

"So we have to get in through there."

"Yes."

"How?"

I frown. "That depends on if the soldiers are on the lookout for us. Have our names and faces and orders to take us in if they see us."

He drops his gaze. "I didn't pass out from the bullet wound," he says, voice low. "My brain just shut down because… I felt…"

"They increased your levels?" I supply, avoiding the word 'anxiety.'

"I've never felt *anything* like that before. I couldn't even rationalize that I wasn't in danger. But now, I don't feel anything. What's going on?" His eyes are pleading.

I take a moment to think, gather my thoughts.

"Do you know the parable about the frog on the frying pan?" I ask.

The look he gives me indicates he has no idea what I'm talking about.

"It's an old one, from before all this," I continue. "If you put a frog in a frying pan and immediately turn it on high heat, it'll jump out. But if you gradually turn on the heat, it won't. It'll adapt. It'll keep adapting as you slowly increase the heat. Until it dies."

His eyebrows are furrowed. "What's a frog?"

"It's a little amphibian creature. Not the point. They increased your levels all the way. It was a massive surge. Your brain shut itself down, did a restart. Just like the frog jumping out. They're going to realize they have to do it slowly. Your brain will adapt. And keep adapting." I stop.

He fills in the gap. "Until I die."

"In theory."

He laughs wryly. "Right."

I risk adding, "Which is why we have to move as fast as possible. Get out of the city before they have a chance to do you much harm."

"And what will getting out of the city accomplish?"

"I have a theory. If we get far enough away from your computer, the connection will break. It'll have to, eventually."

"What happens to my brain when the connection snaps?" he asks.

I don't know. I remember what it was like for them to destroy my connection. Not fun, highly painful. They don't break connections past 16, because it's too risky. Or so they've told us.

"I don't think it will break the connection," I say. "You'd only be out of reach. So, you should be fine."

He searches my eyes. "But I wouldn't be fine if the connection was broken any other way?"

I hesitate. It's a loaded question. I randomly doodle in the dirt as I consider my answer. Finally, I say, "There is one other way to truly break the connection. Get rid of it forever."

"Great!" he exclaims. "Why don't we do that?"

I sigh. "Because it's risky and painful. I would have to destroy your connection from your computer. I don't know how that would affect you. And your computer is in the government section. The chances of me getting killed before even reaching my building are higher than me succeeding."

His shoulders droop.

"Getting out of reach should do the same thing," I say. "With the stipulation that you can't get too close to the city otherwise you'll be in range again."

He's not looking at me.

"You don't have to decide now. But we'll die if we keep stationary. So we need to keep moving." I get to my feet.

He doesn't move. He still can't trust me.

Can I blame him?

I try to be gentle when I say, "This is the second time I could have let you bleed to death. I didn't."

He turns his head the other way.

"Jun, you don't have to forgive me. I'm asking you to trust me. Let me lead us out of the city."

He considers. "Okay. But I want to know the plan. The full plan. And I'm involved in every decision we make. We're equals in this. You swear?"

"I swear."

CHAPTER SEVENTEEN

Jun

Kyra tells me her plan, but it isn't much of a plan. We're going to travel through Sector 5, stock up on what we can, then cross into Sector 3 at a place very close to the Sector 2 entrance, which I approve of. Kyra doesn't know anything about the entrance to 2, though, so she has no clue how to prepare for it. Then we make it through a Sector crawling with soldiers, heavily regulated, to the outside, then somehow escape from the farmland without anyone noticing. All while some government people far away are pushing buttons on a computer and making me more and more anxious.

Yay.

She seems confident it will work. I don't know why. The resentment I have towards the plan might be due to my anger at the plan-maker. But like that's going to change my feelings towards it.

As we cross into Sector 5, she walks by my side, at peace, her air unworried. How can she be so calm? She just completely upended my world!

I try to remain optimistic. Not my strong suit. At least it's something. A tiny sliver of a thing. Plus the opportunity of getting outside the city! You learn early on as a child not to even bother dreaming about it, because no one thought it was possible. Some speculated there *was* no outside of the city, that it was all smoking, ruined wasteland. That the war left scars the natural world couldn't heal from.

But how could we know— Sector 4 has no schools, no one to teach us our history. I scoff. Could we even trust the history? We've been lied to in a massive way. No one has any idea our brains are linked to computers.

I stop short.

Kyra turns around. "What now?" she asks.

"We have to tell people," I say.

"Tell them what?"

I lower my voice. "Their brains are linked to computers. That they're essentially mind-controlled." I make my voice even quieter. "That there are cameras everywhere."

"Why are you whispering?"

"So the cameras won't hear."

She rolls her eyes. "They can't."

I frown. "The cameras don't have audio?"

"They don't need audio when we can see inside your brain."

I shudder. "Good point. Alright, then, but we still have to tell people."

She shakes her head. "Jun, people won't believe. Why would they? They have no reason to."

"I did."

"You had a reason," she says quietly. "For the most part, people in these Sectors are left alone. Their lives already aren't great, so there's no reason to destroy their fortunes and make their lives worse. And they'll never elevate someone from here to a higher sector. So it's only when people here have real potential that they interfere. To inhibit it."

I try to wrap my head around this. I still haven't thought much about what she said about me this morning. My potential and abilities being the reason struggled so much. It's just not right.

I push those thoughts aside. "We still have to try," I insist. "It's not fair to leave them here to suffer."

She just looks at me for a while.

Finally, I get fed up, and say, "What?"

"Can we at least walk while we discuss this?" she says, sounding tired. But not sleepy-tired. Tired of me.

I assent, and we resume walking.

I hate Sector 5. They use their proximity to Sector 6 to try and elevate their status. Ironically, because they purchase so many unnecessary things from Sector 6 (like plastic water bottles) and sell them for higher than people can afford (when you can easily reuse a cup), they keep themselves in a state of poverty almost identical to my Sector. Their clothes are nicer than ours, but everyone only has one pair. They bought above their pay grade, and can only afford one.

And their attitudes are so unpleasant. The way they carry themselves with such ego, as if they were better than us. As if a higher sector number increased their value as humans.

Kyra doesn't seem to notice me stewing in deep-rooted dislike. She continues our conversation. "You have to realize something, Jun. For most of these people, their situations would be the exact same, whether their brains were linked to a computer or no."

"How can you be so *heartless*? Is this just government propaganda you've actually believed?"

"Can you think about what I'm saying for one second?" she snaps.

I clamp my mouth shut and aspire to think. But I'm too mad at her attitude and at being in Sector 5.

"There's a pharmacy," she says. "I'm going to buy some more first aid supplies. They might even have pain killers for you."

"Great." I try to sound sarcastic to make her mad, but I'm actually ecstatic. My shoulder is vengeful, and it's been shooting electricity down my arm and even up my neck. I've been holding my left arm with my right as we walked, to take some of the weight off my shoulder. It's helped, but not much.

We enter the pharmacy. The same one I purchased Mom's pills in only days ago. The difference is electric, but only to me. It's the same building. But I'm not the same. The air in here makes my skin crawl. Everything has changed since a few days ago, when I could barely even ask the guy for the pills.

Kyra sets off with purpose through the aisles, grabbing supplies here and there. How does she know where everything is? Maybe all pharmacies have similar layouts.

I aimlessly wander, glancing at anything that catches my eye. Too often, that turns out to be her.

She confuses me. The confusion frustrates me. At times, I think she might truly care about the people, and their situations. She disobeyed orders to give me a job, which, while it resulted in awfulness, she did out of kindness. To improve my and my family's situation. But then she says the most calloused things.

She saved me twice.

She has enough money to gather an armful of supplies to buy here, but hasn't once given any away to the people we've passed. 5 cords would be enough to change improve someone's life. She could spare that.

She wants to help me escape.

I don't think she likes me beyond feeling like she owes me a debt. I don't think I like her.

"Jun!"

I jump.

Kyra is standing beside me, her brown bag now bulging. Her face looks unimpressed. Or that might just be her resting face.

"Done daydreaming?" she asks.

"Sorry."

She holds out a small, white pill. "Take this. It dissolves, so hold it on your tongue for a bit."

It's the oddest sensation, but I do so.

"It might take a while for the medicine to take effect. But it will. You can take a maximum of 3 a day."

"Thank you."

She makes no acknowledgement of my thanks, and instead heads for the door.

I sigh, and follow. She might keep preventing me from bleeding to death, but she's gonna frustrate me to death.

"How far is it until we're out of Sector 5?" I ask as we head down the stairs and back onto the street.

"With the time we lost today, you should prepare to spend the night here." She says it so matter-of-face, no hint of condemnation at me for running away, but I feel ashamed nonetheless. "We'll have to scope out a safe spot to sleep." She frowns at me. "Are you aware you're doing that?"

"What?" I look down. My hand is on my stomach again.

"Don't panic," she says quickly. "Remember, they have to start small. We have time."

"How quickly will my brain adjust to small, though? How fast will they be able to increase?"

"I don't know," she admits.

That's a terrifying thought. Or, it would be, if I thought about it. But why would I do that? I only have so long before anxiety is my only choice, I'm not choosing it now.

Her brows are furrowed. She's concerned. I sigh. Nothing is ever going to get done if we spend the entire time arguing. I have to be the bigger person and keep my thoughts to myself. If she's willing to help me escape, I'm willing to be nicer.

"Alright, let's get going then." I grab the bag from her, sling it over my right shoulder, and pick up the pace. Already, the pain is improving and I can feel my mood lifting with it.

"What are you doing?" She hurries to catch up with me.

"The faster we walk, the faster we reach our destination, right?" I say.

She frowns, which seems to be her standard response to me.

After a while, she says, quietly, "Thank you."

I grin to myself. A small victory.

The bag weighs nothing to me. Compared to the weight of hauling water, it's like I'm not carrying anything.

I slow down slightly, to make sure we're walking at an even pace. She knows where we're headed. Somehow she's got a map of all the sectors in her head. So I'll follow her.

CHAPTER EIGHTEEN

Kyra

Jun's been chipper since the pain medicine. Bouncing along, carrying the bag, even chatting. I wish we could have continued to walk in silence. I'm trying to envision all the possible obstacles at the Sector 2 entrance and devise solutions. But Jun maintains a steady stream of conversation, asking questions, pointing idiosyncrasies of Sector 5 out to me. It might be interesting if I wasn't concerned with other, more important, matters.

But then he talks about how, for some reason, Sector Five's current fashion trend is putting their hair in a bun on their right or left side of their head, and doing nothing with their hair on the other side. It's even worse in person, if possible. I begin to worry. Is my hair too sophisticated even in the braids? I had been more concerned with putting it up as compactly as possible and didn't give much thought to the complexity. I should have known better

"Should we get food?" he says abruptly, stopping and waiting for my answer.

There's a "restaurant" on the corner of this street which probably inspired the question. I have money aplenty to buy a solid meal.

"Probably," I answer.

"Why'd you say it like that?" he asks.

"Like what?"

"Do you not want to get supper?"

"Yes, I want to eat."

"Oh." He nods. "You're nervous."

I scoff. "What are you talking about?"

He raises an eyebrow.

It's possible he's right. That building will be full of Sector 5 people. I'm not from here. What if they realize? Government workers in the lower sectors have been beat up for where they come from. Out here, on the streets, no one cares about us. Everyone's intent on where they're going. But when people are sitting down, eating, their eyes tend to wander and stare.

He bends down slightly, so he can gaze directly into my eyes. It's patronizing. I'm not a child. "Kyra, whatever you're worried about, don't be. I doubt anyone from the government will be there who will recognize us. We need to eat more than just questionable granola bars."

"I'm not worried," I insist. "So let's go." I start for the restaurant.

I can hear the grin in his voice as he says, "Alright," and follows me.

It's a small, dingy room. They abandoned sweeping the floors a while ago, and they might have never even tried mopping. A few people glance our way when the door opens, but quickly return to their food. Five tables are occupied, leaving two empty ones. Each has only two chairs.

At the back of the room is a counter, and beyond that, a kitchen. We thread our way through the tables to the counter, at which sits a young girl, about 7, doodling on counter-top with a marker mostly out of ink.

"Hello," Jun says.

The girl carefully puts the cap back on the marker, sets it aside, then acknowledges us. She folds her hands, then recites, "The menu today is broccoli soup with a piece of bread, or vegetable stir-fry, or grilled chicken breast."

"Finally, some actual protein," I say.

Jun puts a hand on my arm. It's light, but it's a warning.

"We'll have one order of the soup, and one vegetable stir-fry," he says. "And if we could add one more piece of bread, that would be great."

I want to protest. We're going to be walking all day. We need the protein. But his hand stays on my arm, so I say nothing.

The girl nods solemnly. "That will be 9 cords," she relays.

Jun fishes the amount out of the bag and hands it over.

"Thank you for your business," the girl says. The words sound like they've been spoken many times. She's too young for this. "If you'll wait one moment, I'll be right back with your food."

She scrambles down off her stool. Now looking much shorter and younger, she scurries back to the kitchen.

Before I have time to ask my question, Jun's turning towards me and saying, voice low, "The chicken is fresh. So it's overpriced. We don't want to advertise we have that kind of money, especially since we're already strangers here. We'll buy some protein elsewhere."

I nod. It occurs to me I had the upper hand when Jun didn't know what was going on. Now that he does, he's the more knowledgeable between us. I might have a map of all the sectors in my head, but Jun knows how to survive in them.

The girl comes back out with a bowl of soup, then the bowl of veggies, then the two pieces of bread on a plate. She sets all these on the counter in front of us.

"Enjoy," she says, already returning her attention to her colouring.

We grab the food, and sit down at one of the free tables.

"Who's getting what?" I ask.

"I ordered one of each so you could choose," he says. "I didn't ask which one you wanted because I didn't want to give you an opportunity to ask for the chicken. As long as I get some bread, I don't care. " He grabs a piece and starts munching.

I don't move. He grins and gestures to the bowls, mouth still full. At least he doesn't try to speak again.

I haven't had to pick what I ate in so long. The cafeteria at work served one lunch each day, so you ate what they gave you, or went hungry. Since my job didn't allow lots of time for meal prep, I went with the same approach for supper. Each day of the week had its supper. Breakfast was the same everyday.

Soup is good, though. I like soup. But this is Jun's first full meal in a long time. I've ate well my whole life. Surely I ought to let him pick.

He must have seen me eyeing the soup, because he pushes the bowl towards me. Then he takes the stir-fry for himself.

"Enjoy," he says, then whispers, "Sector 5 might suck, but the food is pretty good."

We barely talk as we eat. I'm hungry, so I can't imagine what he must be feeling. The food is good. At least, better than the previous days in the sectors. It's similar to the cafeteria food at work. Simple, but good and hearty. By the time I'm scraping the bottom of my bowl, I'm more at ease. My shoulders have relaxed. The power of food.

Jun grins. He's got remnants of a pepper stuck in his teeth, and I swallow down a laugh. "Ready for more walking?" he asks.

"Oh, yeah," I nod.

"Is something funny?"

"We were wondering the same thing."

Three teenage boys are approaching our table. They're wiry, hair done in the fashion, and their faces are those of troublemakers.

Jun's face immediately hardens and his eyes hold a known dislike.

"Didn't think we'd see you back in our sector so soon, 4," one of them spits out. He must be the ringleader. He's the tallest, and that's about as complex a hierarchy as I would expect their brains to be able to handle.

"Didn't think you'd be so confident approaching me after our last encounter," Jun responds easily.

It's awesome to see him like this. Without the interference from the computer, the manipulation. This is who he should have been this whole time.

The leader crosses his arms. "Well, it seems you've got another chick with you this time. And seems this one has money."

How could they have known? I'm wearing clothes stolen from someone from Sector 4. They should create the opposite impression.

Jun raises an eyebrow. "What makes you think that?"

"No one here knows how to braid hair like that."

My heart plummets. I was thinking this earlier. I was right.

"Really? That's what you're basing this off?" Jun manages to sound both dubious and condescending.

"I don't need anything else. Cause I'm right." He nods at me. "She doesn't have much to say for herself, does she?"

Jun gives me a quick glance.

What do I say?

I shrug. "You say something worth replying to, and I'll reply."

He places his hands on the table and leans his face into my personal space. I refuse to give him the satisfaction of leaning away. "All we want is your money. Then you can go."

The other people in the restaurant are staring. Murmuring to themselves. Some look ready to jump in if a fight occurs, but I'm worried about whose side they'd be on.

Obviously I can't give him our money. But I can't fight, and I don't like Jun's odds if others decide to give these three jokers a hand.

Jun stands abruptly. His chair falls over. He towers over the boys. He rolls his shoulders. "Last time this happened, it ended with you guys running away. You really want a rematch?"

The other two take a step back. The leader steps closer to Jun.

"You against this whole restaurant? Think you're gonna win?"

This guy barely comes to Jun's chin. Where does he get the audacity from?

"You're crackers if you think we're gonna help you!" cackles an old lady in the corner.

"Take your attitude and shove off!" a man howls.

"Useless boys," another mutters. "They should be working. The lot of them."

The leader looks around. To his credit, his face remains stoic. But he's already shown himself to lack critical thinking, so maybe he's just an idiot.

"You'd better watch your back," he says. "C'mon!"

They leave.

Jun scoffs, and shakes his head. All casual, he gathers our empty bowls and cutlery, and takes them back to the little girl. Then he comes back and grabs the bag. "You ready?"

"You aren't worried about them?" I ask as I follow him out of the restaurant.

"Nah. They're just trouble-makers. They tried to take my Mom's pills from me before."

"And you beat them up?"

He nods. "Punched the tall one right in the throat."

"Wow." I clear my throat. "Thank you. For, you know… keeping them from jumping us."

"They're cowards. I doubt they would have in there. Could they be following us to try and jump us later? That's likely. They've got nothing better to do."

"Woah!" I pull his arm and force him to stop walking. "You don't sound concerned. That sounds like something we should be concerned about."

He shrugs. "Not really. They've not done a hard day's work in their lives. They have no strength."

"Strength is nothing against a knife," I say.

"You're really optimistic, aren't you?"

"Who would be in this reality?"

He shakes his head, and keeps walking.

Despite my fear those three will be waiting for us around every corner, the rest of the day passes uneventfully. Jun finds a vendor selling nuts, and we buy a big bag. Protein acquired. We snack on them as we walk. I ask questions about life in the sectors, and this time, I listen as he explains everything.

We don't get as far as I would like. But in Sector 5, it's too dangerous to be walking around past sundown. I don't want to have only one exit route, but I also don't want to be completely exposed, and we're having a difficult time finding a happy medium.

Until Jun opens the door of a building more run-down than the others. Its windows are broken in, the whole building is listing to the right, and the roof is sagging.

"It's cover, with many exits," he says.

"There's only one door."

"And six windows."

I concede. It's the best option, as long as the roof doesn't cave in on us. And it's getting too dark to search for a better option.

The inside of the house isn't much better than the outside. The floor is caked with dirt and evidence of mice. There's no furniture except a broken chair, and a thick slab of wood, which is about the size of a small bed.

Seeing my eyes on the wood, Jun says, "You place your mattress on it if you don't have a bed frame. It helps create some distance between you and the ground."

"I think outside is cleaner than in here," I mutter.

Jun nods. "Probably. Air flow, traffic. In here it just collects dust." He takes a deep breath, shakes his head, and mutters something to himself.

"Are you okay?" I ask.

He raises his eyebrows, then frowns, then shrugs. "It's fine. I mean, I can feel it, but, it's not affecting me really, yet." Switching the subject, he says, "I'm gonna clean the board for you." He wipes the dust and dirt off the board as best he can, then gestures to it. "Your bed awaits."

"Lovely."

"You can have the floor if you want," he says. "Chill with the mice for the night."

"The wooden bed will be great, thank you."

He chuckles.

I wish I had bought a blanket or something. The wood is hard, cold, and, despite Jun's best efforts, dirty. I arrange my backpack into a poor substitute for a pillow.

Last night was similar sleeping conditions, but between the adrenaline of the last two days, and not having slept the night before due to my sector 5 excursion, I could have fallen asleep anywhere. Tonight might take a while.

"Kyra?" Jun says from wherever he's arranged himself on the floor.

"Yeah?"

He pauses. "Thank you for saving me," he says quietly.

I grin to myself. But I say, "We're not out of danger yet, so maybe save your thanks for when we're free."

More silence. It stretches on long enough I start to feel bad. Perhaps I shouldn't have dismissed his thanks so callously.

"Jun?"

He doesn't reply.

I sit up. Moonlight slices through the many open cracks and holes in the roof. Jun is still, his breathing even, his face relaxed. He's asleep. I lay back down and stare at the ceiling.

My own words echo in my head. We're not out of danger yet. I sit back up. Those guys at the restaurant told us to watch our back. What if they followed us? I know he suspected I had money. What if he tries to steal some?

He'd have a difficult time with my head lying on the backpack, but he could figure it out.

I open my backpack and grab the bags and rolls of coins. If I hide all of them, that would make them suspicious. I put rolls and small bags in different spots on my person, tucking them in pockets, of which this dress has a surprising amount, and in odd places. I tuck a roll in my socks, then stick some loose coins in my shoes.

It will be a pain to get all these coins out tomorrow if nothing has happened. Maybe I should leave them there. There's always been the possibility of getting jumped as we walk along the street.

I shake my head and try to clear my thoughts. I've done all I can for the night. Now I have to sleep.

I lay back down, and rearrange myself into a somewhat comfortable position.

It doesn't take as long as I feared it would before I drift off.

But I don't get to sleep for long before pounding feet, harsh lights, and shouts wake me.

CHAPTER NINETEEN

Jun

Sleep comes fast. Waking comes faster.

Men are shouting. Hands are dragging me to my feet before I am fully conscious.

This isn't right.

What's going on?

I flail my arms and they make contact with somebody's face. In retaliation somebody punches mine. Then my stomach.

Pain clears my head, and my eyes force themselves to adjust to the flashlights shining in my face.

The tiny house is now full of soldiers. Kyra's arms are pinned behind her back, her backpack confiscated by another soldier. The rest, save one, the leader, are pointing guns at us. My stomach plunges into my feet.

I don't try to fight. My shoulder wound is smarting from the rough handling, and I have no desire to give myself another one.

Kyra is stoic, as always. Her face shows no worries. *How?* Is she genuinely unworried, or is she just excellent at faking it?

I try to make my face do the same, but I've never been successful before. I'm sure I'm failing now. But it makes me feel better to try and be brave.

The soldiers marshal us outside.

I see, hanging back on the street, those three jerks from earlier. My face hardens into a glare. They turned us in. I have no doubt. I'd love to beat them up again, but my arms are held fast by soldiers. Even if I managed to shake free, I'd be dead before I reached them.

Why are we still alive? They could have killed us in the house, in our sleep. Removed our bodies in the dead of night. Clean, no fuss. Where are we going, and why aren't we dead?

The flashlights are turned off and we walk the streets in relative silence. The soldiers hold their guns down, but they're still as much of a threat.

I don't know how far or how long we walk. The position they're holding my arms in is uncomfortable at first, then agonizing. The slow, steady throb of the odd position pulls at my wound.

We reach our destination. The soldiers at the front of the procession stop and fan out. Kyra and I are led to a sturdy house with no windows. Two soldiers are standing on either side of the door. One of them opens the door and we're shoved inside.

The door locks behind us.

I freeze. It's pitch black in here. This house has no chinks for moonlight to get through. I can hear breathing, more than Kyra and I. And it smells rough. A coppery scent of blood, not sharp anymore, but there.

"Sector 5's jail," Kyra murmurs by my side. "Try not to step on anyone."

She grabs my wrist and slowly moves to the side. I try to follow as close behind as I can, putting my feet out before I step down. Many times, my toes nudge someone and I recoil. But they're all asleep.

Kyra finds a spot big enough for both of us, and we sit down. The floor is grimy, and I brush away chunks of something I don't want to know the nature of.

Once we're settled, I ask, "Are you okay? Did they hurt you?"

"I'm fine," she says. "I wish they hadn't taken my backpack. I doubt we'll get it back."

"Oh, no!" I lower my voice and hiss, "All our money was in there! What are we going to do?"

"I think we have more pressing concerns." She sounds annoyed I'm even worried about the money. "Money won't matter if we can't escape."

I lean back against the wall and mutter, "There's no way we're escaping this place."

"I didn't mean *this* place, I meant escape in general," she snaps.

"Shut up!" someone roars.

We fall silent.

"We shouldn't both sleep at the same time," Kyra whispers after a while.

"Good idea, you take first watch," I say. It's unfair of me, I know. But I roll over onto my side, facing away from her, even though it's pitch black everywhere in here.

Somehow, around the deafening silence, suffocating air, and uncomfortable floor, I fall asleep.

外

Light floods the room and I wake with a start. My eyes open, but just as quickly I shut them. The transition from the intense darkness to the intense light hurts my eyes. After some opening, shutting, and lots of blinking, my eyes adjust.

Besides Kyra, seven other people lay scattered about the room, in various stages of waking and adjusting. Some haven't even bothered.

"You didn't wake me," I say to Kyra, my tone coming out much more accusatory than I had meant.

Her eyes narrow, and the glare she sends me is piercing.

"You two!" the soldier at the door barks.

We both whip our heads over to look at him.

"Get up," he orders. "Walk out. Come on!"

We scramble to our feet, then thread our way through the people, to the door. More soldiers are waiting for us outside. They line the walkway, guns ready. At the end of their line is something I've only seen twice before in my life.

A truck. It's huge. If I were to stand at the front of the hood, it would be taller than me. The back is facing us, and it's covered by a cloth on top and both sides. We're hoisted and dragged into the back. They shove us to the very back, which only causes me to stumble but it makes Kyra fall.

The sides have benches and the soldiers sit down there, filling them.

One of them shouts an order I can't make out. A door slams and the engine rumbles to life. The truck shakes and sways as it starts moving.

"Are you okay?" I ask Kyra in an undertone.

Before she can reply, a soldier prods my side with the end of his gun. "No talking," he barks.

I shrink back, and resort to staring at the floor, like Kyra is. They'd probably be happy to shoot me for looking at them the wrong way.

Once again, I'm left wondering why we aren't dead yet. And how are we going to escape?

I'm finding it difficult to sit still during what is probably our ride to an execution. The longer the ride stretches on, the more I can hear my heartbeat, getting louder and faster. I begin to sweat.

What if they have plans for us beyond killing us? But why would they make an example out of us, revealing that we're controlled by computers?

That wouldn't be very smart. I glance at Kyra. That's true, the people controlling us know about it. Maybe we won't be an example, but a warning to them. Don't go against orders or you'll end up like these two.

Kyra's face is perfectly calm and reserved. I don't know how she does it!

I try to think of something else, but my mind can't focus on anything other than our imminent death. And how can I try to plan an escape when I don't know what's going to happen? And every soldier has a gun.

The truck lurches to a stop, and my heart drops.

The soldiers marshal us out of the truck. Despite my worries, I can't help but take in the new environment.

We're in a middle sector. It's amazing the difference it makes. How much cleaner it is, how much better-dressed the people are. I suddenly feel filthy and out of place.

Another group of soldiers is waiting for us. They wear the same uniforms as the others, but they look like they shower more often, and have to work a little less. Makes sense, they probably don't have to deal with as many criminals in a middle sector.

Four of the middle-sector soldiers come forward and grab Kyra and I. One of the Sector 5 soldiers goes over to the General. They talk, with a lot of nodding and glancing at us.

My stomach roils and gurgles. I might throw up.

The general shouts, "Take 'em inside and lock 'em up!" To the Sector 5 soldier, he says, "I'll communicate with base, see when they're sending the deployment."

The soldiers shove me forward, and direct me into a building bigger than any I've seen before. It has proper windows, with glass. The floors aren't wood, or any material I've seen before. They're shiny, and made of squares.

It quickly becomes apparent we're in a jail. A more sophisticated jail than Sector 5. This one has cells, with metal rods being the side exposed to the hallway. Many of them have someone in them. And the building has electricity! Lights line the ceiling and illuminate the hallway as if the ceiling were glass and the sun was shining in.

We're brought to an empty one at the end of the hallway. None of the cells around us are occupied. A soldier unlocks a door, which is also made of these metal rods. Kyra and I are shoved in. Then they lock the door behind us.

"Don't get too comfortable," one says. "You won't be here long."

They laugh and jeer, then walk off.

The room has one bed, a tiny window, also barred, and a bucket in the corner.

I look at Kyra.

She looks at me.

"Well," I say, because something has to be said. But I don't know what to say.

She rolls her eyes and sits on the bed.

"Why aren't we dead yet?" I ask.

"How should I know?" she snaps. Then she sighs, takes a breath, and says, "They're probably bringing us to the Government Sector. To make us an example."

Her voice isn't as steady as her face.

"You didn't wake me up last night," I say.

"I was thinking. Then I fell asleep."

I nod. "Okay."

She's staring at the floor. I think she's scared. Has her calm face been a facade this whole time? Of course she's scared. If we're supposed to be examples, our deaths aren't going to be slow. They're going to be public, at the very least. Her friends will see.

I resolve myself. Kyra has been leading this adventure so far. It's time I step up and do so now. I need to figure out an escape plan.

Except, this jail cell looks sturdy. The walls are completely solid and there's no windows. I test the strength of the metal rods, but they're firmly wedged into the walls.

I hold my left elbow with my arm, trying to lift weight off of my shoulder. They took my pain medicine. Kyra spent so much money on those pills and I only got to use two of them.

"It's no use," Kyra says.

"I know, I was just seeing."

"Why would you need to try if you already knew it wouldn't work?"

"Because what if it did?"

She shakes her head. "Jun, no. We're screwed. This jail cell is our best chance at escaping, and even this is impossible. Once they grab us to take us to the Government Sector, there will be too many guns on us."

Fear tightens my stomach, but I refuse to let it take hold of me.

"We can't have gone through all that to have accomplished nothing."

"Trust me," she says, lying down and facing the wall, "we can."

CHAPTER TWENTY

Kyra

Jun keeps pacing, muttering to himself. He won't find a way out of here. It's hopeless.

And it's all my fault. I should have let him die, and run away myself. The Cigarette would have killed him quickly, and I would be alive. As it is, I've condemned the both of us to a slow, public, humiliating death.

It's all my fault. Why did I ever disobey my orders? How is this making his life better? Even if we somehow survived, which we won't, the gunshot wound will be a permanent scar, probably affecting his range of motion and giving him pain.

"I wish we still had your backpack!" Jun bursts out. "All we'd have to do is bribe one guard, and go out through this door!"

"You can't bribe people into doing what you want," Kyra says. "Especially these soldiers. They've been trained."

Jun snorts. "Sure, they've been trained. But they adapt to their surroundings like anyone else. For the right price, you can bribe any soldier. It happens all the time."

I sit and turn to face him. "Does it really?"

My sudden energy confuses him and he frowns. "Yes. Sometimes you're even forced to bribe them otherwise they'll make up some rule to confiscate your stuff. But that doesn't matter; we don't have your backpack."

My brain is buzzing with adrenaline. That could work. It would probably use all of the money I hid on myself, but we could live. My shoulders sag. No, it's no use.

"But what happens once we get outside?" I ask. "No doubt this place is guarded. We won't get far."

Jun shrugs. "It doesn't even matter, we don't have money. It's not an option."

I hesitate. Should I tell him we *do* have money?

I put my head in my hands. Too many thoughts are swirling around in my brain. If we don't escape here, where can we? They will be taking us to Sector 8, putting us on the subway, and sending us directly to the Government Sector, where there is no hope of escape. The subway *might* work, if we could manage to get off at one of the stops. But they're going to send too many guards with us to allow that. They might even shackle us.

When they come to take us out of here and load us on the truck taking us to the subway, there will once again be many armed soldiers. Attempted escape could earn a bullet.

This is our best option. It sucks, but it's the best.

"Excuse me, sir," Jun says.

I quickly look up. A soldier halts outside our cell. Bleary-eyed, he frowns at us.

"What do you want?" he spits.

"Jun, don't," I hiss. I don't know what he's planning, but it can't be good.

"I couldn't help but wonder…" Jun glances around, then lowers his voice, "… if the General would be interested in knowing you're drunk."

The man's face flushes. "I'm not drunk."

"I think he might also be interested in the liquor in your right-hand pants pocket," Jun adds.

The man's eyes flash and he steps closer.

Jun doesn't even flinch.

"I could get whipped," the soldier says.

"Exactly why you don't want him to know," Jun replies, tone even. "Let us out, and he never has to know."

My breath hitches. This is going to get us beat up. How dare we blackmail a soldier?

The soldier's jaw clenches. He looks down the hallway, then back. "I can't just let you out. It'll be obvious you had help."

Jun shrugs. "Have it your way." He gathers his breath to make a shout, and the soldier exclaims.

"Stop, no, wait!" He curses under his breath. "Listen, I've been caught with liquor too many times. This'll kill me."

"But if you're found without your key, it'll probably be much worse." Jun holds up, out of his reach, a plain key.

The man's eyes widen and he gapes at the key. He pats his belt, as if Jun might have stolen a different key.

I didn't even see when Jun took the key! Incredible.

The man's breathing becomes rapid. "Okay, okay. Let yourself out, then give me back the key. I won't go after you. I'll raise the alarm after a few minutes, but I can't wait too long. You'll have to run."

"We're good at that." Jun reaches around the bars, and fiddles with the key in the lock.

I leap to my feet. This worked? No, can't be. It must be a trick.

Jun opens the door. He hands the soldier his key back.

I try to protest. We have to think this through, first. But Jun cuts off my protests.

"We have to run, now!"

He takes off towards a door to our right. Not having any choice, I go after him.

"How did you know he would let us go?" I ask Jun.

"Never underestimate the power of self-preservation, or how selfish it can get."

Then he's opening the door and we're outside. A soldier is standing outside the door. Of course. But before the soldier can sound the alarm, Jun punches him in the mouth. The soldier stumbles and falls.

"We have to run!" I say.

"Running raises suspicion," Jun objects.

"But you'd be surprised how difficult it is to shoot a running object," I answer. Then I take off. Jun will follow, I know he will.

I head straight for the buildings. The jail is in the middle of an empty circle. No other buildings or trees are within the several meters radius. It's smart, making it hard for people to rescue someone and hard for people to escape. Shouts rise up and echo. We've been spotted. A gun sounds and a bullet whizzes past us. Someone howls an order. No other guns fire and I make it to the street where the buildings begin.

It's a shopping area. Why is a shopping area this close to the jail? Too many people are around. They shriek as we run by. Someone tries to grab me, but Jun yanks his hands away.

It's not good they didn't fire more shots. It means they didn't want to risk killing us before our scheduled public torture. This is our one chance. If we're caught, our end will be the worse for having attempted escape.

Up ahead, people are forming a line, a blockade. They're figuring out what's going on.

Quickly, I scan the shops. One appears devoid of people, so I veer to the left and rush in, praying it has a back door. Buildings in Sector 6 and upwards usually have at least two exits.

The shopkeeper greets Jun and I when we enter. Then her nose wrinkles in immediate distaste as she takes us in. We're obviously from a poor sector. I make a face back at her, then head for a back room.

She shrieks and leaps to her feet. "You can't steal from my inventory!"

As if we have interest in frivolous, dyed scarves that do nothing to keep you warm.

There is a door in the back, like I hoped. I exit through it, and Jun follows, the girl shouting curses at us.

Now we're among residencies and little parks. And there are actual streets here. It shouldn't be odd, but after only a few days in the lower sectors, what should feel standard to me now feels out-of-place.

Jun falls in step beside me. "What's the plan?" he asks. "Running raises suspicion, but we're not far enough away from danger to risk walking."

"Our being here raises suspicion," I say. "We have to get back to Sector 5 as soon as possible." I'm just not sure how. I'm trying to figure out where we are in relation to 5.

"Which direction is Sector 5 compared to Sector 6 on the map?" Jun asks.

"South-East," I answer. "But we haven't gone far in yet, so I think it's mostly South."

Jun studies the sky, then points to the left. "Then it's that way."

"Great! Let's go."

"Lead the way."

Something in his voice makes me pause. I remember his insistence we be equals in every decision. So far, I haven't done that well. But I know this sector better than he does. I hesitate.

"Would you rather… do you want to lead?" I ask.

"You know this Sector better than I do, why would I lead?" he asks. Then understanding dawns in his eyes. "Running away from soldiers is not something we can discuss every move on. I'll follow. We need to move."

I nod, then take off. Running at full speed will too quickly tire us, so I go at a jogging pace.

We go past houses that are solid, big in comparison to those in 4. Some have gardens in front, for flowers. Some have big porches, big enough for people to fit underneath, hidden by darkness. I shudder at the thought that a soldier might pop out from one.

People walk leisurely on the streets. Some are sitting and reading. Our presence causes disdain and muttering. People move out of our way and make faces at us.

I want to get somewhere quieter and more secluded. But I don't know if this sector has those places.

"There they are!"

The shout releases a burst of adrenaline. I speed up, but I know it won't help for long. These soldier are trained to give chase. Eventually, we will tire, and they will overtake us. Or get close enough to shoot to incapacitate without worry of death.

We need a secure place to hide, where they won't find us, and we can let them pass by. Or better yet, wait for the cover of night. I force myself to go faster still.

We need to get out of their line of vision, so we can hide. I manage to communicate this to Jun, who's running in step with me.

I risk a glance back and see them spreading out. They're going to try to get ahead of us.

My chest hurts and every breath is on fire. I can't run much longer.

"We'll turn and go under a porch before they see us," Jun says.

It's our best and only chance. I take the next right. In all luck, there's a porch with no one on it.

"There, there!" Jun exclaims.

I dive under the porch. Rocks scrape my hands, and my chin thuds painfully on the ground. I scramble to the back, where the shadow is darkest. I hug my knees to myself to try and get as small as possible.

Soldiers thunder by, feet pounding on the stone of the street.

They pass by, and only then do I allow myself to breath freely again.

And only then do I realize Jun isn't under the porch with me.

CHAPTER TWENTY-ONE

Jun

My lungs are burning within my chest, my feet getting sore from the stone streets. But I can't stop. If I stop, I'm dead.

I don't regret leaving Kyra. If we had both hid, it would have been obvious. They would have stopped running and starting searching for where we hid. At the moment, they still think we split up. I might pay for it if I can't lose them.

I hope Kyra stays under the porch. I hope I can find my way back to her. There was no time to explain.

As I round the corner of a house, a soldier looms out to greet me.

Involuntarily, I shout in surprise. Then I duck as his fist swings towards me. They haven't shot at me yet. I'm grateful, but I don't understand why. It would end this a lot faster.

I punch the soldier in the stomach with my left hand. Regret is immediate as my shoulder burns at the impact. As the man doubles over, I bring up my knee to greet his face. Then I run on. I can't stop. They'll catch up.

My stomach aches with the effort and with hunger. When was the last time I ate?

I don't know where I'm going. The chances of me getting lost are very high.

Up ahead, a house has an open door. Without thinking, I rush up the steps and into the house. A lady is standing in the entrance-way, and shouts in fear.

"Sorry!" I yell as I run by.

I weave my way around furniture and walls. There! An open window. I somewhat ungracefully push myself out the window and jump to the ground.

I keep running without thinking about direction. If they expect me to run logically, with a destination in mind, they're going to be disappointed. Perhaps that way I can lose them.

The sun is making its way down in the sky, but at this time of year, it takes a long time for it to set. I can't rely on the cover of darkness coming soon. But I can't run forever.

The problem is any time I get away from these soldiers, people see me and shout out for them. That's not helpful. And the soldiers are fanned out so much, I usually end up running into one who alerts the others.

Time blurs together as I run, dodge, check behind me, and knock down soldiers, trying to avoid using my left hand to hit. I take little rests when I can, but any rest time brings soldiers closer to me. Too close.

The problem is, I'm pretty sure I'm surrounded. The soldiers are fanning out in a circle, and closing in on me. If I hide, they'll come to the middle and realize. Then they'll search, and I won't be able to run when they find me.

I stop. If they're in a circle around me, then they are spread out from each other. Hopefully. Which means I can break through if I knock down one more soldier. I compare the sun's present position to where it was earlier today when I told Kyra where South was. For now, I'll run South. I'll course-correct once I've lost these soldiers.

I run South, pouring the last of my energy out. I'm ready to encounter someone.

Something hits my chest, and I fall back onto the ground. My breath is knocked out of my chest.

A soldier appears above me, grinning down at me cruelly. He raises a big chunk of wood. That must be what I ran into. Then I realize he's about to hit me in the head with it. I roll onto my side and the wood hits the ground.

Quickly, I jump to my feet.

The soldier has better reaction time, and he adjusts to swing the wood into my leg.

I shout in pain and punch him in the jaw. Not hard enough to knock him out, unfortunately, but he drops the wood.

I'm so tired, and now in pain. One more. If I get away from him, I can be free.

He punches me in my ribs, right side. My reaction time is too slow. But then he aims for my shoulder wound, and my brain clears. I move to the left, and the momentum of his punch causes him to stumble when his fist never connects.

If he causes further injury to my shoulder, that pain will push me over the edge. I'll pass out.

The soldier whirls around to face me, and I kick him in the face. He stumbles backways, eye smarting. His nose is crooked and starts to bleed.

"Sorry," I mutter as I once again punch his jaw.

This time, he goes down.

I don't take time to rest, but take off again. My leg aches where he hit it, but I force myself forward. Forward. Forward.

When it feels like my lungs are going to explode and my legs might fall off, I stop, and find a porch to duck under. My chest heaves as I gulp in air.

My head gets light, despite my increased oxygen. The world spins, and I fight to not pass out. To get this far only for them to discover me passed out under a porch? No.

But I've done too much. Exerted myself beyond my limit. The world goes dark, and I fall into nothing.

When I wake up, it's no longer day, but night. It's still early night. Lamps line the street to illuminate them, so I don't have to worry about not being able to see. The soldiers have passed me by. I'm safe. Unless they're still out searching for me. When would they quit for the night?

I peer out from under the porch. No one is out walking. Hopefully no one is sitting on this porch. That would be awkward. But I don't remember seeing any chairs on it.

What must Kyra be thinking right now? There was no way to tell her, she would have protested.

How do I find where she hid? If she's still there.

My eyes widen. What if she's not there? What if she left to try to find *me*? How will we be able to find each other? What if she got taken back to jail? How will I know what happened? I can't risk going back to the jail to check.

My heart is racing, and my chest hurts. My mind is whirling down a rabbit hole of unknowns.

I duck out from under the porch and stand up. I take deep breaths, forcing my mind to slow down.

"No sense in worrying about what might be," I tell myself. I might find her quickly.

As my heart rate returns to it's normal pace, I take in my surroundings. It looks much like the rest of the residence section I've been running through all day. Pristine, with massive, well-kept houses, trimmed grass, and flowery gardens. Grass hardly even grows in Sector 4.

Then, sore from all the running, I stretch. Passing out immediately didn't help my body. I went from constant motion to complete still. Now it aches all over.

As I straighten, I realize one detriment to waiting for the cover of night. No sun to tell direction.

Anxiety rises again, and I struggle to quelch it. Can you tell direction by the moon the same way you do by the sun?

The moon rises in the east and sets in the west, the same as the sun. Surely I can tell direction with the moon the same way I do by the sun.

The only problem is finding the moon. I have to try and find a dark spot, where the street lights aren't illuminating everything, so I can actually see the sky. The moon isn't high yet. It's still in the east. That means when I face the moon, south is to my right.

Should I head South? We were headed south-east, but how off-course did we veer when running from the soldiers?

I rub my stomach as I think. I can stand here all night and deliberate my options, but eventually, I have to choose and hope. If I go South, I'll know when I hit the border for Sector 5. I can always backtrack from there. Though I hope I won't have to.

I set off Southward, trying to keep to edges where the street lamps aren't playing the role of the sun. People aren't out, but if soldiers are, I want to be hidden. Although maybe a person walking in the shadows is more suspicious than one walking openly in the street. No, they know my face. I'd be caught.

As I walk, I register my nerves My mind keeps questioning. That could be normal, but it also could be my levels increasing. I don't want to think about that. Not yet.

How bad will it get before my brain shuts down?

I *really* don't want to think about that.

Shoving those thoughts aside, I try to focus on keeping my eyes peeled for Kyra, or for the house she hid under.

How long I walk, I don't know. I never see anybody else. A few times, I think I've found the house, but no one's underneath the porch.

Twice, I have to stop and sit on the ground, waiting for light-headedness to pass. I haven't eaten all day, which I've done before, but I've never done so much running in the same day.

I consider changing my direction, but that might do more harm than good at this point. I consider calling out her name, but I can't risk waking anyone in the houses. She's probably not within earshot anyways.

Eventually, I see a figure ahead. They're moving quickly, if somewhat haphazardly, wringing their hands. They're making noise, mumbling words. When I get close enough, I realize it's Kyra.

Relief floods me, and I rush to her. I call out softly, once I'm close enough.

"Jun?"

I reach her. She's been crying.

She's crying? I may not have known her for long yet, but I haven't seen her close to shedding a tear. What's going on?

"Where *were* you?" she demands.

"I had to lead them away," I say. "If I hid with you, and we vanished, they would have realized what we did. They would have searched for us, and we would have been caught. But there wasn't time to explain. I had to go."

She nods. Her eyes, unfocused, slide to observe the distance behind me. "No, I understand. I just—" She hugs herself and takes a few deep breaths. Voice trembling, she tries to explain. "I didn't know what to do, cause you were gone, and I had no way of knowing if you were okay." Her face is getting flushed and she's shaking. "I don't know what's wrong, I can't think straight."

"I'm back now," I say.

That doesn't help.

She flourishes her arms and exclaims, "Yes, but I didn't know if we could find each other again! If you got taken, it would be my fault! Another thing that's my fault! And why would you do that for me?" Her hands are shaking.

Oh.

I'm an idiot for not realizing sooner, but usually I'm the one having the experience, not observing.

I move closer and gently rub her arms. "It's okay, it's okay. I'm safe now. You're safe now. We're okay."

"I know but I—" she has to catch her breath—"I didn't *know* if you would be okay and I was waiting under there and I couldn't know and—"

"I know, I'm sorry. I'm sorry I couldn't explain, but there wasn't time. I'm sorry I made you worry."

My tone is similar to one gently coaxing a wounded cat. If circumstances were any different, she'd probably punch me for it.

"But you could have died and I wouldn't have known!" She wipes her eyes, then manages to glare at the wetness on her hands.

"But I didn't die," I counter gently.

"All I can think about is how unlikely we are to survive." Her voice catches. "It would be all my fault."

Technically, she's right, but it's still a bit unfair.

"Kyra, you don't know what's going to happen. And maybe now's not the best time to be thinking about it. We survived today. That's what matters."

"No." She shakes her head. She's getting her breath back. "No, but we need to plan ahead. Planning is how we survive."

"Well, sure, to a degree. Outside forces interfere with plans, and we adapt."

It's really weird to be the one giving this advice. I haven't followed it well.

"I don't like changing plans," she mutters.

I chuckle. "Just breathe. For now, let's just breathe."

We're silent for a moment as she slowly takes deep breaths. Her breathing returns to normal. She takes a step back and I let my hands fall back.

"I don't usually… do that," she says.

I have to press my lips together to keep from laughing. "You were just panicking," I say, "I'm familiar with the concept." I grin. "It's totally valid, you don't have to be ashamed."

She shakes her head.

"Anyone can have a panic attack," I say. "And these circumstances totally warranted it. Awful. I had one myself."

Her eyes flash. Ah, her old self is returning.

I raise my hands. "Alright, I won't say any more about it. If you're sure you're feeling better."

"Let's find somewhere to sleep," she mutters.

We walk around for a bit, looking for a suitable spot. Out of the corner of my eye, I observe her. She's still shaking a bit, and she's clearly not comfortable with what happened. Probably still feels queasy. It's not a fun experience.

We decide on a little grassy park area. I don't think we'll find a better spot. And we're in no condition to keep searching. Everything hurts, especially my legs. And my shoulder. By the time I sit, I'm convinced I couldn't have taken another step. We position ourselves within a clump of some trees and bushes, so hopefully we'll be a little bit concealed.

As we settle down, it's clear Kyra's still got some adrenaline in her. Her hands keep moving, fiddling with each other, going to fix something on her outfit only to find there's nothing to fix. I'm so used to her being completely still, this change is unsettling. I need to distract her.

"Have you ever heard the story of Izanagi and Izanami?" I ask.

She frowns at me. "Of course I have," she says as she tries to settle down on the grass.

"What? Really?"

"Of course. I've read most cultures' creation myths. They're fascinating, seeing everyone's different perspectives and how they explain different parts of the world. Well, the old world."

I don't know how to respond to this. Does this mean she wouldn't want to hear me tell the story? I'm too afraid to ask.

"Why?" she asks.

"I was gonna… just… tell you the story," I mumble.

"You still can," she says. "I'd be interested to see how you tell it. Maybe it differs in points from the version I read. Many mythologies do vary depending on the teller. Especially Greek."

Surprised, I try to recall how my Dad opens the story. Then I start talking. I don't do a good job, compared to him. And I'm trying to help her calm down further, so I keep my voice steady and quiet. I end up lying on my back, staring at the stars. When I finish, it's quiet.

Has she fallen asleep already? I strain my ears to try and hear her breathing.

"Thanks," she whispers.

I grin to myself. Success.

"Goodnight," I whisper.

She doesn't respond. That's okay.

All the damage she caused in my life, and now we're being friendly. But, was it really her fault? She was only trying to help.

My thoughts slowly become less coherent, and I slip into sleep.

CHAPTER TWENTY-TWO

Jun

The sun is rising and we're already on the move, walking back in the general direction of Sector 5. The longer we walk, the more I think we didn't need to bother with getting up so early. No one else is awake yet. It's so still and it's setting my nerves on edge. Does no one have to go to work? Does the whole sector have the luxury of sleeping in?

We walk in silence. The more my body wakes up, the more it hurts. My shoulder, in particular. It manages to draw attention away from the soreness of my legs, at least. These past few days have been *brutal*. Rest is probably one of the main things a doctor would tell me to do after being shot, and my days have been the exact opposite. I've probably hindered the recovery process.

So far, this venture has been a disaster. How are we supposed to reach the Farmland? Especially since all our supplies have been confiscated. This is gonna be rough.

"Is there an actual plan?" I say, breaking the silence because I suddenly need to have a conversation. My thoughts are threatening to spiral. I know Kyra warned me it would happen, but I was enjoying the break from anxiety. I don't want to return. "Or are we just walking towards Sector 2 and hoping for the best?"

"How could there be much more to the plan?" Kyra asks. "We walk, we avoid soldiers, we make wise choices and evade capture."

"I don't think it was necessarily unwise choices that caused us to be captured," I point out.

She sighs, but doesn't humor me with a response.

"How are you feeling?" I ask.

Immediately, something shifts. It's like a wall goes up between us. Cold wind blows.

"There's no need to ask," she says shortly.

"I really don't know why you're acting like it's such a big deal. So what, you had a panic attack—"

Her punch to the arm is swift and surprisingly strong.

"Ow!" I move away from her. "It's nothing to be ashamed of! In that situation, it was a perfectly normal human reaction!"

She hunches in on herself, and looks down. "Not for me."

I can't believe she punched me. Well, actually, I can. Good to know my previous concerns she might punch me weren't just paranoia. I rub the spot. Will it bruise? That would be crazy.

"I'm sorry," she mumbles, so quietly I almost miss it.

"I get it. It's not pleasant."

"I've never felt anything similar. Usually I can hide my emotions. Quiet them."

I smile. "You're forgiven. Please don't punch me again."

"I'll do my best." Then she scoffs to herself. "I don't think I've apologized as much in my life as I have these past few days."

"What, all of three times? *How* have you gotten through your life with so few apologies? Actually, no, that's concerning. How have you not apologized more? I usually apologize at least ten times a day."

She raises her eyebrows. "There's no way you cause enough damage to necessitate those apologies."

"Okay, fair. But just because I apologize unnecessarily doesn't mean the fact you never apologize is okay."

She rolls her eyes. "How close are we to Sector 5?"

"How should I know? You're the one with the map in your head."

I can't tell if there's tension right now. Are we having friendly banter, or are we arguing? It's a fine line I've never had to walk before.

"The houses are getting more sparse," she says after a while. "I would assume we're reaching the outskirts and 5 is close. People wouldn't want to live close to a poor district. The people in these houses are probably the poor of this sector." When I make a face, she adds, "Well, poor for *this* sector."

I scoff. "These people are richer than the most well-off in my sector."

"But if this life is all they know… it would feel poor to them," she counters lightly.

Anger rises in me, but it quickly dies. We don't know what these people feel like. Why are we bothering to discuss it? Admittedly, the houses are getting smaller. But they're still more well-built than anyone in Sector 4 could dream of. They even still have colour. One's pure yellow. This area doesn't have any street-lamps either, but that doesn't matter, since the sun is rising now.

We both speed up, eager to be back in Sector 5.

"Do you think they're expecting us to go back to 5?" I ask.

"Yes."

My heart skips a beat. "What? But they don't know our plan to go to the farmland."

"It's still the most logical assumption. Why would we go to a higher sector? We'd never blend in."

"I really don't want to do any more running," I mutter. My hand is on my stomach again, and I tear it away.

"How are you—"

"I'm fine."

I'm trying not to panic about the fact that I'm starting to panic again.

The change from Sector 6 to Sector 5 is so subtle, we both miss when it happens officially. The outer sections of 5 are trying to mimic the finery of Sector 6. But we know we're in 5 when we see someone with that *stupid* hairstyle.

"The first thing we need to do is eat," Kyra says. "It's been a long time."

I know it. My stomach is on the verge of digesting itself. But another pain is more insistent than my stomach.

"Well, could you look at my shoulder first?" I ask. Then I quickly add, "Well, it probably doesn't have to be first. We could eat. It's not going to change. If you need food first, I'm fine to wait."

Her eyes widen. "Your shoulder. Running could not have been good for it."

"Yeah, it wasn't. But, what are we even going to do? We don't have any first-aid supplies anymore."

She steps closer and peels back the top of my shirt to inspect the bandage. "We can buy more," she says.

I stare at her. "Did you forget the part where they took your backpack? The thing all our money was in." And the pain medicine. I *really* wish we still had some.

Her eyebrows furrow. "Yeah, but I hid a bunch on me."

"You did *what*?"

"Didn't I tell you?"

"No! When was this?"

"The night we got taken by the soldiers. I kept thinking about those three jerks and how they promised payback. I thought they might have followed us and try to steal our money. So I hid as much as I could in my outfit."

I stare at her. "That's brilliant."

Her cheeks redden. "It was just logical thinking."

"No, it was thinking like someone from these sectors."

She frowns and backs away.

I wish I understood what this change between us was. Something's different since we got arrested. Since she had a panic attack. I can understand that, at least. I always felt embarrassed. Every time. Like I wasn't in control of my own body. Maybe that's it. Maybe it was the fear we were going to die.

Maybe we're both just hungry and sleep-deprived.

"If you did re-tear the wound, it's re-clotted by now," she says. "So we probably should eat first. Then we'll buy more first-aid supplies."

"Can we afford that?" I ask.

Her eyes hold a weight. "You can't afford not to."

A pang of worry shoots through me. "Well… let's buy some food then," I say.

From a few different vendors, we manage to put together a decent, somewhat diverse meal. We eat our fill, not bothering to leave leftovers for later. We don't have a way to carry them, anyways.

I, at least, feel better as soon as we begin to eat. But I'm used to going long periods of time without eating. Has Kyra ever had to skip a meal? She's digging into the food without any hesitation, or even a wrinkle of her nose. This is probably the longest she's gone without. Doesn't mean she had to punch me, though.

She finishes her portion much faster than me. Her lower lip pokes out in the barest pout and she scrapes at the bottom of her bowl. Her eyes dart over at my food, then, just as quickly, she smooths her face into a blank face of contentment.

"It's eerie how you do that," I say.

"Do what?" she asks like I caught her doing something she shouldn't have.

"Make your face so neutral."

"It's a survival skill," she answers.

I understand. If planning to kill her is how her bosses reacted to her helping me, how much better of a life could she have had from me? Taken from her family, trained to enforce misery in all of our lives. What would that do to a person?

"You still hungry?" I ask, holding my bowl out.

Now she wrinkles her nose. "No. At least, not for food with your germs on it."

I raise my eyebrows. "I think those germs are the least of your cleanliness concerns." I shrug. "Whatever." I finish the rest of my food. It's not bad, but it's not great. Doesn't matter, it's energy.

I grab her bowl and stand up.

"What are you doing?" she asks.

"They give you a chord back for each bowl you return," I explain. "Be right back."

It's small incentive, really. The bowls are worth more than that, and I've heard of people buying from vendors so they can steal the bowls. But we don't need them, and while we still have money, our supply shrunk considerably.

The lady is much relieved to see me with the bowls. "Thank you, young man," she says, fishes around in a box on the ground. She brings out two chords and hands them to me. I give her the bowls.

I go to turn away, but she stops me with a "young man?"

"Yes, ma'am?" I say, stopping.

She looks around, then says, voice low, "You ought to tell your lady friend to do something different with her hair. Your business is your business as far as I'm concerned, but others won't think so. Her braids are too fancy for these parts."

That's what made those jerks suspicious yesterday. No, two days ago. Yesterday we were running for our lives, right.

"Thank you, ma'am," I say sincerely.

I go back to where Kyra is sitting, head in her heads. She raises her head as I approach, then stands up.

"Before we go, you need to change your hair," I say.

She frowns.

I go to explain, but she raises her hand and cuts me off.

"I know," she says. "I've been thinking about it too. But a bun or a ponytail are too unstable, and I want to make sure it stays out of my face, doesn't get in my way." She plucks at one of the braids. "That leaves cutting it, doesn't it?" Her words are even, but I see in her eyes she doesn't want to. Her hand doesn't leave her hair. "Does Sector 5 have barbers, or should we borrow a pair of scissors?"

"What are you talking about?" Though I admire her dedication, I'm not about to let her do something she doesn't want to when there's an easier solution. "Just do one braid down the back."

Her eyes clear. "Of course. A standard hairstyle for this Sector."

"For Sector 4, at least. Nothing about the Sector 5 hairstyles could be considered *standard.*"

She rolls her eyes. "You have got to let it go. You keep harping on their hair!"

"Cause it's the worst!"

She looks down, shaking her head. But I can see the smile playing at the edges of her mouth.

"Alright, sit back down," I instruct. "I'll take your braids out."

"Not necessary. I did them myself, I'm capable of taking them out."

"Your capability is the problem," I point out. "You made your braids too refined and people recognized it. You need to pass as someone from these sectors."

Her eyes narrow. "Which means?"

"I'm gonna redo your braids and make them messier."

She relents, and sits again. I get behind her, on my knees. Perfect height. But now that I'm examining her braids, about to attempt to undo all her work, it suddenly looks a lot more complicated.

"Um…"

"Find the ends of the braids," she instructs.

"I can *hear* your grin."

"You were the one who wanted to do it this way."

I manage to find where one braid ends and take out the string tying the end. It's a long process. Some braids blend into others, so I can only undo so much before I have to find the other braid and work on that.

Kyra winces several times, and I apologize profusely. Some people walk by and give us odd looks, but nothing to worry about. No one stares with suspicion. I hope.

Finally, all her hair is out of the braids.

"Wow, you have a lot of hair," I mutter. "It's so curly after being in the braids!"

"Just braid it so we can be moving," she says.

My hands move quickly, having done this for Emi many times. I couldn't do anything else for Emi, not being brave enough or cool enough, but I could brush and braid her hair. She hated doing it, but loved having long hair. It suddenly feels wrong, doing this for Kyra. I've only known her for a few days and she caused the worst time of my life. This feels too intimate, too friendly.

How could she have known? She was just trying to help our family by giving me the job. She didn't know they would all die as I result.

I shake my head and hurriedly tie the end with one of the pieces of string.

"Huh…" Kyra moves her hand down the braid. "After how long it took you to take them out, I thought I would take you forever to braid it."

"I've had—" I swallow down the lump in my throat— "I've had practice."

Kyra tries to cover the awkward moment with, "So, should we get more first-aid supplies?"

I nod, but don't trust myself to speak.

We go back to the pharmacy. Kyra buys less than she did last time, which is wise. She could only hide so many coins on her person, and who knows how many we'll need in the future. But I'm grateful she still considers the pain medication worthy of spending money on. So grateful. It doesn't work immediately, but my body relaxes as soon as I take one. Just the knowledge the pain will soon be gone is enough to ease the tension in my shoulders. She puts the bottle of pills in a little bag she bought at the pharmacy. The pain slowly ebbs away.

After, we find a quiet corner and Kyra changes the bandage. I wish I hadn't been shot in such an awkward spot. I could be changing my bandages myself. I've done it enough. But she works with precision and speed, and once again, we're walking. I hope today is more successful. I really can't wait to be out of Sector 5.

CHAPTER TWENTY-THREE

Kyra

I had hoped to be out of 5 by now. The longer our journey takes, the higher Jun's levels will rise. I know they're rising now, though he hasn't said anything. His head is starting to swivel, scanning his surroundings much more than he was before. He's analyzing for threats. Two days ago, he wasn't. He also keeps rubbing his stomach, then realizing, and stopping.

It doesn't help that he has every reason to be vigilant. We were put in jail, after all. He doesn't know the pain we came so close to receiving. We do have to be on our guard now. Soldiers patrol the streets. Not many and not often, but all it takes is one for us to be captured again and on the subway bound for torture. After the first time we have to duck into an alley and hurriedly run through to the next street, he never stops analyzing.

My appreciation for Jun is much higher. He willing kept running so I could hide. He calmed me down when I was having a— I still don't like to admit it— panic attack. And then he redid my braids so I could blend in even more.

And what have I done? By my actions, caused the death of his family. By looking too conspicuous, caused us to be captured. If we're caught, I've sentenced him to a public death. Even if we escape, the next couple days are going to be rough.

Maybe his life would have been better if I had left him alone. Done my job.

"A public well!" Jun exclaims. "C'mon."

He rushes over to a well, where several people are gathered. I follow reluctantly.

Heavily-used cups are scattered on the ground and being drunk out of. Jun lets down a bucket tied to a rope into the well. Then he carefully pulls it back up and sets it on the ground. He grabs a cup at random, fills it in the bucket, then drinks out of it.

"Kyra, c'mon," he says, lightly, after a sip.

I want to protest. The utter lack of sanitation is appalling. I can't drink out of cups hundreds of other people have drunk out of and have never been washed. People with questionable hygiene and health. I like to think I'm not stuck up, and can handle the grimier sectors, but this is crossing a line.

But Jun's eyes hold a warning. This is a normal practice out here, and I can still be outed by my actions even if my appearance is correct. And there's a deeper urging, too. It's been so long since I've had enough water to drink.

I grab a cup, trying to keep myself from thinking about all the mouths that have used it. I know my face stays neutral, but inside, my emotions are roiling.

I fill my cup and take a sip. It's definitely not filtered water. It wouldn't pass as clean. It has a fine layer of dust and grit I think is from the cup, not the water. But it's water, and my body is grateful for the hydration even as my tongue and stomach recoil and protest.

Jun's already finished his cup and is filling it again. I gulp down the rest of my water, not taking any time between sips to let my body register the taste before I'm already drinking more.

My experience in keeping my face neutral is concerning my emotions, not bad-tasting food or drink, and it's a fight to keep my face from betraying how unused I am to this water. The strong metal taste makes me want to gag, but I force the reaction down. Then I drink more. I'm thirsty. I drink until I'm not thirsty anymore. Then we drop the cups on the ground, not even wiping them or anything.

"Good job," Jun says in an undertone as we walk away. "No one gave us a second glance."

"Is that what all sector water tastes like?"

"No."

Oh, good. Of course it can't. How could people drink that every day?

"Usually, it's worse."

I stop him. "You're not serious?"

He looks at me, his face showing confusion at my disbelief, and a naivety. This is the only water he's ever known, except for the few bottles I bought.

"Right. I suppose you'd be used to better."

How can people live like this?

"The people here don't know better," he says, as if he can read my thoughts. "Well, maybe Sector 5 does. But not 4. It's amazing what people can get used to."

"Yes, it is," I say darkly.

"It's not their fault," he repeats, more passionately than I would expect.

Then I realize he's misunderstood me. "No, Jun, you misunderstood me. I was thinking the opposite way."

"What do you mean?"

"The upper sectors. What they get used to. This water you're so grateful for, we would never drink it. I don't think most would even be able to guess at how bad water *could* taste."

Jun thinks for a moment. "I understand what you're saying. But I don't think it's a bad thing if people haven't experienced hardship. Isn't that what we should be striving for?"

"Not at the expense of others."

"But it's not their fault they were born into luxury, any more than it's ours for being born into poverty."

"How can you defend them?" I snap. I speed up, because I'm not interested in an answer.

"Woah, Kyra, slow down." He catches up easily, then he glances back over his shoulder.

I'm instantly alert. "What is it?"

"What? Oh, nothing. I'm checking to make sure no one followed us."

"Why would they? You said no one looked twice at us."

"Well, just in case."

Just in case. He wasn't before. It's not a bad thing to be cautious, but I'm worried about what this might be. The more we walk, the more it becomes clear he's scanning everywhere for threats. He might not even realize how much he's doing it. He jumps a few times, when people cut in front of us suddenly, or bump into him.

"Can we walk a bit faster?" I ask.

"Sure, why?" He increases his speed to match my new pace.

"I'm done walking through Sector 5. I want to get out as fast as possible, the authorities here know our faces now. We're not as safe as we were before." I mentally kick myself. That's a good strategy, tell the guy who has rising anxiety the situation is more dangerous. That'll keep him calm.

He nods, and says, "Good idea."

My words don't seem to be causing him panic. Good.

I don't mention he's acting more like his old, anxious self, or ask him how he's feeling. Both would only make the situation worse. And what I said was accurate— people are on the lookout for us. It's good to keep our eyes open and minds alert.

However, my concern is increasing. Can Jun make it to the farmland? It's our only option.

Not truly. I could go back to the government sector and break his connection from the computer. I hesitate to count that as an actual option. I'd be killed. It's not worth the risk when the chances that he can get far enough away are much higher.

Other than trying to be constantly on the lookout myself, the day passes rather smoothly. We try to be conservative with our money. I don't think that's necessary. The food quality is only going to get worse. We should spend more money now, before our only food options are cheaper and even more questionable. We don't need to save for anything. But Jun vehemently argues against me, saying we never know when we might need to spend money, so we need to conserve our supply.

I eventually relent. I owe him this little thing. But I'm not looking forward to the food for the next few days. It's easier for him, he's used to this food quality. I'm not.

With a start, I realize I'm thinking exactly what I was getting so frustrated about earlier. This doesn't improve my mood.

As if he senses this, Jun quickly directs us to a vendor. I try hard to appreciate the food and not focus on the taste. It's not as bad as it could be.

We keep moving after that. But sooner than I would like, we need to find a place to sleep. Sector 5 is too dangerous to be walking around after dark. I communicate this to Jun.

"Right. Do we want an alley, or an abandoned house again? That didn't work out too well, but that wasn't because of the place, it was because of those jerks, so it doesn't really count. It could work out well this time."

"Let's be watchful for whatever good option we see first," I cut in before he could go into an overthinking monologue.

He nods, tries to speak, then stumbles.

I grab his arm. "Jun!"

"I'm fine, I'm fine." He shakes his head, then takes a few deep breaths. "I'm fine. Just got lightheaded all of a sudden."

I don't need to say what I'm thinking, I know he's thinking it too.

"You're probably tired," I say instead. "Let's not forget how much you ran yesterday, and then walked all day today."

"Yeah, that's probably it. Just too much exertion."

I want to insist we keep walking. Get as far as we can, sleep as little as possible. Get out of here, break the connection before it can get worse. But we *are* tired from yesterday. We couldn't possibly.

"Look, an alley," I say after scanning the street ahead of us. "Let's sleep there. We're as likely to get mugged there as anywhere else." It's big, too, judging by the distance between the two buildings. One is pretty big for Sector 5, and brick. It looks old, and sturdy.

"Sounds good," Jun says.

We slowly make our way over to the alley. As we get to the entrance— and I was right, it's a decent-sized alley— Jun trips over a trash bag left lying about. He mutters something in frustration. Something rustles in the alleyway. My nose wrinkles. Many trashbag have been deposited in this alleyway, and many random materials lie scattered about. Then a voice, tiny and timid, says, "I didn't steal anything. I promise. I just want to sleep."

Jun and I freeze, and exchange a glance.

It sounded like a girl, young. It's still bright enough to see her, but she's hiding in the shadow casted by the brick building.

"We want to sleep, too," Jun says in a gentle voice. "Is it okay if we share?"

More rustling. "You're not Mr. Ducharme?"

"My name is Jun. And I've got a friend with me too." He looks at me. Then, when I don't get the cue, he motions for me to speak.

"I'm Kyra," I say.

"Could you sound gentle, at all?" he mutters to me in an undertone.

"That was fine!" I snap back, just as quietly.

A figure emerges from the shadows. She's young. Hard to guess how young because she's so small from malnutrition. Her hair is ratty, her face smudged, and her clothes ripped and dirty.

"Oh," Jun says quietly, voice full of empathy. "Don't worry, we won't hurt you. What's your name?"

"I don't have one," she whispers.

"What did your parents call you?" I ask.

The look Jun shoots me is withering.

"I don't know. They died before I can remember."

Oh. I should have thought before I spoke. I could have realized the answer.

Jun crouches down, and smiles at her. "Forgive my friend, she's… not from here."

"She's very pretty," the girl whispers to Jun, as if I can't hear her.

I can't help the warmth in my chest at her words. I'm sure I must look terrible. In the same clothes for days, no shower, hair unbrushed. But her eyes are in awe.

"Yeah, she is," Jun says.

My cheeks heat and my eyes widen. But he doesn't even look at me. I scoff to myself. He's agreeing with her to keep her at ease. Good call.

"Can we sleep in this alleyway, too?" Jun asks.

The girls takes a few tentative steps forward. She's within Jun's arm reach now.

"Don't you have a home?" she asks.

Jun opens his mouth to answer, but words fail him.

"We're on an adventure," I say.

Her eyes bulge. "An adventure?" she exclaims.

I nod. "And… adventurers… sleep outdoors?"

Thankfully, Jun picks up where I flounder. "That's right! What kind of an adventure would it be if we stayed in houses?"

"I've never slept in a house," she says shyly, turning from side to side. "You can sleep here. Sometimes Mr. Ducharme chases me away, but I think you'd scare him."

"Oh no, I don't want to scare anybody," Jun says.

I roll my eyes. "Alright, great, we've got a place to sleep. An alley full of trash, how exciting."

"It can be pretty comfy, if you make sure not to pick bags that'll break," the girl offers.

I grimace. "I'm gonna sleep on the ground."

I move some bags and scraps of wood around to create a space big enough for me to sit. Then I lean against the wall. I don't trust this ground enough to lay my head on it. Rats probably hang around here, scavenging for food. I don't want them anywhere near my head.

"Good idea," Jun says, as if he read my mind. He arranges himself in a similar manner, opposite me.

His building is not as impressive as the brick, though perhaps the wood is more comfortable to lean against?

"Don't get splinters," I tell him.

"I'll do my best," he says with a grin.

The girl crawls into Jun's lap. He momentarily stiffens. His eyes grow misty, but he smiles down at her.

"You need a name," he says.

"Why?"

For a brief moment, I laugh to myself, remembering the frustration of my younger brother going through his 'why' phase. Then my shoulders droop. The initial memory was rose-coloured, but then reality rushed back in. I don't miss anything about my childhood. But I find myself, for the first time, longing for what could have been.

"Well, a name is something other people can call you by," Jun is saying. "It's part of who are you."

She hums, like she's not sure about it.

"We can call you…" Jun thinks, his eyes roaming around, as if the answer's in front of him… "uh, Ally?"

My mouths opens in disbelief. "You're kidding, right?"

He looks somewhat ashamed of himself.

"That's how you name cats, not children!"

"Well, what then? I've never had to name someone before."

"Oh, um…" I've never done so either. "We can call her… Alyson?"

He laughs.

"That's a name!"

"Right, it's so different from my idea."

"It is different, it's a whole extra syllable."

He shakes his head, but asks her, "Do you like the name Alyson?"

"Alyson!" she squeals, beaming at me across the alley.

I can't help but smile at her enthusiasm.

"I love it!" she declares, and the matter is settled. "Alyson, Alyson, Alyson," she chants under her breath.

"Well, it's wonderful to meet you, Alyson," Jun says.

Alyson giggles.

Jun's breath hitches, and something in his eyes change.

"Hey, you wanna see a magic trick?" he asks Alyson.

"Yes!" She claps.

He looks like he's fighting for breath, and I want to say something, but he shakes his head at me. What's wrong?

"Watch this, I'm gonna fall asleep in 10 seconds."

"No way!"

He starts counting, and doesn't make it to six before his head slumps back against the wall.

I jump to my feet. That was not someone falling asleep.

Alyson laughs in delight, and pokes Jun's chest, as if trying to wake him.

As I get closer, I see he's still breathing. He must have fainted. Not good. How are we supposed to get out of this city if he's already fainting from his levels increasing?

Alyson's chanting "wake up, wake up," and I shush her.

"It's time to go to sleep, Alyson, okay," I say. "Jun will wake up in the morning."

"Then you'll keep adventuring?" she asks, eyes shining.

"Yeah."

She pouts. "I don't want you to leave."

I don't know how to respond. She can't come with us, we can't protect her. I can't imagine trying to get Jun *and* this tiny child through Sector 2. But to leave her, alone, in the garbage…

She's still staring at me.

"Go to sleep," I say. "We'll be here when you wake up."

"Okay," she says, her inflection one of disappointment. But she immediately snuggles against Jun.

"Oh, no, Alyson…" My voice trails off. Never mind, who am I to deny her human connection when she might have never experienced it. Her breathing evens out. She's already asleep.

I walk back to my side of the alley and find the spot I cleared. I sit down.

The sun fully vanishes, the stars rise and come out, the night get chilly, and thoughts are still swirling around in my head, my eyes wide awake, sleep far from me.

CHAPTER TWENTY-FOUR

Jun

As I begin to wake up, I become conscious of a weight on me. Did I fall asleep with something on me? Then I remember: I didn't fall asleep at all. I fainted.

As I wake completely, I realize the weight on me is breathing and it has the warmth of another human. Alyson, of course, I remember. I hope she wasn't scared.

The night is surprisingly bright, in a way completely different from Sector 6. No streetlights send down artificial lights but the stars and moon shine brightly. Kyra sits across from me, clearly visible in the natural lighting, her eyes glittering.

"Did it work?" I ask. "Did she panic?"

"She was highly amused," Kyra says. "Not worried at all. Fell asleep right after you." Her voice is flat. Not from anger, I don't think. It sounds like a tiredness and lack of emotion. Has she slept at all? Do we still need to keep watch?

"I should have known she would." I stretch my neck and wince as it complains and creaks. "This position is not comfortable." My muscles are protesting, but I can't move enough to give them relief without risking waking Alyson.

"We can move her."

"No, don't. I'm probably the most comfortable bed she's ever had."

Hopefully I can still fall back asleep despite my cramping muscles. And the torture of my shoulder. It clambors for attention over all the rest of my aches.

Silence stretches across the alley.

"Hey!" I exclaim, then freeze, looking down at Alyson. She doesn't even move. "We have pain medicine," I say.

"Yeah."

"Well, can I have some?"

"Yeah."

Kyra grabs the bottle and crosses the alley. She opens the bottle, and I'm grateful she thought to do it without me needed to ask. I don't know how I would have maneuvered around Alyson. I grab a pill and put it on my tongue.

As she settles back down on her side of the alley, I wait expectantly for the pain to cease. But focusing on it only seems to make it hurt worse. I know I need to give it some time to kick in.

"Can't sleep?" I ask Kyra.

"Too many thoughts."

When she doesn't expand, I ask, "What thoughts?"

After another silence she says, "How are we going to make it outside?"

My first instinct is to reassure her and tell her not to worry. But she's not panicking. Her voice is steady.

"You're worried because I fainted?"

"Yes."

I sigh. "Me too. But I'll die for sure if we don't." I ignore the spike in my heart rate. "If I die on the way, that's alright. Make sure you and Alyson get out safely. That'll be enough."

"When did you decide she was coming with us?"

"As soon as I saw her." I grin at Kyra. "You've decided sometime since I've fainted."

"If you're incapacitated, I can't keep both of you safe."

"She'll be the safest out of the three of us in that scenario."

"Jun…"

"We can't leave her."

"I don't think she has a computer."

Her sentence is so unexpected, my brain blanks on a response. "What— you mean… she…"

"Think about it. She's living on her own, not with a relative. She has no memory of her parents or of living in a house. They must have been extremely poor. How could they have afforded the pills? Her mother probably had to take the risk."

The implications are huge. "How much do the pills cost throughout the sectors?"

"Enough to inconvenience people, but not enough so they won't buy them. In Sectors 1 and 2 they're handed out as mandatory. They can't risk their workers not being under their control. They charge enough in the upper sectors to cover the cost of making them."

I gape at Alyson. She's fast asleep. Her brain unfettered,

undetermined. Free. Are there more out there like her, their parents too poor to have afforded the pills? If they were *that* poor, they may now be free from the computers, but how can their lives be benefited much by that? Are they simply dying off from being in that state of poverty?

"We can't get them all out, Jun," Kyra says, as if she can read my thoughts.

"We could! Once my brain is free, too."

She shakes her head. "You have to know how risky that is. The chances of us making it out alive are so slim, and you'd want to jeopardize that?"

I don't answer. I don't know. I just know it's not fair, how things are right now. It should be different. Everyone deserves a chance to make their own choices.

"Some people's lives would be much worse without the computer," Kyra points out.

"Does that outweigh the people whose lives would be so much better?" I ask, my voice low.

Her jaw works. "You can't help everyone, Jun."

"But you helped me."

She becomes absolutely still. A silence stretches out, widening the gap between us.

"Why'd you help me?" I ask.

She shakes her head and looks up at the sky.

"You had to have known how it could hurt you," I push. "Why—"

"Because I was sleep-deprived and I felt sorry for you," she says testily. "It was a mistake."

Was that all it was? A throwaway mistake was what changed my life? It stings in a way I wouldn't have thought. There has to be more to it. She could have saved herself and left me to my fate. One face among the fifty she kept track of.

"If all I was was a mistake," I risk saying, working to keep my voice steady, "then why did you come for me? Why have you kept saving me?"

Something glistens on Kyra's cheek. The sight gives me chills. I know I've seen her cry before, but she was having a panic attack. This is different. What is she not telling me? I wait. I won't push her further, even though I'm dying to know.

Finally, she says, slowly, "When I first started working it was hard to get used to. I wasn't comfortable messing around in people's brains. It felt wrong to see so many in poverty and do nothing. I was young." She sighs. "There was a family in Sector 4 that gave birth to twins. They already had three children." She chuckles wryly. "Sound familiar?"

I don't dare speak. I don't want to break the spell. So I nod.

"My orders were to—" Her voice breaks— "To actually get the father fired from his job. And I couldn't understand. What could the suffering of one family amount to in their grand plan? But I was scared. I had seen my first demonstration of what happens when someone disobeys their orders. Fear kept me in line, as it was supposed to. And I watched, day after day, as the family slowly starved to death."

"I'm sorry," I say, my heart breaking for her and for the family.

"I was only twelve." Her eyes are faraway. "I cried constantly. They thought they were losing my trust, so they had me do further training. They threatened me and once again tried to stuff their propaganda inside my head. For weeks, I was constantly monitored. I learned I couldn't get involved. I had to keep my distance. I learned to keep my emotions off my face and out of my body language. After a while, nothing felt real anymore."

"Until our family."

"Until your Mom got pregnant again," she agreed. "It brought back to the surface how I felt, doing nothing, letting that family… And, to be honest, I really was sleep-deprived."

A heavy silence falls over us. It's a lot for me to try and wrap my ahead around. It's the first time I really do feel sorry for her.

"I'm sorry," I say again. "That's terrible."

She huffs. "Don't pity me."

"Sorry."

She actually laughs. "No, don't apologize again." Then she raises her eyebrow at me as if daring me to apologize for apologizing.

But instead I say, "Thank you for telling me."

Her smile vanishes and she suddenly finds the ground fascinating. "Yeah, well… I've been inside your head. Telling you about that incident is probably the least I can do."

"You've done a lot for me since then," I say.

"No more than you've done for me."

The silence that falls is comfortable. That's a new experience.

Something tickles the back of my head. I've thought before that she couldn't have known the consequences of her actions. She knew what they'd do to her, but she couldn't have known what they'd do to my family. Right?

I almost don't want to know. If she knew, I couldn't stomach continuing the journey with her, no matter how much she's saved me since then. But the question has attached itself to my brain and it's growing larger. I have to ask.

"Did you know," I whisper, my voice cracking from the sudden stress. "Did you know that they would retaliate by harming my family?"

Her response is fast. "I should have. Based on what they do to us, I should have realized that they might harm the individuals as well. But I had no idea. It's unnecessary to kill the individuals when you can reverse the commands. My bosses are unnecessarily cruel, I knew that much." She shakes her head. "I'm sorry. I wouldn't have done what I did if I had known what they would do to your family."

I'm so glad I did ask. A weight lifts off my shoulders. I didn't realize how much I had been hoping she didn't know.

"Well, like you said, you were sleep-deprived," I say.

"I suppose so." She resettles herself against the wall. "We should sleep," she says. "We need our strength for tomorrow." She closes her eyes.

"Goodnight," I whisper.

Her breathing evens out and she doesn't respond. How does she fall asleep so fast? I wish she would tell me her secret.

But then she whispers back, "Goodnight."

I grin to myself, then rest my head against the wall and stare at the sky.

The night is now quiet except for the soft breathing of Alyson and myself. I smile down at her. She's so little. It breaks my heart she's had to survive on her own.

I remember when Emi was this small and would curl up in my lap. The breath is knocked out of me all at once and I struggle to breath. I desperately blink back tears and try to take even breaths so I don't wake Alyson. The weight that was so comforting before threatens to crush me now.

Emi only exists in my memories now. They all do. It's unfair. We were gonna have a baby sibling. Taro was going to get married. How did his girl find out?

I'll never see them again.

My grief is too deep for tears, but the few that come trickle down my cheeks, making no sound.

CHAPTER TWENTY-FIVE

Jun

"It smells like decaying fingernails," Kyra complains as she accepts the chunk of bread and cheese I hand her.

"That's why it was so cheap," I say as I give Alyson her portion. She exclaims in delight and immediately digs in.

"We don't have to be saving our money so scrupulously. I have plenty."

I shake my head. She's not thinking ahead enough. "Kyra, you *don't know* what's going to happen. What if some of our money gets stolen? Or the painkillers and we need to buy more?" I've already had one this morning and the difference is enormous. I don't think I would last without those. "What if we need to bribe a guard? And, don't forget, now we have a third person to feed. We need to be as careful with the money as possible."

"But—"

"No!" I cut her off. "You never know, and better safe than sorry!"

I try to ignore the way my hand is shaking as I break off a piece of bread and shove it in my mouth. My ears are burning. My mind is flooding with all the potential 'what-ifs' and going over all the ways this could end in our deaths. We have to be prepared. What if we get recognized going into the farmland? We could be shot on sight, or need all the money we have to bribe the guards. We can't fail so close to our freedom! We can't, we can't.

Kyra leans forward and lowers her voice. "Jun, are you okay?"

Everything in me rises in resentment to her question. But I force the emotions back down, and breath out slowly.

"I'm fine, I'm just… re-adjusting." The words have to be forced out of my mouth like they're boulders too big to exit. The few days without the anxiety, as stress-filled as they were, have been enough to de-condition me. Everything in me protests and recoils from these rising feelings, even though they're the feelings that I should be most used to. But louder, above the hatred of anxiety's return, screams the anxiety. To get out of the city. Don't waste time, move now! Break the connection! What are we doing, this is going to go horribly wrong and end in our deaths!

I take some deep breaths, and try to quiet the voices in my head. At least my shoulder doesn't hurt.

Alyson continues eating happily, oblivious to the tension. Kyra picks at her bread. I feel bad for snapping at her, but I also don't know what to say. We've had no good luck on this trip, we should be planning for the worst to happen. But I can't figure out where the logic in my thoughts end and the fear begins.

"We can't reach Sector 2 today," Kyra says, her voice quiet, apologetic even.

My stomach swoops. I suddenly lose my appetite.

"Why do you want to go to Sector 2?" Alyson pipes up.

"What do you mean we can't reach it today?" I ask, ignoring Alyson.

Kyra sighs. "Technically, we could reach the entrance today. But it's already past time to enter for the work day. They wouldn't let us through."

I put my head in my hands. I try to think calming thoughts. My anxiety isn't anything worse than I've dealt with my whole life. But how much can it increase in a day?

Alyson taps my knee. "Can I finish your bread if you don't want it any more?"

"Yeah, go ahead."

I hear her munching. Then, mouth full, she declares, "I'm going to Sector 2!"

I raise my head. "What?"

"I work there," she says. "Not every day, but some days."

Of course. Because how else would she survive?

"What kind of work do you do?" Kyra asks.

"I pick fruit! Blueberries are my favourite. But sometimes I pick other fruits. Not apples, they're too high up." She finishes the bread and licks her fingers.

Some of the bubbly tension in my stomach recedes. This is good. Alyson can give us information. We can plan. This is good. This will help.

"You work outside the city walls?" Kyra asks.

Alyson nods. "Yep! It's more pretty out there. There are trees!"

"We want to get work there too," Kyra says.

"Why?" Alyson asks. "It doesn't pay super well. And you guys are strong, you could get work in a lot of better places."

"Well, that's not exactly—"

Kyra interrupts me, saying, "The pay isn't our motivation. We want to experience the fresh air."

I glare at her, but she ignores me.

Alyson nods. "The air is very nice."

"How do we get the job?" Kyra asks. "Do we have to register to become official workers?"

Alyson giggles. "No, no. You just show up. They pay when you leave at the end of the day."

Kyra frowns. "That's it? That doesn't make sense. I thought Sector 2 *had* to work. How do they enforce it?"

"Do you not have the computers for anyone who works there?" I ask.

Kyra's eyes shoot daggers at me, but Alyson doesn't know what I mean by it.

"Sometimes people fall over in the fields," Alyson says. "The soldiers move them away, and we don't see them again."

Kyra's eyes widen. Is she still unused to the brutality of the lower sectors?

"It makes sense, then," I say. "No contract means no obligation on the soldiers' part. Death doesn't have to be handled properly. It's easier for people to just show up for work, and they want many workers. Sector 2 is probably so impoverished that their choices are work or die. No enforcement necessary."

"It makes sense," Kyra concedes. "That makes it easier for us."

Part of me is satisfied. Some rationality that still persists is glad we will be able to accomplish this easily. But part of me rebels, insisting we're missing something. Some hidden surprise that will be our doom. I try to breathe slowly.

"It will be easy," Kyra repeats, her voice firm and reassuring.

Her eyes peirce mine. I nod, not trusting my voice to speak.

"But we can't get there today," Alyson says, matter-of-fact.

At the reminder, my heart sinks. Another day before we can enter Sector 2. What will I be like tomorrow? I haven't been getting worse in a linear way. The worse I get the faster it worsens. In my spiraling, I miss the conversation Kyra and Alyson have.

"Jun!" Kyra's gripping my shoulder.

My thoughts snap and scatter. I stare at her.

"This is a good thing," Kyra tells me. "We only have to travel a little today. We can rest, get refreshed. We'll wake up early tomorrow and go then."

"But a whole day?"

"You'll be fine."

"How can you say that?" I shout, rising to my feet.

Kyra doesn't respond with words. With her eyes she gestures to Alyson, whose face is drooped and trembling.

"Oh, no, Aly… no, I'm sorry," I say, my voice softening.

I kneel down, but I don't move closer. How can I explain all this to someone so young? She just met me last night, I don't want to scare her. I don't want her to think this is me.

Her eyes are wide as she watches me, waiting.

"I'm nervous," I say finally. "I want to be out. Out of this city. It's hard to wait."

She nods slowly.

"I'm sorry. I won't yell again."

She nods again and grins, a little shyly, but I've been forgiven.

I sit back and sigh. All the energy is gone from my body. My very bones groan with exhaustion.

For some reason, Kyra's eyes twinkle. She stands. "Let's get moving. If we get all our travelling done first, we can rest for the rest of the day."

Alyson hops to her feet. She extends her hands to me, as if to help me up. I take her hands, letting her think she's pulling me to her feet.

"Woah!" I stagger forward, pretending she's so strong she pulled me too much.

She giggles.

"Alyson," Kyra says brightly, "You're in charge! Where should we rest for the day?"

"I know!" She claps. "Follow me!"

We fall in step behind her. "You *are* still planning on bringing her?" I ask Kyra. "Forget all your logical concerns."

"Oh, they're quite forgotten," she answers. "She's definitely coming with us."

"Really? You're not gonna argue at all? Why the sudden change?"

"It's the change she creates in you that changed my mind."

"What?"

She grins to herself and shrugs. "It's good for you to have someone to look out for."

"Hey, I've been looking out for you, too!" I protest.

She rolls her eyes. "Must you take offence at everything I say? It's different and you know it. I am much more capable of taking care of myself."

"Alyson has survived on her own for how long?" I point out. My mind adds, 'And I wish you would let me take care of you once in a while.'

This thought surprises me and I push it away.

"Okay, fine, whatever," Kyra says. "My point was only that it's helpful for you to go into an 'older brother' mode."

My heart pangs at her words. I am supposed to be an older brother. I was an older brother. And I miss it.

Alyson cannot replace Emi. But she and I have both been deprived of family. So has Kyra. We are now each other's family.

CHAPTER TWENTY-SIX

Kyra

Alyson is a beacon of joy. She skips ahead of us, pointing out landmarks important to no one but her. She stops to pet a cat. It's thin, missing an eye and an ear, with fur matted in several places, but she exclaims at how pretty it is. Jun pets the cat too, enthusiastically agreeing with her. I'm starting to feel less complimented about being called pretty last night. I decline her invitation to also pet the cat.

Every street has stories attached and Alyson is happy to tell us about them all. Despite some of their depressing natures, she smiles throughout all of them.

I think I've had the happiest childhood and life out of the three of us. How depressing.

It flashes into my mind that if we encounter soldiers while with Alyson, we could put ourselves in danger. She won't hide from them, but she'll see we do. She could accidentally reveal us.

"Kyra, Kyra, Kyra," Alyson chants as she skips ahead. She tries to gesture me to join in the skipping. She's got Jun doing it.

I should check Jun's shoulder. He hasn't said anything about it, but I can't assume it's healthy with this exercise and dirty environment.

I shake my head and keep walking normally.

Alyson pouts.

"C'mon, Kyra," Jun pleads.

My cheeks heat up and shake my head more resolutely. If I speak, my voice might give me away.

Jun tilts his head, then stops walking. Alyson stops as well, pouting.

"Do you…" Jun hesitates.

I try to warn him with my eyes to drop it. He doesn't get the message. Or he ignores it.

"Do you not know how to skip?"

I grimace.

Jun's eyes flash with amusement. "You don't know how to skip!" he exclaims.

"Skipping and merriment of any kind weren't particularly encouraged in my family," I snap.

"Yeah, but… it's really intuitive," he says. "You jump forward, land on one foot, hop on that foot, then leap forward with the other. Hop. Leap. But fast."

I stare at him. I am not about to embarrass myself by trying something new and falling flat on my face.

Alyson runs back to me and slips her hand in mine. I stiffen, but resist the urge to pull away.

"I can show you!" Alyson grins.

In face of her cheer, I must relent.

Hand in hand, we slowly go through the motions. This is ridiculous. I don't understand how this can have any appeal over walking. Once Alyson determines I understand the basic movements, she lets go of my hand.

"Now faster," she orders. Then she demonstrates.

It's fairly obvious now how skipping works, but I'm worried my thoughts won't translate well into the action.

"Go," Alyson commands.

I try, and promptly trip over my feet, pitching forward. Jun catches me before I fall completely. He holds me as I regain my balance.

"You good?" he asks.

"Yes, well, you're making me nervous," I huff, pushing his arms away.

"Fine, I won't watch then." He turns around. "But that also means I can't catch you when you fall."

"I won't fall again."

I can hear him chuckle lightly.

Determined, I try again, this time trying slowly before going faster. It feels undignified. But fun.

Alyson claps. "You're doing it!" She sounds thrilled. She joins me.

Then Jun joins, and we're all skipping around in circles.

Eventually, I persuade them to move on, with promises we will skip more once we reach today's destination.

We stop to buy food from a vendor whom Alyson has quite the rapport with. The kindly old man wants to give us everything half-off. But Jun won't hear of it. I suppress a grin. Wasn't he just telling me we had to save as much money as possible? But no, his big heart overrules all his concerns for himself. As they argue, I spy a soldier walking down the street. Heading our direction.

A dozen possibilities and reasonings flash through my mind in an instant. It's too late to quickly get out of sight, his eyes are scanning everything in front of him. It would be suspicious to duck away now. We just have to hope he doesn't recognize us. Alyson skips in a circle around us. Maybe she won't reveal us, but be an aid to our cover.

"We can pay," Jun insists. "It's no worries, really. Please, we're not interested in a discount."

I grab the other side of his waist and tilt his body so his back is to the soldier and Jun's face is completely away from the street. Jun flinches when I touch him, but allows me to move him. He keeps arguing smoothly. I reach up and rest my hands on Jun's shoulder, then rest the side of my face on my hands, pointing my face towards the vendor.

Jun must be wondering what is going on. Except for tending to his shoulder wound, which is luckily the other side, we've not been this close. I'm suddenly very aware of how close we are. Does it make him uncomfortable? He's not pushing me away. He must realize there's an important, soldier-evading reason I'm doing this. I don't dare move. We escaped on a chance last time. We might not get one again.

The vendor relents and gives us our food for the regular price. I pay him. Jun turns to tell Alyson to grab her food and my heart drops to my feet. But the soldier is gone. I breath a sigh of relief and grab my portion as well.

We eat as we walk. When Jun gets to the end of his food, which he scarfs down quickly, he asks me, "So… what was that?"

My cheeks heat up and I internally scold myself. No reason for embarrassment, I had logical reasoning.

"A soldier was walking down the street," I answer. "I just made sure he couldn't see our faces."

"Oh." He nods. "Quick thinking."

I can't help asking, "What did you think was going on?"

He shrugs. "I didn't. I just figured you had a reason." Then he yawns a face-splitting yawn.

I don't think he got much sleep last night. He needs as much rest as he can get today. Plus, he can't worry about his anxiety if he's asleep.

"How much further?" I ask Alyson.

"Not far, not far," she says. "There's a spot I sleep. A bunch of us sleep there and we go together."

Yay. A bunch of people.

I hear Jun's sharp intake of breath, but don't say anything. It seems to make things worse when I acknowledge it.

But then he staggers, bumping into my side. I grab his arm, trying to steady him as much as possible.

"Are you okay?"

"I'm fine. Just tired." He tries to grin, but it comes out more as a grimace.

"Do you need my help?" I ask.

He starts to shake his head, but stops. "Yes." He slips his arm around my waist.

I'm briefly concerned at whether I will actually be able to hold him up. But he barely leans on me. I must just be steadying him.

Alyson's face is full of concern. Her hands fiddle with each other.

"I'm okay," Jun says warmly.

She goes to his other side and takes his hand. "I can help."

Slowly, we continue to make our way.

"How am I supposed to pretend to work tomorrow," Jun says in a voice so quiet I barely catch it and I know Alyson doesn't.

"Don't think about that right now," I instruct. "With a little rest, you'll be fine."

"It's only going to get worse. If you have to leave me behind—"

I elbow him in the ribs. He grunts.

"Stop talking," I say. It makes my heart hurt to think of us failing. We can't fail. Not after everything.

"We're almost there!" Alyson exclaims. She drops Jun's hand and runs ahead.

Jun removes his arm from around me. He staggers slightly.

I try to take his arm back, saying, "No, Jun, you're not—"

"I'll be fine." His voice is biting.

I hesitate, ashamed and confused at the hurt that causes. He doesn't want to appear weak as we enter a space full of new people. I understand. And I did elbow him in the ribs. But the tone of his voice…

Alyson pops back out from behind a building and waves us forward. "It's here!"

'Here' is a big clearing with a few small buildings at the edges.

People have tents set up. Bedspreads. Fires with something cooking over them. It's a little camp.

"This is always my spot," Alyson says, leading us to a spot on the edge, near a house that looks like it hasn't been used in years except to grab firewood from.

I survey the area. So far, only six other people are here. Many tents and bedrolls are abandoned, so I know more will come. We shouldn't be recognized.

Jun eases himself down to the ground.

"No, no, we were gonna skip more!" Alyson says. "Please?"

Jun shakes his head. His skin is grey.

"Alyson, Jun didn't sleep well last night," I say. "He needs to take a nap."

Alyson pouts. "But that's not fair! He *promised*!"

Kids. I roll my eyes.

"Later," Jun says shakily.

Alyson makes a face and crosses her arms.

Juns eyes are pleading.

Inadvertently, I make a face of my own. But I immediately correct it. That's not fair of me. He's struggling against someone messing with his brain and I'm frustrated about entertaining a child?

"Alyson, why don't you show me around?" I ask. "I'm sure you have plenty of fun spots around here." Why would she? It's a dusty, broken down part of Sector 5. But she has a way of seeing the positives.

"Can *we* skip?" she asks.

I stare down at her.

"Yes," I say finally.

She cheers and jumps to her feet. "Let's go! I'll show you everywhere!" She waves to Jun as she skips away. "Have a good nap."

I point at him. "Sleep," I order. Then I walk after her.

The first place Alyson takes me is a porch on which sits an ancient woman. It's nothing sort of a miracle she's lived this long.

"Why, do I hear my little alley-friend?" she croaks.

Alyson hops up the stairs. She beams. "I have a name now, Grandmother! I'm Alyson!"

"Indeed, are you? Delighted. Who named you, deary?" So shakily I fear her arm will fall out of its socket, she extends her hand.

Alyson grabs hold of it. "My friends! This is Kyra!"

"Well, I am glad. Alyson suits you, my dear. Kyra."

I wait as she turns her head and her squinting eyes came to rest on me.

"I'm not her real grandmother, you know, but what else could you call a woman so old she's forgotten her name?" She chuckles to herself.

A miracle allowing her to to live so long is a cruel miracle indeed. What quality of life can she have like this? What pains does she cause the person who has to work to feed her? For what? To sit on a porch and do nothing?

"Do you not speak?" the grandmother asks, not unkindly, just curiously.

"I do. Sorry ma'am."

"Ma'am?" She chuckles again. "Have I earned such a stuffy title? Call me grandmother, too."

"Okay…" But the word sticks in my throat and I can't get it out.

Alyson starts chatting, telling the grandmother every detail of her meeting us and everything that has happened since. Seeing this will take a while, I sit.

Alyson has not quite finished telling the story when a group of kids run by, shrieking and giggling. She gasps. "Grandmother, I see my friends! I'm going to play!"

"Oh, yes my dear, go."

But Alyson's already long gone. She's abandoned me and now I'm alone with the grandmother. I have no old-people skills.

"Kyra," she says.

"Yes?"

"Why are you here? What made you leave your upper sector?"

"What?"

I see on her face that this is not a test. She *knows* where I am from.

"How did you know?" I ask.

"You smell too good."

It's such a surprising and odd answer I can't help but laugh. "This is the worst I have ever smelt!"

"Yes, but the smells of perfumes and lotions that you've used your entire life still linger. Someone who knows how to use their nose can tell. Why did you leave?"

"I made a mistake."

I can't tell her.

"Concerning Jun," she says.

How does she know that from only what Alyson has told her about us? "Yes."

"Hmm." She considers this. "Then your mind is not controlled."

I freeze.

She hums. "I have lived long enough that I have observed the changes. Children who were the bravest becoming utter cowards. Children who could make friends with anybody becoming rageful and chasing their friends away." She laughs. "I have felt their attempts in my own brain. It's a wonder they haven't killed me yet. I think they've given up."

My heart sinks. Could her talking like this flag her computer? Will we be found out because of this?

She's still talking, saying, "No, no. I haven't felt them in my brain for years. What have they to worry, I'm but a crazy old woman. Who listens to me?"

I want to tell her our plan. She says no one has been in her brain, perhaps they've abandoned her computer. No, I can't risk it. Can't risk them knowing my plan. The grandmother finds my shoulder and pats it. I want to say something. There are questions I want to ask. But what might the computer flag, if it hasn't already?

And then Alyson is back, pouting, crying almost.

"What's wrong?" I ask. She doesn't appear to be hurt. She all but flings herself into me. I freeze. I've never had such constant physical affection as these past couple days. I wrap my arms around her. "Are you okay?"

After some sniffling, she pulls away, wipes her eyes, and says, "They wouldn't let me be the Princess."

"What?"

"Everyone else got a turn, but I didn't! I really wanted to!"

This confession takes too much and she cries again, burying her head in my shoulder.

"Um… there, there. It's okay." I pat her back.

The grandmother laughs. The fullest I've heard from her yet. "It is amazing what small things can mean so much. Comfort her as though you believe her hurt is valid."

"I'm sorry, Alyson," I say. "That must… suck."

The grandmother sighs. Probably annoyed with my ineptitude.

"Sometimes kids can be selfish," I say. "They don't quite realize the weight of their actions."

Alyson sighs. She's stopped crying, at least.

"Shall we go back and see if Jun is awake?"

She nods.

I wait, but she doesn't move.

"Uh, Alyson?"

"Carry me?"

Why?

"Okay."

I struggle to get to my feet, the grandmother laughing at my attempts. I make it to my feet and readjust. Alyson is clinging to my front like a koala, her head resting on my shoulder.

"Take care of her," the grandmother calls as I descend the porch. Her words hold much weight. How much has she guessed?

"I will. Grandmother."

She nods once, then waves me on.

I walk on, trying to remember the way back to the clearing. I make a few wrong turns, but Alyson is quite content in my arms. The more we walk, the more she relaxes.

Then she puts her hand up to my neck, holding it there.

"Whatcha doing?" I ask.

"Your skin so dark," she mumbles. "More than me."

I chuckle. "It is."

"It's really pretty," she says.

"Thanks. I think yours is pretty too."

"Mine is more like Jun's. Except, not really."

"Because Jun is Japanese."

She pulls her head back so her face is in front of mine. "What are you?"

"Iranian."

"What am I?"

"European."

Once she has a proper shower, her hair will be much more blonde.

"European," she repeats, testing the word. "European." She settles back down, putting her head on my shoulder. "Cool."

I know none of these words have any meaning to her. But sometimes kids just want an answer. I wonder how much these words would mean to anyone else in these sectors. How much history are they taught?

We make it back to the square with no more talking. Jun is asleep. When I go to set Alyson down, I realize she's asleep as well. I put her down next to Jun as gently as possible. Then I sit down beside them. Sleep is far from me, so I stare at the sky. Thinking.

Tomorrow. Either it's our freedom, or our death.

CHAPTER TWENTY-SEVEN

Jun

I wake up slowly. The sun is beginning to set. How long have I slept?

Alyson is way across the square, giggling and dancing with a group of kids her age. People have tiny fires, cooking some scraps of food.

Kyra is sitting beside me. Her eyes are faraway.

I sit up. She doesn't move. She must be thinking hard.

Or she's mad at me.

"I'm sorry," I say. I'm not sure what I'm sorry about yet, but I'd regret anything that made her ignore me.

She jumps and looks at me. "Oh, Jun, you're awake. What'd you say?"

"Uh, I said sorry. I thought you might be mad at me."

She raises an eyebrow. "For what?"

"I don't know."

"Why would you apologize if you don't know what you're apologizing for?" she says with a shake of her head. "It doesn't mean anything."

I think for a second. "So you *are* mad at me?"

"What? No. Well… no. I understand. It's fine."

"I'm gonna be honest, I really don't remember much of what happened right before I passed out, so…"

She laughs softly and shakes her head again. "Don't worry about it."

I scooch closer to her. "Well, now I am worried."

"There are much better things for you to be worried about."

"Please don't remind me."

"OH, right, no, sorry! Don't think about that. Are you hungry?"

I am. Very. So we walk to some nearby vendors and buy supper. I'm so hungry, I completely miss the mold. But Kyra quietly picks as much of it off her bread as she could.

Afterwards, we go back. Kyra gives a little lecture about how we need to sleep as much as possible because we have to wake up super early. Alyson protests because she already took a nap. I want to join the protests— I'm not at all sleepy— but one glance from Kyra and I shut my mouth.

"Try," she says. "The sooner you quiet down and try to fall asleep, the sooner you actually will."

Alyson pouts.

Kyra throws her hands and says, "Fine, never mind, go play!"

Beaming, Alyson races back to play with her friends.

The mood is a little tense. Kyra is glowering at the ground.

"I don't think you need to worry about Alyson," I venture to say. "She's done this many times before. We haven't."

"I am aware."

"But… you should probably go to sleep soon." I wince after I say it, anticipating the glower I'll receive for it.

But her gaze softens. "Good idea. I think I'm tired."

I agree— a little too enthusiastically, I guess, because this time she does glare at me. But it doesn't last for long.

"You'll make sure Alyson goes to bed?" she asks as she lays down.

"I will."

"And you'll go to bed at a responsible time?"

"Definitely," I promise.

I don't. I try, I really try. But my eyes refuse to close. Even as the sun goes down completely, and the moon comes up. Alyson falls asleep. Everyone else in the square falls asleep.

But not me.

My mind is unsettled. I'm spending so much energy trying to think anything but anxious thoughts that I can't relax at all.

Tomorrow. Tomorrow. Tomorrow it either all goes right or all goes wrong.

Too much can go wrong.

My thoughts swirl, getting mixed with emotions, until I can't differentiate between the two.

But I never get anxious enough to pass out. That would have been helpful, at least.

I must sleep. At some point, I must. But the night drags on, and I can't tell when I wake and when I sleep. It's thoroughly unrestful.

Then the sun starts to lighten the east sky.

Kyra said we had to go early. How early is early? Do we need to be moving yet?

People stir. They're getting up, eating. Not everyone, but enough that my heart rate starts to skyrocket.

I go to wake Kyra up, but I stop myself.

She knows when we need to go. Especially after the lecture she gave us last night. She knows.

I try to sit still. I try. But the more people who arise and get moving, the more my heart rate increases. I feel like I'm being choked.

Finally, I give in. I shake Kyra's shoulder.

"Wake up! Wake up, don't we have to go yet?"

She swats my hand away. "What are you doing?" But she's awake. She sits up and rubs her eyes. She checks her watch. "We still have time."

"Oh…" I pinch my shoulders together. I shouldn't have woken her up, that was mean, really. Just because I can't sleep doesn't mean she shouldn't get as much sleep as possible.

She inspects my face. I don't know what she sees there, but concern flashes across her face. She's not as good at hiding what she's thinking anymore.

"Don't worry about it," she says. "Better safe than sorry. We can eat before we go."

I wrap my arms around my knees.

"Jun… how are you feeling?"

"I don't know anymore," I mumble.

What's normal? It's been so long. I can't tell anymore how far I've come. I've always been anxious. How could I ever have felt at peace? When there's so much in this world to be worried about.

"Where's Alyson?" she asks.

Her voice is so neutral. She doesn't even sound worried. She ought to be! Where is Aly?

My head whips around, scanning the crowd.

Oh no.

What happened?

"There she is," Kyra says. Still unconcerned. She waves.

Then I see Aly. She runs over from a small group around a fire.

Relief runs through me, and I slump back to the ground.

Kyra pats my knee. I don't feel comforted. She asks if I was okay, but now she's totally unconcerned. Jerk.

My head clears a little.

"You still sleeping?" Alyson asks me, poking my knee.

An encouraging thought occurs to me. I didn't notice when Alyson woke up or when she ran off. I must have been asleep. I did sleep at some point.

"You hungry?" Kyra asks her.

Aly's eyes widen. "We're gonna eat first?" she squeals, jumping.

"Do you usually not?"

"No, cause I don't have money until after I work."

I sit up. "Let's eat a lot, then!"

Kyra grins to herself. "Alyson, do you know of any vendors open this early?"

Alyson shrugs. "I dunno, I've never checked."

"I'm sure there are some, to get this crowd. We shouldn't have to go far."

Kyra stands up. "Jun, you can wait here, if you want."

I do. I trust Kyra that we have time to go get food before we have to leave. But I don't want to risk it.

"We'll bring you back food."

They walk off.

"Don't spend too much!" I call after them.

Kyra gives me a thumbs up without even turning around. Wow. Why did she care more before? She's not the least bit worried now. We're about to try to get through the entrance to Sector 2 *and* the exit to the outside! So much could go wrong, including what damage I could do. I know I'm not at my best right now. What if I faint and draw attention to us?

I'm a liability. They would have a much better chance if they left me behind.

I should have gone to get food with them. All I do is spiral.

CHAPTER TWENTY-EIGHT

Kyra

Jun is pale and trembling by the time we get back. Everything within me fights to keep my face and body language entire neutral. I don't think it's working. It's been years since I've felt worry like this. It's breaking down my ability to act indifferent.

Will we be able to break the connection in time? What if too much damage has been done?

I push those thoughts aside. I can't think like that. Jun is, for sure, so I need to be clearheaded. If he sees me concerned, it will only make him more concerned.

And hopefully, if I am able to maintain a facade of complete disinterest, he'll be too busy being confused or angry at me to be anxious. Maybe. Who knows. But I do know if I am worried, I will only make him more worried.

"Slim pickings, so here's your food," I say, holding it out.

Jun's hands are shaking as he reaches out. Quickly, I deposit the food directly into his hands, pretending not to notice their unnatural movement.

This is not who he should be. I had a brief glimpse of the man he can be. I want him back. We are going to get him back.

I eat quickly, and so does Alyson. Jun eats as fast as he can without choking, although he still does a few times and has to take a drink of water. I only bought one water cup for us to share, but I'm past being grossed out by something like that. Jun's concerns about saving money got to me, and I couldn't bring myself to buy water for each of us.

The crowd moves as one when the time comes to leave. Everyone gets up, Alyson included. When we don't move, she stares at us.

"It's time to go," she says like it's the most obvious thing in the world.

Jun and I scramble to our feet.

"I didn't think *all* of these people were going to Sector 2," I murmur to Alyson as we follow the crowd.

"Oh yes." She nods. "This is the spot. It's too dangerous to stay in Sector 3 to sleep."

"I know."

"We cut through Sector 3 as a group. So we don't get mugged. Or knifed. Safety in numbers." She beams at me like she didn't just deliver a grim pronunciation.

Jun slips his arm around my waist. At first, my heart jumps. But I quickly realize why he's doing it, and I mentally scold myself.

I do the same, putting my arm around him, hoping to provide even more stabilization. Hopefully it's not obvious to others that I'm holding him up. It would be quite inconvenient for the guards to turn him away because they don't think he's fit to work. Then again, I doubt they care based on Alyson's reports. If a worker does kneel over and die, it's one less person they have to pay.

We follow the crowds. I'm grateful for them. I can concentrate on helping Jun instead of worrying about which route to take. I assume this route is some combination of the quickest and the safest. Alyson sticks close to my side, for which I'm grateful. I don't have brain space to keep an eye on her too.

"Do they check our identifications or anything?" I whisper to her.

"What for?" she asks.

How can they not? Are there no records, no cataloging, no anything?

But then we reach the entrance into Sector 2, and I understand. Sector 2 has a wall around its border. Where we're entering it is nothing more than a gap in the wall. Soldiers stand on balconies halfway up the walls, guns ready. More soldiers are on the ground around the entrance, also armed with guns. And we just... walk through.

How can this be it?

I have greatly underestimated the differences between the upper sectors and Sector 2.

We shuffle through the gap in the wall. I hold in my reaction. It seems impossible there could be such a difference between Sector 3 and 2, but there is. There are barely any houses, and what little there are are decrepit beyond use, falling apart, rotting. No grass. Everyone moving in a mass shuffle to the outside entrance. The only people I see not moving are those too old or infirm to rise, or those too young to walk, being looked after by those young enough to spare.

Jun's grip tightens on my waist as he takes in the surroundings.

"This isn't right," he mutters. "This really isn't right."

"There's nothing we can do about it right now," I say. I can tell he wants to object, so I add, "Focus on yourself right now. You can't do anything for them in your condition."

He grumbles, but doesn't say anything else.

This sector is unbelievably small for the amount of people I thought lived here. When everyone's in here it must be packed.

I can already see the exit. The sun creeps over the edge of the horizon. Jun pulls away from me.

"You good?" I ask, letting my arm fall.

"I have to be," he mutters, adjusting his posture. "What's the plan?"

Too many people are crowding around us. I can't risk saying anything. He seems to understand. At least, he doesn't press.

We're passing through the gate to the outside. The sun isn't high yet, but its direct rays force me to blink and adjust all the same.

Jun stops. His face starts to glow from the sun's rays. Wishing I didn't have to, I prod him forward. He can't stop. We have to keep moving, be one with the crowd. Blend in.

I understand. This air is so fresh compared to the dusty staleness of his sector. Even this close to the city, where the environment is highly worked over and regulated to mass produce food, it's more nature than he's ever experienced before.

We're still within a gate, going forward. Jun's head swivels, taking it all in. I try to take in as much as possible without being obvious. We haven't reached the fields yet. Around us are barns and massive machinery. I would imagine those are operated by paid farmers from one of the middle or even upper sectors. No one from sector 2 could be trusted.

Then we reach a spot where the path splits into two. People move to their different lanes. I hesitate, but Alyson grabs my hand and tugs me to the right.

"Come with me!" she says brightly. "We pick the fruit. It's a good job."

We're not so jostled and pressed, now, since everyone split.

A soldier walks up to us and stops Jun. "Woah. Where are you going?"

"To pick fruit," Jun answers.

I'm impressed. He said that with zero trace of sarcasm.

The soldier looks him up and down. "With those muscles? Aren't you better suited to a job with more heavy lifting?"

"Sir?"

"Is this your first day working here?" the soldier asks.

"Yes, sir."

"He was gonna come with me!" Alyson pipes up, grinning.

The soldier is unmoved. He glares at Jun. "We're not wasting you on blueberries and strawberries. Go down that lane." He jerks his thumb towards the farthest left lane. "Go move some dirt and haybales."

It would be a bad thing to split up. But we can't disobey. Can't risk death or a beating this close to success. And I can't even try to pretend to have enough muscles to go with Jun.

Jun looks at me, his eyes pleading.

"Why do you look at her?" The soldier pushes Jun in the shoulder. He winces.

"I gave you an order, boy."

"We'll see you at lunch," I say. With my eyes I try to send the message of 'it's okay.'

Alyson tugs on my hand. "But you can't see where he'll be working from the fruits fields."

I had already guessed that, no need for her to tell me.

"What's the matter with that?" The soldiers words are close to a growl now.

Jun needs to go before the soldier gets angry.

"Nothing, we were hoping to work together, him and I," I say with a smile. "We just starting dating."

I cringe internally. Why did I say that? What's Jun going to think? I don't want him to jump to the wrong conclusions.

What would the right conclusions be?

Why couldn't I give any other excuse?

The soldier shoves Jun back. "You can survive without each other for the day. Like you said, you'll see each other at lunch. Come on, boy. Don't be more trouble than you're worth."

Jun moves, the soldier following, gripping his gun tightly. Jun casts a glance back at me. I can't read his face, so I give a thumbs ups.

'It's okay,' I mouth. 'See you at lunch.'

He nods.

I grab Alyson's hand and head towards the fruit fields.

"What about Jun?" She's pouting.

"We'll see him at lunch," I repeat. My head is whirling. What now?

Firstly, this operation is much bigger than I expected it to be. I underestimated how much it would take to feed a city of this size. Alyson leads me down a path that branches off from ours, and I can see the approaching fruit fields.

Is there a fence? Posted guards at the perimeter? Where are the fruit fields in relation to the end of this massive farming complex?

Will Jun be okay on his own? How much longer does he have? I don't want to find out. We can't have come all this way to have to turn back. I have to hope he makes it until lunch and find out as much as I can about this place in the meantime. Picking blueberries will be the perfect activity for looking at my surroundings during. I can move rows under the guise of finding a better spot, but in reality, I'm changing locations so I can see something new and continue making a mental map of the area. I'm ready. I won't fail Jun.

But when we reach the blueberry field, I'm not assessing how big it is, or if I can see the end of this farmland. I'm thinking about Jun, wondering what his situation is. What work is he doing? When I grab a bucket from the worker, I'm not scanning to see how many soldiers there are. I'm wondering if Jun will be able to avoid fainting. I wonder if they'd shoot him and save themselves the trouble if he does. My heart skyrockets and I almost drop my bucket.

'He'll be okay,' I tell myself as I find a spot within the many rows. 'He has to be.'

I don't want to think of a world without him in it.

Picking blueberries relaxes me. The guards are content to let everyone work at their own pace, however slow that might be. Why wouldn't they, when they pay each person so little. Alyson shows me what passes for an acceptably-ripe blueberry. It takes little brain power to locate which are ripe and which aren't. And the sun isn't hot yet.

This is pleasant. Lovely.

I settle into a rhythm, thinking about the best ways to escape from this farmland. The morning passes.

I'm no closer to an answer.

CHAPTER TWENTY-NINE

Jun

I shovel the last of the horse manure into the wheelbarrow. Then I set the shovel down and wipe my forehead. This work is hot enough now, but it's going to be brutal this afternoon. I hope my afternoon jobs are also mostly in the stables, out of the sun.

Leaving the shovel on the ground, I take the wheelbarrow outside and dump the manure into its designated pile. They'll use it for fertilizer.

Then I move on to the next stall. More shoveling.

I'm trying to ignore my body, but it's screaming warnings at me. The more I work, the more it protests. My stomach is queasy, my hands are shaking, and I can barely focus. My whole body is vibrating. It feels like I'm facing down a bear instead of just shoveling manure out of empty stalls.

Kyra will have an escape plan at lunch.

My spirits lift for a moment. Yes, she'll know what to do. I grin to myself.

'Except she didn't when the soldier moved you here,' my brain reminds me.

My smile drops and I stab the shovel into the hay.

She did what she could. She tried to use the excuse of us dating. I scoff and shake my head. Did she think some part of the soldier would be moved to compassion and let me stay with her?

If I was a soldier, I would have moved me to this job, too. And if my brain were left to itself, I would be excelling at it right now.

The work is monotonous and laborious. My shoulder winces everytime I lift the full shovel. How long ago was it that I got shot? So much has happened since then.

Shovel. Push. Dump. Repeat.

I wheel out for the last trip. Another man is dumping the contents of his wheelbarrow into the massive and smelly pile. He's too old for this work. His hair is white and his muscles tremble. He ought to be picking fruit or something less laborious. He struggles to turn the wheelbarrow up. I'm too far away to help him.

By the time I get to the pile, he's started leaving. But he doesn't make it far before he stumbles and falls. He doesn't get back up.

My heart rate spikes, a reaction I don't think I can afford. I drop the wheelbarrow and rush over to him. I roll him over on his back. He's breathing, but it's shallow. His skin is pale. He's fainted.

I fan him with my hands.

A soldier calls out, "Just leave him, boy."

We can't leave him out here to lay, unconscious, in direct sunlight after hard labour. That could kill him. He needs to be moved into the shade at least.

I hook my arms under his armpits and attempt to stand. Unconscious bodies are heavy, and I'm not at my best physically.

I didn't hear the soldier approach, but I feel the blow to the back of my head. My vision blacks out for a moment. I drop the man.

"Get back to your work!" the soldier commands.

I take deep breaths, waiting for the threat of vomit to pass. Shakily, I get back to my feet.

The soldier's face is harsh and immovable.

"Back to your position," he spits. "If I see you touch him again, you won't receive lunch today."

The desire to help this man is still strong. But I can't afford to miss lunch. My body wouldn't be able to handle it.

I shuffle back to my wheelbarrow. The soldier returns to his post. I do my work slowly, my head pounding.

Lunch can't come soon enough.

When it does, we all shuffle in a line. I follow the men in front of me. They know where to go. It's a communal lunch space somewhat in the centre of this massive farm operation. No tables except for those that the food sits on. Its bread and some form of stew that probably wasn't made with any fresh ingredients. One table is dedicated to massive bowls of water with only about five cups. We go there first. Everyone grabs a cup, scoops water, and drinks the cup in its entirety. Then the next person grabs the same cup and does the same thing. I do this without thinking. I'm so thirsty. The water might be lukewarm and somewhat dirty, but it quenches my thirst.

Then we go grab stew and bread. I sit off to the side, by myself. It's surprisingly chatty as everyone eats. My hand is shaking so badly, I can't bring the spoon to my mouth. I give up, setting the bowl on the ground. I knaw at the bread. It's hard and stale, but better than nothing.

"Jun!" a voice shrieks, and a figure jumps onto my back. Alyson throws her arms around me. "We missed you!"

I pat her arm. I feel as though I take my the fullest breath I have in hours.

"How was your morning?" I ask, managing to put a lightness in my voice that I don't feel.

"I wish you could have been there." She lowers her voice, "Kyra doesn't talk much."

I chuckle.

"Hey, I grabbed you a bowl, don't make me regret my kindness," Kyra's voice sounds from above us.

My heart jumps, but in a way that's not altogether unpleasant.

Kyra sits down next to me, passing a bowl over to Aly. Alyson lets go of me and sits down. But she fairly snuggles into my side before tearing into the stew.

"You're not eating it?" Kyra asks. She takes a spoonful, coughs, makes a noise, and swallows. "I don't blame you," she says weakly.

"Ingredients gone moldy are very cheap," I say.

"I remember you saying that, yes." She makes a face as she regards the bowl.

"You need it. We've got a long afternoon ahead of us."

She nods towards my bowl. "You need it too."

I don't want to admit why I stopped eating it.

"Did you miss me too?"

I don't know why I asked that.

She ducks her head and fiddles with her spoon. "I was worried about how you were doing."

I grin. It doesn't escape my notice that my anxiety has lessened in their presence. It still pounds away in the back of my head, but it's not commanding my attention like before. It's like they're my safe space.

Taking my bowl, I begin to eat. My hand still trembles slightly, but its hardly noticeable.

"What did they have you doing?" Kyra asks.

I go to make a joke, but I remember the incident with the older man, and the joke dies in my throat. He was still lying there when we left for lunch. Unmoving. I couldn't tell if he was breathing or not.

"What's wrong?" Kyra searches my face.

After a brief hesitation, I tell her what happened. I ramble, pouring out my frustrations. She cuts me off.

"Jun, stop, stop, don't get carried away." She puts her hand on my knee. "For the sake of yourself, don't think about it anymore. Plus, I don't think the soldiers care to hear your feelings about this subject. Lets put our heads down and keep working. Try not to stand out."

"Well… but… you've figured out what we're doing, right?"

She avoids my gaze.

"Please…" My voice fails. "You have a plan. We can't just keep working! We're supposed to… I can't…"

It's suddenly impossible to breathe.

She gets in front of me. "No, Jun, listen, this is a much bigger operation than I thought it would be. The security is tight. I don't even know where the edges are."

"No, no. This was the plan!"

"I know, I'm sorry. I had no idea what it was like out here. We'll figure something out. I'll talk to people, see if they know anything that might help us."

"I don't think I can survive another day!"

Her face drops.

Alyson is watching us, her eyes big.

"Jun—" she starts.

I cut her off sharply, "I'm not kidding."

"I'll figure it out," she promises.

I turn away.

A few soldiers are watching us. I don't care. If we can't figure out a way out, to break the connection, I'm as good as dead where I sit. Maybe I should provoke one into putting a bullet through my brain. That would probably be quicker and less painful than dying by anxiety.

Kyra wraps her arms around me in a tight hug.

My breath cuts out as I register what's going on. Then it comes rushing back, filling me and making every other noise fade into the background. I put my arms around her.

Her chin is resting on my shoulder. She whispers, "I swear to you, I won't let you die from this. I will find a way to free you. No matter what."

I believe her.

The odds are against us in everyway. She might not be able to keep her promise. But I know she'll do everything humanly possible to keep it, and that is reassuring enough. At least for now.

She opens her mouth as if to say more, but then shakes her head, withdrawing into herself again.

Alyson doesn't ask what we were taking about, but she can tell something's going on. She seems unsure whether to move away from me or not. I try to smile at her, but she doesn't smile back. Her eyes are crinkled and her lower lip trembles slightly.

Leaving Kyra and Alyson is harder after lunch than it was this morning. It's like I'm being deprived of oxygen the further away I get from the lunch space.

I try to steel myself. Kyra will figure something out, and soon, the connection will be broken. The anxiety will be a distant memory, and I'll be free. My emotions will be my own. I take a deep breath, and find my boss to get my afternoon job.

He puts me on rebuilding a fence with some other men. Outside. In the hot, direct afternoon sunlight.

The men are quite jovial, despite the work conditions. They laugh and joke with each other. Their ease does some good in setting me at ease, but the sun cancels out their efforts. My strength wanes. My whole body is sweaty.

One of the men takes a hard look at my face.

"Boy, you get out of the sun," he tells me. "Go join someone's work in the barn, the four of us can handle the fence."

"But—"

"If the boss asks, just tell him Billy sent you inside. You're not used to this heat, boy. Can't afford to faint."

My heart drops thinking about the man from earlier. He was gone when we came back from lunch, but I'm not hopeful.

"Yes, sir. Thank you."

I rush back and pick the closest barn.

"Anyone working in here?" I ask loudly.

A head pops up over one of the stalls. "Yeah?" The person sounds confused.

"I was sent to join whatever work you're doing. If there is extra for me."

"Sure."

There's a beat of silence while we just stare at each other before I ask, "So, what are you doing?"

"Well, we're working on helping a horse birth her foal. There's three of us."

On cue, the horse lets out a loud and long neigh.

"Three sounds like enough," I say. Then I turn on my heel and get out of there.

Assisting in my first birth is for another day. When my mental and physical capabilities are not at their weakest.

I make my way to the next barn. Only one person is in here. He's working on repairing a stall door, but he doesn't appear to be making much progress. He keeps cursing under his breath because he can't hold the boards and nail them in at the same time. Then he catches sight of me standing in the doorway.

"Finally," he huffs. "Don't stand there, get over here and help me with this!"

I scramble forward. Under his direction, which I make sure to follow precisely and quickly, we get the stall door repaired. But the ease I had gained from working with the men at the fence vanishes after working with this guy. I'm so aware of following everyone word of his instructions or risk getting cursed at. My body grows stiff and tense.

When we're done, he gives me instructions. "There's a big scrap pile of wood about two barns over. Take all this broken wood out to that scrap pile."

I nod and gather as much wood as a I can, being mindful of big wood splinters and nails.

Accidentally, I head the wrong way. I circle around the barns, but can't locate this big scrap pile he was talking about. It must have been to the left, not the right.

I hurry back, trying not to drop anything and trying not to be seen by him. My breath comes in jagged puffs. Odd, I'm not running that fast.

The pile is two barns over, to the left. I toss the broken pieces of wood onto it, then go to head back and grab more. But my legs are unsteady. I take a few quick steps before I'm suddenly wobbly and my legs feel like they're giving out.

My vision grows blurry.

No, I can't faint! They'll leave me out here! In this heat and sunlight, it's another death sentence.

I fall to my knees.

Maybe dying while unconscious is preferable?

My face goes down to meet the dirt, and my last thought is, 'I'm sorry, Kyra.'

Then everything vanishes.

CHAPTER THIRTY

Kyra

The afternoon is much worse than the morning. The food they served us, if it can be called so, refuses to settle in my stomach. I feel close to vomiting for most of the afternoon. The sun, so pleasant in the morning, now beats down with a vendetta. The energy drains from my body. I can't imagine working a more physically demanding job under these conditions.

How can Jun make it?

A bigger, more important question looms on my mind. How can he make it until tomorrow?

Tomorrow doesn't matter if I can't figure out an escape plan at all. I want to ask Alyson about any information that would help me make a plan, but all my questions would be too suspicious. Too many people are picking blueberries alongside us, or on the other side of the row. They'd overhear. I can't risk that, but it makes me feel guilty. I wish I could help others escape. I don't want to leave them in this state. But I can't risk someone notifying the guards. That would mean a quick, one-way trip to the government sector.

Which might be my only option if I can't find a way to escape from the farmland. It feels like I face death whatever way I turn. This scenario has no easy way out.

The more the afternoon wears on, the less ideas I have. My picking gets slower and slower. Why can't I think of *anything*? There must be a way out of this place.

But the call to leave comes too soon.

Our best shot isn't a great one, but it could work. If he and I could hide somewhere while everyone leaves, then we'd have time to figure out a way to escape, with no one around.

The soldiers will most likely do a patrol after everyone leaves to make sure everyone truly has left. If they don't, then they're all stupid. But this could still work. If we hide well enough. If I find Jun and explain the plan to him and we manage to sneak away to hide in the first place.

"Alyson, be on the lookout for Jun," I say. "Let me know as soon as you see him."

We both keep our eyes peeled as we walk down the pathway to the place where the two join. Many people are walking towards us, but none of them are Jun.

"We should wait for him," Alyson suggests brightly when we reach the intersection.

"Yes."

We move to the edge. Alyson hops onto the fence to get a better viewpoint.

Did something happen to him?

I dismiss the thought. What would have happened? Most likely, he had to finish the last of his job, and got released a little later than everyone else.

We are not the only people who wait in this intersection. Friends and family who work in different sections meet up, and together, head back into Sector 2.

Only a few stragglers are walking down the lanes, now. None of them are Jun.

"Do you think he went through already and we missed him?" Alyson asks.

"No. He would have waited for us."

Something happened.

"You look like you're thinking really hard," Alyson says.

"I am. I'm wondering what happened to him."

As soon as the words are said, Alyson's face transforms. Her eyes widen and well with tears.

"Something happened to him? Is he gonna be okay?"

"Oh, Alyson, no, I didn't mean…"

She messily wipes at her face. "I don't want anything to happen to Jun! He's my friend!"

I pat her shoulder. "Well, I didn't mean… I didn't mean anything bad necessarily, just whatever has caused him to be delayed."

"But what if it *is* something bad?" She sniffs loudly, her big, teary eyes boring into mine.

She jumped to that conclusion fast. It's almost touching how much it's upsetting her.

"Alyson, I don't think this is the time for tears," I say. Then I wince. That's an insensitive to say to a young child who's had a long day of work. "I'm sure Jun's okay," I add, instilling as much warmth as I can into the words. I don't think I do a good job.

"Hey, move along," a soldier shouts at us. "What are you waiting for?"

I turn around, and find the soldier that moved Jun this morning. His eyes register who I am, too.

"What, waiting on lover boy?" he asks with a smirk.

"I'm concerned; he's not passed through yet," I say, keeping my voice level.

"He's probably in the medic tent," he says carelessly.

Alyson gasps.

The soldier turns to another lady, who's been waiting in the intersection for about as long as we have. "Yours too, lady. I'd check the medic tent, both of you. But be quick."

Did Jun hurt himself?

Or did the computer finally—

I can't even finish my thought. For the first time, I begin to worry about him not appearing. I promised him at lunch! I thought he still had time.

After a few deep breaths, I feel composed enough to turn to Alyson and say, "Can you lead me to the medic tent?"

She nods, but she's crying.

I sigh. "Do you want me to carry you again?"

She nods again and lifts her arms up.

I wrap my arms around her and she maneuvers so she's resting on my hip. She ought to be too heavy, as I assume she's six or seven, but she's quite light.

By the time she's settled, I don't need to ask which way. The other lady, who looks to be at least in her sixties, is heading down the path we came from. So I follow her.

It's a long walk. We pass where Alyson and I turned left to go to the fruit field. We walk to the end of the path. Interesting, I would have thought they would want the medic tent somewhat in the middle of the farm, for convenient access. But I do understand why they'd want it far away from everything else.

A few meters behind the medic tent is the tall fence that boarders the farmland. I saw it in the distance when I was picking blueberries.

Up close, it's even more impressive. I also notice a gateway and a truck. Interesting. Maybe this will work out well, if Jun's not too sick. We could sneak off, hide, then escape through the gateway.

The medic tent is huge and white. The lady walks inside, pushing the flap away, and I follow.

She stops short upon entry, and I have to halt to avoid bumping into her. I can't see what made her stop. But then she lets out a noise in between a sigh and a sob. Like she had resigned herself to what she now sees but is still sad to see it. She makes her way over to a man lying on a cot. He's not breathing.

Then I see Jun. He's sitting on his cot, talking to two doctors. He's alive. His skin is pale and clammy-looking, and his hands are shaking. His eyes dart over to me, back to the doctors, then they quickly swivel back and fixate on me. His whole face lights up.

I make my way over to him and carefully set Alyson down beside him. He puts his arm around her, but his eyes are still focused on me.

"You're the girlfriend?" one of the doctors asks. He's quite short, but cheerful-looking. His glasses keep sliding down his nose and he has to keep pushing them up. He doesn't seem to mind.

"Yes," I answer, before my brain registers the 'girlfriend.'

Well, of course he had to say that, he was maintaining the alibi I had already established.

"Something's wrong with this boy," the doctor says. "And I don't know what."

"He's been a bit sick recently," I say. It's not really a lie. "Usually, he's not like this." That one was a lie.

The doctor scratches his head. "Heart palpitations. Fainting. Can't stop his hands from shaking. Sweating. And he doesn't seem like he's all there."

I'm not sure what the doctor wants me to say to this. He regards Jun for a few minutes, then asks me, "How long has he been like this? He couldn't give me a definite answer."

"Two weeks," I say without thinking too much. Who knows what the best time frame is for our cover. I'm not sure what our cover even is. "It got him fired from his old job."

Jun winces. I hope I didn't accidentally hit a sore spot. Then I remember, with a jolt, that I know his whole life. I've been in his brain. It's been so long since I've thought about that. He had just gotten his first job before this mess all began.

"That's not good. I wonder if it's some kind of viral infection or some kind of immune issue."

"Can you help him?" I ask.

The doctor hesitates.

For the first time, the other one chimes in.

"Usually, we don't," she says. "The cost of trying to heal someone doesn't get repaid in—"

The short doctor coughs, and cuts her off. "Yes, well, sometimes it's not worth it. But in his case…" He trails off and his eyebrows knit together.

I know what they're saying. It's worth healing him because of the work he then, theoretically, will be able to do for them. Except they can't heal him. Only breaking his connection to his computer will. But, he'll certainly be cared for. It might be a beneficial environment for keeping his anxiety lower. Keeping him alive longer.

But it would mean that I would have to break the connection.

I stare at Jun. He's talking to Alyson in low, reassuring tones. I promised him I would save him. And there's no way to escape from this place. At least, not in time. I can give him a better chance at life, even if he still has to live here.

"You've seen him work," the short doctor says. "Is he a hard-worker?"

"Of course she'll say yes," the other mutters. "She'll want to save his life."

"I do," I say. "But he is. Ask his boss how much work he did today, despite this illness, then imagine how much more he'll do when he's well. He's strong and hardworking."

"He certainly looks it," the short doctor says. "Well, say your goodbyes. I don't know how long he'll be at the hospital, but my guess is it'll take a while for him to fight off whatever this is."

"The hospital?" Jun asks.

"We send any of our patients to a hospital in Sector 7. Some soldiers will take you there tonight." The doctor nudges the girl. "We'll give you a few minutes."

They walk off.

"I can't go to a hospital," Jun says to me as I sit down beside him. "They can't do anything for me."

"No," I agree. I hesitate, then say, "It could work out well. They'll make you comfortable, it'll be a low stress environment, you'll get a chance to rest."

"I feel like there's a 'but' coming."

"Your chances of being recognized will increase. A lot. And if they ask for instructions concerning you, the instructions will be… to let you die."

He takes a deep breath.

I rush to add, "But perhaps they'll do nothing and let you keep dying as you are already."

"That's supposed to reassure me?" he exclaims.

"It'll give me time to break the connection," I say.

His eyes widen and he grabs my hands. "No! I thought you said that was too dangerous."

"We don't have a choice."

His eyes are deep. "Yes, you do have a choice."

"No!" I say harshly. "I don't."

In the silence that follows, Alyson asks shakily, "Is Jun gonna die?"

I forgot she was sitting next to Jun.

"No, the doctors are gonna fix me up," Jun says reassuringly.

"But Kyra said…"

Alyson's words dissolved into sobs and Jun does his best to comfort her. I cast my eyes over to the doctors. The girl is barely listening, her eyes constantly shifting over to glance at us.

"I have to go," I say, interrupting Jun.

"What?"

"I need to get back to the government sector as fast as possible. It's our best chance." I stand up.

Jun grabs my hand. "Be careful."

"You too." I look at Alyson. But I don't know what to say. She can't come with me, and I can't explain. "I'll come back and find you," I promise.

Then I turn on my heel and rush out of the tent.

"Wait, where's she going?" Alyson cries out behind me.

I make it out of the tent and my heart breaks. I didn't think it'd be so hard to leave them.

This is the only way.

Unfortunately, it means I have to reveal myself and get transported back to the government sector as a prisoner. I can't make it to Sector 7 fast enough to take the subway.

Which means I will then have to escape and shut down Jun's computer while being hunted.

This should be fun.

CHAPTER THIRTY-ONE

Jun

It's harder for me to stay calm once Kyra has left, especially with Alyson weeping into my side. Poor thing. It's been a long day for someone so little, and she has no idea what's going on. I wish Kyra hadn't been so open with the word 'die.' I have no words for Alyson to either explain or comfort. I can barely think.

My stomach roils and my nerves are like hot wires flashing under my skin. I know I'm sweating, and I'm probably pale as well. No wonder they think I'm sick. If I didn't know what was going on, that's probably what I would have thought too.

The doctors return.

"I see she just… left," the man says.

"Odd," the woman comments, her voice sarcastic, but I'm not sure why. She raises an eyebrow at Aly. "Why are you still here?"

With more tact, the man says gently, "You cannot go with him, you know. No need to worry, they'll have him all better in no time!"

It takes some time, but I manage to calm Alyson down. She keeps asking where Kyra went, and eventually, I say, "She remembered something important that she had to do. She promised she'd be back, remember? You're gonna have to go find your friends and stay with them for a little while, until she gets back."

Sniffling, Alyson asks, "When will she be back?"

"Soon."

"What about you?"

Tears jump to my eyes, surprising me. "I'll be back soon, too," I promise. "The doctors will make me all better. You won't even have time to miss me."

But I'll miss her. I already do. She already feels like a little sister, and I know the recent loss of Emi is only contributing to how depressed I feel telling her she has to leave. I might not make it back at all. Even if I live, will we have to run for it again? Will we have a chance to come back and get Alyson? This might be goodbye forever.

Darkness crouches at the edge of my vision and I fight to stay present. I hug her tightly. "Go find your friends, now. I'll see you soon."

Reluctantly, her feet dragging and her head drooping, she leaves the tent.

The doctor start to explain how I'm getting to Sector 7, but my eyes roll back and I hear him no more.

When I come to, I'm lying on a makeshift cot in a vehicle of some sort. I'm staring at the sky, my body shaking from the vibrations of the vehicle. We're still outside the city. The engine rumbles and spits.

Slowly, I sit up.

"Easy," a soldier says, without sounding like he cares much.

I'm in the back of a small truck. The soldier sits near the edge, as if to block my escape. As if I was in the physical condition to jump off a moving truck.

We're still outside the city, but we're driving right alongside the wall. It's huge, grey, and seamless. Intimidating, in a word. How did they build something like this? It's too tall to ever consider trying to climb over and it completely blocks the outside world. Driving right beside it makes me feel small. No, insignificant.

"Didn't expect you to wake up already," the soldier says.

"I thought we were going to Sector 7?" I ask.

"We are. Just taking a short cut."

Whatever that means. I don't know why I expected him to be chatty.

I realize that, for some reason, I feel a bit better. Still terrible, but better than I was before I fainted. Maybe fainting resets my brain a little bit? I have no clue how the science works. Or how it's even possible. It shouldn't be.

"Almost there," the soldier says.

In a minute, the truck rumbles to a stop. I wonder why we've stopped. I can't see anything different about this area compared to everything else. Then, I hear a noise that I can't identify. I just know it wasn't there before. A section of the wall slides backwards and the breath leaves my lungs. A massive square, more than big enough for the truck to drive through, is sliding away. It went back, first, but now it goes right, disappearing behind the rest of the wall.

Now I understand. It's smart, especially for the soldiers who get seriously injured. They'd want to make sure they had access to quick help. And the streets of the lower sectors aren't really big enough for this truck to drive through, at least not without hitting people or the carts of vendors.

The truck drives through the opening. We're in a big, empty room, lit only by the sun coming in through the hole in the wall. The floor looks like concrete. It smells like oil, but there's absolutely nothing here other than ourselves and the truck.

In the front left corner a set of small stairs leads up to a door. The door opens and artificial light enters, making no dent against the sun's rays. A doctor steps out.

Then it hits me.

I'm in Sector 7 already!

Kyra was right to leave when she did. Any second now, someone is going to recognize me. My stomach lurches. No, I'm not ready for that yet. I thought we still had more time. Kyra's probably not even back in Sector 5 yet.

This is impossible.

The doctor is speaking to me, but his words are mumbled noise, far in the distance. They don't matter. Or do they?

I'm going to die. In the next 24 hours. Kyra can't pull this off. It's just not possible. She'll die trying.

I think back to how her eyes flashed when I said she had a choice. It warms my heart for reasons I don't fully understand. But it was stupid. Better only one of us had died than both.

The soldier prods my shoulder.

I whisper words, but I don't know what they are.

The edge of the truck's railing comes up to meet my forehead and pain blooms in my forehead. But I only feel it for a second before I feel nothing at all.

I must wake up fairly quickly again, because I'm still on the back of the truck. The driver is standing on the ground. The doctor and the soldier are gone. When I groan and sit up, the driver turns to me.

"And he's awake again. You didn't tell us you're wanted by the government."

My heart sinks, the nausea rises, and I have to fight not to pass out again. Or throw up. How'd they know? How'd they recognize me so fast?

"Don't worry, they're still figuring out what to do with you. Soldier-boy has gone off to contact the higher-ups directly and get instructions."

"They'll be to kill me," I whisper, my mouth dry.

The driver eyes me. "They won't have to do much. You seem on your way out already."

I am. But I have to give Kyra a chance to make it and destroy my computer. Could she have even reached the government sector yet?

Can I take the risk that they'll just put me in a room somewhere instead of executing me? Why would they take that risk?

What about the risk of being shot if I run away?

I don't know which gamble to take. My brain is scrambled and incapable of analyzing the situation. But the more I try to think, the more my paralyzed-fear turns into adrenaline.

I have to get away. Have to trust that Kyra will make it if I give her enough time. She promised. I trust her.

And I want to see her again. As myself. Whoever that is.

More adrenaline shoots through me. I have a brief thought of 'this can't be good for my heart.' But then my legs are moving. I'm scrambling to the edge of the truck and jumping down.

"Hey!" the driver shouts.

I don't look back. Everything goes blurry, but not like I'm going to pass out. My heart is beating faster than it ever has before and my legs are whirling. They left the wall open and I shoot through the opening. I turn right and race back towards the farmland, which I can see in the distance.

Shouts sound behind me, but it sounds like only one person.

My breath is ragged, but I don't feel the pain. My only thought is to get away. Hide. Wait.

I can make it.

The farmland grows larger. The fence surrounding it is tall and solid. No way to wiggle through it. No chance of climbing over.

I risk a glance behind me. No one's there.

They're probably waiting for me inside.

I find the gate that the truck must have driven out of. It's got gaps big enough for me to squeeze through.

No soldiers are waiting. Of course not. It's the end of the day. They've left. I hope. Otherwise, I'm just as dead here as I was in the hospital.

My eyes dart around. The adrenaline rush is draining from my body and a too-familiar sensation is creeping up.

I rush over to another truck. I drop to the ground and crawl underneath. It's the fourth time today, and I *hate* that. I feel so weak, but nothing I can do can stop me from fainting again.

CHAPTER THIRTY-TWO

Kyra

I run. They can't possibly get Jun to Sector 7 fast. The streets in the sectors were not built for vehicles, if they're using a vehicle. But soon my edge, if it is any edge, will be lost.

This is not going to be easy. But there's no choice. Not for me.

I run especially fast through Sector 3. It's sure to draw attention, but a female travelling alone will also draw attention and I'd rather be moving fast. I make it out of Sector 3 with no incidents and into Sector 5.

This part of the plan is the easiest. Find a soldier, reveal who I am, get captured.

I'm not worried that they'll kill me immediately. They'll want to punish me in front of my fellow workers. Make me an example. I have vague memories of seeing something similar in my first year of working. Unpleasant. If I fail, I have doomed myself to a painful fate.

I try to recall where a station is. Or the 'jail' they put Jun and I in.

My legs are starting to tremble and my chest hurts with every breath. I can't run for much longer. At this point, I'm only jogging. But if I slow down, I'll stop.

I come to a street I recognize. A left turn, and I allow myself to slow down to walking. I'm almost there.

A soldier's station looms up on my right. It's a small building, but it's well-built and maintained. If I walk inside, soldiers will be there. This would be my final chance to turn around. If I had any inclination to do so.

I walk inside. This room is much smaller than I thought it would be. One soldier is sitting behind a desk that faces the doorway. There's a door in the wall to his right. Probably leading to sleeping quarters for the soldiers. To his left there's a small jail cell.

"How can I help you?" the soldier asks. He's reading a book and doesn't bother to break that concentration.

"I wish to turn myself in," I respond.

He doesn't roll his eyes but he gets close to it. "And why is that? Have you stolen a vendor's fruits?"

"No. I escaped from the government sector where I worked as a Individual Overseer."

His eyes slowly raise to inspect me. He regards me for a while. "Is that so?"

I nod.

"But then why would you want to turn yourself in?"

We don't have to have this conversation!

"What does it matter?" I exclaim, walking to the desk. "I'm an wanted criminal or whatever, lock me up!"

My intensity surprises him. "Okay, yeah." He scrambles to his feet. "Uh, right this way."

I follow him to the jail cell which he unlocks with a key on his belt. He gestures to the cell and I enter.

As he's locking the door, I say, "Listen, I know this is also unusual, but can you please let your bosses know as soon as possible. I need to get back to the government sector immediately."

His brows furrowed. "You know they're going to kill you, right?"

"I'm aware."

He stares at me.

"Well, go!" I shout.

He jumps and runs out of the building.

This jail cell is quite tiny. It has no bench or seat of any kind. The ground is clean enough, though. Wood and well-swept. So I sit on the ground.

The time passes by torturously slow. Nothing I can do is distracting me from the seriousness of what I'm about to do. The improbability of survival.

What's happening to Jun right now? Has reached the hospital yet? Have they recognized him?

What if I manage to reach his computer, only to find that he's already gone.

I don't like that thought. I'm sudden anxious to be heading towards the government sector. I have to stand and pace, which is difficult to do in such a small space.

Finally, the soldier returns. I hear the vehicle before he makes it in the building.

Many soldiers steam through the doorway. As if I need that many armed guards.

The soldier opens the cell door. He doesn't bother to shackle me, but once again just gestures. I walk forward. The other soldiers don't share his good nature. They grab my arms and shackle my hands together. With one soldier on each side, I'm marched outside and into a big truck with a covered back. I'm shoved into the back and sat down on a bench. About ten soldiers climb in with me and sit on the bench beside me and on the other side of the truck.

Overkill. What could I do against them, especially armed with guns as they are?

I hope we're headed directly to Sector 7 instead of a stop at Sector 6 like last time.

Could I escape on the subway?

That can't be helpful. No doubt more soldiers are waiting for me at the subway station. But what then? How can I escape from there?

Bah. I'll have to take the opportunity when it arrises. And hope it arises.

The ride is tense. No one speaks. Not that I would expect any of us to speak. Still, it's rather awkward.

But then the truck rumbles to stop.

I sit forward. All the soldiers respond to my movement, either by leaning forward themselves or resting a hand on their gun. Their vigilance is frustrating. How am I supposed to escape when they're so prepared for it?

I am escorted off the truck. To my good fortune, we are in Sector 7. They hustle me down the stairs to the subway and onto one of its cars. All ten of the soldiers join me. I'm not shackled to anything, which is what I would have done. But my hands are still chained together.

I don't see a way I can escape on the subway. Just as well. I don't have my ID on me anymore, so I can't access the building. Oh, that's a problem. I need an ID to operate the elevators. I'll have to find one. Or do… something.

Perhaps some anxiety would be understandable in this situation. But currently, I don't feel anything. This is it. Either I'll figure it out along the way, or I won't.

The subway ride is as silent and awkward as the truck ride was, but considerably longer and with more stops.

The soldiers know exactly when our stop is, which is impressive. They all stand before the train comes to a full stop. I take my cue and stand as well.

The two soldiers on either side of me grab my arms. Four soldiers go ahead of us and exit the subway train. Four walk behind us. They are taking no chances. I'm lead up the stairs.

I can hear murmurings of people. What? I blink rapidly to adjust to the sunlight as we reach the top of the stairs. A crowd is waiting. When I make it fully out, they erupt. They scream at me, shouting, and jeering. Soldiers form a line holding them back, and they all respect it.

My insides shrivel. I didn't think about people's reactions to me. Didn't think people would be waiting. They think I'm a criminal. And technically, I am. But I think my biggest crimes were committed while I was their coworker. How can they stand there accusing me while they work to keep the whole population essentially enslaved? Even if it benefits the individual, it's not okay.

'Now's no time to get philosophical,' I tell myself sternly. 'Now's the time to worry about where they're taking you.'

If they're taking me directly to the torture and execution, that might disrupt my plans.

I wonder how many people I know that are in the crowds. How many distant coworkers. People I've trained. Men that Matthew have tried to set me up with that must be congratulating themselves that it didn't work out.

Then, I catch someone's eyes.

Matthew.

He stands within the crowd, but apart. His mannerisms are unlike everyone else's. He's not shouting. His eyes are big and downcast. It suddenly dawns on me that I have never appreciated how selfless and constant his friendship has been.

I quickly look away. It pains me to see the look on his face. I wish he didn't have to see me like this. He gave me the warning that allowed me to get away, but now he just has to watch me come back.

The crowd follows as I'm lead through the streets. Thankfully, I soon realize where we're going. The jail. I am going to spend my night there. Good. Hopefully I can figure out some way to escape from there. Somehow.

This might not be possible.

Failure wouldn't matter if I was the only person it affected. But I think of Jun and something within me is determined. I have to succeed. The physical pain of torture would be nothing compared to the guilt of failing him.

We reach the jail. It's a small building, pristine and well-built, like everything else in the government sector. It's classy. Except for the jail cell on the outside, you wouldn't realize it was a jail.

The jailer is waiting for us. He unlocks the outside jail cell. His cocky grin is annoying.

One soldier removes my chains before shoving me into the cell. They lock the door.

This cell is made entirely of metal bars, exposing me on all sides. If people wanted to, they could throw things at me, as long as they fit between the bars. If it rains, I will be soaked. There's no additional flooring, so it's the concrete of the road. Nothing is in here except me. No bench, no bucket. Nothing.

The crowd gathers around. They're still shouting and talking, but their voices all blur together and I hardly hear anything they're saying.

That should make it better, but the sounds grate on my soul. This is the first torture. Physical, yes. Concrete is uncomfortable to sit on for long periods of time. But it's emotional. Psychological.

People are on every side. I go to the back wall that is the jail building. I sit in the middle and bury my face in my knees.

How long will people be here? How much longer can they derive entertainment from mocking me?

Some people leave, but that makes it worse. With less people talking, I can pick out individual voices and what they're saying. How people are gossiping to each other about me. And people who've never interacted with me before are telling their companion that they never liked me. That they found me distasteful to be around and it's no surprise I went crazy.

I try to think of something, anything, to distract myself. I can't focus on trying to make a plan. Do I have any chance of succeeding?

An image of Jun and Alyson, skipping, forms in my mind. I smile to myself. Alyson with all her questions and unwavering loyalty to Jun. And Jun...

Nope, I don't want to think about that, either.

What use is it to realize what I might feel towards him when I'll probably never see him again.

What if he doesn't want to see me again? I thought he was warming up to me. But what if he only wants to be rid of the anxiety and he knows I'm how it would happen? Maybe, who Jun really is... without all the mind-control... maybe that person won't want to be friends with me.

"Kyra," a voice says quietly.

My head snaps up.

It's almost dark, now. The sun hasn't fully set, but it's sunk down below the buildings. Everyone is gone. Except for the person who said my name.

It's Matthew. His eyebrows are drawn together and he sits close to the bars.

"Hey. How're you doing?" His eyes are filled with deep concern.

I scoot over to him. "I'm so glad to see you!" I say.

He reaches his hand through the bars to grasp mine. "I'm glad to get to see you again, too. It sucks its in this situation. How'd they catch you?"

"They didn't. I turned myself in."

He gapes at me. "WHY?"

I hesitate. How do I explain? My eyes search my cell, but I don't see any cameras.

Leaning in closer to Matthew, I lower my voice and say, "I'm here to break Jun's connection."

His face goes through many emotions rapidly. "I don't… what? You know— You—" He takes a deep breath, and settles on saying, "Well, you're doing a fine job of that!" He huffs.

I can't help but laugh.

"How can you laugh?" he demands. "You're in prison! And you know what they're going to do tomorrow."

That sobers me. "I know. But listen, they're increasing Jun's levels. Of everything anxiety-related. He's going to die soon."

"Breaking the connection might kill him," Matthew points out.

"I don't need your negativity right now," I snap.

He raises his hands. "Sorry, sorry. That's not helpful."

I sigh and try to remind myself of the feeling that I have taken Matthew for granted. "I am… incredibly grateful that you're here right now," I say. "And I'm sorry for being a jerk sometimes."

Out of all the things I've said, this is what has surprised him the most. He looks like he might even faint from the shock.

"You… you're— you're sorry? You, I'm sorry, *Kyra apologizing*?"

I nod.

He stares at me. "Dang, what did the outer sectors do to you?"

I roll my eyes.

"Oh, thank goodness." He puts a hand over his heart. "She's back. So, how exactly do you plan on breaking Jun's connection?"

I know what I want to say. How there's a way out of this cell and a way for me to get into our building. But I can't put Matthew at risk. But I don't think I can do it without him.

"I'm working on it," I say finally.

"Your ID won't work to let you in, will it?" he asks.

I shake my head. I try not to let my eyes betray me, asking the question I can't force myself to verbalize.

"This area has no cameras, you know," he says.

"None? At all?" I'm not sure why he brings that up.

"None. So that people passing by can do whatever they want to the person in the cage, say whatever they want, and the prisoner can't accuse anyone of anything. No proof."

"Okay, that's helpful, but only if I find a way out of this cell. You don't have a spoon on you, do you? So I can start digging?"

He laughs. "Even better." He winks and stands up. Then he opens the door to the prison-building and enters.

The door shuts as I hiss, "Matthew, no!"

I'm sure his information about the cameras was accurate. It makes sense. But I don't want him involved. Whatever he does, the soldiers inside will know about, and any passerby could identify him. Any help he gives to me, means he has to go on the run too. I couldn't ask him to do that.

Grunts come from inside the building. Oh no, what was his plan? I rush to the wall and press my ear to it, trying to hear. All I can hear is the muffled sound of physical violence. I can't tell who's winning.

Then, silence.

The door opens and Matthew walks out.

"What happened?" I exclaim, standing up.

He's clearly beat up. His lip is split and his forehead is bleeding.

"I got the key," he says, holding it up.

"Matthew..."

"If you thank me, then you won't be at all the person I knew," he says.

I go to the door as he puts the key in the lock.

"Thank you," I say.

The door swings open.

"Does this mean I can hug you?" he asks with a grin.

"In your condition, do you think that's wise?" I ask.

He launches himself at me, even though the action causes him to wince. I hug back, aware this might be the last time we get to see each other. As he pulls away, I something slips into my pocket.

"To get in," he says.

It's his ID.

"You're going to have to run. You know that, right?"

He nods, eyes big, but determined. "I'll go get Jasmine first. Then we'll take the subway out of here."

I want to protest. Getting Jasmine will take time. But if there's no cameras here, he should have the time.

"Hurry," I say. "Take the subway to Sector 7. It's the fastest way to get to the outer sectors. You'll be close and able to enter 6, 5, and 4. If I succeed, Jun will be somewhere in Sector…" I don't know, actually. He was supposed to get taken to Sector 7, to the hospital. I had forgotten about that. I hope they don't kill him.

"Kyra?" Matthew asks.

I jump back to reality. "Sorry. Listen, get yourself to Sector 4. Rip your clothes and rub dirt on yourselves and stuff. Blend in. Don't spend a lot of money. If I live, I'll come find you."

"You'll live," he says. "They have no reason to suspect you'll go into the computer building. Especially using my ID."

"They'll figure it out soon enough," I say.

He hugs me again.

"You have to go." Gently, I shove him away. "Run."

He nods. "Good luck." Then he turns and runs.

I want to give him time, but I also have to get out of here before any of the soldiers wake up. So I run as well.

CHAPTER THIRTY-THREE

Jun

When I come to, I sit up quickly and smack my head into the underbelly of the truck. Groaning, I lay back down. That can't be good for my head.

Then again, no part of this is good for any of me, so what's a little head trauma on top of it all?

I don't know how long I've been unconscious for this time. Last time it was only a minute or so. But when I peer out, the sun looks further down in the sky than it was when I fainted. But it's the summer. The sun takes a long time to go down.

I peer out from underneath the truck. All empty of people. Only barns, machinery, the near mooing of cows and the faint baaing of sheep.

If there's sheep… there must be shepherds. They can't have left all of this completely abandoned. This machinery is expensive. So much livestock. It must have guards during the night, especially if the wall between here and Sector 2 is always open. It could operate like the wall into Sector 7.

Which would make me stuck out here.

That's actually a great place to be, really. As long as I avoid the guards, this is a great place to hide out and wait for Kyra.

It doesn't sit well with me to sit and wait for Kyra to fix this mess. But there's nothing I can do. My insides are humming with anxiety. My hands are shaking again, though it's not so bad yet. I just have to try and ignore it and find a better place to hide.

How does one ignore all of what one's feeling? Especially when it's influencing everything else?

I check my surroundings again. No one is in sight. So I roll out from underneath the truck. Before getting to my feet, I scan for soldiers again. Still clear.

It's weird to stand and casually walk around, but it'd be much weirder to crawl or something. I rush along to the closest barn, which contains, from the sounds, the cows. Should I hide inside the barn?

I shuffle along the side of the building over to a random pile of hay. Leaning into it, I sit down.

Should I see if I can make it back to Sector 2? If anyone sees me out here, it'll be obvious I'm not supposed to be here. I'll be done for. Sector 2 has so many people to hide amongst.

But will they keep quiet when they see me enter? It'll be suspicious to them, too, that I was out in the farmland. And if there are soldiers guarding the entrance? I'll be seen! Then I'll be on the run. From trained soldiers in an area they know well and I know almost nothing about. I wouldn't even find my way to the medic tent. I was unconscious both when I entered and when I exited it.

A clump of hay cascades down on my head. I splutter, shaking my head and watching the hay fall off. I didn't realize I have been hitting the pile.

Then I realize how fast I'm breathing. That's unnecessary. I try to take slower, deeper breaths. In through the nose, out through the mouth.

Nope. Focusing on it only makes it worse. That's not helpful. I'll just ignore my breathing and hope it corrects itself.

How do you ignore your breathing?

I'm just going to have to hide and hope for the best.

My brain is imagining anything but the best right now.

What if Kyra can't get to the computer in time?

No, I trust her. She promised.

She promised.

I have to hide.

I've been hitting the hay again. More falls down and showers me.

Can't hide in this barn. The cows would make too much noise.

Next barn, then.

I peek out from the pile of hay. No one.

What if someone's been sneaking up behind me? I whip my head around. No one there.

I turn back around and jump. I forgot about the hay. Thought it was a person when the corner of my eye saw it.

This is bad.

I creep around the hay and to the corner of the barn.

Slowly, cautiously, I peek around the corner.

More of no one. That's good. Maybe.

I don't know.

There's a barn in front of me. After triple checking that the coast is clear, I run across the empty space.

The big doors are closed.

Is there a small door?

I hear low neighs from inside. Horses. Is this one okay to enter?

Yeah. If my presence was gonna upset the horses, it would have done so by now.

Small door!

Carefully, slowly, I open the small door. Just a crack. I peer through. I can't see anybody.

Are those footsteps? Behind me?

Every muscle in my body jolts. I rush into the barn and shut the door.

Horses rustle.

The sound of my blood and heart beating roar in my ears. I'm trembling.

Have to hide!

The loft! For hay!

This place has so much hay!

I run to the ladder.

Have to hide before they come in and see me. This is it— I could die!

Scaling the ladder takes forever.

I make it to the top and dive into the hay.

I stay motionless for a long time. My ears are straining for the sound of a door opening. I don't dare look.

No one comes.

Eventually, the pounding of my heart reduces. My muscles relax.

I must have imagined the footsteps. Or I made it inside before they noticed me.

I roll over and stare at the ceiling. I've never been this terrified. The terror makes me even more afraid, somehow.

I don't want to think about it.

It consumes me, how can I not?

Hay is not comfortable to lie on.

The doors to the barn slide open.

I freeze, every muscle tensing.

"How many more barns do we have to search?" a voice complains.

"We must search them all," someone answers. "He's hiding here somewhere."

They can't be talking about me, can they?

"He *might* be hiding here somewhere," the first voice says. This one sounds younger. Like a teen boy.

"We have the report from the hospital. He ran towards the farmland. Where else would he go?"

"He could have ran away completely. Why wouldn't he?"

The voices move as they speak. They're searching the barn. For me.

I try to keep as still as possible to avoid rustling any hay. Maybe they won't check the loft. They must be able to hear my heart pounding in my chest.

"He was very sick, he wouldn't have made it far. They're searching too, just in case. Pick up your feet and check these stalls!"

"There are so many places for him to hide," the young one complains.

"With all of us searching, he can't hide for long."

'Kyra, hurry!' I think.

I'm in no condition to play cat-and-mouse with a bunch of highly-trained, physically-fit soldiers. All I feel able to do right now is vomiting and taking a nap.

How long has it been? How long will it take Kyra to break the connection? Assuming she makes it at all…

My stomach does a somersault and twists uncomfortably.

"Check the loft," the older voice orders.

I don't actually fall through the loft and down to the floor, but that's the sensation my body gets at his words.

Slowly, slowly, I creep backwards. What's the point? He'll see me.

My eyes dart around frantically.

There's a window in the wall, about six feet to my left. It's not truly a window, it's more of an empty square in the wall.

Some rational part of my brain tries to explain that jumping out of a window this high could have serious repercussions. But I'm in no condition to fight off two soldiers. Especially if they're armed.

I hear the clomp of the soldier's boots on the ladder. I have no choice!

I scramble to the window, forgoing subtly for speed.

"Hear that!" the boy shouts, sounding excited for the first time. "Someone's up there!"

"Hurry up!" barks the other.

The window overlooks a big pile of hay and a massive fenced area.

"Don't miss," I mutter.

Then I jump.

My body cuts through the hay alarmingly fast. It does something to cushion my fall, but I still thunk unpleasantly against the ground. Groaning, I stumble to my feet.

"He jumped, he jumped!" the young soldier shouts.

I run to the fence and clumsily climb over it. Then I run.

Behind me, I hear shouts. But I don't look back.

Running feels good. Better than sitting still. I should be concerned. This is too much adrenaline for one body to handle. But as I run, I cease to worry. I feel like I could run forever.

But I know it's not true. I need to find another place to hide. A better one. I can't outrun all the soldiers. They know I'm here. I need to hide until Kyra breaks the connection. Then I can escape.

As I race around a silo, I see two more soldiers running towards me. I backpedal, almost tripping over myself. I head the other way.

Where to hide?

I scan my surroundings.

Another barn, I guess. Burrow myself in some hay and hope for the best.

Hay is not comfortable.

Without warning, my legs give way. I stumble and fall to the ground. My head swims and I struggle to breath. The barns are moving, closing in around me, trapping me. The corners of my vision go black.

Somehow, I have this feeling. If I go down now, I'm not getting back up again.

'Kyra, please,' I think. 'You promised.'

Then I hear shouts that are quite different from the soldiers. A girl's voice. Yelling out my name.

"Jun! Jun, help!"

Alyson!

CHAPTER THIRTY-FOUR

Kyra

I know where I am, and how to get to my building. Once I round the corner and get away from the prison, I slow down and walk. Sticking to the shadows, I carefully make my way. No one else is around. Why would they be?

It only takes a few minutes to reach the building. This is it. If the alarm hasn't been raised by now, it will soon. I race down the stairs, which lead to the subway station. The only entrance into this building (except the janitor's entrance) is through here.

I reach the doors. I dig Matthew's ID out of my pocket and hold it to the scanner. It dings and lets me in.

Instead of taking the elevator, I hurry up the stairs. Few people use this building at night (except the janitors), and the fewer times I scan the ID, the better. Somewhere in this building there's a security station, and security guards can see on a computer who scans when. Of course, it'll pop up as Matthew. But let's not raise any extra suspicion.

Of course, if there are any security guards in that station, watching the cameras, then they'll be able to see me. Even if they don't recognize me, they'll be able to see that I clearly got into the building with someone else's ID. That alone will raise—

What if they invalidate my ID? A worker ID is necessary to get onto the computer floors!

Heart pumping, I race onto the second floor and run to the elevator. I hit the button several times. Waiting is a nightmare.

The elevator arrives. I jump in, scan my ID, and press the button for floor 12. It allows me.

I allow myself some deep breaths. They must not have noticed.

Maybe there's only a few guards, and they're all doing rounds right now? That means I might bump into one. I'll try to avoid that.

The elevator opens and I step out into the little foyer-area. One door. That's all that lies between me and Jun's computer. Between his freedom. Well, that and a massive maze made of walls of floor-to-ceiling computers.

I hold Matthew's ID to the scanner. My heart is pounding.

'Please don't have blocked me yet!' I think.

The scanner beeps and the door slides open.

So far this is a lot easier than I thought it'd be.

I step through the door. Something hard jabs into my side. I jump. My adrenaline spikes. Pain blossoms in my ribs.

It's a security guard!

He jabs at me again with his baton. It thunks against my thigh. Another bruise.

I try to grab at the baton, but he pulls it away. I jump back, trying to scan my surroundings for more guards while keeping an eye on this one. He has a gun, but he hasn't pulled it out yet. The want me alive so they can kill me later.

A few steps away is the computer maze entrance. I doubt this guard has it memorized like I do. All I need to do is de-activate Jun's computer. Before more guards show up.

I whirl around and rush into the maze. He can't use his gun in here for risk of hitting a computer. So I run. He runs after me, shouting for me to stop.

But adrenaline is on my side. I make a few good choices. Not to get to Jun's computer, but to turn enough corners so he loses me. It takes a little longer than I would like, but soon, I've lost him.

I keep running. He might be able to hear my footsteps over the whirling of the fans, but getting to Jun's computer first is the priority. I adjust my path to the one that gets me there the fastest.

I turn a corner and physically run into a different guard. We both go tumbling to the ground. I scramble to my feet, kick him in the head, and keep running.

He gets up, but not too fast. He runs after me, but I only have to deviate slightly from my path and I've lost him, too. I take two rights. I'm back on track and safely away from that guard.

I ignore the way my lungs are beginning to burn.

Then I reach the hallway Jun's computer is in. Two guards are waiting. I freeze. I'm not overly skilled in hand-to-hand combat and they're trained in it. Because that's their job.

They've noticed me. They shout and start running at me.

So I bolt. Backwards.

I take a few turns, then double-back. Both guards are behind me. Not a smart move, leaving the computer unguarded, but it's helpful. Or it would be if I could shake them.

I'm getting to close to Jun's computer. I glance back, and decide to risk calling the computer down.

I reach the electronic pad. I scan my fourth finger and say quickly, "Jun Hirano, individual L864k."

The familiar sound of the machinery whirring to life has never made me so happy.

I jump out of the way of the guard barreling towards me. He stumbles. The other guard is also bearing down on me, so I run down the hall. It takes time for the computer to reach eye-level, anyway. Hopefully I can lose them by then.

I try to take turns that have tight corners and short hallways. Easier to lose people on. Breathing hurts now and my leg muscles are shaking. But I have to push forward. I'm so close!

Another guard appears at the end of the hallway I've entered. I yelp, and turn right instead, pouring on the speed. My brain is trying to go over the command for terminating the connection.

I risk returning to Jun's computer. I don't see them behind me anymore, but if they can hear me, they could still be on my tail. The pounding of my feet is nothing compared to the pounding of my heart.

Jun's hallway is empty. His computer is down.

I'm so close, I'm so close!

I'm well aware that if I fail now, I will fail completely.

No one is behind me yet.

I reach Jun's computer. My fingers have never flown so fast. I have to pause for a brief but dreadful moment to remember part of the command. Then I resume typing.

Out of the corner of my eye, I see a security guard enter this hallway.

"Stop!" he shouts.

I barely breath as I finish typing in the command.

'Please don't die,' I think. Then I hit enter.

No sooner do I do, then I get tackled. My head thunks against the floor and I groan.

The other security guards rush up.

"Did you stop her?" one asks.

"What does it look like?" snaps the one pinning me to the ground.

"No, with the computer!" he shouts. "No, no, stop! What's it doing?"

I grin to myself. I did it. Jun is safe.

The one holding me gives me a shake. "Make it stop!" he orders. "Reverse the command."

"It's too late," I say.

From the computer, there emits a long beep. Everyone looks at it. Then the mechanical voice says, "Clearing process completed. The connection to individual L864k has been terminated."

I may be fully captured again, but I can finally breath easily. Jun is free now. That's all that matters.

Of course, his brain is going through a lot. It's enough to harm him. At least make him black out for a long time. Depending on what situation he's in, that could be terrible.

The guards haul me to my feet, cutting off my thoughts.

I have to escape. What if Jun still needs my help?

Also, I've probably caused worse torture for myself. I would like to avoid that, if possible.

We march down the hallways. Only three guards accompany me. Where did the fourth go? Did I lose him? Was there ever a fourth? I don't know and I don't care at this point. I have more pressing concerns.

They have to stop a few times and deliberate which way to go to get out. The one holding my arms behind my back has the maze memorized the best. He eventually snaps the answer after they mutter to themselves for a minute.

I'm marched out and into the elevator. We go down.

One of the guards looks at the one holding onto my arm and asks, "You sure you'll good? Don't need any help?"

He snorts. "Against her? You're kidding, right? I'll be fine."

Hurtful, but accurate.

"Where are you taking me?" I ask.

"Back to jail," he answers.

I could theoretically escape from there again. But they will probably post guards around me this time.

The elevator stops, and the other two get out at the 10th floor. Must be to resume their rounds.

The doors close.

My best chance is to escape from this guard before we reach the jail.

Except I don't believe in my hand-to-hand combat, even against one man.

His grip tightens on my arm, as if he senses I'm trying to plan my escape. I'm going to have a bruise there after this. But, if I don't manage to escape, that will be the least of my concerns.

"How did you get Matthew's ID?" the guard asks.

Something in his voice is dangerous. Beyond a guard asking me how I stole a coworker's ID.

I remain silent. What can I say? To tell the truth would be to incriminate him.

He shakes my arm. "Answer me!"

"I took it out of his pocket," I say. "I stole it."

He gets in front of me. "When?" His voice is venomous.

"When he was… at the jail."

"You just took it? He didn't notice? No one else noticed?"

The elevator doors open. He drags me out, then holds me still. His eyes are glaring at me.

"Well…" Why is he dissecting my lie? "He was the only one there."

"Why didn't he notice?"

"We… we were close."

"Physically or emotionally?"

I make a noise of frustration.

He drags me into a small room and shuts the door.

Where are we? I didn't recognize this floor and I don't know what this room is. It's small. One chair is all that's in it. At the back is a window. Probably two-way. But who would be behind there now?

"This is an interrogation room," he says. "It has no cameras."

My heart sinks.

But he doesn't move towards me.

"Answer my question," he says, the warning in his voice clear.

CHAPTER THIRTY-FIVE

Jun

My brain clears and my body jolts. My eyes focus again. All the anxiety is still there, but it has a direction now. Get to Alyson.

I push myself back on my feet. The soldiers are almost upon me. But I'm able to run again. Towards the sound of Alyson's voice.

She shrieks, sounding afraid.

I run faster, my feet pounding into the ground. I swerve around any farming obstacles, which includes tripping and shoving a soldier bearing down on me.

Then I see her. A soldier is dragging her away. Probably back to Sector 2. She's kicking her legs, but it's not doing much.

"Jun!" she exclaims.

The soldier turns, just in time for me to barrel right into him. He goes down, letting go of Alyson. She falls as well.

I grab her, lifting her and setting her back on her feet. "Run!"

I take off, but remember to slow down so she can keep up with me.

"I thought you were sick!" she shouts.

"I am," I answer.

Another soldier comes at us. I duck under his punch and deliver a blow to his gut. He doubles over and I hit his jaw with everything I've got. He goes down.

"C'mon," I say to Alyson, continuing to run.

"No, wait!"

I stop and turn to her. "Aly, listen, we're kinda in danger right now, so—"

"Are you trying to get back to Sector 2? Cause we need to follow the path." She points.

"You're right. Let's go!"

More soldiers are closing in on us, pouring out from all sides. Alyson runs close to me.

"Why are they chasing you?"

She sounds terrified. She's just a kid. What is she even doing here? She should have been in Sector 2.

"Listen, Alyson, run to Sector 2, okay? Don't stop."

"What about you?" she asks.

"I'll be okay. I'm going to lead them away from you and then I'll come back to Sector 2."

"You promise?" She sounds unsure.

I force the words out. "I promise."

My minds echoes with the words *I swear to you, I won't let you die from this. I will find a way to free you.*

Too late.

Alyson keeps straight, heading back to Sector 2. I veer to the left, which has the fewest soldiers.

This might be it.

Everything blurs as I collide with a soldier. I'm fighting, but I register that only vaguely. Parts of my body are being hit, but the pain is far off. I don't even know why I'm fighting anymore. I should lie down and let myself die.

Suddenly, something inside me snaps.

It feels like part of my brain is being torn away. This pain is like nothing I've ever felt before. It sears like a fire inside of me. Every muscle in my body stiffens and clenches. I scream. My vision goes black, then red.

CHAPTER THIRTY-SIX

Kyra

The guard is staring me down, waiting for an answer.

"We were friends," I say. "So he was visiting me and while we were chatting, I slipped his ID from his pocket."

He looks like he wants to punch me. "You stole from your friend?" He towers over me. "Do you have any idea the danger you could have put him in?"

There's more to this.

I stare at the guard. This is the first time I actually look at his eyes.

"Are you… close to Matthew?" I ask.

"None of your business," he snaps.

If he's a relative, a brother, even… Matthew won't have said goodbye. Does he deserve to know? There's no cameras in here. But I don't know what he'll do.

"What are you thinking?" he asks.

Does Matthew have a brother? I seem to recall… a Braxton. Oh yes. He and Matthew don't get along.

"Your name wouldn't happen to be Braxton, would it?" I ask.

His eyes flicker with surprise and steps back. "I guess you guys *were* friends," he mutters. "Close enough to know who I am, but not enough to keep him out of danger. How can you claim to be his friend, yet steal from him?"

"Hey, I would never put Matthew in danger!" I exclaim. "He's been the only person here who's truly been my friend!"

Braxton steps closer to me. "You stole his ID, explain to me how that's not putting him in danger!"

I bite back the words I'd love to say. I can't tell him Matthew gave me his ID card. If he doesn't talk to Matthew, he might have no qualms about telling his bosses. I need to give Matthew as much time as possible to get away. And what does he care? Matthew never got along with him and Matthew gets along with everybody, so the blame for that definitely lies with Braxton.

He seems to read the answer in my eyes. His shoulders sag. "Matthew gave you his ID. Didn't he? That selfless *idiot*."

"I never would have asked him," I say. "But you'll be happy to know I told him the fastest way out of the government sectors and the best place to lay low. He should already be in another sector."

Braxton's jaw works as he thinks.

He's distracted right now. How mean of a person would I be to take advantage of it? I have no reason to think he will help me just because his brother did. Matthew himself has told me that they don't get along. That's not a good sign.

I steel myself, then reach over and yank his gun out of its holster on his belt. I quickly back up and point it at him.

Eyebrows arching, he holds his hands up. "Would you shoot me?"

"I'm hoping your desire to not be shot is much more than your desire not to let me go," I say.

He steps closer. "What if it's not?"

"Listen, Matthew has been the best friend I have ever had," I say. "I've not been an easy person to be friends with, but he's always been there. But don't think that will keep me from hurting his brother to save my own life."

He stays still.

I jerk my head towards the corner. "Move away from the door."

He moves to the side, always facing me and the gun.

I move towards the door, doing likewise. My gun is always pointing at him. To open the door, I have to take one hand off the gun. I keep my eyes trained on Braxton, ready for any sudden movements.

I swing the door open, then slowly walk backwards through it. What if there are people in the hallway. I try to do a quick scan. No one. When I look back at the room, Braxton is barreling down on me.

Adrenaline courses through me, and my desire to live takes over my instincts. My finger squeezes the trigger. Braxton shouts in pain and falls to his knees.

I gasp and back up. He's holding his lower abdomen. That's good, he can survive that shot.

He glares up at me. "You won't make it out," he seethes.

Matthew must have taken all the nice genes in the family.

Without bothering to respond, I run off.

Going to the subway exit would not be smart. No doubt they will send soldiers there. Oh, but I should make it look like I'm heading that way.

I run the other way. I pass Braxton, who is still on his knees, clutching his stomach. Blood seeps out past his hands.

When I run past, he shouts at me. Then, with some effort, he gets to his feet.

I run faster, into the stairwell.

My legs ache from all the running I've done already. But I'm heading down, so moment propels me forward. No other door to the stairwell opens, so Braxton's not here yet. I get out of the stairs at the next floor.

The janitor's entrance is on Floor One, at the back. I'm on the third floor, so I still have to go down. But I'll find another set of stairs.

The gun feels awkward in my hands. I don't want to carry it anymore. But I need to have the back-up. The reality of breaking Jun's connection is sinking in. Even if it went well, he's going to be majorly disoriented. He'll need my help. I have to get back.

I find another stairwell and go down. My legs are trembling and I have to grip the railing to make sure I don't topple forward.

I make it to the first floor as a door somewhere above me opens. People shout and feet pound on the stairs. I rush out, onto the first floor.

Where am I?

Very few lights are on, and I've rarely been to the first floor. But I know where the janitors entrance is. I can find it. If I recall correctly, the janitor's headquarters, so to speak, are in Wing E. That would mean I go left.

I'm almost in Wing D. Through that is E.

Hopefully it doesn't require ID.

I pass a janitor mopping a hallway.

He stares at me suspiciously.

I grin sheepishly. "Sorry," I say as I carefully step on wet, shiny hallway he's trying to clean. I have to walk gingerly for a little bit, as the floor is quite wet.

Then, behind me, I hear people running.

I risk speeding up and make it to where the corner turns to the entrance to Wing E. People begin to appear at the end of the hallway.

The door is locked.

No!

I'm so close!

I knock on the door.

They're getting closer!

A middle-aged lady comes to the door and opens in. "Who're you?" she starts to ask.

I feel bad about it, but I shove past her and keep running. "Sorry!" I shout over my shoulder.

I toss the gun into a bucket of soap that's sitting there. One gun against the many people running after me won't do me any good. Plus, I'm worried I'll accidentally set it off. Stealth and speed are the important elements right now.

Unfortunately, this place is so packed with cleaning supplies that both of those are rather difficult. I have to maneuver over brooms precariously leaning against walls and around bottles and bottles of cleaning supplies littering the ground. Do they not have closets and proper storage spaces?

A loud crash sounds behind me. Someone has knocked over something. Good. Hopefully that slows them down.

The door!

What if someone's waiting for me?

I rush to it and shove it open.

No one!

I gulp in the fresh air. It was not pleasant in the janitor-area. Too many chemical smells.

But I can't stop now. I keep running. Well, I think how fast I can still go barely qualifies as running, but I push myself on nonetheless. If I can make it to the subway and get on before any soldiers find me, I should be safe.

The closest subway entrance is the one attached to this building, which is not an option. The next closest one doesn't have any turns to reach, so I would still be in sight when my pursuers exited the building. So instead, I turn the corner of the building. I run until I can turn right, pass through two buildings, turn left, and then right again.

People are shouting behind me. I can hear them faintly.

"Fan out! Find her!"

I want to sob. To have come so close, yet to still be so far!

All it will take is for one soldier, trained and not out-of-breath, to catch me, and I'll be done.

Maybe I should hide somewhere?

No, the longer I wait the more chance they have to lock things down! They could stop the subway from running altogether!

I go to round the corner of another building, but I see a guard. He's running away from me, though. I peer behind me. No one in sight. So I peek around the corner and wait until he's out of sight. Then I keep going.

"Hey, stop!" someone behind me shouts.

I curse under my breath. I shouldn't have waited!

"I found her!" my pursuer yells.

And I found a subway entrance!

I veer to my left and hurry down the stairs. My legs give out on the third-last step and I crash down to the hard cement. Scrambling to my feet, I ignore the way my knees are howling in pain.

The subway is here!

I have to take the risk. I rush into it.

Soldiers pour down the stairs.

"Go, go, go," I mutter. As if I have any power to force the subway to do my bidding.

The soldiers are close.

The doors start closing.

Two men manage to leap through before the doors slide shut!

"Woah."

I hurry to the door to the next car. I open it and slide through. The door slams in the face of one of the men.

I rush forward, heading to the next car.

Not many people are on the subway. The few that are openly gawk as I rush past them. Blood drips down my legs. How much more can I withstand?

I make it through to the next car and keep going. I'll have to get off at the next stop and lose them.

I make it onto the next car, but one of the soldiers is now right behind me. The other has disappeared, I don't know where he went.

This one grabs me. I struggle to get away, flailing my limbs. But they don't connect.

People stare, but they won't help. A soldier is doing his duty, apprehending a criminal.

The subway slows. It's the next stop.

"We're getting off here," the soldier orders, holding me tight.

I slump against him, done fighting. I'm exhausted. I want to cry. Some tears do come.

I can't have gone through all that just to fail now!

But what can I do?

The subway stops. His grip is looser, now. Perhaps he realizes I'm not much of a threat. I can use that to my advantage.

As we shuffle off the subway, I try to remember some basic self-defense moves. An idea occurs to me.

The other soldier gets out much further down. It's now or never!

I stomp my heel down on his foot— hard. He grunts and his hold loosens. I'm able to twist enough to jab my elbow into his neck. Then I shove him away from me, whirl around and dark back into the subway.

The doors slide shut.

The soldiers aren't on.

I make my way over to a seat and slump down in it. For the first time in hours, I breathe deeply. I'm safe. For now.

It quickly occurs to me that everyone in this car saw my struggle with the soldier and my subsequent escape. Probably not great.

All I want is to curl up and sleep— after I clean my knees— but I force myself to my feet and stagger to the door between this car and the next. I enter the next car, doing my best to pretend like I have not been on the run for my life for the past twenty minutes. My bloodied knees are probably not helping.

I walk down the length of this car and go into the other one for good measure. Only two people are in this one. I sit down on a chair right beside some doors.

As the subway comes to a stop, I scan the station platform. No soldiers waiting for me. I doubt any of the people who saw me escape from that soldier could notify anyone. I can't risk soldiers waiting for me at any stop. I'd never be able to escape. But what's the best stop to get off on?

This is Sector 10, now. If I get off, I'll stand out with my Sector 4 clothes that haven't been washed in days. Sector 10 has big night life, though. This subway is about to get packed. Already, more people have gotten on than have got off at this stop.

I can hardly think clearly anymore. I need to rest.

The doors close and we keep moving. The stops are going to be much closer together now.

Ah.

I know what to do.

The next stop approaches, and I can see the platform is full of people. The subway glides to a stop and I stand in front of the doors. They slide open. It becomes chaos.

People walk in as we're walking out. I'm jostled on each side. People barely notice me. The ones that do wrinkle their noses and mutter something distasteful to their companion.

I stick close to people's sides, making my way to the bathrooms. Yes, bathrooms in the subway station. Nothing is too good for those in Sector 10. They can't even go up the stairs into the streets to find a washroom.

A gaggle of girls are heading to the washrooms. I follow closely behind. We enter the hallway, and I allow myself to relax. No more security cameras.

I pick an empty bathroom and enter. It's an individual room, and I'm struck by the lavishness of it.

My body is exhausted, but I drag myself over to the paper towel and grab a handful. I pour water over them, then gently use them to get the blood off of my knees. Then I dry my knees with new paper towels. After I throw them in the trash, I can't hold off sleep any longer.

This is not the most sanitary place to take a nap, but the ironic thing is that it might be the most sanitary place I've slept in the past week. No one will notice that this bathroom is occupied for a long time. That's not unusual.

I curl up on the floor, far away from the toilet, and fall asleep.

CHAPTER THIRTY-SEVEN

Jun

I gasp for air, my chest heaving as I take in huge gulps of it. I'm on my knees. Blinking, my vision clears. My whole body is trembling.

The soldiers are standing in a circle around me. Their faces look uncertain. Several shift their weight uneasily.

As the trembling stops and my vision comes into focus, I realize something. My ribs are screaming. My legs ache and tremble, like I can't trust them with my weight. My head pounds with a fierce headache. Worse than that, inside my head, like it's in my very brain, something stabs with pain, like a limb's been cut off.

But I feel better than I've ever felt in my entire life.

The soldiers seem to realize that whatever happened has passed. A few descend on me.

I jump to my feet. My thoughts are so clear, my emotions calm, that fighting them now feels like I've been given superpowers. The blows they manage to land hurt, but they hardly matter.

I cut through them and run, leaving the rest in the dust. They chase after me, but I have energy to burn.

One soldier is standing at the entrance to Sector 2. Many people are crowding behind him, intently watching. A few cheer when they see me.

The soldier pulls out his gun.

If they all have guns, why haven't any of them used it?

I slow down.

Two men from Sector 2 grab the soldier, pulling and throwing his gun away.

I speed back up.

"Thanks!" I shout as I cross into Sector 2 and through the crowd.

"Jun!" Alyson cries.

I skid to a stop and crouch down in front of her.

"Listen, Aly, I have to run, okay? You can come with me if you want." I lower my voice. "Once Kyra gets back, we're gonna escape. But it might be dangerous."

She throws her arms around me. "I wanna go with!"

I grin. "Great!" I scoop her up in my arms and keep running.

Sector 2 is quickly left behind and I race through Sector 3. It occurs to me that since it's night, this is the worst time to be going through Sector 3. Especially since I have to carry Alyson.

But it's uneventful. I have to kick someone, and twice we're shot at. But I'm running so fast, most people don't have a chance to register we're there before we're gone. Alyson is frightened by the guns, but we're unharmed as we make it into Sector 5.

"Alyson, we need to find a place to sleep and hide." I'm panting now, drawing ragged breaths. Whatever high I was on is waning. Fast. I thought I was feeling all the pain before, but somehow, it's finding room to increase.

"Put me down," Alyson says. "I can lead."

I risk a glance behind me, but I haven't heard any sign of the soldiers for a while. I don't see anything now. So I stop and set her down. I stagger. She grabs my hand and leads me forward.

I don't know where we go. Everything hurts. My legs are trembling. I can barely keep my eyes open, and they certainly aren't registering whatever it is I'm seeing since my vision is unfocused and blurry. I don't think I've ever been this tired. I'm not fainting. I'm falling asleep.

"Alyson, can I sleep?" I mumble. I barely have the breath to speak.

"Close, close!" she promises.

I manage to keep going. We walk up a few stairs. I trip, but manage to get back up. We're on wood now.

"We're here," Alyson says, worry evident in her voice.

I land heavily on my knees.

Someone asks a question. Oh, someone's here.

"I don't know," Alyson answers. She prods my shoulder.

"I'm okay. I'm okay. I'm going to sleep now. Stay safe. Okay?" My words are mumbly and might not be coherent.

The someone else chuckles softly. "Safest place in Sector 5, right here, boy." I hope so, because there's nothing I can do to fight off this sleep. I tip forward, meeting the floor. Darkness takes over me, in a pleasant and welcoming way.

CHAPTER THIRTY-EIGHT

Kyra

I wake up refreshed, if sore and hungry. Gingerly, I stretch out my limbs, moving and wiggling them.

When was the last time I ate? Too long ago.

Do I still have money on me?

To my delight, I discover that I do. Not enough to buy meals in the upper sectors, but once I reach the middle or lower ones, I'll be able to eat.

Today is all about speed. Getting to Sector 4 as fast as I can and finding Matthew and Jasmine.

Oh, wait, but is Jun in Sector 7? The hospital? He could be under heavy guard right now. What if they realize he's better and they need to execute him now?

Anxiety shoots through me and I scramble to my feet. That can't happen! Not after I did all that to fix him, it can't end like that!

But there's no way for me to find out.

I rush out of the bathroom. It's early morning, few people will be on the subway.

I take the subway all the way to Sector 7. The last stop. The time goes by fast, and no one bothers me.

Finding the hospital is easy. Figuring out what I'm going to do about it is much harder. But if Jun's in there, trapped, then he needs my help as soon as possible.

But what if he's not?

Either way, I won't be able to get in looking like this.

I wander around for a bit and find a cheap clothing place that sells work clothes. Second-hand, too, I discover when I enter. I inspect the clothes, trying to find the best combination of cheap, my size, and passable enough that I could enter the hospital. I find a shirt that's a little big, but it's got no holes or tears. It's in pretty good condition. Then a pair of pants that has a few patches.

I purchase them. Then, with the money left over, I buy food. Compared to what I've been eating the past week in the lower sectors, this food is amazing.

Once I've eaten, I feel better, my mind clearer.

It could be a fatal decision to enter the hospital. Jun still being in there is a small possibility amongst many more possibilities that all place him outside the hospital. Somewhere.

If I go in there, I could be captured. For nothing, if he's not in there. And if he is, what am I to do?

I stand outside the hospital for a long time, deliberating. I did just spend my money on new clothes so I could get in, after all. But it was probably time for an outfit change. I don't want to think about the fact that I never had a chance to shower and wore the same thing all the time.

It breaks my heart to leave. But it's so much more likely that Jun is somewhere else. I can't risk it.

I turn and walk away.

Getting to Sector 4 is a slow process. I have to avoid soldiers at all cost— without looking like I'm avoiding soldiers. Walking normally, but with my eyes constantly roving. Ducking into alleyways or paths between houses to get out of sight of any soldiers I see. Adjusting my routes from 'fastest' to 'avoids most soldiers.'

At this pace, it'll be hours before I'm back in 4. And then I'll have to find Matthew and Jasmine. I didn't give any specifics on where to hide. I hope I'm able to locate them.

As I walk, I try to think like Matthew. Where would he go to hide?

But this distracts me so much, I almost bump into some soldiers. I backpedal, turning around and adjusting my courses. They didn't see me. But that was too close. That can't happen again.

I put thoughts of them out of my mind. I'll worry about that when I reach Sector 4.

And I don't begin to relax until I cross over into 4. Less soldiers here. Easier to blend in. More places to hide.

It occurs to me as I walk that Matthew isn't the brightest person. But, he would want to make it as easy as possible for me to find him.

I stop walking and sigh. He went to Jun's house. The place they'd expect us to go. Or, maybe they wouldn't, because why on earth would we go there. It's either stupid or the right kind of stupid that turns out to be smart.

I resume walking. The closer I get to Jun's place, the more cautious I am. But I don't see any extra soldiers.

When the house's remains are in sight, I pause. They haven't done anything to clean the area, but it is clear that some wood has been removed. Perhaps what could be was salvaged for firewood. I doubt anything was suitable for much more than that. The sight is depressing, but it captures and demands my attention.

That was his life. My actions caused this devastation.

Well, indirectly. Some other awful people ordered it and others carried it out. Still. However small, I bear a portion of the responsibility and guilt.

I hesitate, wondering if I risk getting any closer.

Then someone taps my shoulder.

I whirl around and try to back up at the same time. The result is me falling.

Matthew snorts. "Calm down, who did you think I was?"

"It's been a rough few days," I mutter.

Jasmine offers her hand and helps me up.

"Glad to see you both made it out," I say.

"And you!" Matthew exclaims. I can tell he's barely restraining himself from hugging me.

"He hasn't stopped worrying about you," Jasmine tells me. "He barely slept. And barely let me sleep, either." She rolls her eyes, but it's affectionate.

"I had every right to be worried! What she was attempting was crazy!"

"It was," I agree. I wonder if I should mention his brother?

"Now what?" Jasmine asks.

"We find Jun," I answer. "Then, we get out of this city."

CHAPTER THIRTY-NINE

Jun

I wake up slowly, lazily. Sleep clings to me and doesn't want to let go. I must have died and went to Heaven— I'm lying in a bed. With a blanket over me and a pillow underneath my head. I sigh and readjust, doing nothing to try and wake up.

Then a heavy force jumps on me. All the breath is knocked from my body and I groan. My shoulder sparks with pain, but the rest of me is so comfortable, I don't really care.

"You're awake!" a young voice shrieks.

"Aly," I say weakly.

My body wakes up, throwing off the protective cover of sleep. My injuries come rushing to my attention. My legs ache. My ribs are only further hurt by Alyson's jump onto me. My head is still sore.

Yet…

I sit up. Alyson laughs and claps.

"You slept for *so long*!" she exclaims.

"Little Alyson, let him wake up," an old voice croaks.

I whip my head over in the direction of the voice. She's so old! She sits in a solid, wooden rocking chair. A cane is beside her. Her face is weathered and wrinkled, but her eyes sparkle with intelligence.

I took her bed!

Immediately, I leap out and get to my feet. "Grandmother," I say with respect, "I must apologize. Did I take your bed? I don't recall going to sleep in one, but…"

She chuckles. "No, you didn't. You passed out on the floor. I got some of my grandchildren to move you into the bed."

"But where did you sleep?"

"So concerned. I haven't slept in that bed in months. It's rather too difficult to get out of for these old bones."

It's incredible that she's survived this long.

Alyson hugs my leg. "I was worried! Are you not sick now?"

I absentmindedly pat her heat. "Am I not—" My freeze, my eyes widening. "Am I not?"

"How do you feel?" the grandmother asks.

I search for the right answer. "At peace," I say finally. What else can describe it?

And what else could I tell her, who has no idea what has been done for me.

She hums. "Good. Good. Well, you may stay here while you wait for Kyra to get back."

"Huh?"

How does she know about Kyra?

She chuckles again. "Alyson told me all about it."

Oh, right. Of course.

Alyson beams at me. I crouch down so we're eye-level.

"Why were you in the farmland again, Aly?" I ask her.

"Cause they came to Sector 2 to look for you. And they kept saying you were somewhere. But you were sick. So I didn't want you to be alone."

Tears come quickly to my eyes. There's nothing she could have done to help. But, actually, she did.

A few tears run down my cheeks. She smudges them away with her hands.

"Did they make you better in the hospital?" she asks.

"They did," I manage to say. "I'm better now."

"Will Kyra be coming back?"

"I hope so."

She grins.

I wrap my arms around her. "Thank you," I whisper.

It hurts. Her love. Too much like a younger sister's. It heals and provokes the wound at the same time.

But they're gone. All I can do now is do my best to protect this new family I've acquired.

As I let Alyson go, I let my family go as well. They're safe.

Someone knocks on the door. Without waiting for an answer, they rush in. It's several kids.

"We're gonna play Princess and Dragons!" the one in front shouts.

Alyson grins at me. "Can I go play with them?"

I'm surprised she's asking. She's been on her own for a lot longer than I've been in her life.

"Yeah, course you can," I say.

She grins and races off with them.

I sit. The floor is hard and grimy, but I don't care. I lean back against the bed.

"So…" the grandmother regards me. "You're free. And you must be hungry." Her arm shaking, she reaches it out to grab her cane from off the wall.

"What… what are you talking about?" I ask.

"Food, boy. When was the last time you ate?"

"No, I meant about being free."

She leans forward, one hand on the cane, one on the arm of her chair. Her whole body strains and trembles.

"Oh, wait, I can do it!" I get up. "You stay seated, just tell me where the food is."

"If you insist." She relaxes back into her chair and sighs deeply.

I stand still, unsure what to do. She hasn't given me any directions and I don't want to go rooting around in her cupboards.

After a minute of deep breathing on her part, she directs me to some granola bars. They're in a bowl, wrapped in a cloth. I grab two.

They're not bad. And my stomach is grateful for the nourishment.

I sit back down on the floor.

"So," she says. "What did I mean by being free. You know what I mean. But you're wondering how I know?"

I nod and continue munching.

"I've figured it out," she says slowly. "I've lived a long time. Seen a lot. I explained better this much better to your friend. Kyra. But I forget now."

"Kyra? How do you know her?"

"Alyson brought her to meet me a few days ago."

Ah.

"How do you feel now?" she asks.

"Worried," I answer.

She raises an eyebrow.

"It's all my own," I clarify. "But I hope Kyra's alright. She broke the connection, but that doesn't mean she's alright now."

"True."

"Aren't you supposed to encourage me?"

She laughs. "What for?"

I can't help but laugh too. What an odd answer.

"You focus on resting, boy. She'll find you soon enough."

I don't know when to expect Kyra, so when the day goes by and she doesn't appear, I don't know how to feel. Is it completely unrealistic to expect her to make it back today? I have no idea.

After thinking for a long time of all I know about this city, I decide: if she's not back two days from now, then I'll start to worry.

That resolution doesn't last long.

It's mid-morning the next day when I start to worry. But this worry is different than past worries in these situations. I'm not just worried because my brain, out-of-my-control, is thinking of all the worst-case scenarios. I'm worried because I don't want anything to have hurt *her*. She needs to make it back. I don't know what to do with myself otherwise.

Especially right now. I'm on house arrest, courtesy of Grandmother. Apparently soldiers are searching all over for me. So I can't go outside. There's nothing to do inside. So I take naps and worry.

Are soldiers searching for her, too? Of course they are. That will make it take longer, cause she'll have to be cautious.

And she has to figure out where to find us. But I know she will.

"Boy, you're going to make a hole in my floor with that pacing," Grandmother tells me as the sun sets on the second day.

With some effort, I stop. "Sorry."

"Have you made a plan?" she asks me.

"Plan? For what?"

She regards me with resigned disappointment. "For your escape. Those soldiers are always going to be looking for you."

Escape. Right. From this city. Out from the farmland. Although, I don't know if we'll be able to make it through the farmland. We'd be easily recognized. We need a plan.

My mind goes completely blank.

"It'll take a lot of thinking," Grandmother says. "Give it time. Keep turning it over in your head. Something will come to you."

But it's a full day later and I've only hit dead ends.

Maybe I don't have enough information to form a plan. Or maybe not enough brains.

The sun is descending, casting the sky with purple and yellow. Alyson may or may not be back. She often sleeps at different places.

I'm staring out of a window at the sky, observing the changes. Trying to convince myself that I'm thinking.

Then the door opens. My back is to it, but I assume it's Alyson.

But then Grandmother says, "Oh, good to see you again. He's been pacing non-stop waiting for you."

My heart does a somersault. I spin around.

It's Kyra. Standing behind her are two people I don't know, but I don't care about them. A weight I didn't realize I was carrying is lifted off my shoulders.

I cross the room in three quick strides and envelope her. She wraps her arms around me.

"It's finally happened!" the boy says, grabbing the girl's arm and jumping in excitement.

I rest my forehead on top of her head. It's like she's the only thing holding me up right now.

"Thank you," I whisper.

"So it worked?"

"Yeah. It worked. You saved my life." I pull back and search her face. "Are you hurt anywhere?"

She shakes her head. "No. I scraped my knees bad, but that's about it."

I bury my face in her shoulder. "I'm so glad to see you."

Her grip tightens.

It feels like time freezes. I never want to let go.

The boy sticks his hand out to me. "I'm Matthew. Lovely to meet you. I'm also on the run from the government who want me dead. How long have you been in love with Kyra?"

CHAPTER FORTY

Kyra

I was enjoying my hug with Jun immensely, feeling the safest I had in days. Until Matthew had to open his mouth. Why would he go through all the risk and trouble of helping me just to embarrass me to death now?

Jun freezes, raising his head to look at Matthew. I can imagine his face. He's probably totally throw off right now, brain short-circuiting. He must be so uncomfortable.

Before I can extract myself from the hug, Jun's arm goes out and it feels like he shakes Matthew's hand. Then he rests his chin on my head.

"Not sure," he answers casually. "My brain has been messed with pretty severely these last few days, so I can't pinpoint the exact time."

My heart does a somersault. What?

An unnatural squeal escapes from Matthew. "I'm so happy! You won't believe how many guys I've tried to set her up with, but she's chased off every one of them! And—"

I quickly extract myself from Jun and turn around to glare to Matthew. My eyes must send the message clearly. He shrinks back.

Choosing to ignore what Jun has said, I say to him, "Sorry about him. That's Matthew. He's my friend from the government sector. And this is his girlfriend, Jasmine."

"Nice to meet you," Jun says. He shakes Jasmine's hand.

I notice someone's not here. "Where's Alyson?" I ask.

Jun shrugs. "Probably staying with friends. She doesn't usually sleep here. She'll be back in the morning."

I understand why Alyson would choose not to sleep here. It's a small room, with a small bed. Grandmother sits on the only chair in it. Jun must sleep on the floor. Is there room for us?

I turn to Grandmother. "I'm sorry for bringing so many people with me," I say. "We can find another place to sleep for the night."

"Why?" she asks.

"Well…"

"I'm sure you two girls can squish onto the bed, and the boys can take the floor. They'll survive."

"What about you?"

"Me? I sleep on this chair."

Jun slips his hand around my waist. I freeze.

"She's right, we'll all fit just fine," he says. "And it's probably too dangerous for us to try and find another place to sleep. I've been on house arrest because of the soldiers out searching for us."

He's so casual about all this. It's different. This quiet, assured confidence. This is who he's supposed to be.

"*So* many soldiers!" Matthew exclaims, sitting on the edge of the bed. "Apparently we're all very popular. We're going to have a hard time evading them." He doesn't sound worried.

"We can discuss plans later." Jun looks down at me. "I want to hear what happened."

We all takes seats. Jasmine joins Matthew on the bed. Jun and I sit on the floor. Then we take turns telling our sides of the story. Matthew jumps in a lot during mine, then completely interrupts to tell what happened after he left me. Jasmine quietly corrects his embellishments and exaggerations.

I don't mention Braxton. I reframe my story so that I stole the gun off a random guard. Jun is amazed and heaps on the praise, which makes me squirm. I don't want his praise, but Matthew doesn't need to hear about Braxton anymore. I already told him about Braxton's involvement in my story and apologized for shooting him. Matthew tried to pretend that he didn't care, but he felt *something*. I wish I knew why they didn't get along. How could Matthew and I be friends for so long and I never inquired? He knew all about my family. My resolve to be a better friend increases.

When Jun tells his story, I can't help getting concerned. I know it's in the past. He's clearly recovered. Yet I feel guilty he had to go through that pain. I'm so glad he never has to go through it again. He only briefly mentions the moment when I broke his connection. I wonder what it was like?

Jun concludes with his side of the story, "And that's pretty much it."

Matthew and Jasmine are frozen. Matthew's face is pale and his eyes are widen. Jasmine is chewing on her bottom lip.

What's bothering them?

"Listen, Jun," Matthew begins haltingly. "I can't imagine... I don't... all my individuals..."

Oh. This is the first time they're hearing the effects the computer can have on an individual. You can dissociate from it when you're on the other side of the computer, surrounded by everyone else who believes what you're doing is right. It's different when you're here.

"Don't worry about it," Jun says. "Your reactions to my story tell me what kind of heart you guys have."

Jasmine is avoiding his eyes.

"Thank you," Matthew says. "It's amazing that you would forgive us for that."

Jun grins sheepishly. "Well, it took me a long time to forgive Kyra."

"With good reason," I mutter.

"I know better now," he says. He smiles at me.

How do I react? I'm still adjusting to him being *him* for the first time, and now he's also being flirty! No, more than that. It's too much for me to wrap my head around. And we still have to figure out how to escape.

"Jun, can I talk to you outside?" I ask.

The light in his eyes dims. He searches mine, then nods.

"Yeah, of course."

Matthew laughs to himself.

"Keep your thoughts to yourself," I snap at him as we get up.

He holds his hands up. "Hey, I didn't say anything."

We go outside, onto the porch. I do a quick visual sweep of the area. No one's around.

Jun closes the door. "What's wrong?" he asks. "Is it about one of them? Can we not trust them?"

"What? Oh, no, they're fine." I don't know what to say to begin this conversation. "I wanted to talk about... um..." My insides are twisting together unpleasantly.

"Did something happen?" Jun asks. His eyebrows are drawn together.

"No. Well, yes. Your connection was broken."

"...yes." He sounds confused.

"How was that, by the way?" I ask. "How was it *really*?" I might be stalling, but I've never had to have this conversation before. And I am curious. We've always been told it was painful and a death-sentence. That the person's brain wouldn't be able to recover from that sudden of a change. Especially for Jun.

"Oh, um…" He leans against the porch railing, crossing his arms. "It sucked. I've never… the pain, it…" He takes a breath.

It was painful.

"I'm sorry."

He blinks. "Why? What, you *saved* me. I can survive a few minutes of pain, even if they were the absolute worst moments of my life. But when I woke up, I felt… invincible. Everything hurt, but I didn't care. I was…" He searches for the right word.

I frown, trying to wrap my head around what he's telling me. Why would he feel good after that, if it's as painful as he says it was?

"Exhilarating," he says. "Like nothing could hurt me. But, that didn't last long. I crashed pretty soon after that. Barely made it to Grandmother's house."

It clicks.

"Of course," I say quietly. The brain is a wonder.

"What?" he asks.

I try to find the words to explain to someone without using too much science jargon. "Your brain, for years now, has only ever experience high or dramatically fluctuating levels of all the hormones that cause or contribute to anxiety and low levels of hormones that help reduce anxiety and generally make a person feel positive. When the connection was broken, your brain was returned to it's true, neutral state. Which, for someone who has experienced high anxiety all his life, would feel like a *high*. Literally. Higher levels of serotonin, endorphins." Seeing his expression, I break off, and try again. "Higher levels of everything that makes you feel good than you've felt in years so yes, it would be a bit overwhelming. But that couldn't last long against the pain. Your body needed to recover."

Jun nods, taking this all in. He stares off into the distance for a bit, and I give him that time to digest it all. Then he focuses back on me and asks, "Did you bring me out here just to ask me what breaking the connection felt like?"

"No, although I did want to know. It felt like you sugar-coated it in there, and I was right, you did. How's your shoulder?"

"Fine, but you're rambling," Jun observes. Not with judgment, but like he's observing an animal out of its usual habitat.

"I am." My eyes dart all over, as if the answer for how to start this conversation is written on this disintegrating porch. What if he gets offended? "This is all new," I say carefully. "Since your connection has been broken, you're a different person that you were before. Well, not entirely. Just, in many ways. Point being, I don't know this *version* of you yet. I saw glimpses of it, but not like this."

Understanding dawns in his eyes. He nods and gestures for me to keep going.

I can't gather my thoughts and I feel like I'm throwing words randomly out. "A lot still has to happen," I continue. "We have to escape."

A little smile plays around Jun's mouth.

"It's not funny!" I say defensively.

"No, it's not, I'm sorry." He grins. "I've just never seen you like this."

"Like what?" I snap.

"Flustered."

I feel my cheeks get red.

"I think I get what you're trying to say," Jun says. "I'll give you some time to get to know this version of me. I'm still getting to know it too." He turns to go back inside.

I grab his arm. He halts.

"I don't want you to get the wrong impression," I say. "It's been a lot. I need some time to adjust."

He turns back to me. "I'll give you all the time you need," he says. "I'm sorry if I made you uncomfortable."

I laugh. "Matthew's the only one making me uncomfortable, but I understand. He's been trying to make this happen for a long time."

Jun brushes away a strand of hair that's fallen out of my braids. "I'm glad he failed," he says quietly.

It feels like my heart stops beating. "Me too," I say, as quiet.

Suddenly, Jun exclaims, "Wait! I have an idea!"

"About what?"

"How we can escape!"

CHAPTER FORTY-ONE

Jun

Despite the odd first greeting, Matthew has grown on me in the few hours since he first appeared in Grandmother's house. But now he's pacing, wringing his hands.

"I'm not sure about this," he says.

"It gives us a better chance than through the farmland," Kyra points out.

"How?"

"They won't be expecting us at the hospital," I say.

"It's a good plan," Grandmother says from her chair. She's being really calm about all of this.

Meanwhile, Jasmine has barely contributed to this discussion. She just sits there, fidgeting with her hands, mouth trembling. I understand. She's in a completely unfamiliar environment talking about escaping the city entirely. Her whole world was changed quickly. That takes a lot to get used to.

"And we get a chance to disguise ourselves in a way that won't draw attention," Kyra adds. "People entering the hospital are expected to be dirty and bloody."

Matthew makes a face. "Whose blood?"

"Well, I could punch your face," I suggest.

Everyone turns to me with varying looks of horror on their face.

"One good punch and he'd get all bruised up," I say. "Much less recognizable. He'd survive. I'd make sure you didn't lose any teeth."

Matthew's legs wobble and he sits down quickly. Maybe I shouldn't have added that last part.

"I hate to say it," Kyra begins.

"Then don't," Matthew says.

"But Jun's right. We need to disguise ourselves. We're going to a hospital. We should be injured in various ways."

"Well, what about you guys?" Matthew asks.

I don't like the idea of punching either of the girls. Especially when I barely know Jasmine. That's not a good way to build a good rapport.

"We'll have to get blood from somewhere," Kyra says. "Smear it on our faces. Concoct a story." She looks at Jasmine. "Is that alright?"

Jasmine looks queasy, but she nods.

"I probably shouldn't do the same," I say. "Matthew, you could also punch me. Our cover story could be that we got in a fight."

"I don't know if Matthew can do enough damage for that to be plausible," Kyra mutters to me under her breath.

Grandmother chuckles.

"Hey! I heard that!" Matthew exclaims.

The door opens and everyone freezes. But it's Alyson.

When she sees Kyra, she yells and runs to her. Kyra welcomes the hug.

We introduce Alyson to Matthew and Jasmine. Alyson sits down on the floor between me and Kyra. We share a look over her head. I nod.

Kyra takes a breath, then says, "Alyson, we have something to explain."

Alyson looks at her.

"We're trying to escape the city. It's dangerous to attempt, but if we succeed, we'll be free. We can live off the land. You can come with us if you want. But it means leaving friends behind. We won't be able to return."

I wish I could see Aly's face right now. It's a lot to put on someone so young.

"No more working?" she asks.

"We'll still have to work to grow food and create a shelter, and live," Kyra says. "But there won't be anyone your age out there."

"There could be," I say quietly.

Kyra's eyes harden. She shakes her head.

I want to keep talking. We could bring people with us! Everyone deserves a chance to be free from their computers.

"We're being hunted," Kyra says. "I'm sure soldiers have orders to kill on sight this time. Now's not the time to try to start a revolution."

I want to argue that it's actually the perfect time.

"You won't be coming back?" Alyson asks.

Kyra refocuses her attention. "No. We can't."

"Then I'm coming!" Alyson declares. She claps. "When are we going?"

"As soon as we can," I say.

"How's she getting into the hospital?" Matthew asks.

That's a good point.

We all stare at Alyson.

"She could be someone's daughter," Jasmine suggests.

"The only person who could pass as her parent is Matthew," Kyra says.

"You mean we don't have to go with the face-punching idea?" Matthew looks like he could pass out from relief.

"I could get my face punched," Jasmine offers.

"What, no!" Matthew objects. "Your face is too lovely to do that to!"

Kyra makes a face of disgust.

I make a mental note. She's not one for gushy talk.

"What do you think about that, Alyson?" I ask her.

She pushes in closer to me. "You mean I won't be with you or Kyra?" Her face is scrunched up.

"I'm not sure yet," Kyra says. "But Matthew's very nice."

Alyson regards him warily. Matthew grins widely. It's slightly unnerving.

"What's your favorite animal?" she asks him.

What a character-revealing question. I can't help but grin at her vetting process.

Matthew takes this question seriously. He leans forward and says, "Jasmine doesn't like when I give this answer, because it's not a real animal. But I love unicorns."

Alyson's face scrunches up. "What's that?"

Kyra laughs.

Matthew frowns. He must have thought that would have been the answer she wanted to hear. He says, "Okay, my favourite real animal is a puppy."

"I've seen puppies!" Alyson says. "They're so cute!"

With that settled, we move on to planning the specifics. Kyra comes up with most ideas. She's so clever. We figure the best way is to split up. Kyra and Jasmine will go in together, all bloodied and dirtied. They'll say they were in some kind of accident. Matthew, Aly, and I will go together. Alyson will pretend to be sick, and I'll be a kindly neighbour who carries her in because Matthew's not strong enough. He tries to protest this point. Jasmine soothes him by saying that of course he could actually carry her, but there needs to be a reason for me to be there. It's too risky for one of us to go in alone. And I don't really trust Matthew to be able to protect Alyson.

Alyson doesn't even pay attention. Once it's settled that I'll also go with her, she falls asleep against Kyra.

Eventually, we settle all the details. And we decide. We go tomorrow. The sooner the better. Before soldiers decide to start knocking at every door.

Grandmother has also fallen asleep by the time we're done.

Kyra says, "Matthew, you take the bed with Jasmine."

"Are you sure?" Matthew asks, but I can tell he wants to accept that offer.

Kyra nods. "Wouldn't want to disturb Alyson. Besides, I've gotten used to sleeping on this kind of surface. You haven't. We need everyone as rested as possible for tomorrow."

Matthew grins in relief. He hops onto the bed with Jasmine, who looks worried. He asks her a question in a undertone. She looks at us, then away at the wall.

"Hey," he says softly. I can't catch the rest of what he says.

I look away to give them what privacy they can get in a small space.

"Can you help me move her?" Kyra asks.

"Yeah." I move over to them.

"Hold her in place until I get settled. Then she can keep using me as a pillow."

I put my arms around Aly's shoulders, pulling her back slightly from against Kyra. She doesn't stir. Kyra lies down on her back. She puts her hand behind her head.

At her direction, I slowly lower Alyson down against her, so that Aly's head is resting on her shoulder. Kyra puts her arm around her.

"You're smiling," she says.

"It's like the exact opposite of our first night with her," I say. "You didn't even like her then."

"I was tired and she was a stranger. Plus, I wasn't exactly thrilled with our sleeping conditions."

"Fair enough."

I get up and go to the counter. The candle's almost out.

"You guys good?" I ask Matthew.

He nods. "Yep. Go ahead."

I blow out the candle. The room darkens. It's kinda crazy how much light one tiny flame can produce.

Carefully, I lay down, making sure to give Kyra and Alyson plenty of space. Hopefully I don't kick in my sleep.

I stare at the ceiling, which I can just make out in the moonlight. I'm suddenly very aware of needing to sleep. Tomorrow is a big day.

I wish breaking the connection meant I never got nervous again. But since I'm still human, I feel the familiar rising in my stomach. It doesn't have the hold on me it used to. I absent-mindedly rub my stomach and try to fall asleep.

But sleep is far from me.

I sigh, and get up quietly. No one else stirs.

Cautiously, I make my way to the door and go out onto the porch.

The night air is cool. The room is warm with so many people in it. A slight breeze ruffles my hair.

I grip the porch railings. What we're going to attempt tomorrow might be the craziest thing I've ever chosen to attempt. Well, it can't be any crazier than what Kyra did for me. She downplayed it when she told me about it, but it must have been terrifying. At least I'll be there to protect her tomorrow. Except, not really, since we're splitting up. I wish we didn't have to. But Jasmine promised she's good at self-defence. They should be fine. Especially if they're unrecognizable.

The door behind me opens and someone steps out. I turn around.

"Jasmine?" I ask quietly.

She jumps. "Jun?" She closes the door behind her. "What are you doing out here?"

"Couldn't sleep. I came out to clear my head. Why are you out here?"

She rubs her arms. "Same reason." She doesn't move.

She looks nervous. Has this whole time, never meeting my eyes, picking at her fingernails. I feel bad for her.

"I'm sure it's a lot to take in," I say.

Jasmine snorts. "That's an understatement. I… I made a quick decision to come with Matthew when he came to me. And I'm still processing it. To try to wrap my head around leaving this city forever."

"Are you nervous for tomorrow?"

"No."

She's clearly nervous about something. Well, I'll let her keep her lie if it helps her feel braver.

"Are you," she hesitates. "You're really okay with us coming?"

If that's what she's nervous about, that's also understandable.

"Of course," I answer. "I meant what I said. You can't help the life you were born into any more than I could."

She nods. "I'm gonna try to get to sleep," she whispers, then goes back inside.

I don't go inside. It's nice out here. In the dark, I locate Grandmother's porch rocking chair and sit. I rock back and forth. The motion is quite soothing…

CHAPTER FORTY-TWO

Kyra

In the morning, as we eat the last of Grandmother's granola bars, we go over the plan one more time. I can't relax. My mind is buzzing and my stomach refuses to settle. But this is the best possible plan we could have conceived. They're probably expecting us to attempt to escape through the farmland. I doubt hospital security has been increased. Aside from whatever increases Jun's previous escape has caused.

We don't have anything to take with us. Jasmine has a small bag with her, but that's it. She looks the most worried out of any of us. This is the first time she's doing anything like this. It's understandable. And maybe she'd rather be paired with Matthew. But she and I have always been friendly. I'll do my best to allay her nerves. Although sometimes you have to let people feel their emotions.

We say our goodbyes to Grandmother.

"I wish I had money to give you," I say.

"What for?" she asks.

"We ate all your food."

She waves her hand. "Don't worry about that. I plan on dying today or tomorrow. What do I need money for?"

I can't tell if she's joking or not.

"You've given me some full and meaningful last days." She pats my hand. "Don't let her mess us your plan." She nods at the clump of everyone waiting at the door.

I'm not sure if she's talking about Alyson's youth or Jasmine's obvious worry. Either way, I say, "I won't."

"Then good luck."

We head out.

We can't even travel all together to the hospital. The five of us in one big group, with soldiers on the lookout for us, is too dangerous. But I outline a path for Matthew and Jun. Between Matthew's knowledge from cameras and his individuals, and Jun's street-smarts, they should make it. Jasmine and I will be fine. But Matthew and Jasmine hug like they'll never see each other again.

I shouldn't be so calloused. They might not, if things go poorly.

"I'll see you on the other side," Jun says. He's so at-ease and confident. I still can't believe it, but it was worth every risk.

Alyson's holding his hand.

I nod. "Good luck."

He grins. "Oh, we'll be fine." He peels Matthew off of Jasmine. "Come on, plenty of time for that later."

"I'll see you!" Matthew calls as Jun drags him along. He waves. "Don't worry! It'll all go according to—"

They round a corner and are out of sight.

Jasmine wipes at her eyes.

She's crying?

"Hey," I say, trying to be comforting, "It'll be alright. They have no reason to expect us to be coming. We'll both be covered in blood, so, why would they recognize us?"

She nods. "I know," she murmurs. "Sorry."

"It's alright." Cause obviously I'm not about to tell her that it's making me feel awkward.

We wait. I want the boys and Alyson to get a good head-start. I don't know how much Alyson will slow them down, and I don't want there to be a chance we accidentally cross paths with them.

After about ten minutes, I ask Jasmine, "Are you ready to go?"

She takes a deep breath. "Yeah, I'm ready."

We start walking. I'm not sure what to do about this. I don't understand why this would move her to such displays of emotion. She's not usually this emotional. That's why she's a good balance for Matthew. Maybe she didn't sleep well?

We move quickly. Part of our plan is messy. The stealing chickens and using their blood to make us unrecognizable. Matthew almost threw up when I revealed this part of the plan. But we would definitely be recognized otherwise.

The chickens are in Sector 7. I remember passing a house that had chickens in a fenced front lawn area. We'll take one. It'll be fine.

We walk along cautiously, keeping our eyes open for soldiers. Well, I am. I'm not sure what Jasmine's doing.

I round around a corner, but I see two soldiers patrolling, walking towards us. Quickly, I backtrack.

"Jasmine, soldiers," I warn. Did they see me? Are they turning down this street? "Let's backtrack and take the previous turn." It's only a small detour.

But she walks to the corner.

"What are you doing?" I hiss.

She peers around the corner. "They're gone. They must have turned."

"Oh, great."

I follow her around the corner.

And run straight into the soldiers.

My heart drops.

"Good morning, sirs," Jasmine greets them.

What is she doing? They'll recognize us.

She lied.

My brain's thoughts turn to static noise. I don't understand.

One of them is staring at me, brows furrowed. His hand is slowly reaching for the gun on his belt.

Jasmine shoots a glance at me. I can't interpret it. "I have an escape plot I must tell you about," she says to the soldiers.

No.

Matthew's going to be crushed.

And I'm in serious trouble.

Without thinking anymore, I whirl around and take off. My knees protest. The scraps I've obtained have scabbed over and my knees hate any bending motion. Unfortunately for them, my life is at stake, so they're gonna have to be bent.

The soldiers shout out. I keep running.

My heart is pounding, but not from the sudden exercise. How could Jasmine do that?

Doesn't matter, doesn't matter. Getting out alive is what matters.

She said she had an escape plan to tell them about… No! She's going to tell them our plan. They're going to alert the hospital.

Jun, Alyson, and Matthew will be walking into a trap.

My brain works fast. I need the fastest route to the hospital. They have to be warned.

But to what purpose? That's still our best chance to get out of the city. If we don't now, we might never.

Hopefully they can get to the hospital before the staff have time to prepare for them. I'm glad we staggered when we left. They have a chance. Maybe.

For some reason, this feels more serious than when it was only me, running for my life in the government sector. I pour all my strength and energy into running. Dodging people. Getting out of Sector 5. Crossing over into Sector 6.

I don't know if the soldier is still behind me. Or if there are more. I can't risk glancing back. It'll slow me down. Or make me bump into something.

A soldier emerges from a building right in front of me.

I yell. I didn't mean too. I was surprised and I'm terrified. Quickly, I duck into the alley right before the building.

What if it's a dead end?

It is, but before I have a chance to freak out about that, I spot a door. It's not locked, so I go through it.

I'm in the back of a shop, surrounded by boxes. Instead of rushing through, I make the decision to take the time to block the door. Straining, I push a big pile of boxes stacking on top of each other over to in front of the door. Hopefully that slows them down.

Then I make my way out of the storage room. The shop owner is busy discussing something with a customer, so I casually make my way to the door. I check outside. No soldiers in sight.

I hear the boxes crash in the back. That's my cue.

I rush outside and keep running the way I had been. My hands are shaking. My feet hurt.

Then I hear a sound I haven't heard in a while. It explodes, then echoes and reverberates. People scream and rush for cover.

Gunshot.

It missed me, but sooner or later, they'll hit their target.

I veer to the left, weaving through alleys and around stores. Just like in the maze, I try to utilize the corners. This is going to slow me down, but staying alive might take precedence here.

Questions rush through my head with every thump of my heart. Should I find a place to hide until they pass? Can I make it to the hospital? Do we have a chance?

My lungs burn and throb like they're going to explode out of my chest. I hate running.

I turn another corner. I've almost lost most of the soldiers.

But one stands in the street, waiting for me. He raises his gun. I almost fall over myself in my attempt to back up.

He fires.

I fall backwards, all the breath forced out of me. Pain. That's all I feel. Before I get my breath back, I scramble to my feet.

The soldier had been lowering his gun, but he raises it again when he sees me moving.

I enter the building closest to me. Another shot fires and hits the door behind me.

It's someone's house. Whoops.

But no one seems to be home.

I run through the house as my body registers the specifics of the pain. He shot my stomach, low, on my left. Right where I shot Braxton. Is this some kind of vengeance? I press my left hand over the spot, trying to apply pressure. A tricky task while you're running.

This is what Jun felt when he was shot. Of course, he didn't have to keep running for his life immediately afterwards.

I'm about to exit through the backdoor of the house. It's a big lawn space that many houses around this one must share. A few people are sunning themselves on chairs, sipping drinks, or reading while their children play.

But the soldier is waiting for me at the base of the porch stairs. Or it's another one.

I back up.

What now?

Deep in my memory, a string of knowledge tugs at me. Something I should know. Something that will be helpful.

I go back into the house, away from windows. When I don't show outside, they'll come in. I need a plan.

I grab a cloth from off a countertop and press it to my wound. The blood is soaking through my shirt. It's not a feeling I enjoy.

Then, I remember. Sector 6 houses are sometimes connected to other houses through a basement. If they have a basement. Sector 6 is the first middle sector, so they still have to share some commodities. Oftentimes, houses will have a connected basement that they share as a laundry space. These people can afford multiple pairs of clothes, but only a few, so it will be a small space. But I can use it to get into the other house. If there is one.

Quickly, I search for the stairs. They're not hard to find and I hurry down. My stomach protests with each step I thump down.

I go around the clothes drying on wooden racks and find the stairs to the next house. These I go up, discovering that my wound hurts a lot more going up stairs than down.

Once I'm in the next house, I find a side door. Before I leave through it, I scan what surroundings I can see. No soldiers in sight. It's a risk I have to take.

Outside, I sneak to the next house. They don't have a side door, so I creep around to the back porch. I peer out. I don't see any soldiers. I rush into the house.

This one also has a basement. This basement is a bit bigger. Two other houses are connected to it. Perfect. I take the tunnel that leads me further, then up stairs into another house.

This house is also empty. Only now do I allow myself a chance to breathe. My wound feels on fire. The pain is unlike anything I've felt before. Now that I'm resting, my head goes woozy. This is not the time to pass out. I need to patch this wound as best as possible so I don't bleed out.

There should be a first aid kit somewhere. In the bathroom?

I find the bathroom and rummage through the cabinets. Aha! There it is.

I haul the bag down and open it. Scissors, tape, bandages, gauze. I place all these out on the floor.

First, I roll back my shirt. The bottom has become thoroughly soaked and sticks to my skin. I clean the area as best I can, but blood keeps spurting.

I can't deal with the bullet right now. It's embedded in my stomach. Besides, it's helping stem some of the bleeding. So, for now, it stays. I use gauze to soak the blood, trying to slow the bleeding more before I put a bandage on.

When I've taken as much time as I can afford with that, I grab some fresh gauze and press it to the wound. Then I use bandages and tape to hold it in place. It's not neatly done, but it's done.

Then I rinse my shirt, trying to get the blood off. It'll be odd to walk around with part of my shirt wet, but it would be more conspicuous for it to be bloody.

I can't take any more time. I must get moving.

Should I change the plan?

I scoff. To what? The hospital and the farmland are the only two options I know of. The hospital is still my best chance. A fool's chance, maybe. I'll be crazy to attempt it, especially if they're expecting me. But to not chance it is to certainly die. I can't hide in this city forever. Nor do I want to.

The hospital it is. Besides, Jun might need my help.

All I want to do is sleep. But I can't.

I find the back door. All clear. I take a deep breath, then push the door open, my goal clear: make it to the hospital. They'll have to admit me. After all, I've been shot.

CHAPTER FORTY-THREE

Jun

Matthew does not stop talking. Which is fine, really. Helps us appear casual. And I'm guessing he's getting some nerves out. While he and Alyson keep up a steady stream of conversation about nothing and everything, I keep an eye out for soldiers. Having Alyson with us is good. Soldiers won't be expecting us to have a small child with us.

Hopefully.

I hope Kyra and Jasmine are doing well. They've got a messy and gross task ahead of them. But it's necessary. Kyra is the most wanted out of any of us. She has to disguise herself. It sounded a bit extreme when she first ventured the idea of using chickens, but I understand her concern. Every soldier everywhere is probably on high alert for her right now.

The more I think about it, the more I wonder if having Alyson with us when we enter the hospital will be enough deflection. It will be if the hospital staff aren't on the lookout for us. But if they are, and nothing is disguising or altering my face, they'll recognize me. Matthew might have to punch me after all. I'll have to think about it. I've got time. It's a good walk to the Sector 7 hospital, and we'll be in Sector 5 for the majority of it, so we should be pretty safe.

"How do you think the girls are doing?" Matthew asks.

It takes me a second to register that he's asking *me* that question.

"I'm sure they're fine," I say. "They know what they're doing."

"I don't know." Matthew's eyebrows are pulled together. "Jasmine was really worried. I've never seen her like that before."

"Well you've never planned on breaking into a hospital and then out of the city before," I say.

He laughs. "Good point." But he doesn't sound convinced.

"How much longer?" Alyson asks. She's on the verge of complaining.

We've been walking a long time, especially for one so little, so I understand her frustration. I want to complain myself, just for different reasons. Every nerve in me is alive. Wanting to be *out*. Wanting to do more than casually walk.

"We'll be reaching Sector 7 soon," I say, though I really have no idea how much longer it'll take. "Once we're in 7, the hospital will be really close."

But when we round the corner, a squad of soldiers is blocking the street.

My heart drops unpleasantly. Matthew and I freeze. Alyson doesn't notice at first. She keeps walking at first, but stops when my hand tugs her back.

The soldiers were waiting for us. Most of them reach for their guns. A few run towards us.

Matthew swears in surprise. I scoop Alyson up in my arms. She barely weighs anything. When we get out of here, I'm making sure she gets three proper meals a day.

We run. Alyson is shaking in my arms. A shot fires, but we're already around the corner.

"What is this?" Matthew shouts.

They knew we were coming. How? How did they know we'd be on this street? Maybe it was a random checkpoint they setup? But my heart knows better. Kyra wouldn't do this. But I can't voice my concern to Matthew. He won't believe me.

"This way," I say, turning down an alley.

I'm not Kyra. I don't have entire sectors mapped out in my head. But I have experience, and I know how to read the terrain.

We race through the tiny alley between two shops and emerge in another street. I locate the next alley and we cut through to another street. Once we make it there, I stop running. Matthew continues, but I call after him. He slows and walks by my side.

"What are we doing?" he hisses. "We have to get away."

"Running raises a lot of suspicion," I answer. "We have to hope they don't know where we're going. Keep your eyes and ears peeled. This way."

We're not walking casually anymore, but with purpose. That's fine. I keep Alyson tucked in my arms. If we need to run, she won't be able to keep up. But if we need to fight… I push the thought aside. Hopefully it won't come to that. I can't fight soldiers with guns while defending Alyson. And defending Matthew, too, whatever he might like to try and insist.

Matthew stops walking.

I turn around. "What are you doing?" it's my turn to demand.

"I thought I saw Jasmine." He's craning his neck, trying to see somewhere.

"No, you didn't. She and Kyra are taking a different path. Besides, they left after us." My eyes don't stay still, roving around, searching for any first signs of soldiers. "Matthew, we need to *move*."

"No, it was her! I know my girlfriend. I'll be right back."

He races off.

I want to shout after him, but that would be a stupid move. Instead, I back up into the shadows cast by the tall shop beside me. If he wants to dig himself a grave, he can lie in it. But I keep an eye on him, not forgetting to occasionally survey behind me.

He goes onto the porch of a store and opens the door. Almost immediately, he shuts the door, falling backwards. Some shots ring out. Alyson flinches.

I rub her back. "It's okay, I promise. We'll be okay."

Matthew runs back to me. I start running before he reaches me. He'll catch up.

When he does, tears are running down his face. "We have to go back."

"Are you crazy?"

"They have Jasmine!"

I screech to a halt. I stare at him. "What do you mean? Was Kyra there?"

"Just Jasmine. Standing amidst all these soldiers."

"Was she tied up or anything?"

"Why would she need to be when she's surrounded by soldiers with guns?!" Matthew shouts.

I try to find a way to put this delicately. I don't like it either, and my stomach twists to think of what might have happened to Kyra as a result. I barely knew Jasmine and I have no reason to trust her when the evidence is against her.

Cautiously, I say, "Matthew, the soldiers knew where we were going to be. They were *waiting* for us. She walked into that store by herself. She knew you would see her."

Matthew shakes his head. "No. No."

"She gave us up."

"They might have tortured that information out of her!"

I concede. "If so, we'll soon see Kyra used as bait." Over Matthew's shoulder, I see soldiers enter the alleyway we've just left. "We have to go!"

Once again, I run without waiting. I hear Matthew's footsteps pounding behind me.

I push thoughts of Jasmine's betrayal out of my head. Thoughts of what's happened to Kyra crowd in instead, making me worry. If Jasmine's caused any harm to come to her!

Jasmine could have been tortured. Perhaps. But I remember last night, on the porch. Was she nervous? Just needing air? Or was she planning on going and revealing our plan then? Getting soldiers to raid the house and take us in our sleep.

In my anger, I mistake a dead-end for a path. My heart rate spikes when I see the wall of another building rising where there should be an escape.

"Back, back!" I shout.

We turn around, but it's too late. Soldiers crowd the entrance, blocking us. They don't draw their guns. Yet.

"Hide and stay hidden," I instruct Alyson, before setting her down. She trembles, but goes behind me.

"What are they waiting for?" Matthew asks.

"I don't know." It's making me uneasy. If they decide to fire, they'll have a hard time missing.

Alyson's presence leaves me. I feel it, but I don't move my eyes an inch. The soldiers are focused on me and Matthew right now. I'd like to keep it that way.

The soldiers stir and part. A girl walks through.

"Jasmine!" Matthew gasps in relief. He starts forward, then stops. Something holds him back. "What's going on?"

She walks right up to us. Her shoulders are drawn in, her face has tear tracks, and she's hugging herself, but physically, she looks unharmed.

My blood begins to boil.

"Did they hurt you?" Matthew asks. I can hear the confusion in his voice. He's seeing the answer, he just doesn't want to believe it.

"No." Her face speaks only guilt. "Please, come in quietly," she begs. "They'll go easy on us. They'll understand."

Matthew shakes his head, taking a step back from her.

"No, Matthew, please." Her voice breaks. "You can't have asked this of me. It's too much. To leave everything we've ever known?"

"I was going to be killed otherwise," Matthew gets out, his voice strained.

"Because of treason *you* chose to commit!" she exclaims. "Why did you come for me?"

"Because I love you. I thought… I thought you wouldn't want to be without me the same way I couldn't stand the thought of being without you."

I haven't known Matthew for long, but my heart breaks for him nonetheless.

Matthew's head hangs and he mumbles, "You could've told me 'no.'"

I don't miss the way the soldiers slowly start to move down further into the alley. As much as I can, I peek at my surrounding with my peripheral vision. I see a door to my left. It's closed, but I could probably break it open if it's locked. Where'd Alyson go? I can't risk looking around anymore.

"How could I have said no?" Jasmine says. "I didn't want to be without you either, but you can't ask all *this* of me. To betray everything we've ever stood for. His connection should *never* have been broken." She gestures to me.

Matthew looks broken.

I don't care what she thinks about me or my proper place in society. "What happened to Kyra?" I ask.

"She ran." Jasmine wipes at appearing tears. "They'll catch her soon, if they haven't already."

She's alive. Relief floods through me. She'll survive. She has so much knowledge. She'll outsmart the soldiers. And she'll keep going with her plan. So it's still my plan. Get to the hospital. Get out.

The door slowly creaks open, then shuts again. No one came out. Alyson must have gone in. There were several trash cans in front, maybe the soldiers didn't see her. They certainly didn't raise an alarm.

"They won't go easy on me," Matthew says, sounding miserable. "Like you said, I chose to commit treason by helping Kyra."

"But they don't have to know that. Say she stole your ID card and you ran because you feared they wouldn't believe you. Please, Matthew." She stretches out her hand. "Come with me."

The soldiers are getting too close. No matter Matthew's answer, we'll be shot soon if we don't move. I don't want to leave him, but I can't wait any longer.

I leap to the side, towards the door. Soldiers shout. Jasmine shrieks. I open the door, jamming it with my shoulder just in case it's locked.

It swings open easily and Alyson tumbles to the ground, making a sound of pain. She must have been trying to hold it closed.

I'll apologize later. I grab her hand and we start running. To her credit, she runs as fast as she's able. I want to carry her again, but these soldiers aren't dumb. They should have the store surrounded. I'll need my hands free.

We're in a store's back storage space. We quickly exit it. A fist swings for my face.

I can't react fast enough and it hits my nose. I hear a gross crack, which bothers me more than the pain. He just broke my nose.

Before the soldier can grab his gun, I grab him and toss him to the side. He crashes into a wall of products.

Blood drips into my mouth. I swipe at my nose and keep going. Alyson sticks close to my side.

"Stop!" the soldier shouts.

I turn, but Matthew's already there, hitting the soldier over the head with a walking stick. He must have grabbed that off one of the shelves.

His face is bruised and bloody.

We run.

Only a few soldiers are waiting out on the street. I leap off the porch into two of them, knocking them to the ground. Matthew, walking stick still in hand, raps on the hand of one reaching for his gun. Then he uppercuts him with the stick.

I have to admire the efficiency.

I sweep the legs of the last soldier, who was aiming his gun at Matthew.

Only now do I grab Alyson, trying to keep my bloody nose from dripping onto her hair. She's crying.

We should have left her. What were we thinking? She had a life. Friends.

No. What life? Forced to work all day for meager pay, sleeping in alleyways, never belonging anywhere?

Doesn't matter. We're on the run for our lives. I can debate the ethics of bringing her with us later.

I'm certain I've never run faster. Hearing Matthew gasp for air beside me, I'm sure he hasn't either.

This is all going horribly wrong.

But, ahead of me, I see where Sector 5 changes to Sector 7.

Can we actually do this?

If Jasmine told them our plan, then they know where we're headed.

Gun shots sound, and bullets whiz around us.

"Ow!" Matthew shouts, yanking his hand in close to his body.

I change directions, going right, past a house. We should not be on the same street as soldiers with orders to shoot to kill.

We serve around houses, changing which street we're on. If we can just get out of sight of the soldiers.

"How close are we?" Matthew manages to ask between huffs of air.

"Not close enough," I mutter.

We're entering a residence section. I can see Sector 7 ahead. To my right, not too far away, I can see the city wall.

Another shot sounds, and again I change directions, leading us around a house, then another one.

People shriek and move as we run by.

The soldiers are probably spreading out. We're going to run into another one soon.

But Matthew's ready. As one rounds the corner towards us, Matthew lashes out with his stolen walking stick. The soldier takes the hit to his face and goes down. Matthew bends down and takes a precious moment to steal the soldier's gun, hitting him with the butt of it when he tries to rise again.

"Matthew…" I take a breath. "I may have misjudged you."

"Effects of a broken heart," he mutters harshly.

I want to say something comforting, but I don't have the breath. I shift Alyson over so she's mostly in my right arm. With my left, I tug Matthew over to follow me. I go around another house. This one has a side door. After a quick scan to make sure we're not in sight of any soldiers, we enter.

Matthew collapses to the ground. I follow, but more gracefully, opening my arms and letting Alyson down gently. She doesn't want to go. She buries her face in my shoulder. I pat her back. But what comfort is that?

"Your face is bleeding," Matthew pants.

"Broken nose," I answer. "Your hand?"

"Bullet nicked me. It's fine."

I lean my head forward. The blood flows down. I rip off a section of my shirt and hold it to my nose. It shouldn't bleed for too much longer. I hope. I've never broken a nose before.

We sit for a few minutes, gathering our breath in gasps.

"What are we doing in here?" Matthew asks once he's recovered his breath.

"There was no way we could outrun them to the hospital," I say. "We'll recover our breath. Try again. They expected us to keep running. We've got time before they think to double-back and start checking houses."

"But they'll be waiting for us at the hospital."

I hate to point it out, but I say, "I think they already were."

Matthew groans and puts his face in his hands. "I'm sorry."

"Kyra will be fine," I say, but I can hear my uncertainty. She'd better be fine. Or I am going to take a lot of soldiers down. "Okay, I hate to be that person, but we need to move again."

I get Alyson back into my arms and stand up. Matthew doesn't move. I nudge him with my foot.

"You can rest when we're outside the city," I say. "Or feel sorry for yourself or whatever. We can't wait much longer."

Matthew brings his hands away from his face. "I don't know what to do," he says. "What does outside the city hold for me anymore?"

"What are you talking about? The same things it always has. Freedom. Life."

He stares off into the distance. "Isolation. No one to share a future with."

My heart goes out to him. Truly. I can't imagine my feelings if Kyra had turned on me like that, and we barely have history compared to Jasmine and Matthew.

"I'm sorry," I say. "And I wish I could give you the time you need to wrap your head around it. But we could *die*. I have to keep moving. You can come with me or not. But you've beaten up several soldiers. I don't think there's any chance now they'll give you a fair trial."

He doesn't say anything.

"Matthew, please, come on!"

I don't want Kyra to lose another friend, one she's so much closer to.

"I don't know," he mumbles.

The weight of Alyson grows heavier in my arms. I'm getting tired. And I have a responsibility to her. To get her out. To give her a better life. To make up for everything.

"I'm sorry. I have to go."

I open the door. No one. I poke my head out and scan the surroundings I can see. No one. I glance back inside.

He's still sitting. Completely still.

"Dang it, Matthew," I mutter.

Holding Alyson closer to me, I step out, letting the door close. Time to get out of this city.

CHAPTER FORTY-FOUR

Kyra

The rest of the walk to the hospital is fairly easy. I only have to swerve a few times to avoid soldiers. I also steal someone's hat off their porch. Not sure how much that helps me be incognito, but it makes me feel a bit better.

The pain of my bullet wound has changed. The sharpness, the drama of the pain has worn away. It's almost worse now. A constant, dull pain that thuds with every step and refuses to dissipate. Maybe I should get them to remove it at the hospital before I make my escape.

A laughable idea. But it would be nice. Outside the city, my options will be limited and primitive. Infection is likely to set in whatever I do. Maybe my tissue can repair around the bullet and I can leave it in. I get the distinct feeling there is no 'right' option anymore. Just a slight possibility of less pain.

I hope Jun, Matthew, and Alyson are alright. My worry for them hurts my heart almost as much as the bullet hurts my stomach.

When I reach the hospital, I'm surprised. How did I so easily make this walk? Why aren't there soldiers waiting outside the hospital.

Ah. It's a trap. Of course.

They might be waiting inside the entrance for me.

I've used servants' entrances before to my advantage. I'm sure the hospital has a side entrance for staff, or deliveries, or whatever.

I make my way to the closest side of the hospital, searching for an entrance. I find one, but realize it needs ID. It must be a staff entrance. That's frustrating. I wait a bit, looking to see if anyone is coming in. But what work shift starts at this time of day?

After a few minutes, I grow impatient. Maybe the building has another entrance on the other side. One that doesn't require ID.

I move away from the hospital, giving it a wide berth as I make my way around to the other side.

There is an entrance. It's not a door, per say. It's a big doorway, big enough for a truck to fit through. It doesn't have a door. It has plastic. But strong plastic, that hangs down from the top, not quite making it to the ground. Interesting.

I walk through.

No one's here. I go up the steps and through the door leading into the hospital.

A guard is waiting on the other side. My body reacts, flinching backwards. Then I realize it's a regular hospital security guard. I don't know if that's any better.

Before he has a chance to focus on studying my face, I gasp and press my hand to my bullet wound. "I need help," I say. It's not hard to sound strained and in pain. "I got shot." I lift my shirt just enough to reveal the bloody bandages.

His eyes widen. "I can't leave my post," he says, "But you should go to the emergency section." He gives me directions.

"Thank you," I murmur, heading down the hallway.

No soldiers yet. That's suspicious. Why weren't there a few waiting at that entrance? They had time to get here.

My stomach is in a lot of pain. Should I risk— no, I can't. That might be exactly what they expect. They know I was shot.

I see a supply closet and duck inside. I can't see a doctor, but I can treat myself. I don't know if I can afford the time, but I definitely can't afford passing out in the middle of the hospital, so I must take the time.

First, I scan the shelves for any pain medication. I find only basic pill bottles. Used for headaches. Oh well, if it's all they have. I read the label and the dosage, then determine it's safe to take 3. Hopefully, that helps lessen the pain at least.

Then I grab new supplies.

Can I risk…?

If not now, then when? I reason. A calculated risk.

I grab some forceps, tweezers, and a scalpel. This is going to get messy.

I remove the bandages and throw them in the trash. My blood isn't flowing as fast anymore. But it's about to be.

Clumsily, wincing in pain, I use the forceps, tweezers, and, when necessary, the scalpel to pry the bullet out of my stomach. It's a messy, painful process, and when the bullet is removed, blood begins to spurt from the wound.

I hold gauze to the area, changing frequently, trying to breathe steadily.

It took so long to get the bullet out, I only allow myself a few minutes to try to staunch the flow. Then I tape and bandage lots more gauze over the wound.

Thank goodness I bought these work pants! They have so many pockets that I stuff with more gauze, bandages, and even a bottle of the pain killers. They may not be strong, but they're all I have. I hope the three I took kick in soon. If I'll even notice now that I've upped the pain.

I wipe my forehead. I'm sweating.

This is not an ideal state to be in. But I'm so close. I just have to make it out of the hospital.

I walk out of the supply closet with purpose, not looking around to see if anyone sees me exiting somewhere I'm not supposed to be. They don't know that. Many times, if you don't look guilty, people won't think you are.

The tricky part will be finding where the exit is. It has to be by the wall, obviously, but it's hard to keep track of direction when you're inside. I think I'm heading East. And it should be on the first floor. Possibly down a flight of stairs.

A nurse stops me. "Hun, you look lost," she says. "Where're you supposed to be?"

Her manner is kind and sympathetic.

"My brother was supposed to have gotten dropped off here," I lie. "From the farmland. He hurt himself with some machinery today and I was told they were taking him here."

"That's not my department," she says. "But I can tell you where they would have brought him first. Maybe someone there knows where he ended up."

"Oh, thank you!"

She gives me directions.

Hardly believing my luck, I hurry on. Did I just receive directions to the exit/entrance? I know more security guards will be there, but, this is going well so far.

I'm suddenly yanked harshly out of the hallway and into a dark room. I'm held tightly, a hand over my mouth.

This is not going well anymore.

"Where are the others?" a voice growls.

I begin to shake, and hate it. But I've lost a lot of blood and my body can't handle me being this scared. I try to take deep breaths, but it's hard around whoever's gross, sweaty hand this is.

"How is she supposed to tell you?" another voice asks.

The hand gets removed from my mouth, but it hovers close by.

"I don't know," I say.

"Liar."

Someone kicks my legs. They buckle, but I'm held up by the soldiers.

"We split up," I say. "From the beginning. I haven't seen them since this morning."

"That tracks with what the girl told us," another voice mutters.

Jasmine. That jerk. How could she turn on us like that? On *Matthew*. He's going to be heart-broken.

"They have to come through sometime," a soldier says. From the gravity and authority in his voice, I assume he's the leader. "And you, my dear, will help us make sure they don't fight back."

I know I can't get free from this. Part of me wants to try and fight anyways. But part of me is so relieved not to be holding myself up anymore. I want to sleep. This is too much.

Can't we just be free?

"Tie her up," the leader barks. "Keep in contact with everybody. We need to know as soon as the boys arrive."

Please don't come, I think. *Somehow, please, know not to come.*

My senses are dimming. Someone's tying my hands together. But the pain rises to greet me and everything falls to the side. I don't faint, but I wish I do. It would be a break from the pain.

CHAPTER FORTY-FIVE

Jun

We reach the hospital with fairly little drama. I walk casually, but keep my eyes peeled for any sign of soldiers. Alyson recovers a bit, and she lifts her head up.

When the hospital is in sight, I pull to the side, observing. No soldiers at the entrance. Or anywhere in sight. Which probably means it's a trap. To lure us in.

But what choice do I have?

Taking a deep breath, I head in, expecting, at any moment, soldiers to swarm around us. Once we're past the entrance, I set Alyson down.

"Listen, I don't know what's going to happen in here," I say. "So if you see soldiers, run and hide. Whatever happens, make sure you get out safely. You can still have a good life in the city, they won't come for you. Okay?"

Her eyes are big and sad, but she nods. "I don't wanna," she mumbles.

"What? You don't want to what?" I ask gently. I know this is a lot for someone so young. It's a lot for me, too.

"I wanna go with you and Kyra." Her bottom lip is trembling.

I give her a hug. "I know. I want that too. This is just a worst-case scenario. Hopefully it doesn't happen." I pull away. "Ready?"

She nods.

"Okay." I take her hand in mine and stand up. "Let's do this."

I stop a friendly-looking nurse and ask for directions to the station they bring people in from the farmland. I say that Alyson's dad was brought in earlier today and we're trying to find him. This wasn't the plan, but if there are soldiers still chasing us, I'm not about to go wandering around aimlessly, trying to find the exit.

The nurse gives me the directions, then casts a glance at Alyson. "Is she okay?" she asks.

"She's worried about her father," I say. "We're hoping he's alright."

"I hope so too."

I thank her, then we move on.

I expected more people to be in these hallways, but we only pass a few nurses and one random citizen. Hopefully that's normal. The rooms themselves are bustling with activity. Full waiting rooms, people lying in beds.

To my left, I notice a soldier emerging from a waiting room. My heart rate spikes as I react on instinct. Dropping Alyson's hand, I punch his stomach. The gun he had been grabbing clatters to the floor. As he doubles over, I put my hands on the back of his head and bring my knee to greet his face. Fast, effective. He goes down.

"Come on, we have to move!" I tell Alyson.

We hurry on.

More soldiers emerge.

My heart sinks. Of course. If they knew where we were going, they could lie in wait for us. "Hide, Alyson," I say as I rush to greet the soldiers.

They can't afford to fire in such a small space. The risk of hitting a patient or doctor is too high. People are screaming and moving into rooms farther in, out of sight of the hallway. I've stopped thinking. Throwing punches, dodging and receiving them is all that fills my mind. I knock down many soldiers. One hits my face, my broken nose, and lights dance in my vision. I kick him away, but take a hit to the back.

I keep moving, trying to get forward, to knock the soldiers down as fast as possible. I don't know where Alyson is, if she's still here or if she's gone to hide. Once again, I have that guilty feeling that we shouldn't have brought her.

Then I hear it.

"Jun."

My name. Not shouted, just spoken. My heart sinks and I whirl around. Down the hallway, where I've been trying to reach, stands Kyra. Two soldiers are at her side, one of them holding a gun against her head.

Everything in me freezes, recognizing the threat loud and clear.

That was all they needed. Soldiers pile on top of me, bringing me to the ground. I don't fight back. They take the opportunity to throw many extra punches.

They drag me over to Kyra and the soldiers.

"Where are the others?" one asks. I think he's the general.

So Alyson did run.

"The girl was here, sir," a soldier to my right says. "But she ran off."

The general rolls his eyes. "Then find her."

Two soldiers leave.

"Why?" I ask. "She's just a kid. She doesn't have any part in this."

The general glares at me. "She wouldn't, if you hadn't brought her along. But you did. And we have discovered that she has no computer. That cannot be allowed to exist. She must also be eliminated."

I try to lunge at him, but I'm held back. "What does that matter, she's a *kid*!"

"Where's Matthew?" the general asks. "And don't lie."

I glance over at Kyra. She's avoiding my eyes. She's also been hurt! Her abdomen is stained with blood.

The general hits my face. "I asked you a question."

I suck in breath through my teeth and gather my thoughts to give an answer. "Matthew was… greatly hurt by Jasmine. We went into a house to rest. He wouldn't leave with me. Her betrayal shocked him too much."

"So you left him."

"I had bigger priorities."

The general chuckles and stands. "Indeed. And how easy to exploit those. Get him tied up."

Rope is produced from somewhere and used to tie my hands behind my back, like Kyra's are. Then my ankles are tied together. Not enough that I can't walk, but enough that I couldn't take long enough strides to run.

"Gentlemen, take these criminals outside the city and shot them. Let's not disturb these good people at the hospital any further."

We're dragged off.

How ironic. They're delivering us to the place we wanted to get to. We're just bound and headed for certain death. I can't break through ropes. The best I can hope for now is that Alyson gets away and can go back to her normal life.

All that. We went through all that to die anyways. It's not fair.

"Are you okay?" I ask Kyra.

"I've been better," she answers.

Someone hits the side of my head. "No talking," he snaps.

But we're about to die.

"I'm sorry," Kyra whispers. "This is all my fault."

She gets hit, too.

I think about what she's said. She right, technically. If she hadn't changed the chemistry in my brain, I never would have gotten the job. My family wouldn't have died.

I wouldn't be free.

I wouldn't have met her.

Is that worth losing them? And now, my life?

I don't know.

The further we get into the hospital, the more I resign myself. No more anxiety, no more fear. This is it. I'm numb.

CHAPTER FORTY-SIX

Kyra

How can this be it?

All of that, for nothing!

Jun hasn't responded to my apology. Maybe he doesn't want to risk being hit again. Maybe he has nothing to say. It *is* my fault. That's not self-pity, that's just what happened.

Death is a necessary step. Does it have to come now? We were both finally going to experience what it really means to be free.

The corners of my lips quirk up, despite the situation. Living free might have eventually been the death of us, anyways. None of us has any experience farming. Alyson has the most, and it's almost entirely picking fruit. No experience hunting. A bear could have taken us all in our sleep the first night.

But now we'll never have a chance to find out.

We reach a door that opens into a massive, empty, concrete space. At least, what the hallway lights illuminate appears completely empty. I hear Jun's breath quicken. This is it.

We have to take stairs down. With our ankles tied, it's an awkward process. At one point, I trip forward. The soldiers catch me, but by placing one of their hands right over my wound. I hiss in pain and my vision temporarily darkens.

Jun, already on the ground, shoots me a worried glance, but he still doesn't say anything.

A high pitch, mechanical whine fills the space. A section of the wall is sliding away, retracting. Daylight streams into the space, and I have to blink against the harsh rays.

"Will you close those doors?" one of the soldiers shouts, walking forward, addressing another soldier who's standing at some kind of control panel over by the opening wall. "We don't actually have to take them outside, this is—"

Whatever he was going to say next is cut off permanently by a bullet whizzing into his head. Blood spurts and he falls to the ground. I recoil.

But who shot him?

Soldiers yell, whirling around to the entrance we've just come through.

More bullets fly towards us, taking out the soldiers on the edges. I don't see who's shooting them. He stays behind the door, coming out only briefly. Only taking enough time to fire.

He could accidentally hit us!

Jun has already moved into action. He's got his hands around the neck of a soldier, strangling him with the rope. He kicks away another one.

A soldier right next to me goes down, shot in the chest. I shriek, and shuffle away. I'm glad we're being rescued, but this idiot might hit me, too!

The door starts sliding shut again, the light growing dim. No!

Next thing I know, Jun's beside me, cutting my hands free with a knife.

"Free your legs," he orders, giving me the knife. Then he leaps onto a nearby soldier.

I drop to the ground and saw at the ropes. In my haste, I accidentally slice my ankle. But that pain is nothing. The taste of freedom is once again in my mouth, and nothing will diminish the flavour.

I cut through the ropes. Someone yanks me to my feet, their fingers digging into my arms. Jun appears at my side, knocking them off me.

I run towards the control panel. The soldier has abandoned it. But as I go, the door slides shut. The area goes dark again. The only light streams in from the hallway. It provides enough light for me to see where the wall is, where the control panel sits on it.

Hopefully the guy on our side isn't silly enough to fire into a dark room where he might accidentally hit the people he's trying to help. I hear sounds of fighting behind me, though. I hope Jun is winning.

I reach the control panel and squint. Why are there five buttons? All that's needed is the door opening. They have writing on them, but in this lighting, I can't make it out. I have to pick and hope for the best.

The biggest button makes sense; biggest button for the primary function. I hit it. Immediately, an alarm blares, reverberating and echoing. It fills my ears and rattles around in my brain.

Wrong button.

I hope that doesn't completely shut down the door. I press the big button again. The alarm doesn't stop. Great. Heart pounding, I hit the second biggest button. To my relief, the door opens.

I turn around. In the light that begins to stream in, I can see the soldiers, all on the ground. Unconscious or worse. I can't help but feel some twinge of guilt about that. They were just men following orders.

But then I'm distracted by Jun running towards me. Two people run beside him. Matthew and Alyson! Relief floods through me even as my mouth drops.

"You were the shooter?" I ask Matthew, shouting to be heard over the alarm.

He gives a modest shrug.

"Let's go, let's go!" Jun encourages. "Too much open field we need to cover."

"Alyson can't keep up!" I shout.

But Jun scoops her up like she weighs nothing. His pace barely changes. Wow. I am going to make sure she gets so much food. Once we figure out how to grow it.

Everything hurts. I want to stop. We're so close! With each step, the woods in the distance grow closer. There we can build a life.

Each of us pours the last of our energy into running.

After five minutes, the woods seems as far away as it was before. I don't know how much longer I can run. My lungs feel like they're going to expand past the limits of my body.

We have to reach the woods.

But I know that's not it. Once we reach the woods then we have to evade whoever they send in after us. Then we have to figure out how to survive in an environment none of us are familiar with. Then we have to keep doing it, every day.

Far behind us, I hear shouting. Then a sound much more concerning. I risk a glance over my shoulder. Vehicles. Vehicles that can reach in a minute what's taken us many.

"We have to move!" I exclaim.

"Almost there," Jun says, his voice somehow steady and calming.

We're at the edge of the woods. Then we're running into it. Branches reach out for me, to hold me back, help our pursuers. They nick my face, but I ignore them.

"Hold on, we lost Jun," Matthew says.

I stumble to a stop. Without meaning to, I sink down to the ground, my chest heaving in air. My legs are shaking, but relived for the rest, however brief it might be.

"Where'd he go?" I ask, looking around. "Wait, is he hurt? Did something happen?"

Then he's there, walking up to us, Alyson now walking beside him. She's grinning. What has she endured today?

"Why'd you stop?" I ask, then wince at how accusatory my voice sounds. "I was worried," I add, hoping that explains and softens it.

"Sorry," he says. "I wanted to observe what they're doing. They're coming at us with a lot of firepower and men. But, their vehicles won't be able to get in here, so that's good. And the woods are so thick, they'll have a hard time shooting at us. But they will get here soon. They're all piled on trucks. We can't stop yet."

I huff.

"You don't have your gun anymore," Jun notes.

Matthew shakes his head. "It was out. No point."

Jun nods.

Blood trickles slowly down one of Matthew's fingers. When he sees me eyeing his hand, he says, "Bullet nicked me. But it's fine."

I frown.

"If you have supplies to help, you can get them out later," Jun says. "I'm sorry, but we have to keep moving."

"No, no, I get it. I'm all for living." I am not confident in the strength of my legs anymore, though.

Jun holds out his hands and I take them gratefully. He hauls me easily to my feet, leaving me feeling like I barely contributed.

We keep moving. We don't say anything, but we all keep a steady pace of a brisk walk. Running makes a lot of noise. But we can't keep this pace for long. Or outrun those soldiers even if we sped up. They're fresh, trained, and under orders. So we have to find a place to hide.

The woods begin to fill with the sounds of harsh, shouted orders. Men communicating as they spread out to cover the most distance. I want to shout at them to go away, but that would reveal our location, so I don't.

"Should we split up?" Matthew suggests tentatively.

Jun, still at my side, says immediately, "No. We protect each other."

"These trees have thick leaves," I observe. "Maybe we could climb them and hide."

"None of us have ever climbed a tree," Jun counters. "I don't think now is the time to try."

"Why not? Death can be an excellent motivator," Matthew jokes, but it's lackluster.

"I've climbed trees," Alyson pipes up.

I grin down at her and ruffle her hair. "Yeah, but that still leaves the rest of us. We'll have to find another place to hide."

"In the meantime, we should probably speed up," Jun says.

"I'm going to sleep for a day after this," Matthew mutters.

But we all increase our pace as the sounds of our pursuers grows louder and more threatening behind us.

CHAPTER FORTY-SEVEN

Jun

Just as I begin to truly worry we won't find a place to hide, I see the trees thinning ahead. We burst into a clearing. My heart breaths a sigh of relief. The perfect clearing.

A bright blue, shallow-looking pool takes up most of the space. It's fed by a small waterfall, a bit taller than me, which flows down from a rocky hill. I race over to the edge of the pool, looking. There's a cave behind the waterfall! Cave might be a generous word, but it's a place to hide. And, unless they look closely, we'll be hidden by the falling spray of water.

"There's a cave." I point.

The others have joined me, but the soldiers aren't far behind.

Kyra doesn't hesitate. She walks in, the water reaching her waist.

Alyson tugs at my shirt. "I don't know how to swim," she whispers.

Me neither, but if it only goes that high on Kyra, then I don't have to know. I crouch down. "I'll give you a ride," I say.

She giggles. Matthew helps her climb onto my back. She wraps her arms around my neck and her legs sort-of-around my waist. I put one of my hands back, helping to hold her. Then I go in too.

Kyra has already made it to the waterfall. She observes the water underneath, then proceeds carefully past it, holding onto a rock to steady herself. Then she slips, going under and past the waterfall.

My heart jolts, but I keep from calling out. The water's not deep, the waterfall isn't strong, she won't drown. But I don't feel calm until I reach the waterfall too and see her behind it.

"It's slippery," she cautions. She holds out her hand.

I grab it and walk slowly. Then we're behind the waterfall, the sound echoing in ripples off the inside of the cave. Matthew enters behind me.

"Is there anywhere for Alyson to sit or something?" I ask, gazing around.

Kyra finds a jutting out of a rock from the cave walls that isn't too slippery. Carefully, I make my way over to it and turn around. Kyra helps guide Alyson down onto the rock. It works really well as a seat.

"I would love for this to be it," Matthew says quietly. A good precaution. We don't know how our voice will echo. "But what if someone notices the cave? We're not exactly in a good position to defend ourselves."

Kyra frowns. "He's not often the voice of reason, but he's right."

"I'll get us a gun," I say.

Kyra protests, but I manage to convince her that it's the safest way. "And I need to go now," I add. "If a soldier sees me wading through the water, I'm dead."

She concedes and lets me go.

I make my way back through the waterfall and wade out of the pool as quickly as I can. There's no way to know what direction a soldier will come from, especially if they've spread out. I have to hide.

I glance at the trees. No, I've never climbed one. But it should be fairly intuitive. Rushing to the nearest tree, I grab the lowest branch and heave myself up. I climb higher up, then wait.

As I wait, I think back to what Matthew said. It's not just if anyone notices that there's a cave there. It's *when* they notice that we've disappeared from the woods. They'll realize we've hidden and circle back. They'll find us.

My mind goes back to hiding underneath the porch in Sector 6. It was the same logic. How long ago was that? It feels like ages, and yet, yesterday. It doesn't help that my memories are a little muddled from all the brain-messing.

I know what has to be done. To ensure everyone's safety.

Branches break and my head snaps up. Someone's running towards me. I press myself close to the tree trunk and wait. As he runs by me, I lower myself down to the ground.

"Hey," I say.

The soldier whirls around, my fist greeting his face. A solid punch, and he goes down. He has two guns on his belt, so I grab both, and a pouch of extra bullets.

Quickly, I return to the cave, careful to keep the guns out of the water. I hand one to Kyra and one to Matthew.

"Stay safe," I say, then turn around.

"Woah, what are you going?" Kyra asks.

I wince. "I'm going to lead them away."

Kyra grabs my hand. "I thought we weren't splitting up! To protect each other."

I face her again. Her eyes are huge. I squeeze her hand. "This is how I'm protecting you," I say. "I knocked a soldier down out there. He's gonna wake up at any moment, and I don't want him hanging around. I'll lead them all away. Leaving you safe. Under the porch."

She understands the logic. I know she does. Letting go of my hand, she swallows. "Just, be careful," she says quietly.

I pull her close, kissing her forehead. "I will. And I'll be back."

"I'm coming with you," Matthew says.

"No," Kyra says harshly.

"You should be here—"

But he cuts me off. "If we both go, then we can split up, drawing them even further away."

He has a good point. And I can tell by the way his jaw is set that arguing won't do me any good. He's small and silly, but he has a strong backbone.

"Then let's go," I say. I wave to Alyson, then leave.

Matthew says a few things to Kyra, then follows.

We reach the shore.

"Let's get to the other side of the woods," I say. "When he wakes up" —I gesture to the soldier— "I don't want him close enough to see that our pants are soaking wet."

Matthew grimaces. "These are not going to be pleasant to run in."

We make our way around the pool, to the edge of the woods. He's kept the gun I gave him. Good idea. Kyra can only shoot one gun at a time anyways.

Slowly, the soldier wakes up. He shakes his head and sits up. Immediately, he scans his surroundings. He notices us, lounging against some trees. He pops up, shouts at us, and reaches for his guns.

"That's our cue," I say.

"More running," Matthew grumbles, pushing himself off the tree.

The soldier chases after us, shouting for everyone to join him.

"How are we gonna find our way back?" Matthew asks me.

"Not the main concern," I say. "Let's focus on surviving this first."

"Fair."

We run wildly, for our lives. Men crash through the woods near us. Matthew takes down several with his gun.

"How do you know how to shot like that?" I ask, my words coming in spurts as I have to breath in between.

"Shooting ranges for fun," he manages to get out.

We're shot at many times, but they all miss. The woods are thick, and we use that to our full advantage, changing directions, dodging around bushes and trees.

We're getting farther away from Kyra and Alyson. I hope we've been successful in leading everyone away from them. If Kyra has to use the gun, the shot is going to be a beacon to their location if anyone's close enough still to hear it.

"Imagine we're heading back to the city," Matthew jokes.

I glace upwards briefly. "We're not. The sun's setting and we're heading away from it."

"Great." I can tell Matthew doesn't fully understand what I've said, but he's been reassured we're not running straight back to the city.

We veer left, continuing our goal in getting as far away from the girls as possible. Soldiers are still on our path. Why are they so dedicated to three, sort of four, criminals who have left the city with no intention of returning? Can't they let us go and hope we die trying to survive in the woods?

Time blurs together. We make sure we don't lose too many soldiers. Matthew and I have split up and rejoined many times. Matthew's run out of bullets, but he hit someone with almost every shot. How many more can there be left?

"Stop, stop, we have to stop," Matthew pants.

We stumble to a stop. The woods are filled with sounds of us panting, regaining our breath.

I survey the area. I don't see anyone. Did we lose them all? Did they give up?

Are Kyra and Alyson safe?

We should probably head back. Night will fall soon, and we do not want to be defenseless and out in the open when that happens. I communicate this to Matthew, who only has the strength to nod.

"Keep your eyes open," I caution as we head back. "There could still be more of them."

After many, many minutes of walking, we haven't encountered anyone. Maybe they got called off, wanting to return to the city before night.

Then someone steps out from behind a tree, blocking our path, gun pointed directly at us. We freeze. Matthew makes some kind of strangled, choking sound. The man is too far away for me to get to before he could shoot us, but too close to try running away. His eyes are murderous.

"What are you doing here?" Matthew asks.

That's an… odd question.

The man's eyes narrow. "Me? I'm doing my job. What are *you* doing here? You had a great life, why would you throw it all away by helping her?"

Matthew scoffs. "Like you care."

There's a really weird dynamic going on here.

"I don't," he spits. "Just wondering what I should tell Mother."

Matthew has a sharp intake of breath. That hurt, as intended. Also, I realize what the weird dynamic is. They're brothers. They don't sound like they had a loving relationship before this, though.

"Tell her I did the right thing," Matthew answers. "And now I'm paying the price."

The man's face was full of hate and barely restrained anger. But it suddenly changes, going cold, blank, impersonal. That's much scarier.

He starts slowly stepping forward. I don't know what to do. He could shoot at any moment.

Then he casually drops the gun to his side. Once he gets close enough, I can jump him. But I find I'm frozen. This seems personal. Like I should wait for Matthew to decide. That also seems like a bad idea.

They're inches apart now. Matthew is rooted to the spot, unflinching. He's trying to put on a brave face.

"How do you intend to survive out here?" Matthew's brother asks. "You have no weapons, no survival tools, no food. No time to make or find decent shelter."

I'm momentarily distracted. Right. That cave is not going to be shelter for the night. In fact, Alyson and Kyra are going to need to get warm and dry. They don't have extra clothes. We'll have to make a fire.

I'm pulled back to the present by Matthew saying, "Doesn't matter. Poor survival out here is better than abundance back there."

A grin stretches across his brother's face. It's cruel and calculating.

I ready myself. He's almost distracted enough for me to jump on him and certainly close enough. I wish Matthew would do something.

"You're going to find out how wrong you are," his brother says.

Wait, is he letting us go?

Then he pulls the trigger on his gun, the sound loud and booming at such close range. Matthew chokes on his own scream, producing almost no sound. I don't think, I just attack, leaping at his brother.

We go down, hard. I throw the gun away. Then I wish I hadn't. I could have used that.

He punches my face. So I return the favour.

"Don't kill him," Matthew wheezes.

How kind. So instead, I punch his face a few more times until he's properly unconscious. I check his pulse, and it's steady.

"He's alive," I say. "For now. He'll wake up in a dark wood. With no flashlight." I grab it out of his belt. "Since we have it."

Matthew makes no reply. The severity of the situation flashes into my mind with a jolt. I make my way over to where Matthew has fallen to the ground.

"Where?" I ask. But it's a needless question. Matthew's clutching his knee, dark with blood.

It was going to be hard enough for us to survive anyways. But his brother has made it way worse. He drew up the death warrant and left it to be signed by time.

I take my shirt off and wrap it tightly around Matthew's knee. He hisses in pain.

"No, Jun, don't," he says. "Just leave me."

I scoff. "Yeah, like I'm gonna do that."

"I'm serious. I can't walk."

"That's fine." I tie my shirt tight and Matthew makes more noises of pain. "I can carry you."

He's so small and light. I pick him up in my arms. This isn't going to be painless. I take a deep breath, then start walking. It's still a ways back to the cave. My arms are trembling after only a minute. I'm exhausted, but that doesn't matter. I'm not leaving him. He's the reason Kyra was able to get into the building to break my connection. He's the reason we're both alive.

He's shaking, too. "Leave me," he says quietly. "It's not worth it."

"Yes, you are."

He doesn't reply. I glance down. He's passed out.

I hope this isn't for nothing. The sun is setting. It's almost night. We have to make it back to the girls, bandage him better, and find adequate shelter. I hope Kyra has something in those many-pocketed pants of hers.

"Hang on, Matthew," I mutter. "Hang on."

CHAPTER FORTY-EIGHT

Kyra

No one has found our hiding place. But my hand doesn't stop trembling, holding the gun up, ready for the possibility that, at any moment, one of them might. I don't trust that I'll hear them get in the water. They've been trained, they know how to be quiet. So I stay still, alert, occasionally reminding Alyson that she has to be quiet. This must be boring to her.

It feels like hours later when I finally allow myself to relax. The light is changing, the sun bidding the day farewell. My body is sore from holding itself in tension for so long.

But then, as soon as I stop, I start shivering. Alyson is shivering, too. We have to get out of the water.

Alyson can't swim.

Should I wait for Jun? I don't know if I can hold her and carry the gun. If it gets wet, it's useless. If someone's waiting out there for us, we'll need it.

"Alyson, I'm going to pop out and look around," I tell her. "Make sure no one's out there. Then I'll come back in for you."

She nods. Her arms are hugging herself.

I hurry out, poking my head around the waterfall. Scanning the clearing, I see no one. I risk walking out a little further to check the rocky hill from where the water flows. No one is waiting for us there, either.

I go back in. I put the gun on a rock, then carefully back up to Alyson. I caution her to go slow, and she climbs onto my back. She's not heavy, but right now, in this slippery situation, it's too much. I decide to come back for the gun. It's safe.

"I can't help you stay on, so cling to me, okay?"

"Okay." Her teeth are chattering.

Slowly, slowly, I walk out, testing my footing everywhere I place my foot, making sure it's not too slippery. I grip the walls for what little support they offer. We make it past the waterfall, and the worst is over.

The water is cold. We'll need a fire. How do you start a fire? Especially with nothing to help.

We make it to the edge of the pool.

How does Alyson get down?

I bend my knees, doing an odd squat. Then I sort of fall to the ground, but gently and almost-controlled. Alyson slips off.

"Stay right here," I tell her. "I'm going back to grab the gun."

She nods, jumping around a bit. Good idea. Get the blood flowing.

I don't like the idea of leaving her out here by herself, exposed, so I rush. That was a mistake. I once again slip and dunk myself at the waterfall. Spluttering, I emerge. This makes the shivering five times worse. I grab the gun and make my way back out more diligently.

Alyson's fine. She's jumping and running about. Chasing a butterfly or something, probably.

"Oh no," I mutter to myself as I reach the shore. That's done, but now there are more decisions to be made. I don't know when or if Jun and Matthew will be back. It's almost night. We need shelter. And a fire. Not that I have any idea how to make one. If we leave this place, how will Jun and Matthew find us?

Alyson runs to me and tugs my hands. "Skip with me!" she exclaims.

I want to tell her no. This is a serious situation we're in and I have to figure it out. But my teeth are clattering and the sound is jarring. I'll warm up, then make decisions.

First, I set the gun on the ground. Then I remember the many first aid supplies I've tucked in my pockets that are now soaking wet. I groan. That's not helpful. As Alyson waits impatiently, I dig everything out of my pockets, laying them out, one-by-one on the ground. Hopefully they dry soon.

Then I join Alyson and we run around. Jumping, skipping, playing tags. My clothes are still wet, but I'm warming up. A good thing, because the temperature is steadily dropping.

Then, I hear a sound in the distance. I freeze and strain my ears. Is someone coming for us.

Alyson notices I've stopped moving. She pouts. "Why'd you stop?"

"Do you hear something?"

She frowns, listening too.

I make out what the sound is. My name being shouted by Jun.

Why's he shouting? What if there are still soldiers in the woods hunting us?

Something must have gone wrong.

"Alyson, can you hide up a tree?" I ask her. "I need to go check out what that is."

It could even be a trap.

She nods and scurries off. I wait until she's found a tree with a low enough branch for her and she starts climbing. Then I take off towards the sound of Jun, still calling for me. My heart pounds as I wonder what happened.

"Jun!" I shout back.

Forget the concern that it's a trap.

"Kyra!"

Then I see him through the trees. He's carrying Matthew in his arms. Why is he carrying Matthew?

"What happened?" I shout.

When I get close enough, I see the blood on Matthew's knee, soaked through Jun's shirt. Matthew's pale, trembling, and cold to the touch.

"Oh no…" My heart sinks. But I shake my personal concerns aside.

Jun's face is flushed and sweaty. Yet underneath that is a paleness. How far has he had to carry Matthew?

"The clearing isn't far," I tell him. "I have some medical supplies." Hopefully they're somewhat dry by now. "You'll have to make a fire." How can I demand more of him? But he's the only one of us who can, and it's necessary. "I'll meet you there." I head back to the clearing, going ahead of them. "It's safe, Alyson!" I call once I'm close enough.

Then I rush to the supplies. They're still damp. Damp material isn't ideal. Dry is the most effective for stopping bleeding, but we'll have to work with what we have.

Jun reaches me and gently sets Matthew on the ground.

"I'll make a fire," he mutters. I don't miss how he's shaking.

A lump rises in my throat. We're alive. The soldiers are gone. This should have been a moment of elation.

I peel the shirt away from Matthew's knee. He's unconscious. Using a damp gauze, I sponge away what blood I can. Then I have to look away and force down the rising bile in my stomach. The bullet went deep. It shattered bone. He was shot right in the kneecap. Blood continues to pour from the wound.

I wrap his knee tightly. Then wrap it again. And again. Stopping the bleeding, allowing the blood to clot, that's first priority. I don't know about getting the bullet out. It's in deep. Even getting it out, his knee will never be the same. Who did this to him?

Jun returns, throwing wood down. Alyson's with him and she also drops her offering of sticks onto his pile. I don't see what Jun does, I focus on Matthew. On rubbing his arms, trying to get the blood flowing better, to warm him up. Soon, a flame rises beside me. Jun did it! Within minutes, and a quick trip for more wood, we have a decent-sized fire.

We arrange Matthew close enough to receive the warmth, but not close enough to burn. I remember the wound on his hand, which does turn out to be a flesh wound. I gently sponge the blood off. The wound doesn't need my attention beyond that.

Then I turn my attention to Jun.

"Is this a good enough place to stay the night?" I ask.

"It'll have to be," he says. "It won't get too cold tonight, so this fire should keep us all warm enough."

Except Jun doesn't have a shirt to help with warmth. He gave it to Matthew. Now it's bloody.

"I'll wash your shirt so hopefully you can wear it tomorrow," I say, rising. "You get warm."

"Yes ma'am." He scoots closer to the fire, wrapping his arms around his knees.

I see his bandage. Now we've both been shot. I'm in so much pain, I can't believe he did all he did the day or two after being shot. That's impressive. I should check his wound today or tomorrow. I'll wait and see if he complains about it.

I go to the pond, careful not to fall in. It's dark now, night truly fallen. The fire and stars provide enough light to see enough. I dunk the shirt, squeezing and twisting it to get as much blood out as possible. I rinse it several times, then twist as much water out as I can. I find a clean, dry stone near me and lay the shirt out. It won't dry much during the night, but eventually the rising sun will warm it up.

I return to the campfire. Alyson is already asleep. Poor kid. She must be exhausted. I sit down beside Jun and rest my head on his shoulder.

"What happened?" I ask.

Jun's silent for a long time. Then, finally, he says, "His brother shot him at close range. It was my fault. I had the opportunity to stop him sooner, and I didn't."

Now it's my turn to be quiet. Could I have somehow prevented this? If Jun had known about Braxton, would that have made any difference?

"Why did he shot him there?" I ask. "Why not kill him?"

"He said we're gonna die anyways. This was to make it worse."

Jun sounds miserable.

"We won't die," I say, putting a confidence into my words that I don't feel.

Jun sighs. "No. I didn't come all this way to die. It's just going to involve a lot of hard days."

He's not wrong.

"Should one of us stay awake to keep watch?" I ask.

"Probably. I'd love to believe they've completely left us, but if they haven't, this fire will draw them to us."

"Great. I'll take first watch," I say before he can volunteer. "I'll keep an eye on Matthew, and wake you when it's your turn to watch."

He doesn't argue.

I stand and retrieve the gun. When I return, he's also fast asleep.

My whole body is sore, my stomach grumbling with hunger, and I want nothing more to sleep. But my family is sleeping, and I need to make sure nothing gets them.

So I stay awake. The whole night.

CHAPTER FORTY-NINE

Jun

When I wake up, the sun's too bright. Kyra was supposed to wake me so I could watch and she could sleep! Did something happen? I jump up, all my senses awake and alert in an instant, a strike of adrenaline going through me.

"No need to panic," Kyra says.

She's sitting on the other side of the long-dead fire, only small, charred remains of the wood left. Matthew is awake, half-sitting up, propped against a rock that must have been a struggle for Kyra to move. His face is ashen, his eyes half-open.

The mood is grim, except for Aly, wading in the pool, water only up to her ankles. She's grabbing at the water, shrieking with delight. I guess she must be trying to catch some fish? She's not going to succeed, but the task is giving her much joy.

They're not in any danger. I take deep breath, relaxing my body, and sit back down.

"Why didn't you wake me?" I ask Kyra. It occurs to me that this is actually the second time I've asked her that question. We're in a much better spot than the jail. Wow, a lot has happened since then.

Kyra shrugs. "You needed the sleep more than I did." But her eyes have dark circles underneath them. She might be regretting her generosity.

"How are you today, Matthew?" I ask.

"Not dead," he says bleakly, and I can't tell if he's happy or disappointed.

I felt refreshed from so much sleep, and the fact that my waking anxiety of danger has completely vanished. Just like that, gone.

Then my stomach starts to growl. Audibly.

Kyra's eyes darken. "That's what we were discussing. We have no way to get food. None of us know which berries are safe to eat. You?"

"Well, I know a few, but you really want to be careful with berries, so not really."

She nods, like this was expected, and continues. "What fruit we do manage to find won't sustain us. We have no way to plant new crops and no way to hunt animals except the gun. The gun has only so many rounds. We have no tools for preparing the animals or for building a shelter."

She's cheery this morning. Of course, I don't know why she *would* be. It seems a grim situation, and I don't think any of us really thought through the struggle to make a life out here. We were just focused on getting here. Plus, she hasn't eaten or slept in a full day. Matthew hasn't either, plus he's been shot, which, from experience, makes everything so much worse. So I perfectly understand why she and Matthew are so miserable, and they're entitled to it.

An idea blooms in my mind. I do know how we can improve our situation. It's a little risky. The payoff would be immeasurable. What use is our escape if we starve to death in the forest? I'm not silly enough to suggest my idea now, however. Nope. Now is the time to procure food for everyone.

I get back on my feet. "Well, I'm going to try and get some food for us. Then we can talk strategy."

I retrieve my shirt, which is surprisingly clean, and completely dry. It has a few dark-coloured spots, but that's alright. It was so kind of Kyra to wash it last night. Oh, I almost forgot Kyra *also* got shot! There's a lot of that going around. I'll check in with her later, maybe after she's eaten, and see how she's doing.

I summon Alyson out of the pond and she's happy to join me. She's also used to little food, so the hunger isn't bothering her. I'm surprised the events of yesterday aren't, though. The perks of being so young, I guess.

I grab the pouch of extra rounds and we head to where Matthew dropped the second gun. Hopefully it's still there. Hopefully his brother isn't.

It's a long walk, especially trying to remember our route. We ran erratically last night. Then we have to manage to find a small gun. That'll be fun. But I think Matthew discarded it as soon as he ran out of shots, so it shouldn't be too far. I tell Alyson to keep her eyes open for a gun or for fruit trees.

We find the fruit first. It's a few apple trees. One has incredibly sour apples that almost aren't even worth eating. But we gather a few, in case the others like them. Who knows what the government sector palate enjoys? We also grab several from the other tree, which has much nicer, sweeter apples.

Alyson finds the gun first and points it out. I grab it, then we turn around and head back towards the clearing. When we're close enough, I give her all the apples, which she gathers in her skirt, and tells her to give them to Matthew and Kyra.

I'm going off to see if I can shoot anything.

This isn't a hunting gun, and Kyra's right, we don't have anything to cut and clean an animal with, but I'll figure it out. If I even find something. We have to eat, so we'll have to make something work for now.

It's many minutes of searching before I see something through the woods. It's a four-legged creature, like a smaller, slimmer horse, except it's got big stick-things growing out of its head. I don't know what it is, but I assume it'll be edible. Plus, those stick-things might be sharp. That could be a temporary solution for cutting the meat.

That's a little grim, I can't help but think.

He stops, sniffing the air. Does he know I'm here?

I have to get this right.

And I do.

It's another matter entirely to get this big guy back to the camp. It's a lot of dragging, switching positions, and I'm a hot, sweaty mess by the time I get back.

Kyra jumps up to help me. Between the two of us, we manage to drag it over to the fire.

"I can't believe you manage to shoot down a deer," she pants.

"Is that what this is?"

She nods.

"What's growing out of his head?"

"Antlers."

I put one hand on his antlers. "Thank you for feeding us," I say.

Thus starts the great debate on how we should cook him. The process is unbelievable messy, and at one point, Kyra has to walk away, taking Alyson with her, saying, "This is too much. This can't be good for her to witness."

"You *said* we couldn't sustain ourselves on fruit!" I call after her.

She waves her hand as she and Alyson disappear into the woods.

Matthew chuckles lightly. "Don't mind her. She's always been grumpy when she gets hungry."

"You're telling me," I mutter.

I build a stove with many stones from the pond and the rocky hill. I build a fire underneath. Then I cook.

"This is going to take a while," I tell Matthew, settling beside him.

"It's more than we were hoping for," he says.

We sit in silence, enjoying the crackling of the fire and the promise of a full meal soon. Eventually. Hopefully. I've never had this much meat before, especially so fresh. I guess it can't get any fresher than this.

"Thank you for saving me," Matthew says after a while, "even though it was the more tactical decision to leave me."

"How could I leave you?" I say. "You're part of the family now."

"I'm not sure if I'm happy to be here," Matthew admits. "Part of me wishes I was back in the government sector, things unchanged."

"I don't blame you," I say.

Matthew sighs in relief at my understanding.

"We'll make ourselves good lives out here," I promise. "It'll just take time."

Kyra and Alyson are gone a concerning amount of time, but I can't go search for them and leave Matthew to fend for himself. Eventually, they return.

"Don't ask," Kyra grumbles, flinging herself to the ground away from us.

I raise my eyebrows and look at Aly.

"We got lost," she informs me.

"Did you now?" I chuckle, giving her a side-hug. "That's alright, you're back now."

Soon, we're ready to eat. It's nothing fancy, but there's more than enough for everyone. Fresh meat is a taste Alyson and I are not accustomed to. She wrinkles her nose.

"Hmm…"

"Keep eating," I encourage. "I promise we'll find a way to grow fruits and veggies. But for now, you need the energy."

She keeps eating, but it's clear she doesn't think highly of this yet. I love it. I've never had this *much* food, either. What a novelty. What a luxury.

Kyra asks about my nose.

"What about my nose?" I ask, reaching up to touch it. "Ow." I'm surprised when it's sensitive. Then I remember. "Oh yeah, a guy broke my nose!"

"Ouch. Did you reset it?"

Full of sympathy, as always.

"Reset it? No, what do you mean?"

"He broke it, therefore it's no longer in the proper position. I can reset it."

She finishes her food and scooches over to me.

I lean away. "Is this gonna be painful?"

Matthew laughs, mouth full of food.

"I'm moving your nose back into the proper position from an improper, broken position. Yes, it will hurt."

"Charming bedside manner," I mutter.

She swats my shoulder and I can't help the grin that springs to my face.

"Hold still," she instructs.

I have to hold back a bigger smile from how close she gets to my face. But she's completely focused on inspecting my nose. She has the most beautiful eyes.

"Ow!" I exclaim, jerking away.

Without warning, she reset my nose, jerking it back into place.

"Done," she says, moving back to her spot.

After a minute, when the sudden surprise of pain resides, I say, "Thanks."

After we've all eaten our fill, I dare to propose my idea to Kyra.

Matthew is asleep, and Alyson is once again fishing in the pond. I get up and move over to where Kyra is sitting.

"I'm sorry I was ill-tempered," she says.

"No worries," I say, brushing it aside. "I have an idea. How we can get what we need."

She regards me warily. "How?"

"From the farmland."

"No! Jun, what are you talking about? We just escaped from that city, you want to risk going back? That's insane! No. You did fine today. We'll figure it out."

"No, you were right. We need proper tools. Seeds. This isn't enough."

She shakes her head. I'm shocked to see tears forming in her eyes.

"No," she says firmly. "They'll be expecting you. You'll die. That's not an option."

"Okay."

"Okay?"

I nod and put her arm around her. "I won't go, then. We'll figure it out."

"That's right." She leans against me. "We will."

"How's your stomach?" I ask.

"It hurts. I gave all of my pathetic medicine to Matthew."

I make a mental note: medicine for the bullet wounds. They should have medicine on-hand at the medic tent. I'll be able to steal some easily.

We talk quietly for a while. Eventually her breathing slows and deepens. I keep talking, requiring no answers for her, just giving all my ideas for how we're going to survive. She falls asleep quickly. I wait a few minutes, for her to be deeply asleep, then I gently lay her down on the ground.

I go over to the pond and wave Alyson over to me.

"What?"

"Is there any chance that you know, based on the sun, when the workers at the farmland will be done for the day?" I ask.

She inspects the sky. She frowns and tilts her head. "Soon. Almost."

That's promising.

"Alright. Aly, can I entrust you with a big responsibility?"

She nods eagerly.

"Can you watch over Matthew and Kyra while I go gather some more fruit?"

"Yes!" she exclaims.

I give her a high-five. "I'll be back soon," I promise.

Then I leave. I hate lying to Kyra, but I know she's wrong. This is worth the risk. All of our survival depends on it. I'm going to get seeds, tools, and medicine. And a bag to put all this in, hopefully.

If I don't, eventually, we'll die. We don't have enough knowledge to survive on our wits and what the forest will give us.

"I'll be back," I promise again, disappearing into the woods.

CHAPTER FIFTY

Kyra

There's no need to stick to any schedule out here, and I'm tired enough to have slept through the night into next morning. But the sun is too bright and it wakes me. Slowly.

As I pull myself out of sleep, first I glance over at Matthew. He's still there and still asleep. Good. Sleep is his best option right now.

Alyson's sitting not too far off, drawing in the dirt with a big stick. She waves at me when she sees I'm awake. I wave back.

The only person I don't see is Jun. Who knows where he wandered off to this time. Foraging for more fruit? Building a better shelter? I'm so glad he's out here with us. He knows what he's doing. And he'll keeping going even when he's tired, so that we're taken care of.

A glimmer of uneasy brims in my mind, but I can't figure out why.

I make my way over to Alyson. "Nice flower," I say, admiring her drawing. "Where's Jun?"

"Gone to gather fruit, so he put me in charge!" she says, confirming my earlier idea.

He's so sweet.

I join Alyson in the dirt, after grabbing a stick of my own. I think of games we can play together, and teach her tic-tac-toe. It takes her a long time to understand the concept, but she's eager to learn. By the time I've taught her the game and we've played a few rounds, it's been a long time since I woke up. Matthew stirs.

Why hasn't Jun returned yet?

As though a trap door were pulled out from under me, my heart suddenly drops. He went to the farmland. I jump to my feet.

Why would he do that?! He promised he wouldn't!

If they catch him, they will kill him. And we will slowly die out here, because there's no way we can survive without him! How selfish!

My anger evaporates and I sink back to the ground. I swipe at my eyes, brimming with tears.

I don't want him to die.

"What's wrong?" Alyson asks, worried by my sudden shift in mood.

"I just miss Jun," I say. How can I explain my worries to her? I don't want her worried, too. I can't deal with that right now.

Everything was supposed to be easier once we escaped! Instead, it's more difficult.

I stand and go over to Matthew.

"How are you feeling?"

He raises an eyebrow. "You don't have to sound so concerned," he says sarcastically. "If taking care of me is such a chore for you—"

"No, it's not that." I sigh. "Jun did something stupid."

I explain our earlier conversation and how I think he's gone to the farmland. Matthew is not helpful.

"Makes sense," he says. "We can't survive on just ourselves and two guns."

"We did alright today."

"*Jun* did alright today."

"All the more reason for him not to risk himself!" I snap.

We go back and forth on this topic for a while. It seems to rouse Matthew's spirits to be in contention with me, and it keeps me somewhat occupied and distracted.

Another day is ending, the trees' shadows stretching out. That's when Jun walks into the clearing. He's carrying a huge bag across his back and an axe in his hand. His cheek is slashed and bleeding, but he's grinning like crazy.

I rush over to him, jumping into his arms. He drops the axe and the bag and wraps his arms around me. But I don't let the hug last before I pull back and punch his shoulder.

"What were you *thinking*?" I exclaim.

He smiles. "That I wanted us to survive. And now we can. Plus, I brought you and Matthew stronger pain medicine."

"I don't care about the pain medication! I care—"

His grin widens. "Yes," he prompts when I hesitate.

"I care about you," I say quietly.

He presses a kiss to my forehead. "And I care about you. That's why I did this."

"Thank you," I whisper. "But please don't leave like that again."

"I won't."

"Not that I'm not excited at all this hugging," Matthew calls out, "But I'm much more excited by the prospect of some stronger pain medication."

"Is he always going to be interrupting us?" Jun grumbles.

He picks the bag back up and brings it over to where Matthew is waiting. We both get our pain-killers, and after only a few minutes, the pain lessens. After a few more, it disappears altogether. I sign in relief and my body relaxes. I hadn't realized how much the pain was affecting me.

Jun shows us everything he managed to grab, assuring us that it was super easy to sneak around and avoid the soldiers doing their rounds. I patch his cheek, wanting to make a snarky remark about how well he avoided them if he got a wound to his face. But I stay quiet. He's back, alive, and that's what matters. And he was right. We would not last long without the supplies he got.

Things like the axe, several knifes, and more bullets for our guns. Matches. Vegetable seeds. More first aid supplies. A few packaged boxes of assorted fruits and vegetables. "Since seeds take a long time," he explains.

Even three books.

I grab one. "Where did you get these?"

"On a table in the medic's tent. I hope they're fun books and not medical books. I figured since you and Matthew might want something to read."

Matthew grabs another one. "These are great! Thanks, Jun."

"Will you read one to me?" Alyson asks me.

"Of course. You'll like this one. It's about princesses, dragons." I glance at Jun. "And knights in shining armour."

CHAPTER FIFTY-ONE

Jun

Progress is slow. The first thing to do is decide where we will live. This clearing is convenient, but I want to check out more of the woods, see where the best place to live really is.

Matthew can't move, so Kyra stays with him while Alyson and I go out to explore, mentally mapping out the woods around us.

We find a large spread of different fruits trees near a running stream. It would be convenient to live so close to so much fruit. A few minutes walk from there, we find an open meadow. Perfect. It has plenty of space to build a house and have a garden.

But then we have to build a house. And that takes time, especially with my shoulder not being completely back to normal yet. Alyson is a great help. Now that she's getting feed more, she's growing a lot and becoming strong. We make the trek every day, making more progress on the house. Matthew's not ready to be moved yet.

I don't like not getting to see Kyra for most of the day, but it'll be worth it.

We plant the garden before the house is done, so the plants can start growing. We water it with water from the stream, which takes only about two minutes to reach.

In the evenings, Alyson and I return back to the makeshift camp where Kyra spends her days trying to keep Matthew alive. She's doing an amazing job, but it's rough for Matthew.

After a few weeks, Matthew is strong enough to be moved, and the house is almost done.

We gather all our things from the clearing, and I carry Matthew as we all make the journey to where we'll live from now on.

At night, Kyra reads to us from one of the books.

Once the house is done, the days become easier. More leisurely. It's an experience I've never had before. The absence of anxiety in my brain is sometimes so jarring. When a situation occurs that I know would have caused me anxiety sometimes that's enough to make me panic. The memory of my heart spiking, the feelings flooding my body and overpowering my rational thought. But, slowly, those go away too.

Matthew gets better every day. But he'll never be able to walk properly again. I fashion him a walking stick, and slowly he learns how to walk with it and his injury. It takes a while for him to return to the fun, sarcastic person he used to be. Kyra informs me he's still not completely himself. He might never be. He went through a lot. But he seems happy to be here.

Alyson is flourishing. She's gained so much weight, now she actually looks her age. She rarely stops smiling. Everything makes her happy and she never runs out of ways to amuse herself. I've almost forgiven myself for everything she had to witness during our escape.

Kyra is also the happiest I've ever seen her, even though her expressions of happiness pale in comparison to Alyson and even, on occasion, Matthew. She's a hard worker, and keeps us all in line. She constantly figuring out creative ways to make use of what we have and not allowing me to go back to the farmland instead. But I'm pretty sure if I keep pestering her, she'll let me go get a cow. I'm certain I could do it. Then we'd have milk.

"And another— huge— mouth to feed," Kyra always counters with.

Solid logic, sadly.

I would have never thought my life would lead me here. It's a future I could have never hoped for, even though I would have never thought about it on my own.

Sometimes, I feel this tug to return to the city. It takes me a while to understand it. Why would I want to go back there? Life is perfect out here. But then it clicks. People are struggling in there. Out here, they'd be free.

I try to dismiss the idea brewing in my mind. We almost died getting ourselves out. I can't risk that. Can't ask anyone to do it again. My heart constricts at the thought of anything happening to Kyra, Alyson, or Matthew. Or to me, that I could no longer be with them. These weeks, or has it even been months, have been the happiest I've ever been. Part of me wants to stay here forever, hidden, enjoying the life we managed to take for ourselves.

But… everyone else should get a chance to enjoy it too.

My stomach twists at the thought of returning to the city. But the idea persists. I find myself turning it over in my mind. Ideas forming and taking shape.

I don't say anything to Kyra yet. But I will. Soon.

This is an idea that refuses to die.

CHAPTER FIFTY-TWO

Kyra

The first few days are rough. Jun and Alyson are gone for most of the day, so it's just me and Matthew, doing our best to stay alive. With Jun and Alyson gone, and nothing else to distract him, Matthew sinks into a stupor. He barely moves and hardly speaks. I can't blame him, with all that's happened in only a few days. He was devoted to Jasmine.

They had been discussing marriage. Her betrayal hit him hard. I don't ask abut it, or his feelings, or try to tell him everything will be better eventually. The psychological wounds from Jasmine and Braxton can be addressed later. I allow him his time to wallow and focus on making him survive his bullet wound. This mostly involves him napping, medicine, and me threatening him into eating more apples. They're pretty much the only food we have a large supply of. Jun tries to catch meat often, which is excellent, but quickly devoured and gone.

I take frequent naps myself. Being shot does that to you. I don't like it. After the first few days, Matthew stabilizes and taking care of him occupies much less of my day. All I do is nap, read, and get startled by bird calls and animals moving around in the forest. I finish one book in two days. I don't know what to do with myself. I want to read more, but there's only two books left, with no chance of ever getting more. I'm going to forbid Jun from going back to the farmland if he ever tries again. My days used to be entirely full— filled with work.

Matthew eventually starts talking more. We spend our days in aimless conversation and playing word games in the dirt. Matthew cheats.

Every night, Jun and Alyson return with news of what progress they're making. I think Matthew can sense how much I want to join them because he tries to insist that he'd be fine staying on his own. We dismiss that idea. So then he tries to argue that he's well enough to travel by now. I disagree with him and Jun backs me up, pointing out that he hasn't gotten the space ready enough for us anyways. That may or may not be true, but I'm grateful for the support. I'm not about to put Matthew at risk of worsening his injury because I miss Jun. I don't think my wound is healed enough to make the walk, either, and Jun can't carry us both.

Alyson and Matthew always fall asleep quickly, especially if Jun's managed to catch us something for dinner. Jun and I take the opportunity to talk. These talks never last long. Jun's exhausted from all the work he's doing. But these moments are the highlights of my day. We talk about our past lives, mostly, and what we want our lives here to be like. It's painful, at first, for Jun to talk about his family. I don't know how to comfort him. It was nothing to me to leave my family behind, all those years ago. He never would have left his.

Sooner than I want, he falls asleep. But I never begrudge him this. He pushes himself too hard, trying to get everything ready as fast as possible. From the stories they tell, Alyson is just as eager of a worker, if a bit lacking in strength. But she seems to grow every day and it's great to see.

When Matthew is actually strong enough to be moved, Jun carries him to our new life. It's almost sad to leave the clearing, but I'm excited to see in person what Jun and Alyson have been doing. The journey takes time. Jun needs breaks from carrying Matthew. I'm ashamed at how winded I get just from walking beside them, but I've had to stay by Matthew's side for weeks, and that meant no walking.

My breath catches in my throat when I see what Jun and Alyson have built for us. A garden and a house. True, it's not done yet, but it's beautiful. Nothing like an apartment in the government sector. Jun apologizes that it's not finished, but I stop him. I wish I could properly verbalize what it means to me, but he appears to understand my fumbling attempts.

Thus commences the happiest days of my life. Sunshine and grass under your feet does wonders for the soul. Matthew, surrounded by the positivity and exuberance of Alyson, gets some life back in him, too. We all work out a routine and do our parts to create our life. It feels like we're a family.

Then an idea captures Jun's mind. Something he's not telling me about yet. He starts staring into space. Then it becomes more frequent. He mutters to himself while he works.

I know what he's thinking about. He's trying to be sly, but he keeps slipping up. Saying things like, "You know, we're really lucky to be out here. Not everyone gets to be this lucky" and "I feel really bad for everyone. They're still in there, trapped."

He has a big heart. Of course he wants to help everyone else. He tried to convince me to save everyone three days after we first met, once he knew about the computers. Then again, when we met Alyson. I knew the day would come when he brought it up again.

Selfishly, I hoped he wouldn't. I want to keep all of us here. Safe and sound. Not to do anything to jeopardize that. Returning to the city is a massive risk and it makes my heart constrict to think of anything happening to him. That's why I won't let him return to the farmland.

I won't be able to stop him. Maybe I can dissuade him for a while, but not for long. Eventually, his good nature would win over, and I would feel too guilty. I do understand his desire to help everyone. This life is something I never could have dreamed of. If we could help make life better for even a few more people…

But I don't tell Jun I know what he's thinking about. I wait. He'll bring it up to me when he's ready. When he thinks I'm ready to agree. Hopefully, when he has a plan. An actual plan. And when he talks to me, I won't stop him.

But for now…

I re-focus on the task at hand: braiding Alyson's hair. It's getting very long now, and she's thrilled by all the different ways I know how to style it. She sits so patiently and still.

Matthew and Jun are arm-wrestling on a tree-stump. Matthew always loses, except for when he uses his puppy eyes and guilt-trips Jun into letting him win. Then he brags about it for a long time, while Jun just shakes his head and winks at me.

For now, I'll enjoy this.

CHAPTER FIFTY-THREE

Jun

One evening, as we're eating supper around the campfire, Alyson pipes up with, "Are you and Kyra gonna get married?"

Kyra chokes on her drink.

I raise an eyebrow at her, an idea occurring to me. "Is that why you haven't kissed me yet?"

She splutters. "Don't be ridiculous."

"You guys haven't kissed yet?" Matthew asks in disbelief.

"None of your business," Kyra snaps.

Alyson giggles. "Your face is red."

Kyra's face *is* red. She looks at me for help, her eyes wide and still shocked.

"Alright, let's drop the subject, okay?" I say.

Matthew, of course, doesn't. "No, no, I insist on knowing *how* and *why* you—"

"Matthew, Matthew," I interrupt, waving my hands in a sign that he should stop while he's ahead. He is very much within punching distance from Kyra and her eyes are starting to narrow.

He relents with a "fine, fine."

And we all drop the subject. Verbally. Now that the question has been raised, I keep thinking about it. Kyra and I haven't known each other for long. But we've been through a lot together. She's the person I know most, and she knows me most.

Once supper is done, I gather everyone's 'plates.' They're pieces of wood that Matthew faithfully did his best to whittle to be proper plates. He has insisted on helping out as much as he can. We clean the plates at the end of the day, doing our best to make them last as long as possible. Though I'm sure Matthew wouldn't mind whittling more, since he's got few other things to occupy himself with.

Alyson grabs a book and brings it to Matthew. He's been reading it to her. I wonder if it's worth it to teach her how to read? Kyra and

Matthew both can, so they've been reading out loud to us. I've been too busy with everything else to think about adding learning how to read. What would be the point other than getting to read the books ourselves? Maybe Alyson will want that eventually?

Kyra comes with me as I go to the river to wash everything. She's quiet, and I don't want to risk saying anything. We wash the dishes side by side. The task goes quickly. Then we sit together, enjoying how the air cools as the sun begins its slow and lazy task of setting. Nothing else is so beautiful.

I know what topic of conversation she wants. But I don't know how she wants to approach it or how to start the conversation myself.

"I have no desire to rush you," I say at last. That feels like a good place to start.

"I know," she replies.

The atmosphere becomes more relaxed.

"But clearly," she says, "You've wondered why I've been taking things slow."

"Not really."

She gives me a look.

"Okay, maybe once or twice, but not really. We've both been busy, trying to build a life here for all of us. You were tending Matthew for a long time. Plus, neither one of us has done this before."

She purses her lips. She's thinking.

I can't resist adding, "But I do think Alyson's idea has merit."

Her face flushes red and she exclaims, "We can't get married, there's no officiant."

I stare at her blankly. "Huh?"

"The officiant," she says like it's obvious. "The one who does the ceremony."

"Is that how it works in the upper sectors?"

"It's a big party. The officiant declares them married, they have to sign a document, and they're married."

"That's it?"

"It's legally binding. What more do you need?"

I shrug. "I dunno. It's just not how we do it. What makes someone an officiant?"

"They have to get their license. What does your sector do?"

I think for a moment, trying to recall everything about the process. Trying to ignore how Taro never got the chance.

"The guy has to ask the girl's father for his blessing. Then, the guy gives her father something valuable to him. Giving away something important to you is a sign that you're going to take the union seriously and will take care of her. Then, the guy has to build or buy a house. Once he has, they invite people over for a meal. They all eat together. Then the parents pronounce blessings. The couple kisses. Then they're married."

"That's sweet. Is there nothing legally binding?"

"Well, what's legally binding about a piece of paper? That's just how you decided to do it. If you don't do what I described, you're not considered married. I think it works the same way."

"Interesting," Kyra says musingly, staring out across the river. "What if the girl's parents are dead? Who does the guy give his important item to?"

"Oh, it can be the next closest relative. Doesn't have to be older, either, it can be a cousin or something. Or even just a best friend if the girl has no relatives, but that's a bit rare."

Kyra looks at me. Her eyes are squinted and a smile plays at the edge of her mouth. "You built me a house."

The grin I grin is immediate, but I try to tamper down my enthusiasm. "I built all of us a house."

"We've eaten a meal in that house."

"Several."

She thinks. "You've given food away to Alyson. You gave Matthew… well, nothing that you didn't get for him, but at great personal risk you went and got things for him."

"That's true."

"Matthew has absolutely given his blessing. Many times. More than called for."

I laugh. "That he has."

"Interesting."

She stands up, breaking the moment I thought was building. She gathers the dishes and turns to leave.

"Wait, where are you going?" I ask, jumping to my feet.

"Back to the house," she answers as she walks forward. "It'll be dark soon and we don't have any light with us."

She's not wrong. I catch up to her. Looking at me out of the corner of her eye, she smiles at me.

I quickly press a kiss to her temple. "Alyon isn't going to drop the subject now that she's thought of it," I warn.

"I know. But we've already eaten all our meals for today."

My heart wants to jump out of my chest and dance around. Containing my excitement, I can only reply, "That's true. Tomorrow, then?"

She laughs. "I thought you were in no rush?"

"I'm not. I was just asking."

"I'll let you know tomorrow."

Photo credit to Pamela Hawdon Photography

Helen Lawrence grew up in a small town in Northern Ontario, on a 60-acre property, and has wanted to be an author ever since she could write. She loves daydreaming about her scenes and then forgetting what she thought up. She is never short of ideas, just short of time. Currently, Helen goes to university for English and Piano, and procrastinates her assignments by writing her books.

READER REVIEWS

An interesting combination of mystery, love story, and horse story, this book is written by a rider for riders…you may even pick up a dressage pointer or two! We've all read the "wanna-be" horse stories, with unrealistic plots and laborious explanations over mundane terms that any equestrian should know. Finally, here's a book that entertains without frustrating the equine enthusiast… describing important details, like the floating feeling of an extended trot, or the power of a collected canter, instead of lamely teaching readers the difference between "bay" and "chestnut."
-*Visionaire at Eventing Nation*

"..rich backgrounds and a cast of characters that jump from the page.."
- *Horse and Style Magazine Feb/March 2013*

Kick On by Kelly Jennings is a non-stop thrill ride, on and off the horse. Set in the lush tropical background of Panama to the lavish equestrian estates of Wellington Florida, Ms. Jennings takes you on a trail ride of adventure, mystery, intrigue and murder. Drug cartels, romance, money and horses… what more could you ask for in a book? Tighten your girth and pick up the reins; its gonna be a hell of a ride!
-*Maureen Fahrenholz - Grand Prix instructor*
Licensed USDF L judge. Located in Florida

Kelly Jennings has created a book that is a rarity, a book with a horse theme that is smart enough to satisfy real horse people with a great storyline that will keep non-horse people reading. So many horse books are filled with flowery horse descriptions and clumsy explanations that make most of us close the book with an eye roll! This is not one of them! The main character, Lauren, reminds me of a more interesting and complex version of Stephanie Plum from the Janet Evonovich series. Self-deprecating with talent is always a likable combination, I found myself rootin for her by page two!
-*T.L. Racich*

I absolutely LOVED this book. Sometimes it's difficult finding a book where the author gets the "horse & riding" part right without making it sound cheesy. Kudos to you, Kelly. Great job! I didn't want to put this book down, and I sure didn't want it to end. Can't wait to read more from this author! This is a MUST read!
-*K. Roberts*

Kick On keeps on giving. I could not put this book down!! I ride dressage and love that Kelly has gone back to basics in describing how movements are accomplished and that the horse's development is thought of! In saying that I also enjoyed that the book was not all about dressage! It had characters that were well developed and a plot that incorporated her love for dressage, her history and have us that intrigue. Thank you Kelly for letting us share your passion! Can't wait for number two!

-Cadie

Great Escape! This book was a great "getaway," fun read, and quite delicious! The characters were intriguing and well written; I found myself truly invested in them. The imagery in this book was wonderful, and although I am not a "horse person," I really enjoyed the equestrian angle and I learned A LOT about the horse world. Can't wait for the next chapter in Lauren's adventures!

-A. Ferrell

Exceptional Read. You get it all—horses, romance, and intrigue. The author does a fantastic job of painting a picture of Panama and all the beautiful horses! This book has it all! From a quirky, down-to-earth main character to a heart-stopping romance with lots of intrigue thrown in to keep you hooked! I grew up riding but have no experience with dressage. I think the author does a great job of bringing you into that world. A well-rounded book!

-Anonymous

Home, horses and intrigue. I, too, grew up I'm the Panama Canal Zone and had horses at one of the local riding clubs. Kelly's book took me back to the steamy jungles of home, had me smelling the salt air and reliving the joys of riding recklessly through the jungle. Can't wait for the sequel.

-Blitchie